MIDNIGHT FIRE

"Come here." His voice was all golden tones; gone were the proper English inflections.

As Kerry cautiously went nearer, Cameron's piercing silver stare unnerved her, but, strangely, it sent pleasurable shivers through her as well. Even in the darkness she saw his smile, dazzling white and confident.

"I would have come back sooner if I'd know that you desired me," he said. "Apparently your hatred of the English is not all-encompassing."

Kerry bit back a retort. "Sir, you must be patient!" she said, trying to hide her shocked innocence and to sound seductive and experienced instead. "We do have all night." With a smile, she refilled his glass and one for herself.

He deftly removed the glass from between her clenched fingers, and before she could protest, his mouth claimed hers, his lips tasting of brandy.

"No . . . I can't," she tried to say, but her words were muted syllables beneath the force of his passion, his kisses now descending greedily down her throat. She gasped as he wound the sheet free, the cool evening air caressing her. A burning desire sparked somewhere within her as he gazed at her, his eyes drinking their fill, yet Kerry knew she should resist. As his mouth took hers again, she struggled to remain coldly calculating as she'd planned to do. But somehow the plan had fallen apart; her body, no longer her own, was yielding to his fiery passion. . . .

TWILIGHT ECSTASY

ROMANCE FOR ALL SEASONS
from Zebra Books

ARIZONA TEMPTRESS (1785, $3.95)
by Bobbi Smith
Rick Peralta found the freedom he craved only in his disguise as El Cazador. Then he saw the exquisitely alluring Jennie among his compadres and the hotblooded male swore she'd belong just to him.

RAPTURE'S TEMPEST (1624, $3.95)
by Bobbi Smith
Terrified of her stepfather, innocent Delight de Vries disguised herself as a lad and hired on as a riverboat cabin boy. But when her gaze locked with Captain James Westlake's, all she knew was that she would forfeit her new-found freedom to be bound in his arms for a night.

WANTON SPLENDOR (1461, $3.50)
by Bobbi Smith
Kathleen had every intention of keeping her distance from the dangerously handsome Christopher Fletcher. But when a hurricane devastated the Island, she crept into Chris's arms for comfort, wondering what it would be like to kiss those cynical lips.

GOLDEN GYPSY (2025, $3.95)
by Wanda Owen
When Domonique consented to be the hostess for the high stakes poker game, she didn't know that her lush body would be the prize—or that the winner would by the impossibly handsome Jared Barlow whose fortune was to forever crave the *Golden Gypsy*.

GOLDEN ECSTASY (1688, $3.95)
by Wanda Owen
Nothing could match Andrea's rage when Gil thoroughly kissed her full trembling lips. She was of his enemy's family, but they were forever enslaved by their precious *Golden Ecstasy*.

Available wherever paperbacks are sold, or order direct from the Publisher. Send cover price plus 50¢ per copy for mailing and handling to Zebra Books, Dept. 1981, 475 Park Avenue South, New York, N.Y. 10016. Residents of New York, New Jersey and Pennsylvania must include sales tax. DO NOT SEND CASH.

TWILIGHT ECSTASY
COLLEEN QUINN

ZEBRA BOOKS
KENSINGTON PUBLISHING CORP.

ZEBRA BOOKS

are published by

Kensington Publishing Corp.
475 Park Avenue South
New York, NY 10016

Copyright © 1987 by Colleen Quinn

All rights reserved. No part of this book may be reproduced in any form or by any means without the prior written consent of the Publisher, excepting brief quotes used in reviews.

First printing: February 1987.

Printed in the United States of America.

For Matthew

Chapter One

"Five pounds! For the purchase of Kerry O'Toole, in exchange for a term of indenture of not less than five years. Done!" Ezekiel Jacobs turned a pleased eye to the well-dressed stranger standing at the edge of the dock near the spot where the immigrants stood. He tugged at his grizzled gray beard and continued in the same thick voice. "Consider yourself lucky, sir. You have made yourself a good bargain today."

The gentleman nodded as the shabby auctioneer grasped the pouch of loose gold coins. His seedy black gloves were worn completely through at the fingers, and his dirty pink stubs could not resist the impulse to finger the coins, caressing them in their sackcloth home with readily apparent greediness. He paused, eying the expensively dressed man before him, and began thoughtfully, "Do you need a good man for your stables?" Ezekiel liked the feel of the stranger's gold and was wont to procure more of it. "Or perhaps another wench for your house?"

"No, thank you." The stranger bowed cordially. "I need only the girl right now." In truth, he had given no previous thought to acquiring another servant, but there was something about this girl—the defiant gleam in her eyes, the way she clutched the torn bag that contained the sum total of all her worldly possessions. He had first spied her disembarking from *The Emerald Express*, balancing the bag and clutching at her worn cloak while the auctioneer herded the immigrants to one side like so many cattle. The man had caught the lass by a slender arm and, with a rude shove, had almost sent her sprawling to the splintered wharves. He'd been about to intervene, but the lass had drawn herself up to her whole five feet three inches and had eyed the seedy auctioneer steadily, showing no sign of fear or obeisance. "Kind sir," she had said, "you'll be keeping your hands to yourself, unless you'd be liking to be without them." While the auctioneer had stood gaping, unable to believe the nerve of this saucy wench, she had smiled, revealing even white teeth between her soft red lips. Then, before he could respond, the young lass had taken her place on the block, her head held high. That had decided the Englishman. Without a second thought, he'd paid the full price for her.

As he looked down at the lass, the Englishman saw that she was glaring at the auctioneer, and favoring himself with a not-too-kind glance in the bargain. Ezekiel Jacobs leered openly at the girl, meanwhile shuffling his ragged boots on the dirty, wet cobbles.

"Aye, sir. She'd be a fine lass in your house. I daresay the wench will serve you well, and she is comely enough."

His intent was clear, and the young girl's eyes widened with distress while her new employer cleared his throat abruptly.

"She is to help in the house and that is all."

He was saying this more to her than to the auctioneer, but the lass was in no frame of mind to be grateful and the auctioneer chuckled broadly.

"Aye, sir. And a prettier lass you could never ask for. Why I had my hands full the whole of the trip, keeping the lads away from her, that I did. Aye, when she's cleaned up a bit, she'll be right handsome. I'd not mind a piece of that myself." The auctioneer reached for the lass, and he fingered the patched shoulder of her cloak in much the same way he had caressed the gold coins. But before he could complete his groping, the girl let out an enraged shriek and Ezekiel found himself sprawling backward against crates of creosote, bundles of sea grass and brine, and parcels and packages from London.

"Blimey! The bloody bitch has given me a black eye, she has!" With a vengeful gleam in his swelling yellow gaze, the auctioneer advanced toward the lass who was facing him defiantly, swirling her bag in the air in preparation for another blow.

"Try it and you'll be rollin' in the river with the rest of the rats!" the tiny lass threatened, wielding the bag with all her might. The auctioneer lunged for her, but the girl's new employer stepped deftly in front of the ratlike old man before the bag could find its mark.

"But, gov'ner," Ezekiel protested," the wench gave me a black un'." His anger quickly abated, however, for the quiet-spoken gentleman loomed before him like an apparition from a nightmare, his silvery eyes blazing and his teeth clenched between his lips. "Blimey," the auctioneer wheezed. He took a step backward as the Englishman advanced, throwing his expensive black cloak over his right shoulder to reveal the polished maple butt of a horse pistol.

"I have purchased this lass for the gold coins you hold in your purse." As the gentleman gestured to the sack at their feet, Ezekiel's eyes flickered to it, wide with alarm. "Now you listen to me and mark my words well. This lass is mine, and if you lay a finger on her you will answer to me. Is that understood?"

The auctioneer nodded quickly, his matted beard dipping frantically against his chest. A muffled laugh came from one of the slaves waiting behind him, but Ezekiel dared not react to it. Instead, he watched the Englishman warily, reserving side glances for the sack of gold coins.

"Good," the stranger continued, tension leaving his face

and his smoldering silver eyes becoming once more calm. "See that you remember it in the future, should our paths cross again." With that abrupt dismissal, the Englishman turned his back on the auctioneer as if the man were so much forgotten trash, and he focused his attention on the girl.

Kerry nearly blanched under the leisurely perusal of those silvery gray eyes, but she forced herself to stand still and show no fear. She was painfully aware of her own appearance, and she blushed as she realized what he must think of her. Her dark black hair, once lustrous, was now a tangled and matted mess tacked casually under her cap. She had tried to keep it clean during the three months aboard ship en route from Ireland to the colonies, but she'd soon found that task impossible. Furthermore she'd quickly learned that loosened tresses attract lice and rats. Her clothing, a ragged piece of cloth that could scarce be called a gown and a tattered cloak, was grimy and it smelled of the fetid debris that accumulated in the hold of the ship. She had but one other dress, her best, lovingly made by her mother who had packed it tearfully into the bag. Kerry remembered how she'd tried not to cry as her only daughter had clambered aboard a ship, never to return. Tears crept into her own eyes now, but Kerry determinedly beat them back and tossed her head high. Her circumstances were not of her making. She forced herself not to think of them and not to be ashamed.

A brief flicker of a smile crossed the gentleman's lean face, and had the circumstances been different, Kerry would have been admiring the fine figure he cut. His face was somber, with a high clear forehead, black eyebrows perched over glittering silver-gray eyes, and a sensuous mouth. His nose was Roman, almost hawklike, while his square-cut chin and forceful jaw suggested a determined and masterful nature. He wore well-tailored garments of a good material, and they fit his broad-shouldered frame to perfection. But today his elegance and control only made Kerry more aware of her own tattered appearance so, when she stole a glance at his eyes and saw that he was secretly amused, her anger flared.

"Have you gotten your fill of staring?" she asked pertly, then softened her tone for it suddenly occurred to her that he might return her to the auctioneer's block if he thought her a troublesome wench. She shuddered to think of herself in the power of someone like Ezekiel, but what fate would she have at the hands of this man? He had assured Ezekiel that he only desired her for housework, but something about the way he stared ... She shivered, but not from the rain-drenched wind, and not daring to examine her feelings too closely, she forced herself to return his stare and retain her composure.

"I beg your pardon." His tone was polite enough, and she was again surprised by his voice. It was so smooth, and polished. English, certainly, but less clipped than the speech of the Englishmen she'd learned to despise and without a trace of the foppishness that affected the speech of so many gentlemen. "You have a strange way of showing gratitude," he continued in the same polite tone. "Had I not paid the coins for your indenture, you might have done much worse. Ezekiel himself had more than your sale in mind, that much was apparent."

Kerry blushed furiously, and it was a full minute before she could speak. "Look you English black dog. I have honored a debt of my family, a debt for which I am not personally responsible. My poor father was taken advantage of by one of your countrymen, a disgusting English landlord, lower than the dirt I tread on. I chose to honor that debt but that does not make me a trinket for any man's pleasure. I need no help from you. I could have handled Ezekiel there with my bag. Indeed, I'd do the same to you should there be a need." As she tossed her head in the direction of the aforementioned weapon, the Englishman followed her gaze.

"I have no doubt." He chuckled dryly. "I'll remember that in the future and see that you are unarmed." Then, before the lass could utter any invectives, the gentleman's hand fell gently on her shoulder. Kerry's face flew up, but something in his eyes brooked no disobedience. He pushed her gently toward the street. "Now before we draw any more attention from those"—he gestured with an absent wave of his free hand, and Kerry glanced in mortification at the sailors listening with amusement and openly leering—"I suggest we discuss this further in the carriage."

A fine coach stood directly in the center of the cobbled street, recently drawn up by a smiling and portly coachman. Kerry hesitated at the door, but before the coachman could dismount, her employer hoisted her unceremoniously into the red leather interior of the handsome equipage. Indeed, she had to grab the window ledge to keep from tumbling headlong onto the seat, so as she settled her small frame on the tufted cushion, she favored the man entering after her with a scathing glance.

"I humbly apologize." He smiled. "I did not mean to cause you to lose your balance. But George, my coachman, is a kind and gentle man, used to favoring ladies. I should hardly think him your equal, should you decide to employ your bag again." When his smile widened, Kerry fumed inwardly but she allowed only a grin to appear on her face.

"And I suppose you have no such fears for yourself," she retorted, hoping to goad him into losing his composure, but he merely chuckled.

"Have no doubts concerning that matter, miss. The Irish," he said thoughtfully, an infuriating grin curling his lips, "are not the most patient breed, and have a complete set of vices that I hardly need to enumerate to you. If they did not, you would not find yourself here. But it has been my experience that they can be trusted to hold to a bargain, and I think I can extend that trust to you."

"Why you . . ." Kerry began, but a large warm hand covered hers and she found herself forced to stare up into the eyes of its owner, now only inches from her face.

"I have business to conduct in this city, before I make my

way home. I cannot afford to be rushing about, looking for you. Do you give me your word that you will honor this debt and your indenture? If not, I will return you to Ezekiel Jacobs."

Silence followed his question so, without pause, the Englishman, as Kerry had already dubbed him, leaned out the small square-paned window of the coach and shouted to the driver.

"George! Rein up a bit! We may have to turn back."

"No!" Kerry shouted, her eyes wide with distress. "No, don't. I give you me word."

"Good." He smiled, and Kerry forced herself not to hit him. "Drive on!" he shouted, and the coach resumed its rumble down the cobbled streets. When he fumbled with a sheet of parchment, his quick eye scanning the contents, Kerry recognized it as her indenture paper. "Now, Miss Kerry O'Toole," he said thoughtfully, "I would ask that you call me by my given name instead of black dog. Is that agreeable to you? My name is Cameron Brent."

She nodded, and even in the dark morning light that filtered through the coach, he could see an embarrassed flush deepen the color of her face. He hid another smile and resumed his reading of her papers. "We shall be at the tavern shortly and then we'll dine. Any questions that you may have, I'll do my best to answer at that time." With that, he turned to gaze out the vacant window, staring into the street and dismissing her like an errant child.

Blundering idiot! Kerry swore silently on, using a host of epithets that her father had indulged in when he'd had too many pints, and there was something so completely satisfying about Irish curses that she soon felt much better.

When the coach rumbled to a stop, Kerry peered out cautiously. Through the already-descending evening twilight, a white and gray tavern was visible, sandwiched neatly between several offices and shops. Its sign was so streaked with rain it was barely legible, but Kerry made out the words:

King's Arms Tavern. The King, Kerry thought in annoyance. Is there anything here that isn't English?

"At your pleasure, miss." George, the driver, offered her his thick hand to assist her from the coach.

Kerry glanced awkwardly at her new employer, Cameron Brent, and with a slight inclination of his head he indicated for her to proceed. As the coachman swung her to the cobbles, he patted her hand reassuringly, and even helped her with the bag. His kindness made her feel warmer so she bravely ventured a smile. Her employer departed the coach too late to catch this exchange, for which Kerry was grateful.

The tavern door spilled open, and a drunken Colonial stumbled out, clutching onto the wall for support. Displaying his yellowed teeth in a grin, he leered at Kerry, but suddenly his leer was replaced by a look of alarm and the man stumbled out into the street, there dispensing of his evening meal. Kerry turned to Cameron Brent, a sarcastic observation on the tip of her tongue, but he was already looking past her, his silvery gaze strangely intent.

"'Tis Saturday night, sir," George stammered apologetically, and Cameron Brent nodded.

"Of course. The dock workers are here. I should have anticipated this. Innkeeper, are the rooms made ready?" The red-faced tavern owner raised a thick finger toward the ceiling and, with a doubtful look, shook his fleshy head. Cameron's face darkened with displeasure.

"We'll have to take a table for a few minutes. George, take care of the baggage. Miss Kerry, will you accompany me to the seat by the fire." She scowled at his overly polite command, feeling that he was mocking her in some way, but Cameron led her around the crowd to a corner of the room, a firm hand on her shoulder. This was the only part of the tavern that afforded any peace or privacy. Pointedly, he drew out a chair for her, leaving her no choice but to be sandwiched between him and the dank whitewashed wall. His proximity made her only too keenly aware of his presence. His masculinity was only enhanced by the elegant ruffles of his shirt, the smooth wool of his coat, and the clean smell of his clothing. Self-consciously, Kerry tugged at the ragged garment she wore—it could scarcely be termed a dress—and she pulled her cap down over her eyes.

"Aye, gov'ner?" The serving wench appeared suddenly, and at the sight of the elegant English gentleman she was all smiles, her wisps of blond hair dancing prettily under her cap. "Two pence a half of brandy. The same for a quart of ale." She leaned over the table to take his order, allowing him a full view of her generous bosom, readily visible because of her low neckline. "What'll it be, sir?" The invitation in her voice was plain, and Kerry scowled in disgust, turning aside and bracing her feet against the wall while fixing her gaze on the fiddlers.

Cameron's eyes narrowed slightly as he watched the lass, but he placed his order, his eyes never leaving the disgruntled urchin before him. "A brandy if you please . . . and tea for the lady." The serving wench, suddenly taking notice of Kerry, gave her the disdainful look reserved for servants although her own status was questionable. Kerry responded by showing her tongue as the wench shuffled away from the table, clearly disappointed in getting no response from the Englishman. As soon as the serving maid was out of earshot, he spoke sternly to the lass before him.

"Kerry, put your feet down." His voice held the sharp edge of command, but Kerry was far too annoyed at the wench's obvious interest in Cameron to concede so easily. Damned English! she thought, and out of the corner of her eye she saw his jaw harden. His eyes sparkled with something other than pleasure as he leaned across the table, and she had to fight to keep from fleeing the room altogether. But something in her nature urged defiance and her broken black boots still adorned the wall.

"Kerry." He spoke now in a strangely quiet voice, a voice that was far more frightening than all her father's rumbling shouts had been, and her eyes widened under the cap at the sound. "If you cannot take your feet down by yourself, I will be happy to assist you." His intent was clear, and her startled gaze met his. In his eyes she saw a threat as well as smoldering anger. Reluctantly, her boots made a scraping descent to the floor, and she sat up more properly than before.

"That's better." His intent regard of her continued as the wench returned, plunking hot tea upon the table, along with a crystal glass of amber brandy. Kerry did not touch the offering, but Cameron's eyes never left her. He waited only until the serving wench departed to continue his chiding.

"It seems to me that you have a lot to learn about obeying. I am accustomed to giving an order only once and I expect it to be carried out. As long as you are in my company, I expect you to act like a lady."

"I thought I'd be doing you a favor, turning me back." Kerry gestured to the wench, who was still staring across the room, with an impudent jerk of her thumb. "The bosoms seemed likely to fall into your lap and I would not want to hamper your pleasure." She grinned, and as that bright red curve graced her lips, an innocent twinkle appeared in her eyes. "After all, there are some things a lady shouldn't see."

Cameron's gaze revealed a flicker of amusement that he quickly squelched. "Drink your tea," he said. His lace cuff waved toward the steaming pot and the plateful of cakes.

"Is that an order?" she questioned pertly, and at his nod she sipped the dark sweet tea, snatching up three of the cakes. Under his amused stare she returned two of them, deciding to eat one before retrieving another. Thus she was more than a little relieved when the bar noise drew his attention away from herself and he turned in his chair.

Two of the louder patrons were engaged in a dispute of sorts which grew more heated and quickly came to blows. Their bodies crashed to the floor, and as they struggled there, the other drinkers scarcely looked up from their brew, except when the rolling combatants struck the legs of their tables. The innkeeper reappeared and, with a tired shake of his head, hoisted one man by the collar and threw him out of the tavern. The other brawler climbed cautiously to his feet, rubbing a black grizzled beard that glistened with ale.

"This is the last time, Jack," the innkeeper threatened, his fist displayed in the air to accompany his words, "or you will find yourself swilling your ale elsewhere. I cannot abide these fights."

"'Tis no fight. I was teaching the young whelp a lesson. A fine thing, this is. You should be thanking me for doing you a service, that you should." The other men roared with laughter while the innkeeper's eyes rolled to the ceiling.

"Your rooms, sir," he then called.

Cameron nodded and, lending Kerry an unwelcome hand with her baggage, he followed the man up a narrow staircase. As she passed the bearded man named Jack, a rumbling roar burst forth from that one's full belly and his flushed face turned in the young girl's direction.

"'Tis a wench, no less. Aye, mates. All the time I took her for a lad, I did, seeing as she had 'er 'air all stuffed up inside that cap." The other men roared with appreciation at this fine jest, but Kerry felt her anger flame. This was too much. She had spent months aboard a ship, been mauled by Ezekiel Jacobs, been sold to this Englishman, and now her womanhood was being mocked. Before common sense could stop her, she broke free from the Englishman's grasp and flung herself in front of the scruffy dock worker, her hands planted firmly on her slender hips.

"You blundering buffoon! 'Twould be your kind would not know a lad from a lass! We have a name for such where I come from, and it's not a compliment!"

"Blimey!" After a startled moment, the man laughed. "Did you hear the brogue on 'er! Thick enough to cut with a knife!" His drunken stare fell on Kerry, taking in the poor quality of her clothes, the comely face that was attractive

17

though streaked with grime. His gaze wandered to Cameron, and with a leer, he reached into his pocket for a fistful of coin. "Are you of a mind to share her, mate?"

Cameron's arm swept around Kerry's waist, barely in time to prevent the Irish lass from assaulting the barrel chest before her. Holding her firmly within his grasp, he spoke calmly to the leering lecher before him.

"The lass is not for sale. And if you would like to question this further, you are welcome to test my pistol as well." At a broad shake of the man's bearded head, Cameron nodded and proceeded up the stairs, the baggage in one arm and the shouting lass in the other. Jack's vengeful eye followed him.

Pushing aside the door, out of necessity with his foot, Cameron strode into the room and plunked Kerry onto the feather tick, depositing the baggage on the floor. The ropes beneath the mattress barely creaked before she was on her feet again.

"That surly no-good son of a fishmonger! Why didn't you let me hit him?" Her eyes flashed and her foot beat a rapid tattoo on the floor.

"Because young ladies do not go around assaulting drunken men," he said patiently. "Now calm down. I've ordered you a bath and a light supper. It appears best that you dine up here, rather than in the tavern. Is there anything else you need?"

Her anger quickly ebbed when she realized he was leaving. She still had no idea where they were going or what he intended, for the tavern noise had forestalled much conversation. "But . . . you were to tell me about my job, where we are going, where you live, what—"

"It will have to wait until morning." A secretive smile crossed his lips, and Kerry had the vague suspicion that his answer was intended to annoy her, as if by some magical method he had found her Achilles' heel. "Nothing else? Then good night, Kerry O'Toole." And with that strange smile, he was gone.

"Damn him!" Kerry thought. Had she had an object at hand, she would have gladly thrown it, but lacking one, weakness rose up in her, causing her shoulders to droop and her head to nod. Despair and fear threatened to overcome her, but they were old adversaries and she fought them with her well-honed weapons.

A slight and darting chambermaid filled a copper tub, but Kerry scarcely saw her, for as her body descended into the pleasantly hot water she was back in Ireland, her mind having soared over a rain-drenched Atlantic. The voyage had made her very aware of the elements—wind and rain, ice and cold—for at sea these things meant one lived or died. Now she saw the soft green carpets of grass, the leafy fronds of the woods, and the glimmer of hidden lakes. Faces rushed up to greet her, five of them to be exact.

Seamus, her older brother. Golden-haired, he stared down from the cloud of steam rising from the tub, solemnly assuring her that all would be well. It amazed her that his image would come so freely, for Seamus had departed Ireland a year ago and was somewhere about on the heathen sea, part of the sassenach army. Seamus had seen far too much poverty in his native land, and he'd chosen to find his fortune elsewhere.

Kerry felt a moment of relief, intensified now that the other faces gathered around, Seamus dissolving in their wake. There was Brian, just turned thirteen and with a devil in his eyes; and there was Eamon, one year his junior, a quiet and serious boy. Kerry saw them running, their fleeting laughter coloring the winds like autumn leaves. They jostled each other as they winked at her now, and Kerry winked back.

She smiled when she thought of them as babies, delightful little creatures to hold and carry on one's hip, to bathe in the clear water while they gurgled with delight. Her mother had grown tired and old from endless work, thankless tasks, and the hopelessness of her fate. But these babies were Kerry's. It was she who could silence their crying by a soft embrace and by the music she hummed to them as she walked across the dirt floor of the thatched hut. Her father would raise a blurred eye when they fussed, then bluster his way back to the wooden table for his ale.

The sounds of the babies, so vivid a moment ago, now dissipated into the vapor, and Kerry quickly soaped a leg, failing to notice the quality of the soap, the soft sweet smell. The thudding of her heart grew more painful now as the last of the ghosts greeted her, the one most dear of all.

Her father's warm and jovial face peered up at her from under his cap, his smile wide and beckoning. It was mainly for him that she'd accepted this indenture, for he had cried and cursed the English landlords for raising his rents and causing them all to starve. He beamed proudly at her now, and she waved back as his spirit dwindled also, returning to the island across the sea. "I'll come for ya, Kerry me darling. Don't be forgetting."

She smiled reassuringly, then the vision disappeared and she was alone.

The bathwater was nearly tepid now, but Kerry enthusiastically set about scrubbing her skin. She felt warm and secure, for she felt she would never be entirely alone in this strange land. Those misty visitors would come when the need arose. She gladly freed her hair from the confines of the black cap, combing it through with her fingers before dunking her head. As the cool water caressed her hot scalp, she generously lathered soap into her dark tresses. Several rinsings later, her hair was finally clean and she emerged from the tub to rub her slender body briskly with a sackcloth towel. After three months of bathing in seawater, living in filth clear up to her knees, and forgetting the sight of clean clothes, her skin now tingled refreshingly. She felt wonderfully alive, and danced across the room to the bed.

Kerry dove into the light supper awaiting her. Some of the foods were unfamiliar but that didn't matter. There was even a small glass of clear liquid that she cautiously tasted and thought it might be wine. When she smelled the drink, she was reminded of the fruits and flowers that grew at the edge of the bay. She savored the clean, crisp taste of it. But as she was enjoying a third sip, the glass midway to her mouth, she paused for a frightening thought occurred to her: what does Cameron Brent want with me? Her experience with indentured servants was limited, and her father had merely advised her to do the best she could. But even with her lack of knowledge, Kerry realized that the treatment she'd received—the room and the bath—was rare.

She placed the glass on the gleaming pewter tray and sat up very straight. She knew nothing of him! Not a thing. Curiosity flamed in her, and it had to be appeased. But how? Her eyes flickered to the door separating the two rooms; perhaps the key would fit. "No!" she said out loud. "What if he should come back?" But the other alternative was equally bleak. Should she simply wait through the night without a clue, and on the morrow be subjected to his whim? No, she decided. It would be far better to be prepared, to have some idea of this man she was forced to work for, and this was the only way to get this knowledge.

When the key turned neatly in the lock, Kerry was suddenly aware of her state of undress, and as a precautionary measure, she took the sheet from the bed, wrapping the rough linen around her carelessly, the way she did at home if she found the need to arise in the night. Her own gown had been removed from the bag and was airing before a window. It was not yet fit for service until the evening breezes had completed their task. Gingerly, she tiptoed through the open door, poised and ready for flight should she hear a sound from within the chamber.

Silence greeted her, silence and darkness. A candle stub sat on the table at hand, gutted to a useless length. Kerry stole back to her own room and grabbed a flickering tallow light, protecting the flame with her cupped hand. Once back inside, she let her hand fall away, and the room sprang vividly to life in the encircled halo of the yellow gleam.

A bed, a bureau, a few tables, and a wingback chair greeted her eye, also a desk and a commode. All were neatly arranged for comfort and had been recently tidied. Kerry's gaze swung back to the desk, and it was here that she placed the light. If this room were mine, she reasoned, these drawers would be the place for secrets.

Downstairs, Cameron had returned to his table and had ordered his meal, the identical one which he had sent upstairs. He glanced about the tavern, seeing, to his satisfaction, the slumbering body of Jack Smith, the docksman.

I needn't watch my back, he thought wryly, aware that the docksman was not the type to let any injury go unavenged. His face darkened as he thought of the way the lout had spoken to Kerry and, as he remembered the Irish lass's unfeigned determination to return the slur, his slightly square, intensely serious face took on an even darker shading. He didn't understand his compassion for the lass, his fascination with the fire that crackled in her every movement, or with the cheerful humor that burst forth freely from her. "Humorless," his father had often fondly called him, and there were many things that Cameron did not think funny. That his mother despised him, he knew, and it puzzled him, for he was the excellent scholar and not his brother Charles. And he was a good worker, and sympathetic to his mother's disappointments. He alone loved his mother, spoke to her kindly, and ignored her less than charitable nature, her chiding remarks to the servants, her deprecating observations on his father. It wasn't until later, when he'd found out the truth, that her behavior had suddenly made sense.

Although his father had tried to stop him, Cameron had

left Philadelphia to make a life of his own, to prove himself worthy. He'd traveled through Pennsylvania to Boston, working on wheat farms and in shipyards. In the latter he'd discovered his love for the sea, and the distance he'd traveled on it had proved a balm to the festering wounds he'd brought from home.

Then his mother had died and his father had moved to his farm in the Jerseys. After a time, his heart condition had worsened and he'd died under somewhat questionable circumstances. He had bequeathed the majority of the estate to Charles, while Cameron had been left the sandy property in the Jersey Pines. "I know you can make it prosper," his father had written in his will.

The lure of having his own land had proved too hard to resist so Cameron had returned home to the delight of his friends and the displeasure of his brother. Charles had always been favored by everyone except his father so Cameron had not understood the source of Charles's rage, but it no longer concerned him. He'd assumed control of Brentwood and he found he loved the clean, white sands of the place, the tea-colored waters, the air filled with the scent of the scrub pine and mountain laurel. Not a moment did he spare from his constant planning, but he worked at molding the village and making crops survive in the heat and the unpredictable weather. Now that he was occupying the house that was built high above the lake on the fifty-year-old estate Cameron had hopes for the future.

His thoughts returned to the ragged lass he had purchased that day and confusion overwhelmed him. He thought of her face, so full of life and laughter, and of her flaming temper. He'd see that it was controlled. That she could feel things so intently was part of her charm, however. Cameron felt a tightening in his groin. It was almost painful, and it alarmed him. After all, the girl was under his protection. With a decisive motion, he called to the tavern owner.

"Send a wench up—a clean girl. You know the room." The

tavern owner nodded solemnly, his thoughts hidden behind expressionless eyes, and Cameron sat back in his seat to watch the dancers, unable to recall the last time he had danced.

A map . . . naval charts . . . books on agriculture. These were the meager contents of the drawer. Kerry sighed with disgust. Were all her efforts for naught? Then the flickering candlelight shone on a cream-colored piece of parchment pigeonholed in a tiny shelf of the desk, and she withdrew the sheet quickly. It was a letter.

"Kind Sir," it began. "In reference to your recent letter describing the peculiar actions of your waterfowl and domestic birds, I have no clear explanation. The pines are occasionally visited by strange happenings, on which even scientific men are unable to enlighten us. The local farmers have their own explanation for them, of course, ridiculous in my opinion, but as you obligated me to furnish you with any available information, I shall render the details.

"The Jersey Devil, most frequently credited with crimes of this nature, is seemingly a legend accepted by the residents of these Pinelands. The Devil is supposedly the offspring of a woman named Leeds. She had twelve children and, upon discovering a thirteenth pregnancy, shouted, "I'm tired of children! Let this be a devil!" On a stormy night, she did give birth to a child, normal at first, but as the midwives watched, the body of the child elongated, became snakelike. Cloven hooves cracked through its feet and its face evolved into a horse's head. After batlike wings sprouted from its shoulder blades, with a horrid shriek, the creature flew out the window, having already consumed some of the Leeds's children.

"Supposedly this is the origin of the legendary creature. It has been sighted occasionally, and is blamed for crop failure and drought, as well as for healthy cows that do not produce.

An exorcism was attempted in 1740, so pervasive is the belief in this diabolical presence, but legend has it that war summons the demon from his sleeping place in the swamp. Before the French and Indian Wars the demon arose and was seen by many, flapping his huge wings and emitting agonized cries as his batlike form swooped through the sky. The residents have even implied that the house of Brentwood, the house you've inherited, stands on the site of the Leeds' house and is, therefore, accursed.

"Utter nonsense, I assure you, Cameron. I only repeat the tale as you requested. Should any further information become available, I will send it speedily."

The letter was signed "Lawrence Chadds," and a postscript stated that the Indians also gave credence to the existence of that creature, that their name for it roughly translated is the Cursed of the Brown Waters.

Kerry's fingers trembled as she read the last lines. She was almost sorry now that Seamus had seen fit to teach her to read. This was her future . . . a house in some godforsaken wilderness which an eerie, satanic creature haunted. Nonsense, the Englishman had written. But then, Kerry thought, the sassenach don't believe a thing. They are not close to the land. They hear none of the whisperings of the life forms burgeoning about them. They see none of the wonders of the earth. She closed her eyes and saw a horrible vision, a creature with a horse's head winging toward her, and she nearly screamed out loud.

As if it were part of her wild imagining, the door slowly opened. Terror gripped Kerry as Cameron Brent stepped into the room, his footfall a little unsteady. She froze, while his gleaming eyes, sparkling like a moonlit lake, peered searchingly around the room, at last falling upon her.

Chapter Two

Kerry stood beside the desk in the candlelight, unaware of the incredibly lovely vision she made, her black silky hair tumbling like an onyx waterfall about her shoulders. Her red lips parted with each breath, and the rise and fall of her small breasts was clearly visible through the linen she clutched about her. Cameron stiffened at the sight of her, and indeed, the sheet hid little from his regard. Standing as she was in front of the only illumination in the ink-black room, her every curve tantalizingly outlined, she stirred his imagination as to what lay hidden beneath the sheet.

Deliberately, Cameron closed the door and walked softly to the bedside, pouring a draft of brandy. Kerry stood motionless, watching the smooth gleam of the brandy glass in the stingy light, afraid to speak until he did so she could decide how best to defend herself. If he had not seen her with the letters, she would have said she'd merely wandered into his room by mistake. . . .

"Come here." His voice was all golden tones, gone was the proper English inflection. Wincingly, she came to stand before him, to smell the fragrance of brandy, as well as the clean masculine scent she had noticed earlier. As she gazed up into his eyes, she was startled by the intensity she saw. His piercing silver stare unnerved her, but it also sent pleasurable shivers from her head down to her bare feet. A heat seemed to radiate from him, a surety, as a moment later his hand fell caressingly on her bare shoulder, softly fingering an errant lock of hair. Even in the darkness she saw his smile, dazzlingly white and confident. "You are lovely," he murmured, and a shiver went through her when he kissed the tress of hair he held. "I would have come back sooner had I known that you desired me." He smiled. "Apparently your hatred of the English is not all-encompassing."

A slow dawning occurred as Kerry glanced down at the sheet clutched between her fingers, her breasts nearly peeking forth from the thin material. As angry words formed on her lips and she prepared to plant a slap on his handsome cheek, an idea took form in her mind and her intuition took over. He'd been drinking, that she knew. And he obviously thought she was here, trespassing in his room, because she wanted to make love to him! That in itself was enough to inspire her wrath, but she paid little heed to it, realizing that fate had sent her a way out of this mess. If she was clever enough, she could play out this charade until the brandy worked its magic. She had often seen the effect whiskey had on her father, and in the one-room cottage, she had heard his most amorous intentions come to a slumbering halt on the nights he'd imbibed too freely. Her smile grew at the thought of using this ploy. It satisfied her to think that she would be deceiving this overly confident Englishman, stealing from him his pleasure in conquering a wench this night.

At the sight of her softly curving smile, Cameron slowly replaced the lock of hair to casually brush the rounded breast thrusting impudently through the thin sheet. He reached for the corner, still tucked firmly under her arm, but with a quick motion, Kerry grasped his hand and stilled it, warming it between her own.

"Sir, abide your eagerness!" She tried to hide her shocked innocence and to sound seductive and experienced as she mimicked his tone, speaking cool English with a melting lilt.

She stirred Cameron no small degree, and he frowned somewhat as she moved away from him in a teasing manner. "We have all night," she continued. "Would you spend it as one would a pence?" With a smile, she refilled his glass and poured one for herself. Then she came to stand beside him, pressing the glass in his hand.

"I'm inclined to agree," he said smoothly, but he drained the glass in one quick gulp and placed it on the desk behind him. With a purposeful stride, he advanced toward her. Kerry backed up, but she was thwarted when the wooden bed frame met the back of her legs. No escape there! She tried to hide her panic, to evade him; but she was trapped. His muscled thighs were so close to her, she was reluctant to move, not wanting to add to his excitement.

"I haven't finished my drink," she declared. Taking a sip of the fiery liquid, she was surprised at the warmth she felt, the throbbing in her veins. He smiled again, somewhat recklessly this time, and she felt his arms encircle her slender waist and pull her against him. Kerry gasped as he removed the glass from her hand. Then, before she could protest, his mouth claimed hers, his lips warm and gentle, tasting of brandy. She struggled, but his well-muscled body was like a solid oak, invulnerable. His kisses became hotter and more insistent as she writhed in his arms, and then his hands descended from her waist to caress her rounded buttocks and to draw her even closer to him. Kerry's eyes flew open as his loins pressed against hers. She was now fully aware of the desire that raged within him, a desire for her.

"No! I can't!" She tried to say, but her words were muted syllables beneath the force of his passion, his kisses descending greedily down her throat, pressing onto her breast, still covered by the cloth. She gasped as the sheet was wound free by his deft fingers and the cool evening air caressed her naked form. A burning desire sparked somewhere within her as he gazed at her, his eyes drinking their fill of her beauty. Kerry knew that she should be resisting him as his mouth took hers, coldly and calculatingly as was her plan, but somehow that plan had fallen apart and her body, no longer her own, was yielding to his ardor. His lips took her breast and she shuddered with pleasure. Helplessly holding his head even closer, she caressed the wealth of curling black hair tied at his nape, wanting more of the passion his muscular body promised.

He pressed her back onto the bed, pausing only a moment to remove his own clothes. But Kerry was only aware of sensory perceptions, the coolness of the sheets beneath her bare back, brandied kisses, the unbearable heat in her loins as he touched her. She thought she'd become mindless when his hands boldly explored her silken thighs. "Please." She feebly attempted to protest as the rational part of her mind registered the fact that he was about to take her virginity, but he simply smiled, lowering his hips between her thighs and plunging mercilessly deep within her.

A strangled cry of pain escaped her lips as reality flooded back. The throbbing in her loins was now a searing tear and she lay perfectly still, frightened of what further torment would greet her should she move. Cameron stopped. Her eyes were wide and fearful, her gasp was neither coy nor light. His mind demanded an explanation, but his flesh would not wait. The firm breasts of the girl drove into him like heated points and her silken body, beneath him, sent his blood singing with desire. He had no choice now but to give in to his flesh and drive himself into the warmth that surrounded him, using all his determination and strength to be gentle and not to make love to her savagely as his body urged him to do. His mouth lowered to hers once more and he kissed her until she was once again his. Then his lips moved to her breasts, in turn encircling the tight nipples with his tongue until he felt her lunge against him and their bodies were forged together by mutual white heat.

* * *

Then it was done. Kerry felt the unfamiliar presence in her bed, the warmth of the man beside her. A wet stickiness between her thighs quickly cleared her mind, and she sought to fling herself away, embarrassed and enraged that she, Kerry O'Toole, had let this happen. But even as she moved, Cameron caught her squarely about the shoulders. Having a few questions to ask, he determinedly pressed her back down onto the sheets.

"No!" Kerry's eyes flew wide open. As she struggled to get free, the door opened and Kerry huddled back in embarrassment as the blond serving wench sauntered into the room.

"Sorry I'm so late, gov'ner." She smiled and swung her hips enticingly as she approached the bed. "But I had me own matters to take care of, if you get me meaning." With a flick of her wrist she made a crude gesture underneath her skirts and leaned against the bedframe. "You got company now, eh? That's all right. I'm not one to complain about seconds. If you can do it twice, I sure as hell can!" With a hearty chuckle, she slapped her knees, her enormous breasts bouncing.

An enraged shriek burst from Kerry, and before Cameron could stop her, she dashed out of the bed and into the adjoining room. The abrupt slam of the door reverberated throughout the room while the serving wench looked puzzled.

She got no explanation from Cameron, however, for going right after the lass, he pounded on the door, mindless of his own naked state. "Dammit Kerry!" he shouted. "Open this door!"

"No!" She yelled back. She was fully aware that he had used her as he would the doxy on the other side of the door. Good Heavens! she thought, as the full realization of what she had done struck her. Unwittingly, she had already served that Englishman's baser needs—almost willingly. Furthermore, she would be in his power for the next five years. Tears rolled down her face, and she hardly heard his fists slamming the door at her back. He *knew* of the desire he'd kindled in her—he had to! What would he think but that she'd wanted the same as he!

"Kerry." His voice was more controlled now, but she was still aware enough to be amazed at the scene he was causing. She didn't think Englishmen ever got riled about anything. "Kerry, I just want to talk to you."

"Go away," she moaned, her head pressing against the door.

The serving wench shrugged and drained the brandy glass, then sat down on the bed, amused. She had seen many a strange thing in her occupation, but this bloke banging down the door in his altogether was something else. She couldn't wait to tell the kitchen girls all about it in the morning.

"Kerry, if you don't open this door, I'll break it down." His voice was cool and composed now, and the wench jumped to her feet.

"I wouldn't do that if I was you, gov! Old Bickford, the owner, don't take too kindly to such and I don't need no blame—"

"Kerry!"

"You have your damned trollop with you!" Kerry shouted, enraged by the thought. "You go have yourself a good time and leave me be! You come through that door, you sassenach bastard, and I'll break every bone in your body!"

"Might I help you, sir?" The tavern owner's voice came through the door and Kerry pressed her ear to the lock to hear what transpired.

"No thank you." There was a smothered chuckle, obviously the wench's and then Cameron sighed heavily. "Here, miss. There's the money for tonight. I won't be needing your services," he said, then called out. "Everything is fine, Bickford. I will see you in the morning."

When she heard a reluctant shuffle of boots in the hall, Kerry scuttled back into her bed, pulling the quilts firmly above her head. She'd witnessed enough of Cameron Brent's actions to know that he meant what he said. He would find a way to enter her room before long. Sure enough, sometime later she heard his voice above her but she kept her eyes closed, her breathing even. "This is not the end of this, Kerry O'Toole. I plan to know the truth and tomorrow you will provide it." With a click of the door he was gone.

Morning found Kerry struggling against the sunlight, the bright shimmer of it just beyond the darkness. Her conscious mind struggled to awaken, but something warned her, told her not to leave this soft, cottonlike dream world, not to enter cold reality.

Too late! A wedge of intruding sun opened her eyes, falling across the red and blue patchwork quilt that lay across the bed. The events of the previous night came rushing up to greet her, and she suddenly knew why she hadn't wanted to waken.

It had really happened. In the course of that fateful half-hour, she had departed from her familiar world and had entered foreign territory, yet she was not mature enough to have done so. A warm flush colored her face, and she quickly drew the quilt over her eyes as she recalled in bold detail the ardor of Cameron Brent, the touch of his hands, the captivating kisses she'd been unable to resist. Her white skin inflamed, she groaned outloud. What did fate have in store for her today? Then, remembering Cameron's surprise the previous night, upon discovering that the wench in his bed was not an experienced lover but a virgin, she flushed again. And what could she tell him? She could hardly explain it to herself. She tossed aside the quilt, irritated and ashamed.

A looking glass adorned the wall of her snug room, and from it a dark-haired young Irish lass stared. Her sea green eyes were wide and frightened, yet defiant. Was it her imagination that today her eyes seemed more knowing, her lips fuller and more cherry colored, almost startling against her skin? Her body betrayed her. It was no longer the slim, boyish figure with which she was comfortable, but a strange, womanly frame. Her hair tumbled over her full breasts, down to the slender waist that enhanced her rounded hips. Unable to bear the sight of her changed appearance, she twirled from the mirror with sudden wrath and snatched the gown that now smelled fresh after its airing. The blue calico, stitched by her mother's hand, brought that woman's tired face to mind, but Kerry quickly squelched the thought. What would her mother, nay her father, say if they knew? What would any of them think? She, an O'Toole, had bedded with a Colonial, a sassenach at that! She could almost hear her father's curse. No, she could not think of that now, for she knew if she did she would be robbed of the fortitude she needed to get through this day and face Cameron Brent.

The dress, though not of a good quality, was clean and new in the sense that it had not yet been worn, and to Kerry it might have been the finest velvet. Straightening her back, she paced the floor, waiting for the frightful moment to arrive.

It came soon, for during her third stroll across the worn pine floor, the knock sounded. Bracing herself, Kerry forced a smile and threw open the portal.

But outside stood no mysterious Englishman with a silvery gaze of burning intensity. Instead, it was his driver, George.

"Miss O'Toole." George bowed, and his florid face flushed still more with pleasure as he surveyed the lass before him. Cleaned of the filth of yesterday, she appeared even lovelier than he'd imagined, and the sight of such a fresh young girl warmed him considerably. "Mr. Brent has gone off into town, having business there to attend, but he bade me to accompany you today so you can fulfill some errands before we leave for home."

"Errands?" Kerry asked, puzzled. "He said naught to me

of it."

"Aye, 'twas not the time. He asked me not to disturb you too early, and he trusted me to see to your tea and the completion of the tasks."

At the mention of needing rest, Kerry found her face growing hot, but George seemed not to notice and if he thought these proceedings strange, he said nothing. He is probably used to attending his lord's trollops, Kerry thought, miffed, but George was smiling benevolently at her, shuffling his feet, and awkwardly toying with his tricorn. She sought to put the man at ease and smiled kindly.

"If that is what Master Brent wants, I will help in any way I can." There was no sense in upsetting George and when he bestowed a relieved grin on her, she knew she was right.

"Aye, that's good, miss. Now we'll take some tea, if you'll not mind an old man such as myself intruding upon your morning meal, and then we'll be off."

"The pleasure is mine," Kerry declared cheerfully, her outlook considerably brighter now. After all, the dreaded confrontation was postponed, she was to have tea with the first kind person she'd met in this America, and perhaps, if she was careful, she could find out more about their destination and about the fabled demon mentioned in the letter. George flushed with pleasure, and gallantly offering his arm, he took her down the steps.

The tavern room below had cast off the sins of the night. It appeared to be fresh and clean, and the tables were set with cones of sugar, with pewter pitchers, spoons and forks, and with thick, heavy china. Even the telltale smoke of the previous night had vanished, along with the disagreeable occupants. Kerry thought of the dock worker who'd assaulted her and she shook her fist at the vacant spot where he had stood.

"Miss?" George asked, his lined face clearly puzzled, and Kerry laughed, realizing she'd been caught.

"'Tis nothing. I was merely thinking of scoundrels that

frequent the taverns at night."

"Yes." George grinned, taking a place beside her. "The master was none too happy about that himself. He likes a quiet life, that he does."

It was on the tip of Kerry's tongue to ask about this "quiet life," but a young girl was beside them, busily stacking teacups and pitchers of milk, plates of black bread, and steaming porridge. As soon as the lass departed, Kerry brought the subject up of her own accord.

"George, where are we going?" She suppressed a laugh as George sputtered in his tea.

"Trifle hot." Holding a linen handkerchief to his face, he tried to evade the question.

With a winning smile, Kerry leaned over the table and removed the large flowered milk pitcher, a convenient obstacle that the coachman was employing as a hiding spot. "George," she said sweetly, "I would like to know—"

George gathered together the fragments of his dignity and bereft of the pitcher, he cleared his throat and replied firmly: "You shall find out everything, miss, in due time." Then, seeing the agitation in her face and the boyish tapping of her hand upon the table, all the more obvious because it contrasted with her feminine beauty, he reluctantly sought to ease her fears.

"Master Cameron has his own reasons for wantin' to tell you himself, miss. You'll have to trust him and you can take it from me that you can. I've been in his employ for well over fifteen years and I've not regretted a one."

"Can you not tell me anything? What am I to do, what kind of a house is this, and what of this devil, this demon that haunts the Jerseys? Is there really such a thing? Did—"

"The Jersey devil!" George's voice lowered perceptibly and he gazed across the table, his small blue eyes widened to the size of a shilling piece. "Where did you hear of that?"

There was awe in his voice, and the slightest tremor. Kerry was instantly alarmed. Her instincts for people were good, and she knew in this short space of time that George was an extremely devoted, practical, and unimaginative man. If such a person could be alarmed by the mere mention of this thing, then Kerry had reason to fear. She replied carefully.

"I heard tales, aboard ship," she answered.

"You'll not be speaking of such a thing here, or at Brentwood," George stated quickly, urgency apparent in his voice. "Do not speak of it."

"Brentwood?" A twinkle appeared in Kerry's eyes, and she shrugged resignedly, trying a new tack. "Well, I know naught of Brentwood, but where I come from, I'm used to speaking my mind so I know I'll be no different here." With a lazy yawn, she glanced about the empty tavern, as if no longer interested in the conversation.

As she suspected, her ploy worked. George's face knotted with frustrated thought, then the lines on it smoothed away and he sighed, sipping his cup. "Miss, you've won. I see that you'll be needing some knowledge of the place where we're heading, before you are in serious trouble."

Kerry nodded, pausing to reassure the man. "Don't worry. I won't tell Cameron Brent."

"Aye, that you won't, because I will. But never you mind, you wanted to know and I'll be telling you. We are going to a place located between Philadelphia and the Jersey shore. It's called The Forks. For reasons of his own, Master Brent does not wish visibility. He desires to proceed with his work in peace and comfort. He has quite a large household and does not venture into the city often. That is why he is making these purchases today. I have a list with me."

A wrinkled sheet of yellowed paper was thrust across the table and, as she finished her porridge, Kerry ran an interested eye over it. For all George had told her, she was little wiser than before and her curiosity was aroused. What was Cameron Brent working on? What required such secrecy? Kerry understood that rumors of the demon might cause attention in a small village, but what kind?

The paper contained a list of foods and other items to be bought: spices that might be difficult to obtain, cottons and other cloths, glassware and cutlery, as well as imported liquors and brandies. Even to Kerry's eye the items were not those a pauper would desire, and she wondered again about this man she would be working for.

"I think we'd better be about it." George did not like the inquisitive look in her widening eyes and he stood up quickly, before any more damaging information slipped from his tongue.

Kerry folded the paper and placed it in her sleeve. As she accompanied George to the coach, her mind absorbed all the facts. After he'd helped her onto the seat so she could ride beside him, she spelled out what she knew of her employer.

He was rich. That much was certain, but from farming? There had to be another source of income. And he was cultured—educated—that was obvious from his speech and manner. What was such a man doing in the wilderness, instead of here in the city where he belonged?

Crowds of well-dressed people loitered in the cobbled streets, peering into glistening shop windows and pausing to exchange a word with passers-by. Carriages lined the street as the horse trotted into the busier part of town, and Kerry gazed about at the lovely red brick buildings with window frames neatly painted white. Gentlemen, dressed in rich brocades and silk stockings, powdered wigs and lace jabots, stood outside the largest rectangular building, their heads dipping seriously. "The State House," George supplied, a queer note in his voice.

Kerry craned her neck for one last look, but already the building was behind them. The carriage turned onto a small street lined with walnut trees and shops of every description. "Here's where we get off."

Kerry swung down by herself, ignoring George's disapproving glance, beginning with the top of the list, they stopped in almost every shop, examining the best of materials and household supplies. As the noon hour approached the coach was filling up, and the top rack was laden with parcels and boxes. Kerry was a shrewd trader, George admired that. For while he had tended to buy the first merchandise offered, the Irish lass had bravely upbraided shopkeepers who offered inferior goods until, grunting and complaining, they retreated to the back rooms and returned with far nicer items. A price was never firm until paid out, Kerry's father had said, and his daughter had remembered it. She had haggled over the price of a bolt of blue cotton chintz until the shopkeeper had groaned aloud. "Miss, this cotton came all the way from London itself! I cannot let it go for a mere pittance!"

But the lass's determined grin made him smile also, and he thrust the cloth back into the sack. "Be off with ye," he grumbled good-naturedly, "before I change my mind." Kerry laughed and ran outside before his wife came from behind the piles of cloth and acidly scolded her husband.

"Miss, I'm truly impressed," George remarked. "Did you find the cotton to your liking?" The sly twinkle in his eye should have warned her, but elated with her successful bargaining, Kerry did not notice.

"Aye, it's lovely. Far lovelier than any bit of cloth these eyes have ever seen." She sighed, satisfied with the day's work, when a sudden thought occurred. "And why would Master Cameron be needing such an item? Does he? . . ." A furious blush followed, for it was on the tip of Kerry's tongue to inquire about her employer's personal life. George's response left her gasping, however.

"'Tis for you, miss. The master gave me strict orders that whatever piece caught your eye was to be yours. You'll be needing a few other things also. Shoes . . ." As his voice trailed off Kerry self-consciously tucked her broken black boots beneath the wooden carriage seat. She realized that Cameron must have noticed their poor condition last night, when she'd obdurately braced them against the wall. Hah! she thought angrily. Now he thinks to appease me with a few trinkets. The thought scarcely completed, she faced poor George, anger in her sea green gaze.

"I'll not be taking any charity from the likes of him!" she bristled. Thinking he had ordered this as payment for services rendered, she let an outraged sound of protest escape her lips, and George gave her a frankly curious stare. They were outside the shop hung with a sign advertising footwear and hats of every description, along with bridles and horse supplies.

"Miss," George said patiently, reasoning with the lass whose nose now pointed toward the heavens, "you'll be needing these things, where we're going. The summers are hot, hotter than any you've ever seen, while the winters—"

"I've managed this long on me own without any handouts from anyone, and I'll continue to do so." From the set of her firm mouth, the coachman knew he was beaten, and flapping the reins of the horse, he did not stop until they reached a solicitor's office.

"Master Brent will not like it," he warned, but Kerry shrugged.

"One can't like everything," she replied flippantly. Her bravado quickly evaporated, however, when she saw the reason for their pause outside the solicitor's, for through the open door strode Cameron Brent.

He was still nodding to and speaking with someone inside the office, and he clutched a walking stick of a peculiar design, with a carved silver handle that appeared to be a horse's head. In the noon sunlight standing on the gray marble step, he looked even more handsome than the day before and an excitement quickened within her, an excitement she could neither explain nor control. His garb was rich, without the extra ruffles some of the men she'd seen in town affected, and his hair, a soft chestnut in the sun, was not powdered but merely tied at the nape of his neck. His features were firm, as if carved, and his expression was serious and unsmiling. He had the stance of one accustomed to giving orders, and that he did so was verified a moment later when Kerry heard his last words. "I want the deed no later than Monday. Good day, Jacob."

As he strode to the carriage, Kerry instinctively withdrew, though her eyes wandered far too freely over his muscular form. Recalling the previous night, she forced herself to stare straight ahead, confident that a gentleman such as himself would scarcely make mention of such events in front of his coachman.

"Miss Kerry, please come down and sit with me inside the coach. I'll need to know of your purchases, so I may see what else is required."

He did not ask, he merely stated his wish. Kerry frantically sought an excuse, but George was already taking her hand and helping her down, then into the soft leather recesses of the coach. As her employer entered, she heard George say, "We've finished most of what you set out, except for one thing. The lass refused the clothes and shoes. She will not accept your charity."

"I see." Cameron's voice was rich with inflection, but he wasted no time in discussion with the coachman. "I'll take care of that. Proceed to the tavern so we can take our midday meal."

As he climbed into the carriage, he saw that Kerry was seated as far away as possible, a crate of tea and spices placed beside her. Cameron glanced at her and at the curious occupants of that seat, then took the opposite one. The coach had barely started to rumble over the cobbles when he spoke quietly.

"To refuse the clothes was foolish, Kerry." His voice was soft but forbidding, and Kerry steeled herself for the confrontation to come. Falling back on her best resource, she replied defiantly.

"I'll not be needing handouts from you, sir. I'm not the

kind of woman that can be bought—for any price." She regretted the words as soon as she uttered them, for he responded with undue haste.

"Ah. I was wondering when we would come to that. I have given considerable thought to what happened last night, and I do see the possibility that a misunderstanding has occurred."

"Possibility!" Kerry's shriek could be heard outside the carriage, and Cameron hastened to explain.

"I meant—"

"I know what you meant." Her eyes flashed green fire, and although her hair was secured in a subdued knot at the nape of her neck, Cameron could picture it falling around her, wild and free as on the previous night. Indeed, a wild animal might envy her fearsome visage as she faced her employer, her outrage evident. "I did not know you would attack a woman in such a manner, or I might have been forewarned. I will certainly bear that in mind in the future."

"Dammit Kerry! I apologize, but you have to take some of the blame. Seeing a partially clothed female in my bedroom, what was I to think?"

"You might have asked," Kerry replied hotly, for she was angry at his suggestion that she had no business being in his room. "Or do you always take what you want and make up for it later?"

A slight throbbing in his neck told Kerry that he was angry too, dangerously so, but it was not in her nature to back down and she did not fear that warning sign. With considerable effort, he controlled his ire and forced his voice to remain calm. "Nevertheless, I feel a certain obligation to you for what happened. I know I cannot repay the damage, but I can help you in some ways. You will be needing the clothes for this climate, and I'd intended to supply them before this incident occurred. I have other servants besides George and I have always seen to their clothing. You will be no exception. If you still can't accept that, George informed me of your talent in the marketplace, and of the considerable sum you've already saved me. Consider the clothing a bonus due to those savings. You certainly couldn't call that charity."

His words penetrated the angry red haze that surrounded her. Partially mollified, she nodded her head, her gaze directed out the window.

"Good," he continued absently, a rare smile curving his lips. "Tell me, Kerry. How did you acquire such a knowledge about buying? I have seldom seen George so impressed."

"I know nothing about it," Kerry answered simply. "But I know a good deal about people. I can spot a man who stretches the truth and that tells me what I need to know."

"I see." Cameron's voice revealed nothing, but Kerry found herself looking up at him, his silvery gaze meeting hers. "I think I shall take you with me then on future trips. Such a skill is most valuable these days." At her inquisitive look, he hastened to explain. "The colonies are revolting against England. They are heavily taxed, and the benefits they receive from the mother country are becoming dubious at best, disadvantageous at worst. Boycotts are becoming common. The colonists are trading their homespun and American-made goods more frequently. There will be many changes in the marketplace, as well as in this country in the coming years." His voice drifted off and he tapped his stick thoughtfully against the door, in a manner that betrayed the intensity of his thoughts.

At that moment George pulled up by the tavern door, and all too eagerly, Cameron departed the coach, helping the lass down into the dining room. Kerry realized with considerable relief that he had been distracted enough by their conversation not to ask her why she'd entered his room. She could only hope he would now forget to do so.

The afternoon sun was beginning to sink when they

entered a small dress shop in the fashionable section of town. Kerry gazed about in disbelief at the shelves filled with bolts of cloth, spools of threads, ermine and beaver pelts, laces and silks, and fringes and adornments of every description. Kerry turned quickly to Cameron and protested. "You said clothes for working! This is the wrong type of shop."

Steadily and slowly, his gaze traveled down the length of her body, then back up, and her face flushed. She was about to upbraid him when she noticed a shopboy watching the commonly dressed girl and the gentleman who eyed her with such a keen regard. The lad continued to stare at Kerry until she felt positively unclothed.

"You . . ." She choked, made furious by the amused glint in Cameron's silver eyes. "If you think for one minute that because of what happened, you can—"

"Kerry, wait outside."

It was an abrupt dismissal, and although she wanted to challenge him, the shopboy was watching and she had no desire to create a scene. The lad's eye was far too bold as it was. With a scuff of her boots she strode out the door to cool her rage in the spring breeze.

Inside the shop, Cameron called to the lad, then held a coin before his eager eyes.

"Aye, mate. What can I do for you? My mother runs the shop, but she's upstairs now."

"Call her down then. But before you go, what size was the lady I was with, would you say? I assume you were staring at her for that reason?"

The lad, a sharp boy to be sure, caught his drift and reddened. "I think I could describe her size to my mother, for the making of her clothes."

"Good." Cameron nodded and tossed the coin to the obliging lad who ran up the stairs.

43

Chapter Three

"Hurry up, miss. The carriage is waiting."

The knock on the door brought Kerry fully awake and she regretfully slid out of the warm quilt. A cold spell had drifted over the land during the night and her toes curled at the icy feel of the floor planks. With considerable haste she pulled on her dress, the blue calico, over her bare skin and saw goose bumps rising. As her feet slipped inside the boots, grateful, Kerry tried not to look at them but merely appreciated the shelter they provided from the cold.

George was waiting in the hall and he quickly ushered her to the tavern dining area. "Master Brent wants to get an early start," he explained. "The roads are unpredictable this time of year, some of them flooded by the spring thaw. The trip can be made in one day, without unforeseen events."

Cameron Brent was already seated at the polished oak table, impatiently glancing out the night-blackened window. The table was decked with steamed clams, spanish mackerel, sea bass, fried chicken, corn fritters, waffles, potatoes, tea, jams, and breads. Indeed, its legs seemed to groan under the weight of the load. "What time is it?" Kerry asked, glancing at the screen of darkness behind them. "It looks like the middle of the night."

"About four," Cameron answered while George silently

departed to ready the coach. "I thought it best to get an early start so as to be home by this eve." His eyes shone as he said the word home.

Whatever this place is, it certainly means something to Cameron Brent, Kerry thought.

"Surely you're not going to eat all this!" she exclaimed, seating herself and taking a cup of tea. Her stomach lurched at the sight of so much food at such an early hour, but Cameron nodded seriously.

"Yes, and I suggest you do the same. The inns are few and far between on the trip, and should ill luck befall us, a meal is far less missed if a good one had preceded it."

Kerry's nose wrinkled at the thought, and she watched in silent protest as he dished some fish and a mountainous portion of waffles and crispy fritters onto her plate. "I've seen a fair sample of your appetite," he continued dryly. "So please don't be shy."

As soon as his gaze left hers, Kerry allowed herself the indulgence of a scowl, which Cameron missed only by a few moments for he quickly looked up. Noticing, she smiled sweetly and indicated her compliance by raising the chicken to her lips. A fleeting smile graced his mouth, but was gone in an instant and his brooding again took hold. He's the oddest Tory I've ever seen, she thought, taking advantage of the opportunity to observe without being observed while she ate. His dark chestnut hair was fine and straight, but around his neck and at the base where his locks were tied, a few curls broke rebelliously loose from their confinement. His face was a cleanly chiseled masterpiece of elegance and breeding —the high forehead and Roman nose, the jawline that marked determination and forcefulness—but this was at odds with his eyes, dark gray and brooding one minute, silvery and glinting with suppressed amusement the next. His rare smile, showed strong white teeth, and his hands, rougher than most gentleman's, were dexterous. It was like two personalities forged into one being, the strong, serious one taking precedence due to the owner's persistence. He seemed to feel her gaze for he looked up, studying her as intently as she had him.

"Hadn't we better go?" she asked as she finished up her plate, becoming unnerved under his steady stare.

"Yes, I think we should." He stood up to lend her assistance, but Kerry leaped out of the seat before he got to her and walked past him out the door.

George was waiting in the morning cold. He yawned, his ample face disappearing into a cavernous opening before he covered his mouth and held open the door. Strong hands clasped Kerry's waist and before she could make a sound, she was handed into the carriage and immediately joined by Cameron. It then dawned on her that she was to be closeted with this man for the rest of the day in such a confined space. Kerry had never been alone with any man except Cameron . . . that night. . . . She refused to allow her thoughts to follow *that* course any longer, but a shiver sped along her spine and her pulse raced. Even at home, she'd never been courted for most of the lads had avoided marriage, being concerned mainly with survival. And now, this man who had taken her virginity, would be her private companion until long past nightfall!

Well, if he thinks I'll show fear, little he knows me! Kerry thought bravely, lifting her chin and fixing her gaze defiantly on the dark window.

"Are you cold?" Cameron asked solicitously, placing the wooden panel in the window opening and hooking it firmly into place. "Springtime in Philadelphia can be chilly."

"No," she answered, a little too quickly. A fleeting smile curved Cameron's face; then he leaned closer to her, his hand braced directly on the seat beside her. "What do you think you're doing?" Kerry sputtered, but she immediately clamped her lips shut in embarrassment for he was drawing a lap robe from beneath the cushion and handing it toward her. Her face was averted so he spread the warm fur over her legs, then sat back in the seat opposite her. When she dared to look once more, he was no longer watching her. Indeed, she might not have been present for his attention was concentrated on the papers that lay in his lap. The only audible sounds in the coach for the next hour were the scratchings of his quill on parchments as he made notations next to the neatly summed columns of figures or the paragraphs written in a scrawl she soon recognized as his own.

The pen did not cease until the sun was high in the sky, and then Cameron paused only to open the window a bit. His attention was drawn to the countryside for only a few moments, however, and then he was back at work on his papers. Kerry's curious glances afforded her little information, but when he withdrew a familiar-looking parchment, she quickly sank back into the seat and riveted her gaze outside. She had no doubt as to what *that* letter contained; it was the one she'd foolishly opened in Cameron's room. From the corner of her eye she saw his forbidding frown as he once more scanned the letter's contents before rolling it back up and placing it deep inside his breast pocket.

"'Tis the Delaware." His clipped voice broke the silence and Kerry glanced up at him, startled.

"What?"

He gestured with his hand toward the river. "We are on a ferry crossing the Delaware river into the Jerseys." He leaned forward, expanding on the subject while Kerry listened with interest.

"The place where we are going also lies on a river, but one a bit different than this. The Mullica river is a narrow, twisting channel, a haven for smugglers, a deathtrap for the unwary. Brentwood, the place where I make my home is actually a small village rather than a house." He drew a diagram on the back of a sheet of parchment as he spoke. "This is the main house, a short distance from the road. There is also an ice house, a stable, a general store, and the barns. In the village section down near the lake"—a circle was drawn on the table with a roughened thumb and Kerry nodded—"there's a sawmill, a gristmill, a blacksmith's, and the workers' cottages."

"Workers' cottages?" Kerry asked. "For farming? I've never heard—"

"No." Cameron answered, amused at her blatant curiosity. "No, not farming. Iron."

"Iron!" Her incredulity was apparent from her arched brow as she studied the Englishman before her. "Here? In the Jerseys?"

"Yes," he explained. "The Pine Barrens of West Jersey have considerable iron deposits below the rivers and bogs. The waters of these pinelands are tea colored and very soft, because of the accumulation of these iron deposits."

"And you mine and produce iron?"

"Yes, although not the way a mine would. The waters actually do this. They percolate through the stream beds, picking up the iron and bringing it to the surface where it is relatively easy to remove. The workers dig out the ore, bringing it in flat ore boats downstream to the furnace where it is melted."

"And there is a great demand for this iron in the colonies?" Kerry asked.

Cameron Brent's elegant smile appeared. "Presently, the furnace sustains the community, producing firebacks, pots, kettles, and things of that nature. It should make you happy to know that the English government is very much against iron production here. They have, so far, been unsuccessful in enacting legislation to prevent it, and they have enough trouble here now."

Kerry grinned at his mention of the English government's discomfiture, but she had a feeling he had not told her all. "'Tis strange that England should be so concerned about a wee bit of iron," she mused. "Unless . . . could the ore be used to make munitions?"

His face darkened almost imperceptibly, and Cameron gave a quick nod of assent. "It could."

His curt reply warned her not to ask more so Kerry changed the subject.

"What kind of work . . . I mean, what is it you want me to do when we get to your home?" Kerry became flustered when his gaze passed boldly over her, a strange smile apparent in the silver of his eyes as well as on his lips.

"Fear not," he declared. "I have no intention of dishonoring you further. I shall find work suitable for you."

The smile, which still adorned his lips, provoked Kerry to glare at him. "I'm happy that you take the matter so lightly. 'Twas not your honor ruined."

"Kerry, I will do everything in my power to make it up to you."

"That's grand!" Wide, sea-colored eyes sparkled at him, no laughter in them, but a different emotion entirely. "There are some things your money can't restore!"

"Dammit Kerry! What would you have me do? The deed is done. There is nothing I can do to erase it, nor would I." Seeing that he'd provoked further outrage, he laid a restraining hand on her arm so she would not leap from her seat. "I cannot lie to you, Kerry, and to say that I regret that night would be doing so. But I realize that I'm as indebted to you as you are to me."

Kerry tried to maintain her anger, but the pleading look in his eyes, for the briefest moment, was tantalizingly warm and human, and extremely attractive contrasted with the sternness of his face. He had leaned closer to her so she could see his every feature clearly, and she recalled his sensual smile, the soft, silvery glimmer of his eyes when they grew dark with passion. A shiver passed through her as the intimate details of that night with him were suddenly real again, and she experienced that spark of excitement his very presence seemed to generate.

This is madness! she thought, turning her face quickly

away, embarrassed that he might have seen her emotions on her face. He is an Englishman! Shame flooded through her as she realized her weakness, wrought by the touch of an English hand. He was her enemy, a living example of the people who caused her own so much suffering. Nothing should have brought her so low, yet his mere glance set her to trembling. No other lad's kisses had ever set her aflame, set her senses reeling, and drawn her very will from herself. It was a hard thing for her to face—she desired him. This won't happen, she resolved. But her body seemed out of accord with her mind, and her veins still throbbed with a frightening heat.

But Cameron was burying himself in work once more, dismissing her as he turned to his books and figures. A discerning eye would have detected the slight throbbing in his cheek, his tightly clenched jaw, but Kerry saw none of that, her own turmoil clouding her mind. She chafed, for reasons she did not entirely understand, and she slung her small frame back into the corner of the coach. She was rewarded for the noise she made with a frozen glance, so she shrugged in half-hearted apology as her nerve fled under his steely gaze.

"Just getting comfortable."

His eyes remained on her a moment longer, then returned to the parchments as if they were of great interest. Damned English! She thought, drawing the fur over her shoulders and presenting him with a fine view of her back.

A soft yellow light glowed in the distance, slowly becoming definable as a candle glowing in a window. Cameron's eyes narrowed at the sight. He was puzzled by the sign of someone awake in the house. Almost before the carriage stopped on the soft sand path, he leaped out, impatiently extending Kerry a hand from sheer politeness. George seemed equally baffled as he swung down from the coach, lantern in hand.

"Aye, 'tis a light all right. Were you expecting anyone? Perhaps Eliah or Richard Westcoat?"

"No." Cameron's firm mouth was set, and in the lamplight, Kerry saw an ominous gleam in his eyes. His hand tightened on hers as they strode toward the house, and his annoyance was clearly reflected in the sharp click of his boots on the gravel walk. Kerry's free hand clasped her bag as she struggled to keep pace with him. A slight tension was apparent in his manner, a tension that increased a moment later when the door swung open and a handsome, light-complected man a few years younger than Cameron smiled indolently in the doorjamb.

"Cameron, my dear fellow. I am so glad to see you! I've been waiting up for you." His amiable features relaxed, and in the lamplight, Kerry saw the silvery glint of his powdered wig, the smooth, fashionable brocade of his waistcoat, the impeccable linen of his shirt. Ruffles dripped from his sleeves and about his neck, emphasizing the fairness of his skin, the regularity of his features, the innocent blue twinkle of his eyes. Cameron seemed anything but pleased to see the man, however, and his fingers tightened painfully on Kerry's wrist. With a small maneuver, he ushered her before him, gathering up her bag himself.

At the sight of Kerry, the man gave a twisted smile.

"Well, what have we here. An Irish maid—and a pretty one at that." A strange inflection colored the seemingly innocent remark, and as she stood in the hallway, Kerry saw Cameron's face harden. "My, my," the young man continued in that casual way. "History does repeat."

"Charles, that's enough," Cameron said softly. He turned reluctantly to Kerry. "My brother," he said by way of explanation, as if almost unwilling to part with the information.

"Cam, you never change." The young man called Charles turned to Kerry, fixing a clear blue gaze on her, his guileless eyes shining. "Happy to meet you, miss. I'll bet Cameron hasn't told you anything about me, has he?" He turned his knowing gaze on his brother, while Cameron's features remained immobile. "He doesn't like me," Charles continued, as if the matter was amazingly funny. "But that's because I'm all fun and he's all seriousness and work."

Cameron said nothing. He simply watched the two as if determined not to influence Kerry. With a quick smile, Kerry took the proffered white hand and tossed back her hair, gazing up at Charles. "I'm Kerry O'Toole, and I'm happy to meet you also." She gazed up at him speculatively, then continued. "I think there's more to you than meets the eye, so I'll be sure to keep me eye on you." Her tone was properly teasing, but her eyes were not, and Charles broke into delighted laughter.

"Maybe you should Miss Kerry. And Cam too, otherwise I might be inclined to steal you for myself." With a wink, he turned back to Cameron, still chuckling. "Helga's gone to bed. Now that this lass is here, do you think I might have tea?"

The annoyance increased in Cameron's face, and he took Kerry firmly up the arm and guided her to a staircase. "Charles, even in this house servants do not work past midnight, not even indentures. If you want tea, get it yourself."

"I don't mind . . ." Kerry began, but Cameron's face darkened ominously. Having glimpsed his anger before, she thought it best to obey him. From the corner of her eye, she saw Charles bow in a mock apology.

"Terribly sorry, lass. So blinded by your beauty, I scarce thought of time. And the thought of a good meal sent my mind in a frenzy."

"That's its permanent state," Cameron replied bluntly. A hoarse cough came from the doorway, and Kerry saw George there, struggling to repress his laughter. At the sight of the coachman, Charles drew himself up with all the dignity he could muster and left the room.

"Which are the servants' quarters?" Kerry asked as she stopped at a landing that turned to the right off the steps. A long hall stretched before her, illuminated by the candle in the window alcove. Without replying, Cameron opened the second door, placed her bag inside, and lighted several smaller tapers. Instantly, the air was filled with a sweet, lingering scent.

"Bayberry," Cameron explained. "The bushes grow freely in the pines. This room hasn't been used for quite some time and the candles help sweeten the air. Do you like it?"

"Oh, yes." Kerry breathed in the refreshing smell.

Cameron smiled and strode across the room to place several logs in the grate and start a fire. In the flickering light, Kerry glanced about the room and saw a bureau, a dressing table of wood so dark and shining it appeared to be of glass, and a rocking chair with a spoked back. Under her feet was a braided rug made of every imaginable color and material, sure protection against the cold on a winter's morn, and the adjacent windows against the farthest wall were hung with soft white curtains, tied back and promising a view.

In the center of the room, drawing the eye magnetically, was a four poster bed, hung with a crocheted canopy of wool so fine it dangled like the web of a spider and created a jagged scallop at the top. Pineapples were carved on the tips of the posts, and the bed itself was covered with a quilt of white edged with green leaves and red flowers. A chamber pot stood to the side and behind that, a washstand with a pitcher standing in a bowl. It was by far the most gracious room Kerry had ever seen and she could scarcely believe it was hers.

"There must be a mistake." She turned, nearly coming into contact with his broad chest as he stood up from the fire. Cameron grasped her waist, helping her to regain her balance, and as his eyes met hers in the firelight, a thrill of excitement coursed through her. Alarmed, she pulled away from him.

Taking a deep breath, she continued. "This cannot be a servant's room." She glanced once more at the lovely surroundings, then looked up at her employer for an explanation.

Cameron strode past her. Pausing for a moment at the fireplace, he fingered an oval object for a moment, his face softening in the pale moonlight shining from the window. Then, carefully replacing the object, he went to stand at the window itself, peering absently into the night. Moonlight silvered his face, lending him an eerie quality and casting every line and crease of his skin into shadow. He slowly turned toward her, and he gestured to the room with a flick of his hand.

"It is where I wish you to stay. Do you have any objections?" He spoke as if he expected none, and under his fearsome glance, Kerry voiced none.

"No, but—"

"Then it's settled." With a nod of his head he quit the room, closing the door softly behind him and leaving only the aromatic fragrance of candles as a reminder that he'd been there. Still feeling as if she were dreaming, Kerry fingered the fine quilt, then the draperies and the tables. As she touched each in turn she wondered at this mystery that was Cameron Brent.

However, a tired yawn persuaded her to prepare for sleep so she availed herself of the fresh water in the pitcher on the washstand. The water was chill but pleasantly so, and after she dried her face on a soft linen towel she felt tingly, warm, and refreshed. The air, heated by the fragrant logs, caressed her bare flesh as she gazed out the window into the courtyard below.

Moonlight bathed the scene, softly touching the tips of the pine trees and reflecting on the blackened waters of the nearby lake. Several tall buildings stood nearby, and from what Cameron told her, she knew them to be the furnace and the mills. Below, in a puddle of lamplight she saw George handing down the bags to an unseen helper. As that man stepped into the light to assist with a large trunk, Kerry withdrew, for she recognized the tall lean figure of Cameron Brent.

'Tis strange that he would prefer to help a servant rather than speak with his brother, she mused. Then again, the brothers' behavior was also strange. She gathered from their conversation that they had not seen each other recently, yet Cameron gave the impression they were meeting too soon. Remembering the love shared by those in her own family, Kerry wondered at these brothers. Then she sighed and shrugged. Just one more mystery to solve.

Moving the candle to the mantelpiece, Kerry drew down the bed covers and tossed her boots under the bed. She had carefully hung up her dress, but the rest of her belongings were still in the bag. Seeing the clean, cedar-lined bureau, polished within an inch of its life, Kerry could not bear the thought of placing her old clothes in the drawers until she could wash them.

For a moment she stood before the fire, and her gaze came to rest on the item Cameron had picked up from the mantel. Curious, she reached for it and held the wooden object to the flickering light. Startled, she saw that it was a miniature portrait of a woman!

Chapter Four

Kerry examined the intricately carved frame, the soft, smiling countenance of the woman. She was young, but a serenity was apparent in her soft dark eyes, the calm contentment of one who has all she desires. Her smooth brown hair was piled up in a cascade of ringlets, and her throat was unadorned. There was a simplicity about her, something comforting in the calm acceptance of her eyes and of her soft smile.

A chill ran through Kerry as she gazed on the picture, then a sudden suspicion. Who was this woman? She recalled Cameron Brent's odd manner. Was this his mistress? His manner had not indicated such a relationship, but this picture was not to be dismissed. She removed the oval portrait, tucking it into the bureau drawer and closing the soft smiling face away. Was there a chance, even a slight one, that Cameron had given her this room so she might be a substitute for this woman? Perhaps he thought to press her into performing the functions of this missing or dead person?

The soft cry of a whippoorwill was her only answer, so she sighed, blew out the candles, and slipped between the cold sheets. Instantly, she drew the warm quilt over her. The bed was exquisitely comfortable, the soft mattress creaking on a rope frame. Yet in spite of the unaccustomed comfort, it was a long time before Kerry fell asleep, and in her slumber she imagined she heard footsteps outside her door.

When morning dawned, warm and golden like a yellow rose, Kerry snuggled under the comfort of the white quilt, reluctant to leave its embrace. Finally, with a shiver, she arose and slipped on her dress, moving very quietly. She opened the door to find herself in the corridor she dimly recollected from the night before. At the squeak of a neighboring door, she quickly closed her own, waiting until the footsteps reached the landing. Peering out through a sliverlike crack, she saw Cameron Brent's dark head disappear downstairs.

Her wonder increased as she stepped out into the hallway. The corridor contained only three doors, the middle one her own. Cameron had apparently just come from the first as she'd heard no footsteps pass her door. The third was most likely Charles's. Incredible as it seemed, he had given her a room, not in a servant's quarter, but next to his own!

With that disturbing knowledge in mind, Kerry descended the stairs, looking about the house as she did so. It was a mansion, its splendor visible in the daytime. Indeed, from the few quick glances she'd caught of the house last night before she'd been led upstairs, Kerry had had a feeling of doom. She'd found the lower rooms somber and depressing. Only her room was not, and the reason for that seemed tied in with the picture.

The picture. She hadn't been able to forget her startled surprise upon finding the miniature, and she could only wonder what it signified.

She was now in the foyer, a room paneled in dark oak on which brass hooks had ben placed to hold hastily discarded clothing. A tall mirror graced one end of the room while oil portraits of ancestors clung to the walls, giving her disapproving glances. A mustached cavalier with a hint of Charles's mischievous eyes smirked at her from the far side, while the closer forebears appeared disgruntled at having been hung there at all. A coat of arms swathed in red cloth graced the center of one wall, and Kerry stepped nearer for a better look. On the shield was the family name of Brent, with the head of a horse as its symbol. But there was something strange about the head. On closer inspection she saw that the animal was shaped normally enough—but the eyes! These blazed out of proportion with the rest, appearing as two flaming orbs, crystal-like and not of this world. Kerry shivered, an involuntary rushing of ice through her veings, as she thought of the letter she'd found that night in the tavern. It had contained an inscription, but it was in another language and she could not make it out. . . .

"Eques noctis," an amused voice rang out, and Kerry's heart leaped then eased as she saw Charles leaning in the doorway, an indolent smile gracing his fair face. He strode toward her to stand before the coat of arms, a smirking interest dancing about in his pale blue eyes. He was still in his dressing gown, a blue brocade garment that was open enough to reveal his neatly tied cravat and his matching waistcoat. His hair was powdered to perfection and his hands, locked behind his back as he stared up at the apparition, were manicured. He smiled at Kerry as if sharing a secret joke.

"The Night Horseman," he said. "Egotistical things, are they not?" He gestured at the wall with his hand, covering a yawn with the other.

"What's that?" Kerry asked, and Charles chuckled.

"Arms, portraits, all of it. It's as if some feel by reaching into the past, one might secure what is no longer present. Ridiculous, is it not?" He lifted one eyebrow while Kerry shrugged.

"I don't know . . . they're nice to look at."

"Yes, they are," Charles agreed amiably. "But then there's that business there." He pointed to the glaring horse, and Kerry's attention perked.

"You've heard the legend of the Jersey Devil?" Charles

asked, and Kerry nodded quickly.

"Aye, a bit."

"'Tis said to be a curse upon this land, a diabolical being with the shape of a horse. I told Cameron to take the damned thing down but he refuses. Feels some sort of family loyalty to the arms and won't even discuss it."

"Why would you want them taken down?" Kerry asked curiously. "You don't believe the legend yourself?"

"Hardly." Charles laughed, his amusement apparent. "But the workers and the servants are inclined to listen to such tales, and they need little further excitement. I see no reason to add fuel to that fire." He grinned pleasantly, and Kerry walked away from the portraits, taking one last look at the arms. It seemed strange, but no matter where she was in the room, the cold flaring eyes followed her so it was with considerable relief that she found herself in the kitchen with Charles.

"Now you must meet our cook." Charles waved to a large German woman working at a table. The cook did not stop to smile, but flipped a round ball of dough up into the air, slapping it with a vengeance when it returned to the table. "She really runs this place," Charles continued, a trace of condescension in his voice. "She only allows us to think we do. Isn't that right, Helga?"

"If you say it's so." The woman finally finished kneading the dough and placing it in a bowl. She then came from around the side of the table to peer at Kerry. She wore her light hair wrapped in a bun on top of her head, and her face seemed pinched, as if the knot was too tight. Her blue eyes made a no-nonsense appraisal, and when she smiled approvingly, Kerry felt herself exhale as if she had just passed a difficult inspection.

"*Ja*, and a pretty thing you are. I am Helga. Vat is your name?" Her head cocked as she awaited an answer and Kerry found herself smiling back.

"Kerry. Kerry O'Toole."

"Kerry O'Toole. *Ja,* it is a nice name. Vat does the Master vish for you to do?"

"I don't know." Kerry shrugged, confused herself. "He didn't say exactly."

"Ja, that is just like him! Vat does that man expect—a young girl like you must vait forever! Here you are, in a strange house with new people and he does not even take you about. Vell, I shall see to him!" Helga ushered Kerry toward a stool near the red brick fireplace, and indicated that she should take it. Kerry complied. "Now you sit here vith me until the master returns. Then ve shall get to the bottom of this!"

Her eye returned to Charles with a questioning stare, and even he grew nervous under her scrutiny. "Do you vish something else, Master Charles?" she asked, and Charles shook his head.

"No, just my breakfast." Regaining some of his dignity, he clicked his heels together. "See that I have it in the dining room shortly." Then he stalked out while Kerry smothered a laugh.

On her perch beside the warm stove Kerry drank tea and tasted samples of whatever Helga was cooking. The kitchen was warm and comfortable. It was not gloomy like the rest of the house, and it radiated cleanliness. Before Kerry was a vast assortment of food, quantities of flour, sugar, molasses, and rum, articles that were rare during wartime. Besides the red brick fireplace, there was a Franklin stove, a long work table, several cupboards, and some chairs. Dried herbs hung from the ceiling, their spicy scents wafting about the room.

Soon the maids began to appear, yawning and avoiding Helga so she would not question them about their whereabouts and scold them if given an unsatisfactory answer. They quickly disappeared, to go about their tasks or to hide in the vacant rooms upstairs until Helga called for them.

"These girls! They vant to do nothing! Vat do they think they are here for!" She pointed to several casks of rum and some flagons of wine standing in the corner. "That must be put avay and not one of them in sight!"

"I'll do it," Kerry volunteered. She slipped down from her seat, having finished the last crumbs of a teacake. "Just tell me where they go."

"Down the hallvay, there is a vinecellar. Thank you, Miss Kerry." Helga beamed at this new lass, nodding as Kerry hoisted the bottles and headed in the direction specified.

It was only a few steps down into the cool room, and Kerry lined the casks and bottles next to others on a stone floor. The cellar was filled with wines of every description. From their dust-covered necks, Kerry knew them to be very old and quite valuable. The last cask in place, she started for the hall and shut the door, turning accidentally to the right instead of to the left where the kitchen lay.

The corridor ran behind the main rooms of the house, the parlor she had barely glimpsed the night before and the dining room. She realized her mistake and started to turn back, but a single beam of sunlight etched across the wall from a diamond-paned window and a glint of metal caught her eye. There was another room back here. It was locked but a key protruded invitingly from the keyhole.

Glancing both ways down the corridor, Kerry found it reassuringly empty. Helga was busy, and Charles was upstairs dressing. He had said Cameron would not return until later. With a slow, careful motion she turned the key, her curiosity now out of control. A click sounded and when she pushed slightly on the door, it softly opened.

At first she saw nothing. Then, gradually, she became accustomed to the dim light. The lack of windows in this room was readily apparent on this spring morning, yet she saw it was a sort of a study. Books lined the walls. Maps, globes, and charts were tacked to the red cedar paneling, and a desk occupied the room's center. A quill was jammed into the ink bottle as if its user had recently departed. Stepping closer, silencing her footfalls, Kerry saw rolls of parchment on the desk, some with fresh ink blots. Carefully she unrolled one, only to find it to be a diagram of a ship's hold, arrows and lines idicating its storage capacity, while notes concerning the cargo were scrawled in Cameron's decisive hand. The other papers were of the same nature, and Kerry felt a quiver of disappointment. Nothing here to shed any light on the mysterious woman whose picture lay upstairs. No references to the Devil. Nothing of any interest except these drawings of boats. Tossing them aside in disgust, she was about to examine another when a voice rang out of the darkness, harsh and coldly accusing:

"What in God's name are you doing?"

Kerry glanced up, then stood frozen as Cameron loomed in the doorway. His black cape, lined with red, was thrown over his shoulders, his face was a mask of fury, and his thick black eyebrows were drawn down over smoldering eyes. Furrows of anger were so deeply etched upon his face that his features seemed carved of granite. He was satanic, magnificent in his rage, and Kerry shook with fear.

"Nothing! Not a thing! I was just in the hallway, putting things away in the cellar when—"

"Out!" he thundered, and for a moment Kerry thought him mad. "Out! Wait outside!"

Kerry did not have to be told twice. She rushed past him into the kitchen, there to await her fate.

It seemed hours before he finally returned from the corridor and securely closed off its entrance with the key he clutched in his hand. Kerry swallowed hard and Helga fled the room, leaving the two of them alone. For a long time Cameron said nothing. He merely tapped his walking stick upon the floorboards until Kerry thought she would scream. When at last he spoke, his voice was not at all what she'd imagined.

"Miss O'Toole, I apologize for shouting at you. Since I had no opportunity to speak to you this morning, you could not have known that my study is my personal domain. I am very particular about my things, and I do not like them disturbed. Will you accept my apology?"

"Certainly," Kerry said, puzzled. She knew that it was she who should be apologizing, but she sneaked a glance up at him and saw that he was sincere. When he continued in the same tone, she stared up at him wonderingly.

"Good. Now I would like you to accompany me to the furnace. I have a job for you, one I think you won't overly mind." Kerry obediently followed him through the door, suspecting some connection between her type of employment and snooping through his things. Did he fear that she would find something? But at his next words she dismissed this idea.

"I need someone to keep a record of the workings at the furnace and of the employees. I assume you can write?" At her quick nod he continued, though she well knew he should not have taken this for granted. Only due to the generosity of her older brother was she supplied with this knowledge, and among her shipmates she had discovered it was rare. "I want to use this information as a comparison to judge the efficiency of the operation, and as a checklist against the workers' wages."

"Sort of a diary?" Kerry asked, and he nodded.

"Precisely." Together they walked in silence past the barn and the stables, and in the distance Kerry could see the general store and the gristmill. From Cameron's description that day in the carriage she had little difficulty recognizing any of them as she rushed to keep up with his long strides.

The workers' cottages lay down the road, a grouping of neat little clapboard houses, each with a porch and its own privy in back. Just beyond was the lake, a tranquil sapphire gem nestled among green pines and softly scented cedars.

"What a beautiful place!" Kerry exclaimed, and her employer slowed down a bit, gazing outward at the scene with a curious glance.

"Do you think so?" he asked. Kerry looked up at him surprised.

"Yes. Don't you? Look at that lake! And the white ducks and the trees and the sky! It's like a bit o' heaven on earth!" She declared this last firmly, and Cameron favored her with a slight smile.

"I suppose it is," he replied, but his face darkened a bit as he spoke, some hidden shadow creeping over him, and he started once more toward their destination, Kerry following.

The furnace itself was now in sight, and she saw workmen hauling a wagon full of ore into the pyramid-shaped, brick building. The men stopped and stared at her appreciatively, the only reason for their silence Cameron's presence. He held open the door for her, taking her inside where a rush of heat greeted her.

"Problem, suh?" A black-bearded man with a pair of burning black eyes shuffled over to them. His mouth formed a permanent scowl for lines had dug trenches about his lips, and his yellowed teeth were bared like those of a feral dog. Kerry visibly withdrew, watching his approach with considerable apprehension, but when he reached the doorway he sent her a disinterested glance, then faced Cameron. "Something you find wrong?"

"No. Bill Seldon, this is Kerry O'Toole. She will be helping with the record-keeping here."

"Ain't been no record-keeping before," Bill replied, wiping his mouth with his sleeve. "At no time."

"There will be now. Any objections?"

With a surly grunt, Bill scuffled off to the furnace, his growl still audible over the blast of the furnace.

"What a nice man," Kerry said deprecatingly.

Cameron nodded.

"He has reason to behave like that. Or so he thinks." At Kerry's puzzled glance, he continued. "He used to own the place. Part of it, anyway. But he lost so much money on the furnace that he was forced to sell."

"And you let him stay on?" Kerry asked, wondering at this.

"Yes. He is an excellent ironmaster. I saw no need to dismiss the man, as long as his grudges do not affect his work. So far they haven't." Kerry's eyes wandered over to the furnace and to the surly bearded man who watched the molten blast. She shivered, then turned away as Cameron called to a boy.

"Trevor. Come here."

The lad seemed only too glad to leave his chores and he ran over, his face smudged with charcoal and dirt. At the sight of Kerry, a broad grin broke out upon his face, revealing startlingly white teeth. His mass of black hair fell in rude disarray over his eyes, and with an impatient flick of his wrist, he tossed it off his face. When Cameron scowled at the pleased, casual look about the young man, he fought to assume an innocent expression.

"You called, sir?"

After giving the jaunty lad a penetrating look, Cameron introduced him while Trevor grinned.

"This is Trevor Shanahan, one of your countrymen." At the lad's antic expression Cameron sent him a quelling glance. "He's an errand boy, an indenture. He will help you in the work I described, and I hope doing so will prove more fruitful than his other endeavors."

"Oh now, sir, you be knowing that's not true. Why just today I swept the floors, lugged the charcoal, worked on the ore boats 'til dawn—"

"That's enough," Cameron said abruptly. "What I would like you to do now, Trevor, is give Kerry a brief accounting of the furnace activities and the employees. You seem to get about quite a bit; therefore you should prove an ideal candidate for the job. Do you think you can manage that?"

"Why, me heart's a bleedin' at your lack of faith." Trevor grinned.

"See that I have no reason to regret offering your services. Good day." Cameron's eyes met Kerry's in a lingering look, as if he wanted to say something else. Then he turned and walked quickly away, leaving Kerry with an odd feeling of disappointment.

"What do you make of that?" Trevor's dark eyes danced, his gaze following Cameron's path. "Now, Miss Kerry"—his insouciant grin reappeared and he whispered to her out of his cupped hand—"what do you say we quit this place and go out for a jar? There's a tavern not a mile down the road."

"Trevor!" Kerry grinned at the lad's audacity, then quickly smothered her smile. Having three younger brothers of her own, she knew when it was better not to laugh. She indicated the furnace room decisively. "We have a job to do."

"Ah, well. You can't blame a lad for trying. Though I think it's far too hot a day to be hobbling around this furnace instead of sipping a cool ale."

"And I think you give a new meaning to the word blarney. Shall we?"

Feigning profound disappointment, Trevor gallantly offered his arm, after brushing away the cinders that dotted his white shirt. Together they walked to the stone furnace, and Kerry strained to hear the urchin's explanation of its workings.

"Up there at the top is where the batches of ore, flux, and charcoal are dumped in to make the charge. Here we use the oyster shells for the flux. Those large bellows up there, they're used to blow hot air into the furnace, which fans the fire to where it is so hot, hell would be envious." At Kerry's startled expression, Trevor covered his mouth with a sheepish grin. "Sorry. Then the iron separates and comes into the crucible there, at the bottom. You should see it when it pours out . . . look!"

At the lad's excited expression, Kerry glanced about just in time to see a cascade of molten metal pour over the hearth like a blinding, fiery waterfall. The iron hissed and crackled, red streamers of it flickering like a dragon's tongue toward Kerry and the young lad. They withdrew a few paces, hearing the searing metal strike sand as workers stood by to ladle it into pigs. Kerry had to admit that Trevor's description was accurate . . . it did resemble hell.

Heat penetrated her face and clothes, leaving the cloying calico plastered to her body by sweat. Kerry pulled the material away from her, but her discomfort continued and her hair was beginning to cling to her face. Seeing her position, Trevor took her hand and led her past the angry furnace, now belching up white clouds of steam after dispelling the last of its fiery remnants.

Behind the chimney was a door, and it was here that Trevor led her, into a neat little office lined with books, papers, and a desk.

"Cameron's," Kerry guessed, and Trevor nodded.

"Aye. That man's always working. They say hard work ne'er killed anyone, but it did me own parents. And it will kill him, if he doesn't slow down. Scarce a day of fun does he have. Always at the fields, at the furnace, over at the forge town—never saw a body so keen on working as that soul." The foolishness of such a notion was very real to young Trevor, who idled around the desk, glancing at papers and documents.

"What about Charles?" Kerry asked, more than a little curious about this mysterious brother. "What does he do?"

With the air of importance inherent in a good gossip, Trevor replied eagerly. "Not a damned thing. I don't even know why he's here. He never comes down until well into the summer months, and then it's just to go drinkin' and wenchin'. Knows a hell of a lot more about having a good time than old Master Cameron there."

"Master Cameron doesn't . . . go out?" Kerry asked hesitatingly, not willing to place too much trust in a lad she's just met, and one with such a loose tongue at that. Shaking his head ruefully, Trevor sighed.

"No, not at all. 'Twas a piece o' luck for us that he went up to Philadelphia for a time. To think, the whole city at his feet and he never stays more than a day or two. Master Charles loves the place. Master Cameron's just married to his work, I guess." Trevor shook his head, remarking once more on the ridiculousness of such behavior.

For all his meanderings, Trevor proved as sharp of mind as of tongue. He deftly withdrew a book in which she could keep her records, and it became evident that he knew all of the workers and their activities. Furthermore he parted with that information with no show of embarrassment at the disclosures.

"Old lady Dunlap's making a muster today." He pointed to the column reserved for the worker's activities. At Kerry's confused, sea green gaze he hastened to explain. "Having a baby. You got to enter it. It affects the wage."

"Oh," Kerry said, after sneaking a look at the lad to be sure he was not teasing. "What about this entry? For the oremen?"

"Well, McIntire's out today with apple palsy. Drunk," he explained patiently. "Stevens and Cramer're all right. Then there's Murphy and McAllister. They get only half a day's wages for fighting. Watch out for Ed Smythe too. He's a ten fingers—made off with two sacks of flour from the store last week. It comes out of the pay."

Kerry marked all the entries, totaling the figures neatly in a single column.

"And did you add them up already?" Trevor scanned the sheet in disbelief, then handed it back, his skepticism gone. "You're as bright as you are pretty, miss. 'Tisn't a wonder Master Cameron wanted you for hisself."

Kerry would have tossed him a scathing glance, but she herself was unsure of Cameron's motives so she was unwilling to meet Trevor's eyes.

Chapter Five

Kerry had been at her job for a few days when, on a sunny Thursday morning, Trevor strolled into the furnace office, the ledger book jammed under one arm.

"We have to go down to the ore boats." He gestured toward the river with a crook of his thumb, not too displeased to spend a day in the sunshine. "The men are hauling ore, and we can't get their names from here."

"Let's go then." Kerry finished up the ledger for the men working in the furnace. Securing a quill and the necessary ink, she then followed Trevor outside and down to the stream.

The furnace workers were busily engaged in unloading and hauling the ore, passing the rust-colored chunks in an efficient assembly line process from the flat ore boats to the platform on the banks. The platform was actually connected to the gristmill, all parties using the same small stream as their water supply. A paddle wheel splashed freely while overhead the wheat chaff poured, like gold dust, into a chute that led back into the mill. Trevor made himself comfortable on the corner of the platform, dutifully calling out the worker's names to Kerry, his hands folded behind his head.

"Hey!" a dark, bearded oreman shouted, taking exception to the lounging position of the Irish lad. "Why the hell aren't you doing some work? Are ye special or somewhat?"

"He ain't special; he just hasn't the muscle for it," his companion in the boat shouted. Trevor, not at all shamed by these accusations, merely rolled up his sleeve and flexed his muscles for all to see.

The surly voice came from behind them. "I've see better than that on a sick goose."

Kerry turned about to face Bill Seldon. The sinister-looking man drove a wagon loaded with ore, and in his hand he clutched a whip. The horse pulling the heavily loaded cart strained under the weight. From her position at the stream, Kerry could see one round white eye in the animal's chestnut head. The horse was blind.

"Come on, you lazy mule," Seldon shouted as he whipped the animal mercilessly. The horse strained and champed at the bit, but the ground was soft due to the spring rains so its hooves only dug deeper into the mud. "Why you good for nothing!" The whip flew so quickly that Kerry's eye could not follow it, and the horse snorted pitifully, in pain as blood-flecked froth flew in the air.

"Leave that horse alone." Kerry yelled, dropping her quill and ink in her anger. Unfortunately, the ink bottle broke, sending a dark cascade of liquid all over her dress and shoes.

"Hee, hee, hee." Bill Seldon laughed. It was the first time she'd ever seen him indulge in humor. "Why you look more like a lad than ever. Look at ye—all dirty and full of the ink." The smile that creased his face was worse than his customary scowl. However, he quickly turned the horse away, toward the furnace, while Kerry shook her fist in a mute gesture of outrage.

"'Tis a shame about your garb, miss." The miller stepped over from his work. He had heard the altercation and wished to lend a hand. "That Bill Seldon—he's a blight on this place, he is. Master Brent should get rid of him. A real menace, he is." He retrieved the quill, then took Kerry's hand. "Come inside. There's a bit of fresh water in there. You can try to clean the dress."

"Thank you," Kerry said wryly, for she doubted that even her best efforts would get out the stains. The ink was already drying, and sure enough, even with the water the miller so generously heated, the dark pigmentation remained.

"It's just going to have to do." Kerry shrugged, scrunching the material into her fist and letting it fall back against her legs, a wet inky mess. "There's no sense bothering about it." From the window of the grist mill, Kerry could see Bill Seldon returning, the horse still flagging under his whip. With an oath, she pulled away from the sight, her green eyes sparkling with fire.

"God, I'd like to give it to him," she fumed, while the miller shook his head, his hands occupied with the stones.

"You'd be wise to stay away from him, miss. Bill's a dangerous man. You don't want to arouse his wrath."

"I know." Kerry nodded, then walked to the door. From inside, she could see Seldon saunter down to the oar boat and order the men about. "I'll have to return for more ink," she said aloud, pushing the door open and walking outside.

As she started for the furnace, a shrill whistle broke the silence, and when she looked about, she saw Bill Seldon standing in the oar boat, one leg hoisted up on the platform.

"Look at 'er! Would you lads ever know that was a woman, tried and true?" He chortled at his own wit, while from his perch Trevor shouted back angrily.

"Leave her the hell alone, Bill. She's done nothing to you."

"Come over here and say that, ye Irish lout."

Before Trevor could arise, Kerry rushed down to the platform, halting his progress.

"Don't bother, Trevor. I'll not be needing protection from the likes of that." She sneered in Seldon's direction, which Bill found even more amusing. From the look on his face, a frozen, almost plastered grin, Kerry had cause to wonder if he hadn't been dipping into the furnace rum supply a bit too freely.

"From the likes of this!" He gestured to his own barrel chest, then indicated her slender form with a belittling leer. "Listen who's talking. The way you stride about 'ere like some lad, 'tis no wonder the army hasn't claimed such as you."

"Come on, Bill. Let's get this ore unloaded." The other oreman seemed bored. He passed a load to Bill. The foreman was uninterested in work, however, not when he could indulge himself in baiting a lass.

"And I ne'er heard of any woman gettin' a job here, at the furnace," he continued, wiping the snot from his nose with his sleeve. "What did you do to get such a light job, bed down with the boss?" A hearty chuckle escaped his lips at this fine joke, but he had not kept an eye on the Irish lass as he spoke. Before he saw what was happening, Kerry, forgetting reason, had hiked up her skirts, and run down the riverbank. With a well-aimed kick, she sent the ore boat on its way downstream.

Her action had the desired effect. Bill Seldon's left leg was on the platform. As the boat sailed out from under his right, the barrel-shaped man fell, with a huge splash, into the stream, sending a cascade of water rippling far over the bank. A flock of disgruntled ducks vacated the water at this unwarranted intrusion, the mother duck giving Seldon an unkind glance as he rose to the surface like some fabled monster.

"Why you . . . I'll get you for this!" he bellowed.

Kerry turned and ran up the hill as the dripping Seldon, cursing and yelling, charged out of the stream, fully intent on revenge. Trevor, who stood alongside the dock, tried to stop him, but Bill brushed him aside as if he were a gnat, his huge frame hustling after Kerry with a speed one wouldn't think possible for so large a person.

Her heart pounding, Kerry looked back and saw he was gaining on her. In a few moments, he'd be right on top of her. . . . That was when she ran right into the tall figure of

Cameron Brent.

Her employer had just come from the fields. He caught Kerry with a quick motion, immediately noticing the mountainous figure following her.

"It's you, sir! I didn't see . . ." She was breathless, lost when Bill Seldon ran up, his face coarse, blood red, and furious.

"She tried to drown me, the Irish slut!" He lunged for her, but Cameron drew her away from his flying fist, and sent the foreman sprawling with his other arm.

"None of that!" Cameron shouted, his voice firm and angry. "Have you taken leave of your senses, man? You don't strike a girl." At the foreman's glare, Cameron spoke more quietly, his authoritative words carrying more weight than any fist. "Now settle yourself and tell me what happened. That is, if you're calm enough to make sense."

At that, Bill Seldon snorted, then pawed the ground like an angry steer.

"She kicked the boat out from under my feet, she did." He gestured to his still-dripping hair and clothes. "That wench needs a beating, she does. Came running down the hill, her skirts pulled up, and she kicked out the goddamned boat." His expression became incredulous as he told the story. He seemed unable to believe it had happened himself.

"I see." Cameron glanced at Kerry, saw her ink-stained dress and her outraged expression. He then turned back to Seldon. He was aware of the man's rum-soaked eyes and slurred speech, and he could easily envision what had happened. He had not doubt that Kerry would not patiently remain the brunt of this man's jokes, yet the lass should know better than to antagonize such a brute.

"I'd like you to return to your job, Bill. You have my word that such an incident will not be repeated." Cameron dismissed the man abruptly, but Bill Seldon's thirst for vengeance was not appeased. He crossed his huge arms that resembled the trunks of two trees and stood obdurately in their path.

"You don't mean she's to get off, just like that!"

Cameron shook his head. "I did not say that. As a matter of fact, I plan to take care of this matter myself." He faced the menacing lout before him, one thick eyebrow raised as a thought occurred to him. "I have already given you my word that the incident will not be repeated. Is my word not enough?" Cameron's manner was an insult, and Bill Seldon immediately backed down. Brentwood belonged to this man, and to question his word would be folly indeed.

"No, sir. Your word is fine." Bill could not keep the anger out of his voice. He sauntered off, tossing back a glare at Kerry. The Irish lass's face betrayed her satisfaction, but the rather pretty crinkling of her nose disappeared when Cameron's blazing gaze settled upon her.

"Come with me." The interested oremen were still standing upright in the boats, listening to every word so Kerry complied immediately. The tone of Cameron's voice was so forbidding that she could not suppress a tremor of fear. Whereas Bill Seldon had not frightened her at all, this man did, and her fears grew worse as he led her past the frankly curious gazes of the workmen to the furnace office, closing the door behind him.

"Now what have you got to say for yourself?" His manner was stern, but Kerry faced him defiantly. She'd heard enough tales of masters who lashed, even beat recalcitrant servants, and though she was not sure what he intended, she was determined to fight him every inch of the way.

"What's the difference? Your man answered you. You won't believe me." Green eyes flashed, and she locked her arms stubbornly at her sides, her fists unconsciously clenched.

"I asked you, didn't I?" Cameron said quietly. "I wish to hear both sides of the story."

Kerry's eyes widened in disbelief, then she haltingly complied. Cameron's eyes narrowed as she mentioned the beating of the horse, Bill's taunting of Trevor, and his last insults to herself. These she was strangely unable to repeat, stumbling over her words until Cameron said helpfully, "Just tell me exactly what he said."

"He said . . ." She faced the wall, embarrassed to repeat the slurs and half believing them herself. "He said that I looked like a lad, and that I must be bedding down with the boss to be working at the furnace."

An awkward silence fell between them until Kerry's lilting voice continued. "I don't think he meant the last, I think he was just blowing off. It made me angry, that's all."

Relief softened Cameron's granitelike face, but then he gestured to her dress, still hiked up around her hips and he spoke. "So you ran down there and pushed him into the water. A man three times your size, who'd been drinking."

The way he put it, her actions seemed ridiculous. Kerry shrugged, embarrassed.

"Dammit Kerry! What if I hadn't come down just then? He might have hurt you!" Cameron's face darkened as that possibility occurred to him, and even Kerry had to admit to herself that she had not done the wisest thing. "Now you've made an enemy. I'm shorthanded at the furnace with the war going on so I can't let Seldon go right now." He favored her with a glowering glance while Kerry shuffled her feet on the dust-covered floor.

"What am I going to do with that temper of yours?" he said, more to himself than to her, and he strode angrily about the room.

Kerry ventured to remark, "It won't happen again."

"I'll see to that! And look at you! Your dress . . . I thought I told you to act like a lady?" He stopped pacing, his gaze more distracted than he wanted to admit by her shapely legs. She tugged uncertainly at the dress, pulling it down over her well-formed limbs while Cameron forced his glance away.

At the sound of scraping wood, Kerry glanced up to see him dragging a chair out from behind the desk. As he faced her once more, she trembled with fear, but she was far from beaten and met his glare with one of her own.

"Don't touch me!" she shrieked, backing away from him as he approached. Cameron stopped in midstride and looked at her strangely.

"I mean it! You touch me and you'll be sorry!" She was now against the wall. Nonetheless he continued his advance, thrusting the chair before her.

"Sit," he commanded. After an uncertain moment she obeyed, her eyes never leaving his muscular form. "Now I want you to stay there until I get back. Think about how a lady acts in such a situation, and when I return, I expect you to have some well-thought-out ideas on the subject. Agreed?"

"Yes." She sighed audibly in her relief, unable to believe that he would be so lenient with her. With a shake of his head, he walked out, and Kerry let out her breath and then leaned weakly against the wall.

Outside, Cameron paused, an amused expression lending a sparkle to his eyes. He could not dismiss the sight of Bill Seldon, his hair soaked and his rage apparent, from his mind. The man's dip, courtesy of the Irish lass, was deserved. Only due to fear that Bill would attack Kerry had he kept his composure. Smoothing back his hair, he resumed his normal aloof expression. For one small Irish lass she certainly had a way of getting herself into trouble, but she had made his day considerably less boring.

Chapter Six

As the days slowly passed, Kerry learned the inner workings of the furnace, and soon became a familiar face to the villagers as well. The hands at the furnace were wont to start the day with no more than a passing nod, but slowly they began to confide in her, discussing their troubles, their lives, and their sweethearts, wives, or children. The wives of the furnace men sometimes invited her for tea or milk, warm and fresh from a cow, and although these women could scarce spend the time to sip it with her, they enjoyed company and would stir a vat of soap or dip candles or spin thread while talking. Kerry's quick wit and her understanding were qualities these people valued, so instead of dreading the sight of someone recording their doings, they welcomed her.

On a warm, early summer's morning, Kerry and Trevor set up the pages for the diary of that day. Trevor was in a bragging mood, his topics ranging from his prowess with women to the amount of spirits he could safely imbibe. "Why I could drink all these men under the table before the morn's end," he declared, determined as always to avoid work.

Kerry yawned, not impressed. "Aye and be asleep under the table too, no doubt." She grinned when Trevor warmed to the subject.

"Not me. Although there was one time, in the tavern at Haddonfield, where I met me limit. Do you recall the Indian King?" he asked, and when Kerry shook her head to indicate she didn't, he smiled. "'Twas there I took a sound knock on me head, is all. Why I fell down behind the three rear tables, onto a wall, and you'll never guess what happened."

"Everyone left you there," Kerry guessed, and Trevor's nose lifted indicating he was insulted.

"No, miss. Now I was about to tell you an interesting fact, but if you don't care to hear..." His voice trailed off enticingly, and Kerry took the bait.

"I know I'll regret this, but what happened?" She lifted her eyes from the sheets of parchment, and with her undivided attention, Trevor gleefully continued. "I fell into a trap door." At Kerry's wide and appreciative gaze, he rubbed his hands together, impressed by his own story. "I did! There's a secret entrance to that tavern. They use it, the Continentals, I mean, to smuggle goods and munitions. The British have control of the town now, and I think it a fine joke, that right underneath their noses"—he pointed to his own rather pug nose—"a trail of weapons and food go right to the men they're fighting."

"Do they not know of it?" Kerry asked. Trevor shook his head, his natural love for mischief showing in his black eyes.

"Not a thing! But that is not the only time I took a wee bit much. Then there was the time—"

"Trevor," Kerry interrupted, seeing another long-winded speech coming. "Hadn't we better get started?"

"All right, miss, if you insist." He followed her begrudgingly through the office door, glancing about the furnace. "McIntire's not here. You'd better go see if he's sick or just drunk. There's Kindle, Luker, Townshed, and Haeger, all carting pigs." He pointed to the men who were dragging a wagon filled with finished bars of iron to the forge. "Then we have—"

"God, no!" A shrill cry rent the air and Kerry froze as the man by the furnace dropped his ladle and clutched his arm, his feet dancing in a pained frenzy. John Craig was the man, Kerry realized. "Jesus God, someone help me!" he shrieked, then his teeth bit through his lips till a red stream of blood coursed down his chin. Luker dropped his work and ran outside with a bucket, returning a moment later, a moment that the poor man spent writhing in pain, his hair glistening with sweat, his distended eyes bulging from their sockets. When a splash of water descended upon his arm, the man sighed gratefully and pulled his hand away from the injury. Kerry gasped at the sight of the wound. Charred black flesh stuck to John Craig's cotton shirt, and a section of bone was fully exposed.

"That's what ye get." Bill Seldon scuffled out from behind the furnace, his jaundiced eye fixing on the man. "Ye should watch what the hell you're doing."

"I did watch," Craig whispered, his pain returning as the water's cooling effects diminished. "It's just that I'm tired."

"Tired! Hell, we're all tired. Luker, take 'is place."

Kerry glared at the back of the departing Seldon while she lent John Craig a helping hand. The man's normally florid face was now pale and white, and she feared that he would faint.

"Here, I'll help," Trevor volunteered and together they walked the man slowly down the path to the worker's cottages. John Craig said nothing on the way. Indeed, every step was an effort and an agony in his present state. Kerry saw his face become even paler when his injured arm inadvertently brushed hers, and she prayed that he would not fall.

"John! Oh, John!" A young brown-haired woman rushed out and clasped her husband in a worried embrace. "Are you all right? Tell me that you are."

"Yes," he whispered, trying to reassure her while Kerry spoke for him.

"He's had a bad burn at the furnace. Can you send for help?" She and Trevor led the injured man to the cot his wife indicated, then lowered him inch by painful inch. Up close, the wound looked even worse; Kerry clearly saw splotches of dried iron clinging to the once-healthy skin. She was reminded of the coal workers in Ireland. They often incurred such burns, and Kerry knew these wounds could easily become infected and could develop into gangrene.

"There's only Granny. She tends to the births and may be of some help." The young woman twisted her handkerchief in her hands as she stared helplessly at her injured husband. At Kerry's nod, Trevor ran out the door to find the old woman.

"He's strong and healthy," Kerry said bracingly. "I'm certain he'll be all right."

But Craig's wife only walked silently about the room, finally resting her elbow on the fireplace mantel.

"This time mayhap. But what about tomorrow? He hasn't a day off, except for Christmas and election day. Even when the furnace is shut down, the foreman finds work. 'Tisn't any wonder he's tired, and this is the result." Her tears fell freely as she went to her husband and cradled his head in her arms. John's coarse hand reached out to comfort her, but the effort cost him his consciousness and he slipped into oblivion.

The minutes passed like hours, and Kerry thought no more welcome sight had ever greeted her eyes than Trevor returning with the midwife.

"Aye, it's a bad un'," the old woman remarked. Her toothless gums rumbled against each other while she examined the wound. "It's a good thing he's out. 'Twill be better for him when I sear the wound."

"Is there no other way?" Mrs. Craig cried, and Trevor's face took on the color of snow.

"I ain't no doctor." Granny's voice crackled like a flame. "When a birth makes a bad tear, I sear. 'Tis the only method I'm knowing." She turned her watery blue gaze toward

Trevor, who shrugged, then to Kerry. As the Irish lass silently cursed her own lack of knowledge, the old woman gave her a raisinlike grin, then shuffled over to the fire. "Have you a blade?"

Without a word, Craig's wife retrieved a knife from the pantry. She handed it reluctantly to the old woman, and Granny stuffed it into the meager fire, twisting and turning the handle until the metal glowed with a white heat. "Looks ready," she remarked, withdrawing the implement and laying the blade full across the arm of John Craig.

Even in his mindless state, the man felt the pain and he groaned, his cry becoming louder and more agonized by the moment until finally he was silent once more. Kerry held his wife as he screamed, and the air was filled with the stench of burning flesh. Mrs. Craig sobbed for some time, but finally she quieted and Granny took a seat near the fire.

"We can now only wait," the old woman stated, not too dissatisfied with the proceedings. "Have you any rum?"

"For his wound?" Craig's wife nodded and then brought out a jug.

Granny pulled out the cork. "No, for the wait," she said. When she took a long pull from the jar Kerry grabbed Trevor and started to leave. Pausing at the door, she glanced back at Mrs. Craig.

"Please let me know if there's something I can do."

The woman nodded, silently transmitting her thanks as Kerry softly closed the door.

"Happens all the time," Trevor said, his quick glance taking in Kerry's heavy breaths, the righteous sparkle in her eyes. "There's nothing to be done."

"Aye? We'll see about that," she said smartly, tucking her book firmly under her arm and heading up the hill.

Trevor was behind her in a moment, his worry evident in his words. "You're not going to do something, are you? We might get into trouble, that we might. I don't know how the Brents will take to interference. And I ain't even mentioned

Bill Seldon. If you think he'll let you get away with—"

"I'm not afraid of Bill Seldon or the Brents," Kerry declared, her eyes flashing with all the fires of hell. She only half meant what she said. She was, indeed, afraid of Cameron, but not allowing herself to dwell on that, she fed her anger instead. "Ridiculous!" She threw out her right hand, pointing toward the furnace. "These are men, not cattle to be branded. Working about in that furnace without any rest—it's a wonder someone hasn't been killed!"

"Men have," Trevor stated. Kerry stopped in her tracks.

"Not since I've been here," Trevor continued. "But I've heard of it happening before, and at the other furnaces."

"That's all I need to know." Burning with outrage, she stormed into the house, her hair falling freely about her, intent on finding the master of this place. Helga gave her a quizzical glance, but Kerry marched right past the cook. Cameron was not about so there was only one place he was likely to be.

Sure enough, the door to the study was closed, but a light spread out from under it. Kerry had the presence of mind to calm herself for a moment, then she knocked.

"Yes. What is it?" The voice on the other side of the wooden barrier was impatient, annoyed. Kerry felt her courage flag, but she held her ground and answered quickly.

"It's me, sir, Kerry."

A shuffling of papers was audible, then a gruff, "Come in."

Kerry stepped into the study, feeling like a lamb entering the den of a lion. Cameron Brent was seated at his desk, intent on his work. He glanced up, his eyes scanning Kerry in that peculiarly thorough fashion he'd employed the first day they'd met, and he placed aside his quill, resting his hands together as his eyes searched hers.

"Well, what is it?"

His words were spoken curtly, but Kerry had come too far to retreat and approach him at a more convenient time. And it was not in her nature to worry about such subtleties when she had something to say; so, fortified with a deep breath, she let the words rush out all at once.

"Sir, I know you probably think it's not my place to say anything to you about the way you run your business, but I know Bill Seldon oversees much of it and things go on that you don't know. I'm sure if you were there everyday you would understand, but since you have so much else to take care of—"

"Please come to the point." Cameron leaned back in his chair, his gaze narrowing.

Many a meeker lass would have fled from such a stern visage, but Kerry was made of sterner stuff. "Surely. You see, there was an accident today at the furnace."

"An accident?" Cameron's eyes widened and concern softened his chiseled features. "Was anyone hurt?"

"Yes. John Craig was hurt badly." Picturing the man anew, Kerry's anger flamed and she declared in an accusing voice, "Aye, and a lot anyone cares! These men don't get any time off so they're dropping in their boots half the time. John's a good worker, but because he was exhausted, he dropped a ladle of hot iron on his arm. Seven days a week, eighteen hours a day they work!"

"That is the accepted practice," Cameron replied, but his thick eyebrows knitted thoughtfully while Kerry ranted on.

"'Tis also the accepted practice for men to be killed by these accidents! 'Tis common knowledge, sir. You can ask about for yourself."

"I see." Cameron gazed at the young girl before him. "And how is the man? The one injured?"

"John Craig? As well as can be expected, considering there's no doctor for the men. A midwife came and burned the flesh from his arm, right before these very eyes." She pointed to her own flashing eyes, and Cameron's expression revealed her surprise.

"They have no doctor?"

"You didn't know?"

"No, I didn't. You see"—he turned his gaze toward her and his glance made her flinch—"the workers don't come to me with their problems. Bill Seldon's in charge of running the furnace, but he has said nothing. Of course, this really is not his responsibility." Returning to his desk, Cameron picked up his quill and pointed to the book she still carried. "Let me see that."

He took the diary, and scratching down a few figures and making some notations, he performed a series of calculations with lightninglike speed. Staring thoughtfully at the result, he then added a few more notes and handed the book back to Kerry.

"I cannot hire new men at the present time. My quota is filled. The army has exempted only fifty men from the military to work in the furnace. But I am willing to try something else. I have adjusted the schedule, giving every man a day off, although not the same day. And instead of changing the schedule daily, each man will work either day or night for a full week, then alternate the following week. That should help the men's fatigue and it may also improve the working of the furnace." At Kerry's questioning glance, Cameron gestured to the figures with his quill.

"From the information you've collected about the workers, I've been making some careful computations. It seems that on the days when the men have adequate rest, their production is greater. Therefore, it would be to their benefit and mine to make a change. It should also cut down on injuries, if what you've told me is correct."

Kerry hugged the book to herself, unable to believe an improvement of this magnitude had come so easily. Only one other furnace in the area had adopted so radical an idea as a day of rest, and she thought it was exemplary for Cameron to provide it, particularly during the war when resources were already strained. "I can't wait to tell them. Now if only there could be a doctor . . ."

"There's a man in Somers' Point," Cameron said

thoughtfully. "He is retired and an old friend of mine. I am certain that, for a reasonable amount, he would agree to stay here and tend to the men's injuries."

"You would do this for them, your workers?" Kerry asked incredulous, and Cameron smiled softly.

"Yes. Had I known sooner, I might have prevented other injuries. Are you pleased?"

"Oh, yes!" A warmth grew within her as she gazed on his stern countenance. Impulsively, she leaned toward him, brushing his cheek with a kiss.

When Cameron's face lifted to hers, she noted the intensity of his piercing gray gaze. His hand touched her face, then fingered a stray lock of black hair. The diary trembled in Kerry's hand as he carefully replaced the tress, his fingers brushing the tip of her breast.

"Please don't," she whispered.

Immediately he turned away. "Why don't you tell the men?" he suggested in an even voice.

Kerry rushed out of the room, and sped across the velvety green lawn, her heart full.

At the furnace the men cheered, tossing up their hats at the news. Only one person did not appear pleased: Bill Seldon spat a wad of tobacco into the fire and, with a grunt, ordered the men back to work.

When the sun had long since set, Kerry could be found in the kitchen of the great house, taking her meal with Helga. The furnace men who boarded at the house ate their meals in the large dining room, and Charles could often be heard complaining about their boisterousness, their bad manners, and their boastful stories. Cameron usually ate alone, often appearing when Kerry was helping the maids clear the dishes away and Charles was sipping his coffee.

Wrinkling his long nose in repugnance at the brew, he glanced up at his brother. "I say, old Cam. Would you care to join me in the library for a brandy? Without it this coffee is nigh unbearable."

As always, Charles was impeccable. In a dark blue waistcoat, velvet this time, his wig tied with a ribbon of the same hue, he made a strange contrast to his brother, for Cameron's garb contained none of Charles's fashionable ruffles or silks. His trousers and coat were made of black homespun material, against which his shirt was startlingly white. The severity of his clothes lent him an air of sophistication, and their effect was decidedly masculine. He favored Charles with a nod of compliance, then paused before Kerry as he was leaving the room.

"I've arranged to have Trevor show you some of the land tomorrow. I assume you can ride?" At her eager nod, he continued in the same businesslike tone.

"Good. Trevor has my permission to arrange the mounts. If you need anything else, please let me know." Having said this, he proceeded to the library with his brother.

"Those two . . ." Helga shook her head as she swept the crumbs from the table, while easily balancing the remaining dishes in her other hand. "Vill you take them the brandy, Kerry? Then I can get this mess cleaned up."

Kerry set out the crystal decanter on a silver tray, along with two glasses. Unused to balancing such an object, she proceeded cautiously to the library, then paused outside the door to grip the tray carefully in one hand so she could reach for the doorknob. As she did so an icy voice came from the library.

"No. I will not reconsider and sell this place! If you want to live in Philadelphia, do so! I certainly won't stop you." It was Cameron's voice.

"Why in God's name you persist in clinging to these memories—"

"Charles, that's enough." The threat in Cameron's voice was clear.

Reluctant to intrude on such a personal discussion, Kerry

started away from the door, but suddenly Charles's voice had grown calmer.

"Really, Cameron. I was only thinking of you. Locked away in this godforsaken place . . . I don't know why you do it. You are a shipping merchant. You could be making a fortune right now."

"I have some prospects here."

"Oh?" Charles could not hide his interest.

At this point, Kerry thought it safe to enter. She placed the brandy and the glasses on a small table, aware that both men's eyes were upon her.

"And may I ask what they are?" Charles continued, allowing his appreciative gaze to remain on Kerry.

"With the war activity increasing in Massachusetts, we have been called upon to furnish supplies for the Continental Army. Here, at the iron forges."

Charles was obviously shocked, and Kerry grabbed the back of a winged chair for support.

"You don't mean to say you won't be loyal to the crown." Charles gazed, horrified, at his brother.

"Is it really that bad, sir?" Kerry asked. "Is the war coming this way?" She could not hide the fear in her voice, for she had heard many war tales aboard the ship that brought her to America.

"Yes, it is, and I intend to help the Continental Army." Cameron looked at his brother as he spoke. "But if it's any consolation to you, the iron supplies are so important to them that we will not have to enlist. And"—this last he directed to Kerry—"for that same reason, this area will be well protected."

"It's that Franklin's fault." Charles took a pinch of snuff from a silver case and sniffed, inhaling deeply. Then he waved a lace handkerchief before his nose and grinned, his good nature restored. "Well, we haven't a worry here in any case. The army hasn't a chance against the Jersey Devil."

Kerry's eyes opened wider at the mention of the Devil, and

she carefully watched Cameron for a reaction. He merely looked skeptical, however, and his dark eyebrows rose as he lifted his glass.

"And what, pray tell, makes you say that?" Sarcasm laced Cameron's words but Charles shrugged.

"Eliah Clark stopped to see you today, but of course you were too busy out working somewhere. He said that he found several chickens torn up on his property, and that the servants and workmen claim it to be the work of the Devil."

"That's certainly conclusive." Cameron snorted. "I don't imagine anyone suspected a fox, when there's a much more Mephistophelian explanation at hand."

Charles smiled.

"Could be. Although Clark says there was something strange about the way the chickens were mutilated. Their heads were cut straight off as if . . . something had bitten them off."

Chapter Seven

Kerry's gasp rang out in the room and both men looked up, seeing the startled paleness of her face. "I'm sorry. It's just . . ."

"Irish superstition," Cameron replied. "Sheer nonsense."

"Of course it is." Charles sighed, dropping into the lounge chair and turning it toward the fire. "It's pure rubbish! These peasants indulge in primitive beliefs."

"I should not like such rumors spread," Cameron stated. "They could have a bad effect on the workers."

"They already have," Charles declared somberly. "I've heard some of the workers' tales of a cry in the night, a curious scream that wrests them from their sleep— Oh, sorry, miss. I didn't mean to alarm you."

"You didn't," Kerry said, hiding her true feelings.

"Well, I plan to correct any such notions I hear," Charles announced.

Since she had given them their brandy, Kerry started to leave the room. She did not see the devouring glance Charles bestowed on her, starting with her feet and not halting until it came to rest on her well-curved bosom. He actually licked his lips, as if in anticipation of a feast, and then he rose to leave also.

"I feel quite tired tonight. I think I shall retire early," he said. He yawned and then retrieved the brandy flask he'd placed in his pocket. Kerry had just reached the door when Cameron's voice rang out.

"Miss O'Toole, I would like you to remain."

Kerry glanced up, puzzled by the closed look of his eyes. Even Charles glanced at his brother strangely before shrugging and abruptly leaving the room. Kerry waited, but Cameron said nothing else. He merely sipped his amber-colored drink as if she were no longer there.

"Sir?"

When she finally broke the silence, he glanced up. His eyes had been fixed on the fire, and they now seemed to contain many of its lights as he stared in her direction.

"I merely wished for your presence. Is it so difficult to humor me?" His face shrouded as if the question contained a hidden meaning.

Blushing for her impertinence, Kerry quickly shook her head. "No."

"Then wait here," her ordered. "I will tell you when to leave."

Kerry sat in the large winged-back chair, but her nerves were tense and its roomy seat was uncomfortable. Her agitation grew as she thought of Charles's tale of the beheaded chickens, of the strange horse's head hanging in the hall, and of the cryptic words: *The Night Horseman*. What did it all mean?

After moments of fidgeting, Kerry got to her feet and paced about the tiny room. But Cameron remained immobile, staring into the flames, while Kerry was about to burst. Was it her imagination or was there really some subtle change in the air?

Suddenly, a cry arose from somewhere beyond, a cry so harrowing it made her skin crawl. It wasn't just a scream or a ghastly howl, but seemed a combination of both, a sound wrought in hell itself. Cameron glanced up, his face white and pale in the firelight. It seemed that all sounds were stilled except for that cry.

Something broke inside of Kerry, and hysteria overcame her. As she began to sob, strong arms encircled her, embracing her. He held her close as one would a frightened child, his hand softly caressing her back, soothing her fears.

Somewhat of a stranger to women, Cameron relied purely on instinct as he sought to comfort Kerry. The horrible cries had ceased, but he could still feel her tremble in his arms like a terrified creature. Cameron knew her to be a lass of rare courage. She had endured a long voyage and being sold into his service. It appalled him to see her crying. Never before had he seen her shed a tear, but now devastating sobs racked her small frame.

"What is it?" she asked, her voice breaking, and when he peered down into her tear-streaked face he felt compassion arise in him, as well a desire to prevent her from being hurt again.

"It's nothing," he whispered, his hand brushing the strands of black hair from her wet cheek. "It has stopped." His hand slipped down to her neck, to brushing away a tear that had rolled down from her chin. She stared up at him, her eyes wide and sea green and sparkling with tears. Her mouth was parted so it seemed the most natural thing in the world for him to kiss her.

His lips met with hers, softly at first, barely hinting of the passion that he'd kept under control these past days. His arm tightened about her waist, drawing her closer, more intimately against him. Kerry felt her breasts press firmly against his hard muscled chest, and he held her possessively while he kissed her gently at first, but with an ever-warming heat. Like the cessation of a cold wind, fear left her body, and a warm, glowing heat started deep within her, spreading like hot oil through her skin. Her eyes closed, she could smell the clean, masculine scent of him, taste the lingering essence of brandy as his tongue played with hers, testing, questing. Her entire being was stimulated by his nearness, by the potency of his kiss; then his lips eased their pressure as if waiting.

Her response startled him, for instead of withdrawing, she slipped her arms about his neck, and stood on tiptoe to return his kiss. The warmth of her response left him reeling. Hot blood surged through his veins and his mind was filled with the scent of her hair, the feel of her soft body pressed intimately against his. His hand slid down the coarse cotton of her dress and cupped her breast, feeling the round fullness of it in his hand, the beating of her heart beneath his fingers. Moisture beaded on his brow for he was overly conscious of the soft nipple that peaked beneath her gown and it was becoming increasingly difficult to maintain his control. His flesh cried out to him to take her.

"Kerry." He spoke hoarsely, his lips brushing her hair, his fingers sliding through the black silken strands of it. Then his hand slipped back, cupping her head while his lips tasted hers once more. Kerry gave him no resistance, all reason having long since fled, and their kiss intensified, so much so that they never heard the door creak open or the footsteps that intruded on their privacy.

"Excuse me." Charles's amused voice dashed their passion.

Startled, Cameron broke his embrace, while Kerry flushed in mortification. As she felt hot color stain her cheeks, she quickly smoothed her gown. She wondered how much Cameron's brother had witnessed and, worse, what he thought.

"What in the hell are you doing?" Cameron's voice shook with anger, but Charles smiled politely, his brows lifting as he picked up his brandy glass.

"I merely returned for my drink. I would have been more discreet had I had any idea—"

"That'll do," Cameron cut in coolly.

Charles shrugged. "Well, I really didn't mean to disturb you." His smile cool and secretive, he held the glass firmly to his chest, then gave Kerry a parting bow. "I apologize Miss

Kerry, if I've cause you any embarrassment, but I must say I'm surprised at my brother—he's usually far more controlled."

"Charles." Cameron's voice was calm, but his unuttered threat was clear.

"Certainly, Cameron. Good night." With a satisfied chuckle, Charles quit the room, closing the door firmly behind him.

For a moment, Kerry said nothing, but discomfited at being discovered in Cameron's arms, she finally sidled to the door.

"I think . . . I'll be going now, if you have no more need of me."

She froze as Cameron sent her a searching glance, his eyes raking over her as if he were trying to read something in her cringing form. He was not happy with her, that much she could tell, and his voice sounded almost sarcastic as he spoke.

"No, Miss Kerry. I have no further need of you."

Blushing furiously, Kerry picked up her skirts and raced from the room. She could hear him pacing inside from anger and frustration, and she could not forget the way his eyes blazed at her, silvery one minute, gray and flintlike the next.

Shivering, she reached her bedroom and was tugging on a nightgown when a sound outside alerted her. She pushed aside the curtains and gazed down into the yard below. The night was still, the moon full. Suddenly, a horse thundered by and Kerry recognized Cameron, riding with all his might across the fields.

A small frown crept across her mouth and she sighed, then turned and climbed into her warm bed. Her youthful body still warm and tingly from Cameron's heated caresses, she fell asleep and soon was dreaming of warm lips upon hers and the heady embrace of Cameron Brent.

The following morning, Kerry descended the stairs to find

Cameron already gone. She was more than a bit relieved, after what had happened between them the night before and a faint flush pinkened her cheeks as she thought of it. Fetching a cup of tea and a slice of warm bread, she gave Helga a slight smile, then sped out the door, nearly falling over the slender body of Trevor Shanahan.

"Morning, miss." He swept his arm wide before her. "Are you ready for our ride?"

She recalled Cameron saying something about arranging for her to go riding, but her mind was still reeling from her last encounter with him.

"Didn't he tell you?" Trevor asked, observing her bewildered glance.

"Yes. I just forgot," she responded absently.

The lad impishly fell to his knees, placing his hand over his heart. "Me heart's broken," he sighed, trying in vain to look distressed while Kerry giggled freely. "To think, I've been looking forward to this all night, and you haven't given it a thought."

"You've been looking forward to a day without work," she teased. "Shall we?"

"With pleasure, miss." He rose from his inane position on the lawn and took her arm, leading her with all due ceremony to the horse stables.

The morning was golden, soft and sweet, the spicy scent of the pines crisped the air, and the azure sky promised a brilliant day for the excursion. Kerry's heart lifted at the sight of the chestnut stallion, whose nose was lifted inquiringly over the top of the stall.

"Caledonia," Trevor replied to her unasked question. "Scottish. Master Brent thinks them the finest." He led the horse out into the sunlight, the saddle already in place. Tossing the reins to her, Trevor retrieved his own mount, a sturdy bay, and swung up into the saddle. Then he saw her hesitation. "Oh, I'm sorry, miss. Let me help you."

"No. That's not it. It's the saddle." She pointed to the

sidesaddle that graced the horse's back and frowned. "I hate those things. They are so uncomfortable after an hour or so."

"I see what you mean." Trevor nodded, and his black brows knitted into a cloud over his twinkling eyes. "But what can we do about it?"

"At home it was easy," Kerry said in disgust, throwing her hands up. "I would just borrow me brother's breeches for a ride, and there was no one to say a thing. But here . . ."

"Say no more," Trevor announced gallantly. Dismounting and tying his steed, he disappeared into the stables, returning a moment later with a pair of tan homespun pants. "Here you are, miss." He tossed them to her, but relief faded quickly from Kerry's face.

"I can't. What if somebody sees me?"

"What if they do?" Trevor grinned, leaning against the post, his face colored with mischief. "You have no husband about, no father or mither. So who's to say?"

The thought of Cameron flickered through both their minds, but at the daring grin on Trevor's face, Kerry marched toward the barn. "I'll do it." She smiled to herself, inside, upon hearing the lad's loud and approving applause. Standing within the cramped quarters of Caledonia's stall, she quickly donned the pants, and was delighted to find that they fit her slim hips snugly. When she tied her dress up around her waist, she was reasonably comfortable.

"All right, Trevor. If you laugh, you'll have to answer to me." She gave him a sparkling grin as she walked out, breaking into laughter at his leering whistle.

"Miss, I think you'll be starting a new fashion, looking as you do. In fact . . ." When his gaze lowered appreciatively, Kerry raised a small fist.

"Trevor," she threatened, and his smile broke wide as he refitted the mare with a proper saddle.

"'Tis only the truth I speak." He helped her up onto the horse, then jumped onto his own mount and led the way down the path to the main road.

As she'd noted before on her trip in the carriage, the roads here in the pines were of soft, white sand, shifting and silent. They passed the charcoal hut where a man turned and chopped trees into furnace fuel, heading down past the mule barn to the wire fence. Trevor let his horse step daintily over the wire and Kerry followed suit to find herself, for the first time, free of Brentwood manor.

The woodlands flourished around them, the ferns, brilliantly green, rising about a foot and a half and creating the illusion of a pale misty cloud settled on the earth. Cedars and pines were joined by an occasional oak, huge and spreading. A stream flowed past, silent and dark, its amber-colord waters whispering the secrets of the pines, the unspoken mysteries of this land. No skies were reflected in its waters, no bright leaves or sharply thrusting pine needles. But shadows rippled across them, like ghosts escaping from their crypts.

"Batsto river." Trevor pointed to the stream. "It joins with the Mullica farther down. 'Tis a fine place for a swim. The water's soft as me mither's tears. But ya can't go too far downstream, for therein lies the swamp. One step in the wrong direction and . . . death."

Kerry glanced down at the spot where the stream formed a pool. On the surrounding banks, green velvet moss rushed down to greet the waters, small pink flowers grew, and an array of lavender blooms filled the air with a sweet scent. The tranquility of the place was enhanced by the song of a warbler and by the soft lapping of the waters.

"It's beautiful." Kerry sighed.

"Do you think so?" Trevor asked, his mocking grin reappearing. "Now there's a beautiful sight." He pointed to a tavern, amidst the trees. From the smooth, packed sand that surrounded it and the fence that had been chewed by many an impatient horse, Kerry surmised that Trevor was not the only one aware of this treasure. "Bodine's." Trevor continued, his eyes rolling upward to the heavens as if recalling some of his fondest memories. "Are you sure you would not like—"

"No." Kerry laughed.

A lingering colonial slapped his hand awkwardly over his eyes, shading them from the dubious sun as he staggered out of the barroom. His eyes were red, and his full, black beard still dripped with ale. Even from a distance, Kerry felt a chill run through her for she recognized him as the lout who'd accosted her that night in the Philadelphia tavern. "Trevor, come on." She quickly kicked her horse as the drunkard's gaze fixed on her, his squint deepening as he seemed to recognize her.

"Please Kerry," Trevor pleaded, already dismounting. "Just one jar and we'll go."

At the sight of the advancing bearded colonial, Kerry shook her head and started for the road. "I'll come back for you in a few minutes," she replied hastily as the drunkard approached. "And so help me, Trevor, if you're not ready . . ."

"Never you fear," Trevor assured her, racing into the tavern to procure his ale and have a bit of fun with the furnace workers.

Kerry's horse broke into a full gallop, eager to have its head after long weeks of confinement, and Kerry thoroughly enjoyed the run, the cold feel of the wind breaking over her skin. She did not slow down until she felt the horse beginning to tire. Glancing about, she found herself surrounded by bogland. Cool, floating islands of soft, green-colored moss drifted amid towering cedars, and she suddenly knew where she was—the swamp.

The air was deathly still, but a sudden, strangled cry overhead chilled Kerry to the quick, for it recalled stories of the Jersey Devil, the demon haunting this place. However, her fears subsided somewhat when she noted the sound was caused by the wind rushing through the tangle of cedars. Small splotches of sun fought to penetrate this living cavern, without much success, and finally the sunlight was no more. A creeping sensation tingled along Kerry's spine as the horse trod, sure-footed, along the path, for she recalled Trevor's warning that one step in the wrong direction would plunge the unwary to a drowning death.

Shivering, she grasped the reins of the horse and was carefully turning it around when a voice broke the silence.

"Stop or I'll shoot!"

Drawing back on the reins, Kerry froze, unwilling to move and risk a warning piece of lead. A rustle came from the brush straight ahead, followed by the snap of a twig. Kerry scarcely dared to breathe, as she waited for this apparition to appear.

At length an old woman sauntered out of the brush, a rifle tucked under her arm. She resembled a living twig herself, and a rustling, as of leaves, seemed to accompany her every movement. Yet her black eyes glistened, mysterious and full of life. They seemed an entrance to another world, a passageway to some ancient and forgotten time. When this strange being sighted Kerry, she nodded as if she'd been expecting the girl and then tucked the gun safely beneath her arm. She was clad in dark trousers, and she pointed to Kerry's breeches with an odd grin.

"Seems we have something in common."

Her voice was soft, musical as a warbler's, and Kerry found herself smiling back.

"Yes, it does. I'm Kerry O'Toole. The new indentured—"

"I know who you are," the woman said seriously, touching a pointed finger to her cheek, unwrinkled despite her obvious years. Then she shook her head and sighed with the wind. "Come on down, lass. That fool you are with will not be ready for a time."

With a puzzled wrinkling of her nose, Kerry complied, slipping down from her horse. That this woman knew about Trevor did not surprise her, nor was she surprised that Caledonia nuzzled her freely, as if glad to see a friend.

"Come to my hut. We'll have tea." The woman slipped her hand expertly under the nose of the horse and took the reins. "My name is Enid," she said, and the leaves rushed about in a whispering frenzy.

Although fleet of foot, Kerry struggled to keep up with the old woman's rapid movements. Then in the midst of a wall of trees, she turned abruptly and a tiny hut was suddenly visible. At first glance, it was not obvious, but a thin wisp of smoke curled up over the thorn bushes, showing the way. Sandwiched under the briars, the house appeared much the same as a rabbit hutch, its rounded roof covered with thorny green leaves and vines.

Opening a small door, the woman slipped inside, instructing Kerry to leave her horse. "He will be there when you are ready," she promised.

Inside, the hut was cozy and warm. The floor was of packed earth, covered with rushes found in the nearby streams, and a fire burned cheerily in the stone hearth. On a hook above the blaze, a kettle of stew bubbled merrily, emanating delicious odors. A small wooden table and two chairs graced the small dwelling, and there was a cupboard neatly stacked with baked goods, boxes, and sacks. Tiny plants grew everywhere, some in pots or boxes, some merely springing from the walls and floor. Glass jars filled a case near the fire, clearly labeled as teas or herbs, or by strange sounding names that Kerry could not fathom.

"Sit down, sit down," Enid crooned, and Kerry took a seat to watch as the wizened old woman brewed the tea. A scuffle from a corner startled Kerry, and she laughed as a tiny raccoon scampered forth to sit up on his hind legs and study her dubiously.

"Is he your pet?"

When Kerry held out a bit of candy that Enid supplied, the raccoon took it readily, holding the sweet with two paws, and eying her the whole time it was eating.

"They all are." Enid smiled, her eyes liquid and full of

warm lights. "I choose to live out here alone . . . I will ne'er live elsewhere," she remarked, as she poured the tea and placed a cake nearby. "I can make a living here, in the woods. They provide food, wood, cures . . . whatever one needs."

"Cures?" Kerry asked, sipping the pale liquid in her cup. The tea was excellent.

"Aye. Foxglove, hoarhound, dandelion. And this swamp grows a moss, a rare kind not oft seen."

"Do you mean the soft green floating moss?" Kerry asked, and the woman nodded.

"Yes. It can hold its fill of water, water that pours out as you squeeze it over and over. The waters here are pure, and the moss can be used as a bandage."

"The flowers are lovely here too. I saw a small pink one down near the banks," Kerry said.

The woman sat opposite her, close enough to the fire to dip some of the stew into two bowls. "That would be a lady's slipper." She nodded, affirming the matter to herself. Without looking behind her, she reached up onto a wooden shelf and withdrew a salt cellar, then sprinkled the crystals over the meal. She handed Kerry a fragrant bowl, and proceeded to enjoy her own while she talked. "Yes, there are many flowers. Wild orchids. A moss called sweetbay, a pink moss that flowers in June, with scent like ye'd find in heaven."

"In June?" Kerry asked. "I'll have to look for it."

"No!" Enid threw her a startled glance, her eyes wide and shining. "No, this place is dangerous, except for those who know the way. I will take you," she declared solemnly, the matter done.

A tapping sounded at the door, and Enid sighed, pushing herself away from the table to greet her expected guest. A woods owl waddled inside, glancing with a yellow eye at Kerry, before, with a whirring of wings, taking his place on the mantel. Kerry laughed and Enid shook her head.

"Pest, he is. He always waits 'til I set down and then comes in. In or out bird. I have company today and will not be hopping for you."

The owl drew his feathers indignantly about him, cleaning their soft brown sheen with his hooked beak, while Kerry scraped the bottom of the bowl. Having finished her meal, she felt quite comfortable and full and she leaned back, enjoying the tea and the odd company. Then a thought occurred to her, and she asked Enid speculatively, "Do you know Cameron Brent? My employer?"

A quick birdlike nod of the head followed, and the old woman spoke. "Aye, that I do. He's a fine man, but his eyes are set on earthly sights. He does not take the time to live."

"You mean he works too much?" Kerry asked, and the woman nodded.

"Aye, that and much more. He needs laughter in his life. Ever since his mother . . ." She sighed, sipped her tea, and gave Kerry a shy smile. "I'll not want you thinking I'm a gossip."

"I wouldn't," Kerry protested. "After all, I asked you."

"Yes." Enid smiled, staring into her cup. "Yes, Cameron Brent is a fine man. The best of the lot."

Since only Cameron and his brother were at home, Kerry could only assume that Charles did not meet with Enid's approval, but something in her new friend's manner did not welcome further questioning.

"Enid, you've lived here a long time." At the woman's affirmative nod, Kerry continued. "Have you ever heard, or seen anything of this Devil they speak of? Charles was saying just last night that a neighbor had chickens—"

"I know." Enid's face changed and she seemed sadder, her skin resembling the color of leaves that have fallen to the earth to die. "I will say this"—she chose her words carefully—"there is naught to fear from such. Not for you."

Kerry wondered at her meaning, but she shook her head, her crisp black hair shining.

"Ah, it's old I'm getting, Kerry. But I am glad you came

today, and I hope to see you again. I choose my friends carefully, as you see." The raccoon stretched, as if amused by her words, and Enid scratched the creature behind its ears while it rubbed its nose against her wrist.

Reluctantly Kerry stood up, and the two women went outside. Caledonia was waiting, as foretold, and Enid glanced up toward the hidden sky.

"Your young fool will be waiting now, full to the brim with ale. Do not let him work today or the troubles will be many."

Kerry nodded, taking the reins from the earth and, with Enid's help, swinging up on the horse. She gazed about her, her fears gone, and she saw that this place was indeed beautiful, mysterious and still. Thanking Enid for the meal, she let the horse set his own pace, a brisk canter, as she started off down the path. Without looking back, she knew Enid was there, and she felt comforted by having found such a friend in such a place.

As Enid had predicted, Trevor was mounting his horse in a peculiar fashion for his legs were refusing to cooperate. "Oh, wonderful. Look at you." Kerry's disgust couldn't be greater as she hoisted his sliding foot over the horse and into the stirrup. With deliberate patience, she placed his hands on the mane, herself taking the reins and leading his mount back to Brentwood.

"Kerry, me darling lass," Trevor, emboldened by ale, sang. "Have I told you lately that you are as fair as the morn? Your hair's as black as the shining coal, your eyes the color of the sea—"

"Trevor," she warned, putting a finger to her lips. "Will you be quiet?"

"Quiet? How can I be quiet when me heart's aching with your beauty?" His hand wavered forth, and Kerry thrust it impatiently back to the mane as his body shifted. It took considerably longer to get back to Brentwood, but there was no one about and they made it successfully to the stables.

"I have to get to work," Trevor stated, slumping to the

earth like a sack of potatoes. Kerry unsaddled the horses, returning them to their stalls while Trevor pulled himself up with the aid of the hitching post. "I've got to—"

"You're not going anywhere," Kerry said pointedly.

She assisted the youth into the stables, and at the feel of her arm about him, Trevor slowly moved his hand upward from her waist but Kerry's free hand caught his before he could make any serious contact.

"But, miss . . ." Trevor protested, as he found himself bedded down in a bundle of straw. "Master Cameron will kill me if I don't get to work."

"Master Cameron will kill you even more if you do, in that condition. Now get some sleep. Maybe you can make up your work tonight, at the furnace."

A slumberous sigh was her answer so Kerry shook her head, then tended to the horses herself. Slipping out of the pants, she adjusted the dress around her just before Cameron walked in.

"Kerry?" His gaze flickered around the stable, and not wishing him to find Trevor in his inebriated state, she nodded and strode quickly outside, hoping he would follow her. The ploy worked. The sharp crunch of his boots on the gravel behind her was clearly audible, and she braced herself, ready for the battle sure to come.

"What is going on here?" His eyes narrowed quickly, taking in her wrinkled dress, the straw that clung to her hair and clothes. "Where have you been all this time and what have you been doing?" He stepped even closer, his head cocked sideways. "You look like you've been rolling in the hay." This last remark caused his eyes to narrow even further as he considered the possibilities. "Where's Trevor?"

"He's not here," Kerry answered quickly, alarmed by the direction of his questions. But Cameron did not believe her and started purposefully for the stables, not pausing until she grabbed his arm.

"Trevor didn't do anything. . . ."

"Then why are you stopping me?" His eyebrows lifted sharply, but he paused, awaiting her explanation.

"Well . . ." Kerry stumbled, her foot kicking at the sand while her mind spun frantically. "I didn't want you to find out—"

"What?" He waited patiently, brushing aside his waistcoat and letting his hands rest on his firm hips. "I asked you a question, Kerry."

"Don't rush me!" She stared off toward the stables, then smiled ruefully as an idea came to her. "I didn't want you to find out that I couldn't ride. I fell off the horse and Trevor had to help me. That's what took so long. That's why the straw." She bit her lip, and being unused to lying, she hoped fervently that he would believe her.

A slight twitch twisted his lips, a twitch that changed instantly to a smile, and then to full-blown laughter. In a huff, Kerry turned her back to him, having no choice but to stand and bear his chuckling, for a sin that wasn't even hers. Finally after what seemed to be an eternity, his laughter faded away to a slight tremor and his hand fell comfortably on her shoulder.

"I'm sorry, Kerry. I didn't mean to laugh. Let me take you up to the house and I'll order water for a bath." He was still smiling and Kerry's cheeks burned under his amused stare. Silently, she flung several choice names at him and at Trevor, whose fault this all was anyway.

The bath itself was a delight. Purring as softly as any kitten, Kerry lifted the sponge and let the water trickle across her shoulders, luxuriating in the soft warm feel of it. For a while she could forget work, forget Trevor, and forget the troubles that had been plaguing her the last few days, troubles with the name of Cameron Brent. She could not fathom this man. After working all day, he still took the time to help Helga fill the large kettle and shuttle hot water to fill the copper tub. He had even managed to dislodge Charles from his permanent position beside the brandy in the parlor by inviting him to take a walk about the grounds, thereby leaving Kerry free use of the kitchen for her bath.

Nightfall was rapidly approaching and the firelight flickered from the brick hearth, reflecting in shimmering orange streamers across the liquid surface of the tub. Tiny beads of water glistened like crystals on Kerry's white shoulders and arms, then wove precarious paths down to her breasts before plunging back into the bathwater from which they came. Contentment escaped her in a sigh as she secured a stray lock of black silken hair under the blue ribbon tied atop her head; then she sank blissfully into the tub to totally enjoy the water's warm caress.

She leaned back and closed her eyes, a smile on her face, imagining that she was no longer an Irish serving girl but a lady, regally gowned in a dress of blue silk. Her hair was curled, and pinned high atop her head, and sparkling diamonds dangled from her ears. She was dancing—breathless—to a sweet and lilting music that wafted around her and she was in the arms of a handsome man whose arms held her possessively. He left her trembling with desire. She lifted her lashes coyly, and his face swam closer, until it became Cameron's face. His steely gray eyes were warm and welcoming, shining with pride and passion as his arm tightened and he swirled her around the floor. Their steps became faster and faster, until the other dancers disappeared and they were alone together, the swirling mists clearing to form a white draped bed.

Slowly, Cameron removed her gown, the gray of his eyes turning dark and smoky with passion. Kerry shivered as she found herself clasped once again in his arms, and she felt near pain as his chest pressed against her bosom. His mouth took hers and his hands began their descent, playing, arousing, titillating until she was breathless with passion.

Kerry's eyes flew open with a start as she glanced about the room. The water was rapidly cooling and she abruptly sat up, disturbed that the memory of Cameron's lovemaking should arouse her so completely. Indeed, that memory, allowed to ferment in her woman's body, was now all the more intoxicating. Damned English rogue! she thought, but it rang shallow even in her own mind. She recalled the way he'd helped the workers, his fairness in dealing with her, the restraint he had shown just last night in his study when she was completely in his power. Yet how long could he maintain that restraint, when her own body cried out for the very same thing he desired?

When a sharp knock interrupted her reverie, Kerry moved so abruptly that water splashed freely over her face. Frustrated, she wiped the droplets from her nose and faced the closed door.

"Well, what is it?" she called impatiently, miffed to be robbed of even one second of this unaccustomed joy.

"Miss Kerry?" George's voice rang out uncertainly in the silence, and Kerry frowned as she recognized his voice.

"Aye, George. It's me. I'm bathing."

"Yes, miss." Even from this slight distance Kerry could hear the servant's heel scraping, the persistent clearing of his throat, as if he knew not where to begin. "Ah well, miss, you see—"

"Out with it, George." Maybe if this interruption was not so important, she could still enjoy her bath before the rapidly cooling waters forced her to leave it. "What is it?"

"Well, miss. It's the wee lad. Young Trevor."

"Trevor!" Kerry cried out in surprise. She distinctly recalled the lad's slumberous state when she'd quit the stables. She'd been certain he would sleep through the night. "What about him?"

"Well it seems, miss, that though the lad's taken ill of spirits he's gone back to work in the furnace. Master Brent was walking with his brother and they caught the lad. There was no denying the smell of whiskey, and his staggering walk was obvoius. Then Bill Seldon . . ."

"Go on," Kerry called as George's voice drifted off in confusion.

"Well, he ne'er liked the lad from the first, you know. Doesn't care for the Irish, Bill doesn't. Sorry, miss. But he made sure that Masters Charles and Cameron saw Trevor's poor state, and before Master Cameron could stop him, Master Charles applied his fist to the lad and sent him sprawling to the earth."

"Oh, no!" Kerry cried. Slipping her dress over her still damp skin, she flung open the door, pulling the ribbon from her tangled hair as she faced George. "I'll go see to him right now. Maybe I can help."

"No, miss. I mean . . . that's it. After this row, Cameron managed to get Charles away, but when the lad came to he ran off in a rage."

"What do you mean he ran off?" Kerry demanded, tapping her foot in unconscious impatience as George rubbed his round face.

"I don't know, miss! He took the horse, not the good one but the bay. Master Cameron does not yet know, and I thought mayhap you might have an idea where he'd be." At her questioning glance, George hung his head, scuffling his boots against the hard wood floor. "Aye, I knew you went for a ride with him today and you've spent some time with the lad. He's a good sort so I'd not like to see him get into any more trouble than he already is."

"George, don't apologize. You did right." Tugging on her tattered boots, Kerry gestured toward the door. "I'll take Caledonia with me and try to find him. I have an idea where he might be." Tucking her hair inside the collar of her dress, she strode to the door. "In the meantime, ask around here. Try the sawmill and the gristmill. And there's a lass in the village who's rumored to be sweet on him . . . why, I don't know. Maggie Cramer's her name. A light-haired lass. Her father runs the store."

Grateful at having something concrete to do, George nodded and ran after the lass, his large bulk making its way through the barns toward the village. Kerry herself wasted no time in running to the stable. Startling the composed Caledonia, she threw a saddle on his back. She had no idea how long she had before Cameron returned and discovered her absence, but she pushed the thought firmly from her mind as she clambered upon the horse. A runaway servant was a serious offense indeed, and she was certain Trevor would suffer sorely for this deed. His discovery was almost certain, for indentured servants were the life blood of the colonies and neighbors far and near banded together to watch for escapees.

Kicking the horse into a frenzied gallop, she leaned forward, allowing her body to move with the horse the way she had as a child. Her dress flapped behind her, but she paid little heed to it, grateful that she was not confined to a sidesaddle. The gate loomed before her, but the Scottish mare, sensing the urgency of this mission, neatly gathered up her legs and cleared the fence, hardly pausing in her stride before resuming her gallop. Horse and rider were as one, exuberant and determined in this night enshrouded race against time. Guilt gnawed at the back of Kerry's mind as she thought of Trevor. Although she was aware that his condition was by no means her fault, she nevertheless could not help feeling that if she'd been more insistent about leaving Bodine's instead of panicking at the sight of the drunken colonial, none of this would have come to pass.

Bodine's, she said to herself, reaffirming her destination, for she had little doubt as to Trevor's course. Being alone, angry, and abused, he would surely come to the only place he regarded as friendly in the midst of these pine barrens, there to quaff his ale and plan his next move. She could only hope that fatigue would induce him to spend some time there before he went forth.

The tavern came into sight. First as a yellow, lamplit glow, then she saw the fence and the place itself. The porch sagged in an open leer while the gaudy sounds of music and drunken laughter spilled forth through the open window. Tethered horses stamped their hooves at the approach of the Scottish stallion, and seeing the poor condition of some of the steeds, Kerry wisely led her mount behind the building, then tied its reins to an apple tree. Compared to the noise out front, here it was strangely still. Kerry slipped cautiously into the shadow of the tavern.

Her hand upon the wall, she felt a weakness in her knees—relief. There, innocently returning her stare, was the bay Trevor favored, its reins tossed casually around the hitching post. Secure in her belief now, Kerry softly opened the wooden door that sorely lacked paint, cringing at the squawk elicited from the leather hinge. As the door swung shut, her horrified gaze fell on the table before her. Packed around the single flickering candle were a half-dozen leering coal buggers grasping black-smudged cards, their leader the drunken colonial from Philadelphia!

"Well, well. Looky here. 'Tis the lady from Philadelphia." The well-remembered yellow-toothed grin appeared, surrounded by a forest of black beard. Kerry edged backward toward the door, but to her dismay she found her way blocked by a scrawny little coalman. His whiskey-drenched breath caused her to gag.

"You're not thinkin' of leaving us already, are you?" the bearded lout continued, while chuckles erupted from the other men. "Now that wouldn't be perlight."

"I only came to find someone," Kerry replied defiantly, tossing off the scrawny one's hand when it came to rest upon her shoulder. She shivered in distaste when some of his grime remained on her fingers and she wiped them pointedly on her dress. "Now, if you don't mind . . ."

She brushed past the skinny man who blocked the door, only to find her way obstructed by the bearded ruffian. I would have to be a mountain climber to traverse his broad belly, she thought.

"But we do mind," he jeered, obviously enjoying himself. "You see lads, I offered for her for a price, but her master would not take it. 'E wanted the lass all to himself, 'e did. But me . . . I don't mind a wait. And now it willna' cost me a farthing." Kerry's sea-colored eyes went wide and her skin blanched white as his meaning came clear. But just as he reached for her, his fat sweaty hands dripping with charcoal dust and ale, the door swung open and Trevor stomped in.

"Is this where the game's going on . . . ? Kerry!" His astonishment was apparent as his eyes fell on the dark-haired lass, and the bearded coal bugger scowled, his face rapidly assuming the same hue as his beard.

"And wot do you want, you wee lad? You're far too young for such." His hands wrapped like snakes around Kerry's wrists, heedless of the pain he caused, while Trevor's black brows gathered in rage.

"You'll be keeping your hands from her, you black-haired lout! She's a good lass and not for the likes of you." Bravado winning over sense, he charged into the sprawling tormentor, his head landing squarely in the center of the big man's soft belly.

With a roar, the drunkard leaped up and swung his meaty fist, and before Kerry could even cry out, the Irish lad's body flew across the room, pausing only on contact with the wall, then slumping to the floor. Kerry's heart sank as a renewed roar rattled the tankards of ale on the table, but she ran to Trevor's side and tried to wrest his body from the floor. Smirking at her efforts, the bearded man pointed a sausagelike finger and roared, "You'll be saving your strength for me, lassie. Do not be wasting it on himself there. Scanlon, take them up."

At his command, the surly lout at the beefy man's elbow swung to his feet and complied, tossing the lad over one shoulder while hoisting the girl under his arm. Kerry fought and kicked, but her fists did not even penetrate the barrel-like frame of the coal worker. "You want them in your room?" A knowing leer spread across Scanlon's face when the bearded colonial tossed the cards haphazardly upon the table.

"Aye. And Scanlon"—a shining black eye widened for emphasis—"come right back doon."

Guffaws and much thigh slapping followed, and Kerry was carted unceremoniously up the stairs, around a bend, and then dumped onto a straw bed in the center of a dingy room. Gathering herself together after her fall, she glared at the man called Scanlon whose face still loomed in the doorway.

"Don't be bothering to move from that bed, lass. You'll be landing there soon enough again anyway." Chortling at his own drunken humor, he descended the stairs, wondering how long he would have to wait for his turn.

Trevor had landed on the floor, tossed there by Scanlon before he'd rid himself of Kerry. Her first thought now was for his condition. In the moonlight, the paleness of his face was alarming. Groping about, Kerry found a stub of a candle and a match on a nearby table. Cupping the precious light, she knelt beside Trevor to survey the damage.

When a groan issued from his lips, Kerry felt immense relief. Welts arose from his fair face and both eyes seemed swollen, one due to Charles no doubt. Kerry snorted in disgust. The groan increased in volume and the lad's eyelids flickered, then slowly opened. The blue orbs focused uncertainly on Kerry.

"Where . . . what the hell happened?"

Kerry slipped an arm under his body, gingerly helping Trevor to his feet and to the bed. He tried to sit up on the straw mattress, but his body slumped backward of its own accord. "Kerry . . . I'm sorry. I didn't know . . . I thought to run."

"Shhhh," she whispered, placing a finger to her lips as a renewed boom of laughter echoed from below. "We have to get out of here."

Understanding crept into Trevor's eyes as he realized the danger they were in, but he was as yet too weak to do anything but follow the Irish lass with his eyes. "The window?" he croaked, but Kerry was already at that aperture, her hands clawing numbly at the latch.

"It's bolted on the outside!" she groaned, recalled that tavern owners did this to prevent paying guests from escaping witout settling the bills. "I can't get it open."

Taking the candle with her, she tried the door, sure that it was locked. She was right. The doorknob gleamed at her—a brass leer. She struggled with it, but was unable to maneuver the lock free. Frantic, she glanced about the room, looking for something—anything—to aid their escape.

An empty tankard, a jar, a chamber pot in the corner, the bed, the table. With a sigh, Kerry stepped over to the table, her mind spinning frantically. Automatically, she dampened the corner of her gown with the remnants of liquor remaining in the jar and she daubed it across Trevor's wounds. Placing the candle on the table to better aid her, she concentrated on this task until her eyes returned to the candle. A distracting gleam caught her attention. It was a knife!

Sandwiched between the jar and the wall, it had first been invisible to her, but now it glistened like silver. With a glad cry, she snatched it up from the table.

"Kerry . . . do you think? . . ." Trevor struggled to speak but Kerry would not listen to him, would not hear her own fears put into words. Grabbing the candle, she shook her head.

"I'll try to wedge it in the door or window. Surely one of them will come free," she said, with considerably more optimism than she felt. She proceeded to wedge the knife blade deftly between the wood holding the two panes of the window, the place where the latch was. But the lock was old and rusted from neglect, and although she pushed and jimmied the blade through the narrow slit, the latch did not loosen. Pulling away in disgust, she went to the door, still clutching the candle. She felt rather than saw Trevor's distraught interest. His eyes strained to follow her movements, but she had no further success here. The bolt was strong. Of Jersey iron, Kerry thought derisively as the immobile metal made a mockery of her thin blade. Glancing back at Trevor's worried face, Kerry tried to sound confident. "I'll keep trying at the window. It has to come free." Secretly, however, her heart sank and her hope for freedom waned.

Chapter Eight

Cameron turned away from his brother upon reaching the house, trying to keep from hitting Charles.

"I daresay, Cam. You would be a fool to let the Irish urchin get away with this. Stout discipline is the only thing these lads understand." With an oath, Cameron flung his hand up to silence his brother, glaring at him full in the lamplight.

"'Tis the result of your discipline that we're now missing a servant," Cameron retorted, his disgust plain. "Do me a favor, Charles. From now on, leave the servants to me. I can't afford to be losing them right and left, not due to your temper."

With a click of disdain, Charles strode toward the library, muttering under his breath as to the danger of such leniency. As soon as he was out of earshot, Cameron ran into the kitchen, calling for Kerry.

"Kerry! Kerry where are? . . ." But the tub stood at the hearth, the waters long since cooled. Cameron was starting for the stairs when a voice rang out behind him.

"Sir . . . she's gone."

Cameron whirled about to face George. The servant stood awkwardly in the doorway, twisting his tricorn in his hand, his face a deepening red.

"Gone! What do you mean?"

"Do not blame the lass, sir. 'Twas my fault. I told her what happened to Trevor today, thinking she might have a clue as to where the lad went. She gave me a few suggestions, then she took off on the horse and has not yet returned." Wincing under the glare of his employer, George bravely went on. "I've got the coach ready outside. Let's be off and I'll help find them."

Muttering an oath, Cameron snatched up his pistol. He ignored Charles's jeering laughter behind him. Having heard the commotion, his brother had sauntered out of the library and he couldn't be more delighted with Cameron's predicament. "This is the result of coddling servants." Charles sniffed, but George gave him a look that silenced him. Not pausing to retort, Cameron ran out the door, George at his heels.

"Stop at the furnace first," Cameron yelled, grasping onto the side of the coach to keep from tumbling off as the conveyance lurched. "Perhaps one of them will know which pub Trevor frequents."

With a determined set of his firm lips, George slapped the horses into an even faster pace and they soon came upon the furnace. Before the carriage came to a stop, Cameron jumped down and flung open the door.

The workers froze in startled surprise at seeing their employer in the doorway, his black cloak tossed over his shoulder, his pistol protruding from his hand, his eyes silver and blazing. Indeed, his gaze evoked the fires of the furnace itself, and more than one mouth gaped as Cameron strode into the room.

"Trevor. Where does he go? Which pub?" The men's heads turned toward Bill Seldon, whose lips pursed in a negative snarl. His eyes cast noncommittally down to the iron, he calmly ladled the liquid metal into the sand molds, ignoring the irate Cameron. Not one to be long denied, Cameron crossed the floor purposefully, and before Bill Seldon could draw two breaths, a hand clenched his shoulder with such force that the metal sizzled to the floor. Then Cameron shook him roughly.

"Tell me now, I'm warning you."

"Bodine's," Seldon snarled. No Irish lad was worth this. "Right down the road."

Without another word, Cameron stalked out to the carriage and swung up beside George. "Bodine's," he shouted, and with a frenzied motion, George flapped the reins.

The horses lurched toward the road, almost rushing over the gate boy, who though warned of the oncoming carriage by George, was nevertheless stunned by this apocalyptic vision of wildly galloping horses and a carriage that veered madly from one side of the road to the other. A sleety rain was beginning to fall. It pelleted the lad as he hastened from the gate, glad that this vision of hell was far down the path. He ran for the house, shaking his head.

"Can't you go any faster?" Cameron shouted as the rain pounded his back and the horses strained at the bit. He did not bother to question himself about the urgency he felt, the pounding of his heart, but perhaps it was good that he did not. For the answer would have disturbed him. It would have made his self-image as indistinct as a reflection in a pool into which a pebble had been tossed.

Rolling thunder came from the east as rain beat relentlessly upon them, changing the soft sandy roads into mires. Once the left rear wheel of the carriage sank hopelessly into the muck. The horses pulled frantically and suddenly burst free, racing along the road. Cameron mentally urged the steeds on, his eyes straining for the slightest light in the all enveloping icy rain.

Then it came. A tiny gleam identified the tavern, and soon they were galloping into the yard, the carriage swinging to a frenzied halt beneath the apple tree. Cameron's quicksilver gaze caught sight of the Scottish stallion. With a deep breath, he withdrew his pistol and headed determinedly for the door.

"Wait!" George scrambled down from his perch in the carriage to follow Cameron. The windows were shuttered, and only a thin ray of light escaped through the tiny slit between them.

"I don't like it," George muttered, searching about the rain-spattered grounds for a weapon. A stout chunk of wood was the only thing that presented itself, but George was from the old country and had fought many battles armed thusly. With renewed confidence the two men crept toward the rear door, halting at the sound of voices.

"Throw that card back a spell, or I'll take off your hand," a surly voice rumbled.

An equally inebriated man responded, "Aye, he's just in a hurry for that lass 'e's got upstairs." This remark was rewarded with chuckles and then the eloquent one continued. "Aye, wouldn't mind a bit of that mesel'. How about it?"

"We'll see," was the noncommittal answer, followed by a loud belch. "If she has any strength left after me." A rumbled roar broke out as these words were followed by the scraping of a chair, then the clinking of glasses. Cameron had heard enough. With a decisive tug on George's coat, he pulled his servant close to his ear.

"Go around front and into the tavern. Ask about for a game, and when they lead you back here, stand guard by the door and make certain that none of them venture upstairs." Cameron tested the well-oiled trigger of his pistol, then pointed toward the door. "If all goes well I'll meet you back here."

George slipped through the shadows to the side of the tavern, then sauntered into the bar.

The room was full to the rafters with charcoal burners, sawmill workers, laborers, and lumbermen. Clammers and fishermen from the Jersey shore took half of the space, sacks filled with fish and oozing water betraying their livelihood, as did their peculiar aroma. "What'll it be?" The bartender winked, thrusting a long-necked jug at a clammer waiting nearby. He absently marked the clammer's slate with a bit of chalk, blowing away the dust so the mark was clear under *q*.

"What'll you recommend?" George said, knowing the way to an innkeeper's heart. It wasn't often the man had the opportunity to appear an expert so he leaned over the polished oak bar, warming to the subject.

"We got some good, wholesome ale coolin' below." He nodded, polishing a pewter tankard as he spoke. "Also some rum, newly smuggled from the frigate. But if I was you"—he winked conspiratorially and George leaned closer, assuming an impressed air—"I'd take the lightnin'."

"Hard cider?" George asked, and the bartender grinned.

"Aye. We have two kinds. Depends if yer goin' courtin' or fightin'."

"Well, I'm not going courtin' so give me the other." Remembering his business there, George kept the stick well secreted beneath his coat and assumed an only mildly interested air. "Would there be such a thing as a game in these parts? I know it's illegal but . . ." Looking askance, George deposited several shining coins on the bar. "You see, I just learned this game called poker, and I'd be liking some practice."

The bartender's suspicious glance disappeared at the sight of the coins. Sweeping them deftly into his apron, he jerked his thumb toward the rear door. "Tell them I said you're invited." He winked, then turned to fill a jug for a coal bugger.

"Ah, you damned coal bugs, you cannot wait for a fill, nor can you hold your ale!" a clammer jeered, and a ripple of drunken laughter erupted as George ambled to the closed rear door. He could only hope that a fight would not break out and interfere with their plan.

Heads turned as he walked into the smoke-filled room, and the scrawny coal worker was beside him in an instant. "I inquired about a game out front," George said, assuming his most foppish manner, "and the barkeep sent me back here. I cannot play very well, but I think it jolly good sport." At his bashful smile, scowls broadened into grins and a man obligingly vacated a seat for him, their eyes never leaving the pouch that dangled from his belt.

"Welcome aboard, mate." The closest set of tobacco-stained teeth grinned. "And don't worry none about not playing too well. We can't either." At this fine joke they all laughed, then pulled their seats up to the table.

Upon hearing this, Cameron strode around to the door. When he sauntered inside, the workers scarcely looked up for their insults were growing hotter as the ale flowed and running feuds were being renewed. To get the barkeep's attention, Cameron Brent waved a gold piece before him.

"Yes, sir. Whatever you say, sir."

"I want a room upstairs. The main room." Cameron nodded to the door while the bartender sighed.

"I'm sorry. It's already been taken."

"By whom?" The gold piece danced before the bartender's eyes and the man's reluctance vanished.

"Jack Maxwell. He let it for the week."

"I want the room," Cameron declared, with a voice long used to giving orders. He tossed the coin to the man and started for the steps, but the barkeep was at his shoulders in an instant, his thin angular face knotted into a frenzy of anger.

"You cannot! I said the room was let, and I mean—"

"Either you retreat from my path or you will test this bit of lead I carry." The barkeep's eyes fled to the pistol aimed directly at his heart, and his courage fled. "Or," Cameron continued pleasantly, "I would be most happy to call the law. I have it on good authority that you have an illegal game running here, as well as a lass being held against her will. The choice is entirely yours."

The barkeep scuttled quickly out of Cameron's way, returning to his jugs and whistling distractedly. He had a bad feeling about all this, a very bad feeling.

Up in the room, Kerry heard the icy pinging of rain upon the shuttered windows, then a low growl of thunder. When lightning flashed, she shivered, pulling her arms more closely about her shoulders. Then the dreaded sound came. Above the noise of the rain and wind, heavy footsteps were approaching. Now they were at the door. Thrusting the slim dagger beneath the straw mattress, Kerry tried to ignore the wide-eyed alarm in Trevor's eyes. With a roar, the door burst open and the leering, obese Jack sauntered into the room.

"Well, well, me lady. Methinks the Irishman's been keeping you occupied for the time." His yellow leer traveled to Trevor, whose face flushed from suppressed rage. "'Tis a shame, lad. Now the lass will know a real man and be forgetting the likes of you." With one stroke of his hand, he swept Trevor to the floor like a discarded piece of clothing. Darkness mercifully overcame the injured lad, and he was spared the pain of seeing what transpired.

"Oh, no you don't." Jack's yellowish eyes observed Kerry's rapid flight toward the door, and for a man of his bulk, he moved remarkably fast, blocking the exit with his ample figure. A surging laugh started from somewhere in his belly as he observed the panic in her soft green eyes, the rapid rise and fall of her breast. As he took in her soft curves his face became distorted by lust, and Kerry backed away in revulsion as he dangled the key before her.

"Have no thought but these, lady. You're mine for the night, and I will not let you go." With a toss, he deposited the key in the chamber pot and advanced purposefully toward her. His hands fumbled with the buckle of his belt while his lips dripped with ale and saliva, seemingly watering for a taste of her soft skin. "You might as well get out of them clothes, lady. Or I'll do it for you."

"Never!" Kerry hissed, bolting in horror as Jack let his belt dangle and grabbed for her. A low chuckle rose in his throat as, with one tug, he split her calico dress right down the center, leaving her breasts bare to his greedy gaze. When his meaty hands pawed at her soft round curves, Kerry screamed, clawed, and kicked. Her knee struck his groin at the same time her fist clamped down on his hand. Jack snarled like a feral dog. "Why you bloody bitch!" He threw her upon the bed, forcing her knees apart.

In that last frantic moment, Kerry remembered the knife! Slipping her hand free as she struggled to breathe beneath his crushing weight, she grasped its silver handle and sank the blade in his meaty shoulder. A flash of lightning revealed yellowish eyes boring into her face, then with a little effort, he took the knife from her hand before she could do further damage.

"Try to kill me, will you? When I get through with you, you'll wish you'd a been good to me, you will!" Without raising himself from her body, he wrapped his shirt roughly about his shoulder, which had been merely scratched by the slender blade. Then, ignoring her screams and laughing evilly, he wrenched up her skirts, meanwhile tugging at his unbelted trousers.

A thundering shot ripped through the air and Jack's large head swiveled over his shoulder, his eyes blinking in disbelief for a man stood boldly in the doorway. "Why, you bloody beggar, I'll kill you mesel'!" In frustrated rage, Jack prepared to charge the intruder, but he soon changed his mind.

"Unless you're willing to join your ancestors in hell, I suggest you stay where you are." The voice was cool and deadly calm.

No blustering lad was this, but a man prepared to kill should his wishes be thwarted. Warily, Jack eyed this incipient assassin.

"Now get up and walk quietly toward the door."

Rising warily to his feet, Jack obeyed, his hands tugging at his trousers.

"Leave them." The gun indicated his pants and Jack's round yellowish eyes widened, his jaw gaping in disbelief. "You heard me!" Cameron nodded, fingering the silver trigger as if steeling his fingers not to shoot. Seeing this gesture, Jack dropped his idea of assault and shuffled comically out of the room, his speed considerably hampered by the rumpled trousers bagging around his knees. He descended the stairs awkwardly, grumbling to himself as Cameron stood above him, the pistol still focused on the broad target he made.

"You'll pay for this!" Jack shouted, once out of range, and as he adjusted his pants amid gaping stares, he allowed himself the luxury of shaking his fist. "That's twice you crossed me. You'll pay for both times."

A shot rang out behind him, the bullet ricocheting from the plastered wall and then imbedding itself in a wooden beam directly behind him. Favoring prudence more than his reputation, Jack made a hasty retreat through the back door, trying to ignore the humored guffaws that followed him.

"Are you all right?" Cameron turned back into the room, the gun in his hand still smoking.

Kerry nodded. She stood beside the bed, biting her lip and trying to hold the two flimsy pieces of her gown together. The drunken lout had rent its thin cloth, and despite her attempts at modesty she was displaying more than she covered. At the sight of her gleaming shoulders and the rounded bosom almost spilling forth from her crossed arms, Cameron's restraint was sorely tested. Seeing his wandering gaze, Kerry turned her back to him, clutching the tatters of the gown tighter.

"If you had any decency you'd look away," she declared,

sensing his approach. With a sigh, he doffed his cloak and placed it around her shoulders, one hand lingering caressingly in her soft black hair.

"'Twas your comfort that concerned me," he stated, fastening the cloak. Then, as shimmering green eyes looked up at him searchingly, he continued in the same manner. "He did not hurt you, did he? For I will kill him if he did."

"No." Kerry said, her wondering gaze never leaving his serious face. His eyes were cast down now, for he was intent on working the fasteners of the cloak, but when they joined with hers she saw the warmth in them. "Trevor." Kerry smiled weakly, trying to ignore the strong reassurance she felt in his arms, the desire to be drawn into his embrace. What was the matter with her? She shook her head, and her black hair fell about her shoulders in a most attractive manner. Then she stepped uncertainly away from his disturbing presence, the warmth of his body. Gesturing to the slumbering lad on the floor, she said, "We have to get him up."

With a grimace, Cameron crossed the room and scooped the injured Trevor Shanahan from the floorboards. He placed the lad carefully on the bed, forcing open his closed eyelids with a thumb. "The bottle." He gestured with a nod of his head to the table, and Kerry handed him the dark whiskey jug. Withdrawing the cork with his teeth, Cameron forced a bit of the liquor between Trevor's lips. Immediately, the lad sputtered and his white pallor was transformed to a healthier hue. He coughed, but was unable to rise. Indeed, he could not even force his eyes open due to the painful swelling.

"Charles?" Cameron directed his question to Kerry as he examined the purple contusions.

"One side," Kerry answered. "The other was from Jack. Trevor tried to save me."

"As well he should. 'Twas his fault you were here at all." His annoyance and anger softened, however, as Kerry favored the lad with a worried, maternal glance. "Fear not for the lad, Kerry. My anger is due to his having placed you in jeopardy, but I well understand the reason he ran. I will deal with him fairly, you have my word."

She nodded. Strangely reassured, she watched him from the bedside as he tended the Irish lad, a mere servant. Even with her limited experience, she knew that another man would not have been so kind. Most masters would have thrown Trevor in jail for running away, and herself too, as an accomplice. But Cameron went to the stairs and called for a tavern wench, ordering the shy girl to bring both hot and cold water and several cloths. The sound of her scurrying footsteps died quickly away.

"He should be all right." Cameron again plied Trevor with whiskey, and was rewarded by the soft flicker of his eyelids. "It's ourselves I'm concerned with now."

"What do you mean?" Kerry asked.

"With the weather outside, the roads are sure to be washed out. It seems we have no other choice. We will have to wait until morning to leave."

"Does that mean we must stay here?" Kerry could not suppress the wrinkling of her nose as she surveyed their surroundings, and she shuddered as rain dashed against the windows. "Surely we could make it—"

"The carriage got stuck once on the way up here, and that was over an hour ago. No. I'm afraid we're staying here."

Kerry sighed, and dutifully swallowed her repugnance at spending another minute in the tavern. Settling herself on the one chair, she watched the tavern girl enter, cautiously balancing a bowl of heated water, and bearing a pitcher and several white rags.

"Will that be all, sir?" If the lass thought it strange to see Kerry huddled in a chair while this elegant English gentleman tended to the injuries of a poor working boy, she hid her feelings admirably, placing the bowl and the pitcher on the table and carefully averting her eyes.

"Yes, miss. I'll need this room made ready for the night, along with two more." Cameron scarcely looked up. He was now applying the cloths to Trevor's mottled face.

"But, sir"—she flushed, still refusing to meet his gaze as if she expected to be struck for her impertinence—"there is only one other room tonight. There are only four rooms total, and the others are occupied by some of the men downstairs." She trembled violently as she spoke, waiting for a blow to descend.

"That's quite all right," Cameron hastened to assure her. "Just the two rooms then. And when you go down for the linens, in the back room where the men play cards, you will find a rather broad, merry fellow who is undoubtedly beating the trousers off those boors. Do send him up. I guarantee the others will not raise an argument at his departure, at least if they plan to keep some of their money."

The girl slid sideways to the door, still unable to believe he was not angry that she could not supply the extra room. But as he was now applying cold cloths to Trevor's head, she sidled to the stairs and then raced down before he could change his mind.

"The lass appears to be scared to death of you," Kerry mused, troubled concern wrinkling her brow. "I wonder why."

"She's been ill used by those ruffians below, no doubt." Cameron frowned, placed one more cool cloth on Trevor's brow and then stood up. "'Tis said I have a rather formidable appearance"—he smiled—"and that I would frighten more than a lass away."

A timid knock sounded on the door and the tavern girl staggered in, this time struggling with linens and fresh towels. She scurried about the room, straightening up the mess and attempting to change the sheets with Trevor still abed. Kerry joined her and together they lifted Trevor just enough to adjust the sheets below him. As they did so, the cloak Kerry wore fell open and the tavern girl's wide-eyed gaze fell on the ripped material beneath it and on her exposed bosom. Emitting a frightened squeak, she tore out of the room, eager to avoid the same end.

Kerry could not stop a fit of giggles at the girl's erroneous conclusion, but Cameron scowled. "And now I'm a molester of women."

"'Tis a charge you cannot deny," Kerry answered pertly, glad the bed and Trevor's body were between them as he lowered a piercing gaze in her direction. He studied her far too closely for Kerry's liking so she glided quickly to the opposite side to the room to answer a knock.

At once he was at her side. "Let me," he said quickly. "Who is it?" he called, pushing her to safety behind him.

"Me, sir. George." At the sound of his servant's voice, Cameron opened the door just a crack, then, certain it was indeed the coachman, he bade him enter.

"You needed me, sir?" George's eyes fell on Kerry and relief relaxed his broad features. "Good to see you're all right, miss. The master run over here right away, as soon as I told him you'd gone."

A scowl came to Cameron's face at the coachman's words, but Kerry smiled in delight, returning George's eager handclasp with one of her own.

"Due to the rainstorm"—Cameron interrupted this reunion—"I have deemed it advisable to spend the night here. Unfortunately, the tavern girl informed me there is only one more available room."

"There will soon be more than that," George assured him, his hands covering his round belly as he chuckled. "More than one lad's taken his leave already, since I have his coins, and by the end of this night many more will follow. 'Tis amazing how many lads insist upon playing a game they know nothing about." A wrinkled brow accompanied his words, but the twinkle in his eyes showed no true remorse and Kerry smiled at the thought of the coalmen's discomfiture. "Now if you don't mind, I've kept them waiting long enough."

As George bowed, Cameron said in a strangely choked voice, "I'll make a pallet for you here, since Trevor's occupying the bed, you may need it. It must be a strain to carry your new-found wealth." With a wink, George departed and the sound of his heavy footsteps slowly died. As Cameron closed the door, Kerry was already fluffing up the linens and pillows for the pallet. He watched her admiringly. When she'd finished, he nodded toward the neat little bed.

"Now that George has sleeping quarters, we have only ourselves to worry about."

Taking up the candle and a bundle of linens, Cameron stepped through the door, holding on to Kerry's wrist. Fortunately, the very next room was vacant and they slipped inside.

"This is an improvement," Kerry remarked, for even in the dancing candlelight the cleanliness of the large bed was apparent. Cameron placed the candle on a small wooden table, and the flame was clearly reflected in its polished sheen. In spite of the room's tidy appearance, Kerry was not willing to leave anything to chance. She quickly stripped the sheets from the bed, smoothing the new ones into place. She was amazed to find that she had a helper, for in a matter-of-fact way, Cameron's strong, tanned hands came to her aid, pulling the quilts over the new sheets and tucking them under on the opposite side. These fresh linens exuded the aromas of cedar and lavender, and Kerry wondered at this, particularly in light of the condition of the room next door.

"That was Jack's doing, no doubt." Cameron answered her thought as if he'd read her mind. "He doesn't seem the kind to care overly much about fresh sheets."

"Aye, that's the truth," Kerry said with a shudder. "'Tis a shame to leave poor Trevor there in his bed. He'll be in for a fright when he awakens."

"It will serve him right," Cameron answered, annoyed by her concern for the lad. "Maybe he'll think twice before he goes rushing off again and dragging you with him."

"He did not!" Kerry protested, but Cameron was at her side, his hands on her shoulders, turning her toward him.

"Which brings me to something else, Kerry." From the ominous tone in his voice, she knew what was coming but winced when it came.

"Why did you keep his expedition to the tavern a secret?" He peered directly into her face, his silvery gaze penetrating.

"I didn't think it was my business," she began lamely, but he pounced on her words.

"He could easily have been injured, or have caused harm to others at the furnace. Surely from your daily work there you are aware of the dangers involved for a sober man. But a drunken lad! His life could have been forfeit! You obviously hold some affection for him, yet you chose not to come to me. By hiding his secret, you endangered his life!" His eyes blazed now, and Kerry's chin rose in defiance. "Why, Kerry? Why didn't you tell me?"

"And how was I supposed to know what you'd do?" She lifted her nose primly. "What I know of the sassenach is not flattering, of that you can be sure!"

Amazement fought with anger in Cameron and from the strained muscles at the sides of his neck, Kerry feared she'd gone too far. Indeed, his voice was barely recognizable when he spoke, so choked was it with anger.

"A sassenach? And all the time I've spent with you means nothing? You still consider me your enemy?" His face darkened ominously and his piercing gaze narrowed. Kerry was not a lass to fear most men, but she could not suppress an involuntary shiver.

With a deliberate movement, Cameron reached out and undid the fasteners of his cloak, letting the garment drop to

128

the floor. Kerry gasped as the cool night air caressed her partially clad body. Then she glanced up and found his eyes wandering boldly over her rounded curves. When Jack had gazed at her lustfully she'd felt nothing but repulsion, but this man's gaze was strangely exciting. She reached for the cloak, but his hand stilled her movement and his boot kicked the cloak away from her feet.

"Take off the dress." His voice was firm and low, and as Kerry glanced up at him in astonishment, his gaze met hers and brooked no refusal.

"But . . ."

"Take off the dress," he repeated. As she toyed with the folds of the torn calico, his voice rang out so sharply that she jumped.

"I am not a patient man, Kerry."

With trembling fingers, she obeyed and slid the dress from her shoulders. The soft blue material slipped down to her waist, catching on her rounded bottom before falling down to the floorboards. Her breath caught in her throat as his eyes caressed her everywhere, drinking their fill of her exquisite beauty. At last his hand reached forth and removed the concealing lock of black silk hair that lay curled about her breast, his fingers brushing the tight nipple in their path.

"I want to see all of you," he murmured, his hand dropping to her slender waist, then pausing at her hip. Before Kerry could react, he had grasped her buttock and pulled her to him. She was in his embrace. Her mouth opened, but her protests went unaired for his lips captured hers, their touch sparking a fiery heat in Kerry. She would have pulled away, but Cameron took advantage of her slight movement by reaching up to grasp her silken tresses and hold her head while his kiss deepened. His hips rubbed hers most intimately, and in spite of the breeches he wore, she was well aware of his arousal. Her head swam with a giddy excitement, yet she struggled against the intoxication of his kiss. The logical side of her brain voiced its arguments, but passion laughed at them and desire ignited deep inside of her.

His lips eased a bit, then trailed a fiery path to her throat while Kerry gasped for breath. "Master Cameron . . ." Her voice was a husky plea, and she leaned against him shakily, her world spinning. But her eyes told a different story. Cameron smiled at her.

"I've been far too patient with you for too long," he said thickly, passion racing through his voice. Kerry looked up and saw the hard, silvery gleam in his eyes. "I must have you now."

His lips traveled lower, past her throat, and Kerry trembled in his arms, fighting for sanity. "Master, wait—"

"Cameron," he said hoarsely, tumbling to the bed with her in his arms. Somehow Kerry found herself pulled onto him, her arms braced on either side of him as his fingers traced a molten path to her breasts. Kerry shuddered, and her thighs entwined with his as he rolled her beneath him, his hands pressing her shoulders down into the bedclothes.

"Cameron," he repeated.

"Cameron," Kerry whispered, her voice shaking.

He smiled, then lowered his head and his mouth caught her breast, his tongue flicking slowly over each nipple until both stood erect and were achingly sensitive. Meanwhile his hands continued to caress her. They moved boldly over her creamy flesh, arousing, exciting every fiber of her being until she thought she could no longer bear it. She felt the warmth of his hands on her waist, then on her belly and lower still. A gasp caught in her throat as his hands touched her intimately, but at the same time his lips brushed the peak of her breast, teasing the nipple. A hot, scorching flame raced through her, and when his mouth met hers, her kiss was savage and fierce, hungrily impatient.

As he left her arms for the briefest moment, rising to rid

himself of his clothes, Kerry leaned up on one arm, shyly watching his body emerge, the muscles rippling in his legs and arms. He was a magnificent specimen of a man, his body firm, his waist lean, his chest lightly furred. She felt a stirring within her at the sight of him, and she blushed as he looked up, a broad smile coming to his face.

When she looked away, he was beside her in a second, his hand softly cupping her chin and turning her face back to his.

"Kerry." His voice was low and soft and Kerry gazed up at him, wide-eyed, wondering at the gentleness of his tone. She saw the anger had left him and something different shone in his gaze, passion, aye, and something else, something that warmed the very essence of her. "Kerry, I have never forced a woman, until that night with you in the tavern, and the thought that you were unwilling has haunted me ever since. I plan to keep you with me tonight, to make love to you. But I would rather you were willing to share this night with me than face regrets upon the dawn."

Kerry stared up at him in amazement as he drew her into his arms. His mouth nuzzled her throat and she sighed, drawing him even closer to her, reveling in the way the hardness of his flesh complemented the silken smoothness of her own. Her eyes fluttered closed as his lips and tongue moved over her skin, patiently arousing her until she was breathless and panting beneath him. When his lips took hers, she welcomed him with open arms, and his tongue teased hers, tasting of her sweetness until she writhed against him. Kerry could only wonder at this man. He made her want him. Fiery tension built in her with each fevered caress, and her own hands explored the firmness of his chest, the muscles of his legs. She heard his hoarse groan and she smiled at the thought that, inexperienced though she was, she could still give him the same incredible pleasure that he was giving her.

When his hands parted her thighs, she shivered, unable to stop the flood of pleasure that raced through her. Her body arched, eager to meet his, and his legs entwined with hers. His arms embraced her, and every inch of their bodies touched. She could feel the ragged beat of his heart answering her own, and she waited for his thrust.

Cameron pressed deep within her, the first sharp ache quickly passing, and then she nearly sobbed with pleasure. She moved instinctively with him, her body catching his rhythm, her passion raging higher until she wondered wildly where it would end. His tongue ravished hers, and she wanted that. The tension within her became a red-hot fervor, then burst into ecstasy as the driving force of his body brought her reward, surging waves of pleasure flooding through her. She heard Cameron cry out her name, and he clasped her tightly to him as if he would draw her into himself, merging their bodies.

Kerry huddled next to him, her heart still pounding, her breath slow and uneven. An odd feeling of contentment and security came to her and her arms tightened about him. She dared not think logically now—there was no need. She felt euphoric, whole, and complete, and she drifted into undisturbed slumber.

She woke drowsily some time later, hardly aware that he was awake, but the firmness of his flesh against her thigh assured her this was no dream. She smiled, her eyes half-closed, as he cajoled her, softly arousing her as if the earlier part of the evening hadn't even taken place. He treated her as if she were a virgin still, seducing her with soft words of love until Kerry clutched him to her, begging him to take her again. She heard his husky chuckle; then she shivered as he kissed every part of her body: her face, her throat, each finger, her wrist, and on and on until she thought she would become mindless. Even though she'd never experienced another man, Kerry knew that Cameron was different. Not all men were as caring or sophisticated in their lovemaking.

He made a wanton of her as she cried out for him, feelings of ravishment traveling down to her toes and every inch of her tingling with excitement as he took her again. She buried her fingers in his hair with a sigh, never feeling so much a woman or so completely innocent in all her life. She found new amazement in every moment; then together they slept, deep in each other's arms, until morn.

Chapter Nine

Morning broke early as an uninhibited wedge of sunshine poured through the shuttered windows, and Kerry awakened sleepily upon hearing strident voices somewhere outside. The recollection of the previous night bringing a bright flush to her face, she turned around to find empty space next to her. Confusion and shame struck her as she saw the dented pillow, testimony that he had been with her. "He cannot even face me!" she declared. Wrathfully, Kerry picked up the pillow and flung it across the room, letting it strike the wall and fall in a crumpled heap to the floor. She thought of her dream of herself as a grand lady waltzing in Cameron's arms, and she laughed derisively. There had been little that was ladylike in her behavior last night, she mused, aware that a true lady would never have found herself in such a predicament. Her anger at herself grew, and she pictured her father, what he would say if he knew what she had done . . . tumbling into bed with that Englishman like any common dockside trollop!

Why is it he I respond to? Kerry asked herself. Why do I tremble at his nearness? He is one man among many! Yet, try as she might, she could think of no other that aroused these feelings within her. Agitatedly, she went to stand beside the window, trying not to hear her own thoughts.

Below, she saw a group of young lads assembled in a line, some of them still bearing telltale peach fuzz upon their chins. They were garbed in the blue of the Continental Army and from their movements, Kerry realized they were being trained. They were a ragged bunch, unaccustomed to duty, and they scattered quickly when a skunk sauntered up the path.

One of the soldier's glanced appreciatively toward her window, reminding Kerry that her dress was still torn. With an embarrassed flush, she moved away from the aperture, tucking the gown down around her neckline in an attempt to repair the tear. But her efforts to repair the damage were futile so she glanced about the room in frustration. Her eyes found no bit of cloth or thread, and with an oath, she stamped her foot just as the door swung open.

"Good morning, Kerry."

She glanced up quickly, feeling a hot flush race over her body as Cameron entered the room. His eyes scanned her with a burning perusal, and a warmth burned brightly within them as he came to stand beside her.

"I trust you slept well." His hand caressed her arm lightly. "I took another room this morning so as not to disturb your rest, but I cannot always promise to be so considerate in the future. I find my own sleep disturbed by the want of you beside me."

Regaining a bit of her composure, Kerry glanced quickly upward at his last words, her eyes wide with astonishment.

"You don't think this can continue?" Her mind had fully received the import of his words, and her mouth sagged open.

"And why not?" Cameron smiled, his voice warm and coaxing.

Kerry felt her resolves flagging, but her pride saved her and she spoke more rapidly. "Last night . . . it was a mistake!" she insisted hotly, her courage rapidly giving way when she saw his jaw twitch and his eyes turn cold. "It just happened! We cannot let it happen again!"

"Kerry." Cameron tried a lighter tone. "Kerry . . . I want you. You know I want you. I want to hold you in my arms. Last night can be one of many. Why do you deny this thing between us?"

"No!" Kerry said, agonized. When he drew her to him, she turned quickly away, not trusting herself or her unpredictable emotions. His hand came to rest on her shoulder, and he slowly turned her toward him. Kerry's skin burned where he touched her. She felt like wax, pliable and melting beneath his touch, and he smiled at her warmly.

"Kerry." Cameron lifted her chin and forced her to look at him. "I can do much for you . . . treat you the way you should be treated. You should not have to toil, to wear these rags." His hand gestured toward her gown. "I can dress you as befits your beauty. Name your desires."

Kerry stared at him incredulously, and her anger grew. Appalled, she pulled away from him, her eyes flashing green fire, outrage pouring from her small form.

"I thought I made it plain to you once, Englishman," she taunted him, not caring that his own rage, newly kindled, could flare into a frightening anger. "I can't be bought—for any price! Not by you or any other of your kind!"

"So that's the way it's to be," Cameron growled, his voice low, his manner menacing. "You will return to your world of English and Irish, disallowing all that happened between us! By God, Kerry, you try my patience!" He took a step closer to her, but Kerry held her ground, glaring up at him.

"Well, I'll try it no more! I'm but your servant, master! There is little need for you to be concerned over me! I'll stay well out of your way . . . you can be sure of that!"

Cameron's fingers tightened about her shoulders, and Kerry thought he meant to strike her. Her eyes met his and held for a brief second; then a discreet knock sounded at the door. Cursing under his breath, Cameron looked at her gown, scowling at the sight of it.

"Cover yourself," he commanded, tossing his cloak to her. "Unless you want the men to see you as I have."

Hurriedly, Kerry obeyed, tossing him a well-earened glare for his crudity. She lifted the cloak and as she drew on one ragged boot, she heard Cameron's grunt of impatience. The sight of her shapely limbs set him to thinking about other, more pliable parts of her body and his foot tapped impatiently on the floor. When she finally finished, Cameron flung open the door to see George standing there, twisting his tricorn sheepishly in his hands.

"Beg pardon, sir. But I thought we should be on our way . . . we should see to the wee lad, Trevor."

Cameron did not respond, but strode past George into the room where Trevor lay.

Kerry entered the room, undecided whether she was relieved to see Trevor sitting up though his face was mottled with yellow and purple bruises. "How are you feeling?" she asked, rushing past Cameron to the lad's side.

"Well enough, miss." Seeing the darkening glower on his master's face, Trevor pushed Kerry aside and whispered furtively, "I'll not be needing more trouble, miss." Then louder, for Cameron's ears he added, "Good morning, sir. I do apologize for last night. It will not happen again, of that you can be certain."

"I don't need your word for that," Cameron grumbled, glancing from Kerry to Trevor with disapproval. "I'll see to you myself. You've a lot to answer for, lad." With a brush of his hand, Cameron indicated Kerry, and Trevor placed his hand over his heart in a dramatic gesture.

"Upon me life, sir. I had no idea that the miss would come after me. 'Twas a foolish thing I've done, indeed. Can you ever forgive me?" His ingratiating grin was completely lost on Cameron, especially in light of the danger in which he'd placed Kerry, as well as the men at the furnace and himself.

"We'll discuss it at the house. You and I and your mistress there"—Cameron indicated the whiskey jug, ignoring

Trevor's innocent glance—"will come to a meeting of the minds. Otherwise, I shall take you off furnace duty and give you something safer, such as tending the hogs. Do I make myself clear?"

"Aye, sir." Trevor nodded, then began hesitantly, "Sir, about Master Charles . . ." His voice trailed off uncertainly and Cameron waved his hand quickly.

"You have no further fears on that account. Any problems with you or any of the other servants I will handle myself. Master Charles now knows this too."

Trevor gazed at Cameron in astonishment, while Kerry hid her own surprise. That Cameron should take a servant's side over that of his own brother was singularly unique. Trevor was doubly pleased, for while Charles was unpredictable, Cameron was always fair and he smirked openly. Kerry's own pleasure was tinged with a bit of doubt, however. Was Cameron's offer genuine, or was it merely a ploy, designed to take her off guard? Was he trying to prove a point? Time would tell. Kerry sighed inwardly and wondered why life at Brentwood was always fraught with tension.

They ventured downstairs, Trevor leaning heavily on George until, once they were outside, Cameron came to his driver's rescue. "He can walk out here on his own," Cameron remarked dryly. "He has no broken bones, and I've yet to meet a man who couldn't walk with a black eye." George turned an outraged glare on the lad as if suddenly realizing he'd been had, but Trevor looked piteous.

"'Twas me eyes! I could scarcely walk for seeing! I couldn't make it down those steps alone!" Under Cameron's gaze the lad quickly regained his legs, however, and hastened to the carriage, unwilling to allow his master an opportunity to vent his wrath.

When Cameron approached the equipage, however, Trevor was sprawled comfortably across one of the seats. "Do you mind?" Cameron asked pointedly. "There are two more of us."

"Sorry." Trevor grinned. "I just thought you might be more comfortable sitting close." At Kerry's glare, he found himself stuttering, and he hastened to explain. "'Tis a cold morning, and ye don't want your legs chilled." He gestured toward the slender white calves that were displayed beneath the cloak, but his grin disappeared a moment later when a slender foot kicked him sharply.

"What was that for?" he asked, rubbing his abused member.

"You keep your eyes to yourself, Trevor Shanahan." Kerry was in no mood for his antics, especially since Cameron had taken the seat beside her and was sitting far too close for her own peace of mind. "Or you will dearly wish you had."

Nodding, the lad turned a reddened face to the window, his eyes properly downcast. He was already in trouble with Cameron, George, and the workers at the furnace. He decided to quit while he still had one friend.

When the carriage passed the men training, Kerry's eyes traveled once more to the ragged group. Trevor was now slumbering across from her.

"They are young," Kerry remarked as Cameron sat stiffly beside her, hating the stilted silence between them. Dammit! Let him rage at her, shout . . . anything was better than this coolness! But Cameron merely nodded.

"Perhaps you will get your wish," he answered calmly, and Kerry turned her face quickly toward him, relieved that he'd answered. He gestured outside at the men. "They intend to send us all back to England."

"Would they harm you?" Regretting her words, Kerry covered her mouth, then sputtered, "I mean . . . the house."

Puzzled, Cameron watched her for a moment, a strange smile curving his lips. "I didn't think you were so fond of me, Kerry." He leaned closer, his voice barely a whisper but to her it was as loud as a shout.

Kerry threw him a heated glance. "I was simply worried about the house. Imagine whatever else you wish." Content when she saw his scowl reappear, she tucked his cloak more firmly about her and gazed out the window, upon hearing George's shout from above.

"Ho, man! What's that?" At first, Kerry could see nothing. Then, as the carriage tumbled closer, a man stood beside the roadside, waving a lantern. Here the cedars were deeper and she surmised their location to be near a swamp.

"You there!" The man with the lantern called. "Stop, man! I need your help!"

The carriage slowed to a creaking halt and Cameron leaped out, while Trevor aroused himself. The man was talking to Cameron, and his manner was extremely agitated. His hands slashed at the air, and his voice squeaked with fright. Kerry leaned out, then gasped upon seeing the cause for his upset. Right beside the man lay a body, between the roadside and the woods.

"Holy Mother of God, someone's been killed!" Kerry exclaimed, jumping out while Trevor sank deeper into his seat.

"Not me," he muttered. Remarking under his breath on the foolishness of a certain Irish lass, he retrieved a bottle from his pocket, sighed, and sipped the whiskey he had hidden there.

Outside, Kerry walked cautiously toward the men, seeing Cameron's frown of disapproval but ignoring it.

"You say you found her this morning?" Cameron asked, while the little man danced up and down in fright.

"Aye, that I did. And I know they'll be blaming me! Though I don't know why they'd think I would want to do such a thing! But I couldn't just leave her there—that would not be Christian! Oh, I know I'll suffer for this! I know it!"

"Now, now, man. Calm down," Cameron spoke in an authoritative voice and at once the little man's agitation lessened, though he still twitched. "Now tell me from the start exactly what transpired."

"Well, I was driving out with the teams, me and Rufus Booy. Rufus, he seen the body a-lying there and we pulled over to take us a look. Well, Rufus did not like what he seen and he asked me to drive off, pretending like we didn't see a thing. Well, I couldn't do that. I mean, Enid Leeds was a nice woman, and it wouldn't do to leave her bones here for the wolves and foxes."

"Enid!" Kerry exclaimed. Cameron turned a surprised glance on her as she rushed to the body, and lifted the woman's head from the sand. She looked upon the silent and staring gaze of Enid the woodswoman, the black eyes subdued, the fire in them ever stilled. She seemed more than ever like a broken twig, an uprooted plant doomed to die like a weed a farmer pulls up and discards.

Forgetting her anger at Cameron, Kerry felt an overwhelming sense of loss. Enid's body had left a patch of moist gray sand, a wet depression, in the road decorated by broken pine needles. Gone now were the cheery tea, the boiling pot of stew, the animals who treated her home as their own. An overpowering sadness filled Kerry, but there was little she could do. Silently she watched as the men wrapped Enid's body in the carriage blanket, then lifted the weighty bundle.

"Rufus, he wouldn't stop, so he and I went to Harrisville," the man continued. "To drop off the charcoal for the furnace, ye know. So I walked back myself, not a wagon passed by until just now and they wouldn't stop, though I waved my arms and yelled. Then you came."

"You didn't see anyone in the area from the time you got here besides the wagon?" Cameron asked, and the little man's head shook vigorously, his agitation returning.

"No. That's why I'll be blamed! I know I'll be arrested!" He turned to flee, but Cameron caught his shoulder, his eyes meeting the man's firmly.

"Be sensible now! For what reason would you be jailed? It seems to me that you acted reasonably enough." To further relieve the man, Cameron added, "I am not without influence in this colony, and I will see you come to no harm if you're telling the truth. But one thing does puzzle me." His brow knotted, and the man stopped his pacing.

"What is that?"

"Why was Rufus afraid to stop? If there was no one else about, what frightened him so much that he insisted upon driving all the way to Harrisville and not stopping?"

At this, the little man's face paled and he looked both ways, as if afraid to impart this information. He gestured for Cameron to come closer. Then furtively cupping his lips, he whispered, "'Twas not the body he feared. 'Twas what was beside it."

Cameron looked to the body, but saw nothing out of the ordinary. Pine needles carpeted the earth, except for the sand-filled road, and the leafy fronds of spring ferns waved softly. Yet he saw no object nearby, no weapon or clue. Cameron frowned and turned back to the man.

"And? What was it?"

Cameron's growing impatience was clear, but the man was genuinely shaken and his voice broke with fright as he replied, "Just beside the body were the cloven tracks of a horse!"

George crossed himself in unison with the man, but Cameron snorted in disgust and walked away, to stand beside the body.

"I don't see a thing." Cameron challenged the workman, who continued to nod vigorously.

"Aye, not now! But I saw it this morning, and so did Rufus. We know the signs of the devil. Didn't Eliah Clark find such outside when his chickens were killed? Their heads cut clean off—"

"That's enough," Cameron snapped, but Kerry turned to the man.

"The Devil? The Jersey Devil?"

Cameron's disgust couldn't be greater, and he tossed

Kerry a stern glance before addressing the workman.

"They say this Devil's got horse's feet, cloven and sharp. But there aren't any tracks. I've looked for them myself."

"But there were!" The workman insisted, now upset that he wasn't believed on this count. "I saw them! And so did Rufus!"

"But if you went directly to Harrisville, walked right back this way, and saw only two wagons that did not stop, how do you explain the disappearance of the tracks? This is the only way the wagons would come, so you would see any others passing. Or did the dead woman obligingly get up and remove them?"

"No. I guess she couldn't have done that." He shrugged. "But I know what I saw."

"Of course!" Cameron said in a disbelieving tone. "George, would you mind transporting the body back to the house, where it can be prepared for burial? We can place it inside the carriage." Cameron suppressed a smile at seeing Kerry's white face. Then, remembering what had transpired between them last night and this morning, he replaced it with a frown. Observing the change in him, Kerry scurried quickly to the top of the carriage, glad to be away from his disturbing presence.

While George hoisted the body into its traveling place, the corpse's companion, Trevor, appeared at the window, his eyes saucerlike at the prospect of traveling with this ghastly cargo.

"But sir!" poor Trevor cried. "You don't mean to say that I have to ride alone with that." He jerked his thumb toward the old woman's body and Cameron nodded abruptly.

"Yes. I apologize for the inconvenience," Cameron replied sarcastically, then to Trevor's surprise, he waved on the coach. "I'll return on foot."

Glancing over her shoulder, Kerry was amazed to see Cameron take his silver cane and sweep the ground with it as he walked. His face was downcast, but even from her precarious position, Kerry could see that it was intense, and that he was studying something on the ground. Trying to get a better view, she got to her knees on the driver's seat, craning around the side of the coach. Just then the wheels rolled into a rut, and the carriage lurched, sending the lass in a whirling somersault, down the side of the carriage and into the smooth sand below.

"Stop!" Trevor called, his quick gaze catching sight of Kerry as she tumbled past him. "Stop the coach!" The upper half of his body was thrust through the square window, and George, suddenly aware of his missing passenger, obligingly pulled back on the reins.

"What the devil!" Cameron strode quickly toward the girl, yanking her to her feet as she ruefully tried to steady herself, like a newborn fawn. Cameron's gaze swiftly assessed the minor damage; then his eyes narrowed and his cane tapped pointedly into the moist ground. "What the hell are you about? Do you wish to break your neck? That fall could have hurt you!"

"It did, sir," she muttered, rubbing her abused posterior. Aware that her injuries evoked only a wince when she touched a sore spot, she glanced up at Cameron's face and found that he was maintaining a severe expression with considerable difficulty. "Just a wee bit."

"As long as nothing's broken." Cameron said, his manner changing as he forced his gaze from her. "I suggest the next time you want to see behind a carriage, you wait until it stops." His voice was more abrupt than he'd intended, and Kerry's eyes blazed at him.

"Why, I . . ." She was furious, but even as she spoke the color drained from her face and her lips paled. Unable to speak, she pointed blindly at a smooth patch of sand behind Cameron, her hand shaking and trembling. Cameron's eyes followed her horrified gaze. There, at the roadside, were the cloven prints of a diabolical horse!

* * *

"Kerry, are you all right? Charles, get the brandy."

Her eyelids fluttering, Kerry awoke, amazed to find herself at Brentwood, lying on the brocade sofa in the parlor.

"Here you are, miss." Charles's face appeared, shimmering in the light of the chandelier, a glass of golden liquid in his hand. Sweat clung to Kerry's brow and skin.

"I fainted?" she asked, astonished, for she'd never fainted before. Charles nodded, disgust clearly written across his face as he glanced at his brother.

"I am hardly surprised after what you've been through this past night; chasing after that Irish convict, being assaulted by a drunkard, enduring the horrors of a tavern for the night, and then being rescued by my brother, the rusted knight in shining armor. And once you are within his care, what does the noble knight do? He picks up a corpse from the roadside, thereby forcing you to ride home in the cold morning, clad only in a cloak."

Kerry's face grew hot as she glanced uncertainly about the room. Trevor was watching Charles, his annoyance evident, while Cameron's jaw was clenched. He appeared on the verge of violence, as Charles continued in the same chiding tones, his voice thick with insinuation.

"Forcing you to stay the night in that wretched place, stopping to listen to the babblings of illiterate workmen about demons and devils, and then allowing you to see some tramplings in the road."

At that point Cameron stepped past him to remove the cloth from Kerry's head.

"That's enough, Charles," he said coldly. "You've had your say."

"'Tis a good thing I happened along when I did. Otherwise, who knows what would have happened to the girl." Charles peered into Kerry's face, disapproval in his gaze. "You poor dear! Is there anything else I can do for you?" He placed the brandy in Kerry's hand, patting it comfortingly.

"For God's sake, Charles—she's only fainted." Cameron

sat on the sofa beside Kerry. Raising the glass to her lips, he said, "Drink."

"Yes, sir." Kerry obeyed. She gasped as a bolt of hot, fiery liquid dashed down her throat. Then slowly the burning sensation was replaced by a warm glow, her head cleared, and she felt better. "I'm fine," she insisted. "I'm sorry I fainted. That's not like me."

"Why, there's certainly no need for you to apologize, my dear girl," Charles said emphatically, smoothing his silvered wig as he spoke. "'Twas none of your doing to be sure. It was all—"

"Charles." Cameron's chiseled features assumed a granite-like severity. "There has been a murder committed. Would you be so kind as to take the carriage and ask John Cox in Batsto to come down tonight? He's Assistant Quartermaster General in the Continental Army, and he should have some advice on the matter. And," he continued smoothly as Charles tried to protest, "do stop for Eliah Clark and Richard Westcoat. I would like them all to be present."

Cameron abruptly turned his back on his brother, placing the glass to Kerry's lips once more. In a huff, Charles took his leave, dragging the complaining Trevor with him as a guide. When the door slammed closed, Kerry laughed nervously.

"What's so funny?" Cameron asked, his annoyance clearly evident. "There seems little enough to laugh at."

"Your brother." Kerry struggled to sit up, smoothing the silky mass of black hair that tumbled about her shoulders. "He did not seem too eager to venture out. Perhaps he'll think twice next time before he baits you, lest he be sent on some other dire mission."

Cameron's chiseled features softened, then he, too, laughed. "I hope you're right. There is something about that brother of mine that gets under my skin. 'Tis a strange thing to say about my own kin, but it's true." With a sigh, he glanced down at a strand of silken hair he'd been absently caressing. He dropped the curl, startled to see what he'd been doing; then he continued more abruptly. "With Clark and John Cox here, along with Westcoat, we shall be able to decide on a course of action."

Kerry glanced up, puzzled, so he went on.

"They are all businessmen in this area. They, too, are aware of the folly involved in allowing stories of the Devil to spread. And with the British occupation of Philadelphia, it would not be wise to involve the authorities at this point." Dropping into an armchair opposite her, Cameron thoughtfully tapped the wooden window sill with the tips of his long tanned fingers. "Yes, Livingston has enough on his hands as the newly elected Governor. And with Brentwood furnace supplying munitions for the war . . . too much attention would be disadvantageous. It could spoil everything." On that mysterious note he became silent, and Kerry gazed up at him, puzzled. Turning a slate-gray gaze toward her, Cameron smiled.

"Will you be up to an inquisition this evening?" he asked curtly. "If it was not necessary, I would not trouble you. But the men are certain to want to hear your story from your own lips as well as my own. However, if you do not feel well . . ."

"I'll be fine," Kerry responded primly. She struggled to her feet, determined to show him the indifference he was demonstrating to her. She stood up, amazed at the solid feel of the floor beneath her, and she paled in spite of her brave words.

"I think a rest is in order," Cameron said in a commanding tone, raising his hand to stifle any objections. "Sleep now. Tonight's ordeal is yet to come."

"Yes, sir," Kerry replied, and with a swish of her skirts she left the room. Climbing the stairs to her bedroom cost her her remaining strength, and she'd barely laid her head on the quilt when sleep came to her, a sleep haunted with dreams of horsemen and of death.

A nap did much to refresh her in spite of her dreams, and

Kerry slipped out of bed to fill the bowl with water from the pitcher. A noise outside on the road drew her attention and she was surprised to find as she gazed out the open window, that it was nighttime. Cool evening air rushed through the white billowing curtains to caress her naked shoulders and arms. A carriage rattled up to the door. From her position, Kerry could easily see George dismount and assist two gentlemen to alight. These were followed by two more, apparently not in need of help, and Kerry could see that the latter of these was Charles. Brushing his brocade jacket free of the dirt accumulated on the trip, he glanced anxiously about the house and grounds. His gaze wandered freely until it rose and came to rest at the very window Kerry leaned out of. She saw his interested gaze fall on her unclad bosom, and she hurriedly shuttered the window before his eyes could claim more of her. Breathlessly, she leaned on the now-closed aperture. Charles had looked at her so possessively—as if he had already claimed her as his own.

"Nonsense!" She told herself, remembering that Charles was a well-known ladies' man. "He looks at all women that way." Cameron's searching gaze brought a tingle to her blood, but Charles watched her as a cat does a mouse. With a shiver, she stepped over to the washstand and bathed quickly.

Donning her last cotton working dress, she stood before the mirror and saw the thinness of the cloth, the worn places. She'd never been one to fuss over her garb. Indeed, her brothers had been wont to tease her about being a tomboy. 'Twas true that she never took much care in her dress. She hiked her skirts about her waist to go wading in streams, and she often let her hair blow free, scorning the hours involved in carefully coiffing her raven locks. But suddenly she cared deeply about her appearance, although refusing to admit that had anything to do with the events of the previous night. She told herself she should look well for Cameron's friends, that it would be no good for them to think her a common

Irish wench.

But that's what I am, she thought suddenly, a heaviness in her heart as she recalled Cameron's anger that morning, then his coolness toward her. But the woman staring out of the mirror negated her estimate. Her dress showed the effects of toil, true, but the somberness of its color only heightened the beauty of the lass who wore it. The good food Cameron had provided, and the frequent baths she'd taken had made her complexion blossom. Her cheeks were warm and pink, the strain gone, and her lips were red and full. Even her hair was glossy and shining, though it was pulled up within her cap, with just a few stray curls escaping to dance prettily about her face. Her sea green eyes sparkled with a myriad of colors, first blue, then emerald, then both colors flecked with gold. They stared back at her now from beneath full black lashes, daring her to deny the mirror's statement.

"Even if he never thinks of me as a lady," she told herself, not pausing to wonder why that concerned her, "he would see little to remind him of the scrawny wench he purchased in Philadelphia."

That thought gave her comfort and her mind turned to the people below. She wondered what questions they might ask. "I saw what I saw," she said aloud, reaffirming the sight in her mind. "And if they ask, that is what I'll say." Forcing the memory of the hoofprints from her mind, she stepped quickly out of the room, quelling an urge to race down the steps.

Voices came from behind the parlor doors. As Kerry entered, she was grateful for Charles's absence, although Cameron's presence was unsettling. He stood at the fire with three other men. The four of them were engaged in deep, friendly conversation, tankards of warm rum in their fists. At a slight sound at the doorway, Cameron looked up, his sharp features tensing when he spotted her. His eyes quickly scanned her attire and Kerry could have sworn she saw a flash of warmth in them, a flash of passion, but he covered it quickly. With a nod of his head, he indicated that she should come forward.

"Kerry O'Toole . . . John Cox, Eliah Clark, and Richard Westcoat, and of course, Jane Clark."

All three men bowed in sincere appreciation while the elderly woman on the sofa nodded graciously. Richard Westcoat, a dashingly handsome Englishman, stared at Kerry with interest. He then made it his business to see to her comfort, securing a chair for her by the fire and earning a glare from Cameron.

"Would you like to join us in a rum, Miss Kerry?" Richard asked, his blue eyes lingering on Kerry's striking beauty. "Or perhaps a brandy?"

"Rum! Brandy! The last thing that poor child needs now is spirits!" With a start, Kerry glanced up at Jane Clark, whose watery blue eyes peered kindly from behind spectacles. Her hair was so white it appeared to glisten.

Eliah Clark went to stand beside his wife and laid a fond hand on her shoulder, chuckling deeply. "As you can see, Kerry, when my wife has an opinion she does not keep it to herself. She could fight the entire British army alone and win. A firm hand she has, but it is not always appreciated."

Jane Clark smiled at her husband's description, her wrinkled face smoothing like a warm white rose. "Perhaps I could," she agreed. "This was a hard land when we settled here—beautiful but filled with danger. Indians, wolves, bears, every sort of wild beast you could name. But the land has proven prosperous, and we wouldn't live anywhere else. Now we face other dangers—war and highwaymen and ruffians. It seems you only trade one kind of trouble for another. Now," she smiled, blue eyes twinkling behind the glasses, "I hear you've been face to face with some of these troubles this past evening. My cure for such is a hot meal and sleep. The rest you've had, but I've not seen anyone supply you with a meal. With your permission"—she smiled at Cameron—"I'd like to speak with your cook."

"Certainly," Cameron replied coolly. Kerry sensed that he was annoyed with her for some reason, and she noticed with surprise that he refilled his cup as soon as he drained the contents. It was uncharacteristic of Cameron to imbibe heavily and she wondered at his mood.

"Now Cameron," said John Cox, his soft warm features belying his military stance. Dark eyes peered out of his expressive face, concern etched on them. "What of this murder? Enid Leeds, I hear. A terrible thing, that."

"Yes," Cameron answered abruptly, taking a seat by the fire, his expression changing as Richard Westcoat obligingly seated himself beside Kerry. Sending a cool glance in his direction, Cameron briefly related the circumstances surrounding the old woodswoman's death, ending with the hoofmarks.

"Cloven prints!" Richard's clipped voice broke the startled silence following Cameron's testimony, and he glanced quickly to Kerry for verification.

"'Twas that," she answered. "Not far from the body."

"Enid probably crawled several hundred feet just before she died." Eliah shook his head, slapping his hand down on his breeches. "God bless her." He cast his eyes to the heavens, his voice filled with compassion for the old woman's fate.

"Have you told anyone else of this?" Richard asked suddenly, turning quickly to Cameron. "This is the first I've heard of it. Does anyone else know?"

"Charles, my brother. George, my driver. Kerry. And the workmen that originally discovered the body. As far as I can discern, that is all."

A snort of disgust from Richard followed; then he crossed his long legs and leaned back on the sofa. "You may as well say the world. Those workingmen gossip from dawn 'til dark, being at the furnace all day. And Charles! He'll be blabbing it about at every tavern and bordello this side of the Delaware. Oh, beg pardon, miss." Richard's face turned a brilliant red as Cameron's eyebrows lifted. "They're all still talking about those chickens found in your yard last week, Eliah," he continued. "When they hear of this—"

"I know," Eliah Clark said unhappily. "Already my slaves are spreading blood over the doorways and windows of their houses. 'Tis said to ward off the demon. If this keeps up, we'll have all of them afraid to work."

"That's not my main concern." Richard Westcoat's eyes met Cameron's and the two seemed to concur silently. "My main thought is for *Polly's Adventure*."

"Aye." John Cox stood up now, warming his rum before the fire. "That and the *Hazards of Industry*." The four men exchanged an amused glance, while Kerry leaned forward on her perch, her eyes wide with curiosity.

"Who is Polly?" she asked.

Richard and Cameron looked at each other, then the two broke into laughter, delighted and masculine. "There are some things," Cameron said, "that a gentleman does not speak of in front of a lady. It seems you've erred twice, Richard. Your injury at the Battle of Trenton has affected your manners."

"It would seem that." Westcoat grinned, while Kerry glanced from one to the other, unable to comprehend their joke. But her thoughts were interrupted as Jane Clark reentered the parlor, a maid following her and bearing a tray loaded with a pot of the scarce tea, cold meats, cheeses, a dish of red berries swimming in cream, and hot oat cakes. Forgetting the mystery when faced with these scrumptious delights, Kerry generously offered Richard Westcoat his choice of the mouth-watering assortment of treats.

"You are as kind as you are beautiful, miss." He smiled, securing one of the cakes and finishing it off quickly. He then brushed his hands together and leaned back, his gaze skimming over her in an appreciative manner.

"Kerry O'Toole. What a beautiful name! What part of the Emerald Isle did you call home?" At her look of surprise, he grinned roguishly. "Living in America has not diminished the lovely lilt in your voice. And you should change your name, if you truly wish to remain a mystery."

"Donegal." Kerry laughed brightly at his inanity, and when she dropped her napkin he nobly retrieved it. He returned it, hanging on to one end of the linen as his eyes met hers.

"Should you ever tire of working for your scowling master there"—he gestured to Cameron, who was indeed scowling—"just send me a message. I'll rush your indenture papers to my house so quickly Cameron will scarcely know what happened."

"I'll keep your kind offer in mind," Kerry retorted. "For himself there has been in a temper quite a bit of late."

"Just say the word." Richard picked up her small white hand and pressed a kiss to the back of it, and Kerry blushed, then glanced up. Cameron was staring unconcernedly into his cup, but as he glanced up, she shivered at the rage she saw reflected in his silvery gaze. He was distracted by John Cox, who quietly discussed business matters with him, but his eyes kept returning to Kerry, his expression far from pleased.

Jane Clark glanced from the smiling lass, whose small pink mouth appeared strained, to the scowling ironmaster across the room, and a pleased twinkle came into her blue eyes. 'Twould seem that for all his cool composure, Cameron Brent was caught in the age-old trap, and with a serving girl at that. Jane nearly giggled. She loved intrigue and romance of all sorts, and she'd thought for some time that Cameron should marry. This Kerry was exactly right for him. Delighted, she mulled over a plan, while the principals involved remained ignorant of her thoughts.

Time passed quickly and the guests were soon ready to leave, their departure hastened, no doubt, by the arrival of Charles. As soon as the younger Brent entered the room, the men stood up and gathered their cloaks.

"Not going already?" Charles yawned, and helping himself to a brandy, he posed jauntily near the mantel. "'Tis hours 'til dawn."

"Yes, but some of us have to be up and working," John Cox answered stiffly.

Mrs. Clark stopped beside Kerry, taking her small hand in her own. "Do come down and see us, dear. I've enjoyed your company." Kerry promised she would.

"About the matter we discussed," John was saying to Cameron at the door, "I feel that silence is prudent at this time. Should the need for further inquiry arise, I shall get in touch with you and the lass promptly."

"Thank you, John." Cameron opened the door for his guests, and as they stood by it saying their last goodbyes, a harrowing shriek rent the silence.

"What is that?" John Cox asked, his face cocked to one side and listening.

The sound emanated from the bogs, but it seemed to come to a halt right above the house.

"Good heavens!" Eliah Clark murmured, gazing about with a white face. The cry filled the hallway, echoes of it remaining long after the original sound had died.

"It seems to come from all the demons of hell," Richard said softly, glancing through the open door into the darkness. "What in blazes could it be?"

"An animal perhaps?" Charles stood framed in the hallway, his head turned and alert. "Or the wind through the trees?"

"Hardly," Richard replied, somewhat indignantly. "I've not heard any animal like that and I've been living in these woods all my life. No wind sounds like that."

The coach rumbled up outside and George entered the hall, doffing his tricorn. "Did you hear it, sir?" His voice was shaking and sweat glistened on his broad forehead. "You know what they say it is."

"Oh, bosh!" John Cox snorted, his usually amiable face showing his annoyance. "We need no legends."

"What, George?" Cameron's voice cut through the soft

conversation. "What do they say it is?"

"They say . . . it is the Jersey Devil, crying for revenge."

A long silence followed George's words. It was interrupted by Charles's amused chuckle.

"The Jersey Devil! Crying for vengeance! I daresay, Cameron. You and I, being Brents and residing on the creature's birthplace, are in serious trouble. I, for one, have no intention of being a meal for this local demon, so I guess that leaves you. Unless we could set out a small buffet for the creature—do you think that would do? I suppose—"

"Charles," Cameron said sharply.

"There's been enough talk about demons for one night," said Eliah Clark. "You've upset the poor girl."

Cameron glanced quickly to Kerry and saw the fear in her wide eyes. But Richard hurried to her side and placed one arm about her in a reassuring embrace.

"Don't let all this talk trouble you, miss. And if you ever need me, you know where I'll be."

Kerry gave him a fond smile and he kissed her cheek, ignoring Cameron's glare. Then he bid his host goodbye along with the rest of the guests, puzzling at the furious expression on Cameron's face while Jane chuckled softly.

After the guests had gone and Charles had retired, Kerry stared up at her employer, a small smile coming to her lips. "It was a nice evening, Cameron. In spite of that . . . sound. Your friends are very kind."

"You seemed to enjoy yourself," Cameron said coldly. It was only then that Kerry realized he was in a fine rage, for anger glimmered like steel in his eyes. "In fact, you seemed to enjoy Richard's company more than was proper. Do you enjoy being petted by strange men, miss? Does the excitement wear off if attention is paid by a lover?"

"Oh . . . you . . ." Kerry sputtered. The crudity of his words left her speechless. She whirled about, intending to depart, but one hand shot out and grasped her shoulder, turning her around. Furious, she struggled to break free, but his grip was like iron and he dragged her closer to him.

"Oh no, my little vixen." Cameron murmured, pulling her against him. Kerry struggled more now, aware of his raging desire as she felt him, hard and hot against her, but Cameron was relentless and he held her firmly in his arms. "You'll not run away this time."

"How dare you accuse me of . . . I was just being kind to *your* guests! And Richard was just being a gentleman," Kerry protested, twisting in his arms, but she was aware that her actions had an arousing effect on him and that he was still furious. Fear swept over her at the look on his face, and she felt his grip tighten on her waist. As he secured her in his hold, a smile crept across his lips but did not reach his eyes.

"Aye, a gentleman. But I've found being a gentleman with you, sweet Kerry, leads to naught. I wonder at your motives, sweet, rejecting me as your lover, then taunting me by flirting with my friend in my own house. I think I owe you something for that." His voice was thick with emotion, almost as if he no longer ruled himself, and Kerry became frightened.

"Well, go ahead. Hit me then! 'Twould prove to me that you are little better than your brother!" She faced him bravely, her green eyes meeting his, locking and refusing to give ground.

"Ah, but there you are wrong, sweet Kerry. I have other ways of dealing with recalcitrant young lasses like you, especially when they don't know what they want." Cupping her head in his hand, his lips crushed hers in a punishing kiss.

Kerry frantically tried to stem the swirling tide of emotion that threatened to drown her, but she was powerless against the intoxication of his kiss. Knowing that he was kissing her to punish, to prove something mattered little; her wayward will disappeared and a sense of tormenting pleasure seeped through her as if it had a will of its own. Her lips parted helplessly under his assault and his tongue thrust through them, arousing her, raping her mouth until she felt she might swoon. In their past times together, Cameron's kisses were never like this! Though she still struggled against him, she wanted him to continue, wanted more of the burning, melting feeling that was spreading through her loins like heated oil. . . .

She stopped struggling in his arms, letting him have his way, and one of his hands slid over her rounded buttock. Helpless to protest, she pressed her warm body against his, all sense of righteousness and sanity gone. Cameron muttered a hoarse groan of triumph; then his kiss deepened as he was caught up in the passion that raged between them. Blindly his hand reached under her gown, pushing away the worn cotton chemise she wore, seeking the satin softness of her flesh.. He found the warm triangle between her thighs, and his fingers aroused her with fevered yet gentle caresses, his hand slipping beneath her . . .

Sanity returned in the form of shock as she realized his intention. He meant to take her here and now, on the floor if necessary! Kerry struggled to break free of him, but he refused to release her, his hand fumbling with the neckline of the gown. She heard a slight tearing sound, then his fingers plunged beneath the frayed material of the dress to caress her breasts, his thumb stroking the nipple into a tightening hardness.

Frightened more of herself now than anything, Kerry kicked and pushed against his chest, but physical resistance proved useless. Vaguely she knew Cameron was compelled by more than just lust: he wanted to claim her as his own, brand her as he would any other possession. And Kerry didn't want to let that happen . . . she was far too vulnerable to him now.

Clutching upwardly, Kerry felt her hand touch something small—the pin of his cravat gleaming in the dark hallway. Without another thought, she plucked the ornament from its bed of lace and jabbed Cameron's hand. Startled, he withdrew the hand from her gown, rubbing the bead of blood that appeared, while his eyes searched her, blazing silvery in the night.

"Are you mad?" He glanced at the gash in his thumb, while Kerry quickly removed herself from his grasp.

"I told you, not again!" Kerry reminded him, backing away when she saw something harden in his eyes. "I will not be your paramour! I am here as your sevant, nothing else!"

"As my servant?" Cameron took a step closer to her; then Kerry took one farther back, her foot striking the steps. She eyed him as an animal would a predator, and seeing the look in her eyes, Cameron advanced no farther but held his ground.

"Kerry, why can't you see it my way? Is this really your desire, to function merely as my servant?" He gestured to the house about them, and Kerry looked up at him, her smile incredulous.

"What I desire?" She laughed ruefully. "What does it matter what I desire? What if I should get with child? Will you then forget yourself as my master and marry me?" At the darkening look in his eyes, Kerry nodded. "Aye. That's what I thought. No, sir. I will be your servant, I will keep your house and your books, but I give you no other rights! Unless of course, you wish to force me. But I will be no more yours then than now."

Her voice held a firm promise and, although Cameron was sorely tempted to act upon her suggestion, to force her submission and make her admit— But he realized that he would only earn her undying hatred from such an act. Coldly, he reached inside his pocket and withdrew a white linen handkerchief which he wrapped around his injured thumb. His eyes never left her until he completed the task; then he smiled icily.

"You shall have your wish, miss. I shall not bother you with my intentions again. You will remain here as my servant, and do not fear that I will force you into anything. I will see you in the morning at the furnace. Please bring your books."

With that Cameron stalked off and Kerry quickly fled up the stairs, seeking her own room. But once there, she found little comfort within the four walls. Despondent, she flung herself onto the bed, ignoring the coverlet, and she sobbed bitterly, unable to stem the flow of her emotions. Her only consolation, if it was one, was the sound of Cameron's door, closing quite early in the morning. 'Twould seem that he found little sleep this night himself.

Chapter Ten

The spring weeks faded into summer, and the death of Enid Leeds was forgotten by most. Kerry's burdens were considerably diversified at the furnace, for with the coming of the warmer months the workers not only engaged in the making of iron, they also tended their own gardens, drove to the shore for shells to provide flux, and delivered their goods, camouflaged with plenty of salt hay, through the eerie pine barrens. It was a fearsome time because of Tory spies and British inspections, for often as not the wagons were secretly delivering material to Washington's armies. If a British officer was inclined to look too closely under a suspicious parcel of salt hay, he was never seen again. Such was the law of the woods.

One fine June morning, Kerry was perched in the kitchen beside Helga who had never become accustomed to Kerry's position at the furnace.

"Ah, a lot of good that does, vorking up there vith all those no goods. The master must be out of his mind! Such a place for a young girl." She shook her head while pouring Kerry a cup of strong coffee, her pinched face even more drawn due to her lecturing.

"I don't mind." Kerry grimaced, sipping the strong brew with distaste. She preferred tea, but it was considered unpatriotic now, and except for the rare package Cameron provided, it was no longer available.

"You don't mind! Those men—drinking and fighting. *Ja,* this is no good. The master must think you one of the boys that vork there. No place for a girl."

Kerry winced involuntarily at Helga's words. The woman had struck far closer than she knew, for Kerry half-believed that was true. Since the time at the tavern, Cameron often worked in the furnace when Kerry did, sometimes even in the same office. Yet he seemed to completely forget the girl was present and to concentrate totally on his books. Kerry could not so easily dismiss his presence, however, a fact she attributed to his nationality. English! She thought derisively, sipping at the coffee without tasting it. Cold as a morning in February.

"I'll be off now, Helga." Kerry started for the door, but the German woman was not about to accede so easily.

"Ja, off to that den of tosspots. You stay out of trouble, miss!" In spite of her words, Helga's face wore a worried, maternal frown, and she stopped polishing a pewter tankard to admonish the lass. "Keep clear of those vagabonds!"

"Don't worry, Helga. I will take care of myself," Kerry assured her, giving the cook a sparkling smile before disappearing through the door.

"She vill take care of herself!" Helga repeated, rolling her round blue eyes at the ceiling. "That's vat I'm afraid of!"

Kerry rushed down to the furnace, for her delay with Helga had cost her a few precious minutes and she had no doubt that Cameron would be punctual as usual. The woods were alive with the sounds of the teams, and in the distance, Kerry heard the great clang of the forge, its huge hammers slamming down to shape the metal. Grimacing, she hurried onward.

The workmen, with the exception of Bill Seldon, gave her warm smiles, for each man remembered that this lass had braved the wrath of Cameron Brent for them. Any doubts they'd had about a young girl working among them had been quickly dispelled, for Kerry never lacked courage. They now treated her as a favored companion. Trevor ceased his bragging long enough to glance her way, pointing to the office and rolling his eyes. That small gesture told Kerry everything: Cameron was, indeed, inside and had been for some time. With a nod, she picked up her books, then ventured in to the office.

The quill was scratching furiously against parchment, and Cameron scarcely looked up from his labors. "You're late," he said tersely, his lean features knotted into a frown as he surveyed the figures before him.

"Aye. I had a bit of a delay." Not wishing to involve Helga, Kerry said nothing about her. "It won't happen again."

"See that it doesn't. I have enough work to do without chasing you down." He still did not look up from his books, and from his tone, Kerry had the impression he was annoyed with her for some other reason. She searched her mind as to the previous night when Richard Westcoat had stopped by for a visit. He had thoughtfully presented Kerry and a few of the other serving girls with some lovely wild roses that bloomed in his garden, laughingly comparing Kerry's beauty with that of the flower. Shortly afterward, when Cameron had appeared to be brooding, Richard had taken his leave.

Cameron reached out and, with a flick of his wrist, sent the diary in a smooth slide across the desk.

Kerry snatched up the book, her glance betraying her attitude toward his brusque manner, but when he glanced up, magically the scowl was erased and a look of angelic innocence had replaced it. "Do you require anything else, Master?" she asked sweetly, and was rewarded with a glower.

"No. See to the work before nightfall is upon us."

With an elevated nose, Kerry swept out of the room, slamming the door behind her. She missed the oath that followed her exit when several books toppled from the shelf behind Cameron, landing smack in the papers before him. That lass is more trouble than any ten I ever knew! he fumed, righting the books and cleaning the ink spots. But it never occurred to Cameron to have her work at the house, where he would be free of her pesky presence.

"Trevor!" she called, and the sauntering Irish lad reluctantly left his comrades to call out the names.

"Cross and Emons down getting pork. Richard Phillips drunk. Warner and Gilliam on teams. McIntire making molds. Seldon—"

"I'm right here," the surly voice called, and Kerry gave the man a disdainful flicker of her eyes. But recalling Helga's words, she kept her comments to herself and inked in the entries.

"Ventling home. His wife put to bed with a daughter."

"Aye." Jacob looked up from the wagon where he was readying a load of pigs. "He has a daily increase of his family, he does."

At this hilarity all hands laughed and Kerry hid a smile. Mick slapped his knee and showing his full appreciation, he shoved Jacob freely across the room.

"Watch it!" Jacob roared, but it was too late. A handful of burning coals flew through the air in a shower of orange cinders, and where they landed a small flame started.

"Fire!" the hands yelled. Kerry dropped the diary. Spying a bucket, she rushed out to the pond and submerged the tin while the workers sought other containers. "Fire! Furnace fire!" Men rushed about in a frenzy, in spite of the fact that the fire was yet small and contained.

"What the devil's going on?" Cameron stepped out of his office and was greeted with a deluge of water as Kerry tossed the bucket at the flames. The tiny fire immediately sputtered and died, but the blaze in her employer's eyes was just beginning to kindle.

"There was a fire," Kerry said lamely, clutching the bucket guiltily. One by one the workers coughed, then choked, then broke into full laughter while Cameron Brent started purposefully toward her, his dark hair clinging to his face, his elegant clothes dripping. With a yelp, Kerry dropped the bucket, which fell with a clatter to the floor, and ran for the door. The workers roared full strength now as Cameron's pace quickened to a run, and they gathered about at the windows to watch their conscientious employer chase the young Irish lass who flew like the wind.

Kerry reached the mansion in a matter of minutes, but a quick glance behind her told her that Cameron was hot on her trail. Wasting no time, she dashed into the kitchen, causing Helga to drop her peeled potatoes as Cameron rushed in behind her.

"You little vixen! You did it on purpose!" His gray eyes were blazing so Kerry sought the safety of the opposite side of the table.

"I did no such thing! There was a fire, I tell you!"

"Aye, a fire! I've been far too lenient with you up to now but I'm about ready to remedy that this instant. How do you expect me to manage these men when you are making me a laughingstock?" He reached for her across the table, his long arms almost catching his prize, but Kerry was too quick for him. She dashed under the table to the farthermost side.

"'Twasn't I that made you a laughingstock, it was yourself! What do you expect when someone calls fire?" The menacing look in his eyes told her how much he appreciated her logic, and with a muttered curse, he rounded the table.

"Sir! That's enough of this! Chasing the poor girl about the table like she's some lost chicken or something!" Helga cried, flapping her apron at this sight. Kerry took full advantage of Cameron's distraction and with a quick step, evaded him completely and slipped out the door.

"Get back here!" he called, but Kerry's floating laughter was his only response. That sound, much like a brook in early spring, was now joined by Helga's scolding, and Cameron's fist met the table.

"Enough!" he shouted, and even Helga fell silent. "I'm going to the study where I can get some peace! And I don't want to see anything even slightly Irish until I come out!" Snatching up his cane, he retreated wrathfully to his study while Helga shook her head disapprovingly.

"*Ja,* that young girl in there. Vat does he expect?"

Kerry did her best to avoid Cameron the rest of the day. She had seen the vengeful gleam in his eyes. It had been there the first day they'd met, when he'd ordered her feet down from the wall with an unspoken promise of retribution if she did not obey. Fearing that his patience had been stretched to the limit, she had no desire to see him fulfill his threats so she decided distance was prudent.

The separation did not last long, however, for when Kerry burst into the house that evening, her stomach knotted with hunger and her youthful buoyance renewed, she found an unwelcome stare greeting her as she slammed through the door.

"Helga, you should have seen what happened at the furnace today with Mick," she began, then froze as a silvery gaze measured her disapprovingly. Cameron normally took his meals alone in the study, barely pausing from his work to dispense with this necessity. But tonight he was seated in the dining room, where the workers were fed and into which even Charles disdained to venture. With her hand still clutching the door handle, Kerry gulped and returned his stare with all the bravado she could muster.

"The shoes," Cameron said blandly. A confused wrinkle appeared on Kerry's nose, and he indicated her boots with a distasteful glance. "You're tracking mud from the lake. Why do you insist upon wearing those ragged boots? Did you not get the clothes I ordered?" His lifted eyebrows hovered over eyes sparkling with something other than amusement, and at Kerry's lofty reply, his gaze darkened ominously.

"Aye. But these boots will serve me fine. I have not been in your employ long enough to deserve others."

"Dammit girl! We've been all through this! Those ragged things could scarce be given the name of shoes and you cling to them with that damnable Irish tenacity . . . have you no pride?" He was leaning far across the table now, his fork gripped unconsciously in his left hand. "Well?"

"Aye, I have that, sir, and that is why I will not accept your charity. When I have earned them, I will gladly wear them." She tossed her head pertly, but had reason to doubt her braveness when he spoke a moment later, his voice peculiarly strained.

"Leave them at the door." She opened her mouth to object, but he repeated in that same deadly tone. "I said leave them at the door."

"Ja. Those boots good for nothing." Helga joined in as she placed a hot bowl of chicken and noodles on the table. "I think you leave them."

With two such determined adversaries watching her every move, Kerry sighed and removed the irksome boots with a petulant jerk of the laces. At once they came apart in her hands and she dared not look up, but her cheeks burned as she heard Cameron's amused chuckle. Tossing him a well-deserved glare, she dropped her skirts self-consciously as his reproving glance reminded her of her bare ankles. Damned English! she thought resentfully, taking the seat farthest from him and praying that the other workers would arrive quickly.

As soon as her small frame met the seat, Cameron was up, and before Kerry could protest, the loyal boots were taken by the tips of his fingers and tossed unceremoniously into the kitchen fire. As Cameron returned to the dining room, wiping his hands as if glad to be done with this chore, he met the young lass's righteous glare.

"You had no right to do that! Those boots were mine!" Gray eyes, now calm, appeared from under heavy black brows and locked with sea green ones.

"Beg pardon, miss. But you see, refuse around here is customarily disposed of in that manner, and I'm too old to change."

Helga coughed loudly, but when the two faces peered up at her her face was composed and she seemed preoccupied with pouring gravy into a bowl. Kerry chafed on the edge of her seat, but once again outnumbered, she bided her time until the cook whisked back into the kitchen.

"You! By what right . . ." she sputtered, then stopped as he spoke more quietly.

"That's enough. You have new boots, and now you'll have to wear them. I wish to tell you something so please be still and stop glaring at me."

Kerry stilled her movements, but the glare remained. Cameron shook his head.

"You have got to be the most stubborn female I've ever laid eyes on." He spoke almost to himself, but Kerry seized upon his words.

"I thought, sir, that you wished to discuss something with me. I did not realize we were here to speak of my temperament." She smiled sweetly, a full red curving of her mouth, and Cameron scowled at her righteous demeanor.

"Aye, we'd be here for weeks if we attempted to discuss your mettle. Enough!" He lifted a hand as she opened her mouth. "I wanted to tell you that we have a guest arriving."

"We do?" Kerry asked bluntly, searching his face for some clue to this mystery, but he seemed reluctant to speak, then proceeded as if there were no other choice.

"Philadelphia is under seige. Loyalists are no longer welcome in the city, and we have no idea how long the British occupation will last. I have made it known to my acquaintances there that should there be a need, they are welcome to find refuge here. Charles has taken the carriage to the Camden Ferry and should be arriving here shortly."

His face was slightly averted, as if the matter was not

entirely pleasing, and recalling his secretive nature, the way he'd shouted when she'd been in his study, Kerry idly wondered if he was loath to open his house to strangers. Her thoughts were to go unanswered, however, for the workmen who boarded at the mansion piled into the kitchen, their boisterous voices permitting no further conversation.

Despite the surrounding cloak of human companionship, Kerry ate her own meal uneasily. She was ever aware of her master directly across from her, and when she glanced up, she found his unflinching stare following her every move. Sitting more properly, she forced herself to eat daintily under this scrutiny, then breathed a sigh of relief when he finally turned to pour out the brandy.

No one heard the knock on the door, so great was the camaraderie, and it was a moment before anyone noticed the stranger coming to stand under the lamplight. Charles followed, and his smirking posture caught their attention. Only then did the faces turn, and one by one, the men fell silent. Kerry noted their behavior and whirled about in her chair, her half-raised fork freezing midway at the sight that greeted her.

A petite, slightly rounded woman stood in the doorway. She was dressed in a fashionable gown of ice blue brocade, parted in the middle to show a petticoat of crinoline embroidered in a matching blue. Her brocade shoes were made of the same material, decorated with silver buckles that glinted softly in the candlelight. This lady's golden hair was dressed with ribbons and scented powder, then set in an elegant pompadour above her finely chiseled face. Her cool blue-gray eyes were set above an English nose and delicately shaped lips. Poised, remote and beautiful, she surveyed the room from under pale gold lashes before turning, not to Charles but to Cameron, for an explanation.

"The furnace workers," Cameron stated, rising to his feet with decided reluctance. "They board here at the house. May I present Miss Caroline, from Philadelphia."

The woman bestowed a rather brittle glance on the men while Charles laughed quietly.

"My dear Cameron, aren't you being a little modest? You should introduce her as your fiancée, Miss Caroline."

Although Charles addressed Cameron, he was watching Kerry while the workmen, much in awe of this golden beauty, staggered to their feet, offering congratulations. Cameron did not acknowledge the statement. His stance was rigid, his face stern; and only Charles seemed unperplexed by his manner.

Kerry got up from the table and began to clear the dishes. Her fingers seemed numb and the plates clattered against one another, causing the Englishwoman to turn a slightly cool gaze upon her and to look at Cameron. But he offered no explanation. He merely conferred with Charles as to the disposition of her baggage and trunks while Kerry fought with the plates, glad to have something to do. It seemed that a great weight had fallen upon her shoulders and all light had gone out of the world, leaving her in perpetual grayness, as she'd been aboard ship. She departed for the kitchen with the plates, attracting Helga's attention when she tossed them forcefully into the bucket and proceeded to scrub them with a vengeance.

From her position at the window, Kerry saw George drag several trunks from the carriage, then deposit them inside the door. The woman's wardrobe, Kerry guessed, envisioning the costly clothes Caroline was obviously accustomed to. George returned to the carriage for the next load, which consisted of several oddly shaped boxes and bags. When Kerry finished the dishes, the man was still struggling with his loads. He was now bringing small pieces of furniture and other items of comfort into the house.

"I'd better see if he needs help," Kerry remarked, and Helga nodded for she, too, had been looking out of the window. Reluctantly, Kerry rose and headed outside in her bare feet. The coolness of the grass instantly reminded her of her state, and she was pointedly aware of the vast difference between herself and this grand lady.

"Will you be needin' a hand, George?"

The servant smiled his gratitude, and he soon handed down an armful of parcels to her. Trudging toward the mansion, Kerry tried to see between a hat box and a fur muff, but the latter slid persistently toward her nose, tickling it and causing her to sneeze.

"Lord!" she murmured, for the force of her sneeze had sent some of the packages rolling in the hall. A grunt sounded as a particularly heavy box broke loose from her arms and toppled straight onto Cameron's foot.

A grimace of pain crossed his face, followed by a look of disbelief and anger. He surveyed his molester, but Kerry was already backing away, colliding with the assortment of parcels that cluttered the floor. Trapped between the trunks and two cherry end tables, Kerry could do naught but stand still and face the wrath of Cameron.

"Good God, woman! You'll be the end of me yet! First you douse me at the furnace, now you nearly break my foot. What are you about, proceeding in such a manner?" His glower traveled down the length of her, stopping with a scowl at her bare wet feet. Kerry self-consciously tucked them beneath her, but she was too late. He'd already noted them and his voice rose.

"You went out in the dark without anything on your feet? Kerry, you test me sorely!" He was now only a few feet away, and Kerry backed up as far as she could, the trunks impeding her progress.

"Since I annoy you so much I'll make it a point to stay out of your way! Will that appease you, Tory?"

Enraged, Cameron crossed the space that separated them, and placed his hands on both sides of the wall so this recalcitrant Irish lass could not escape. Quaking beneath his glare, Kerry dropped the remaining packages.

"Kerry, I swear—"

"Cameron, what is this?"

Caroline stepped into the room and surveyed Kerry coldly. She was none too pleased to see a slightly guilty look upon Cameron's face while a defiant one graced that of the Irish lass. Her voice was exactly as Kerry had imagined it, polished and elegant but glasslike, without any warmth or color.

"Never mind, Caroline," said Cameron impatiently. "We were just having a disagreement."

"Oh?" Caroline appraised the Irish lass and her lips curled slightly. She saw a young, raven-haired beauty, natural and uncontrived. Her dress was poor and marked her as a servant, but it did not detract from her uncommon good looks. Caroline's hatred grew with this assessment, for she also saw that the girl possessed boundless courage, revealed in her proud uplifted chin and in the optimism that gave her the strength to rise above her circumstances. And all of that showed in the lass's defiance, her determination and her fiery glance.

"Perhaps you should dismiss her, Cameron," Caroline said evenly, and was rewarded by the scarlet coloring that poured over the girl's face. "If she presents a problem?"

"No, it is far from serious. Kerry, take yourself upstairs and tend to the matter we spoke of. I'll have the boxes tended to." With a last chiding glance at her feet, he cleared the way to the stairs. Mustering her dignity, Kerry swept past them, making certain her gown touched the floor as she passed Caroline.

A short time later, from the confines of her room, Kerry saw Cameron's night-enshrouded figure stride across the lawn. A whinny came from the stables, clear in the warm summer air; then a rider clothed in black flashed across the fields. In a moment he was gone, and only the heavy thud of hooves verified this vision.

Strange, Kerry thought, sitting on the edge of her bed and hugging her knees. The very night his betrothed arrives,

Cameron rides off into the night. Such behavior made no sense, but it lightened Kerry's spirits just a notch and she quickly undressed and slid into bed.

Cameron's whereabouts would have surprised Kerry greatly had she known of them, for far from being in the embrace of some taproom wench, he was seated in the home of Richard Westcoat. Firelight poured over a pile of parchments and diagrams, while Cameron's quill busily scratched figures and adjustments on a separate sheet.

"Let's see now, *Molly's Adventure,* the *Dispatch,* and the *Industry* are set for sale tomorrow. We should secure a handsome profit there." Cameron smiled, a flash of white teeth showing in the limited light, while Richard Westcoat agreed.

"Then there's the *Canester,* the *Speedwell, Prince Frederick, Jenny,* and the *Carolina Packet,* all for tomorrow," Richard added, surveying the list with a gleam in his eyes. "There's one more, but I'm not sure you'll wish to enter it." He smirked, and Cameron glanced up from his work with a puzzled frown.

"Why?"

"Well, the ship's a schooner. The name is the *Bachelor.* Now that Caroline is down here, at Brentwood, perhaps you won't be in a position to handle such a ship." Richard wisely hid his grin behind his tankard of grog while Cameron favored him with a meaningful stare.

"We'll see about that," he remarked, listing the ship's name with a flourish. "Well, I think that takes care of it." Cameron scanned the sheet with immense satisfaction while Richard poured him another drink. "Will you be able to handle all the sales work here?" he asked while the tall Englishman opposite him nodded easily.

"They know of my place, but so long as the channel proves

dangerous for their ships they've been loath to try a seige. In any case, Eliah Clark and I erected a fort on Chestnut Neck. 'Tis far enough downriver to prevent the British from reaching Batsto and the other furnaces, your own included. Now that the Delaware river's been closed off by the Redcoats, Washington is depending upon the Mullica for goods, and on the wagon trails through Burlington." Richard sipped his drink, enjoying the rum all the more because it was captured from an English ship.

"Aye, privateering is not without its rewards," Cameron mused, his thoughts traveling upon much the same path. "But I still think it wise to keep most of our methods a secret. Tory spies are abundant here, and these damned woods are a perfect haven for them and for the Hessians."

"German louts," Richard remarked, his voice filled with loathing. "The damage they do is incredible. Bayoneting unarmed men, molesting women . . . there is nothing beneath them."

"Aye. But some of the local thugs are hardly better. Mulliner comes quickly to mind, and he's Tory as well. Perhaps it would be better if I took the *Morning Star* out myself. I am beginning to become alarmed at the reports I've received of Captain Stark, and I would like to command the ship once more. I need to get away for a few days." Cameron said nothing more, but that one remark spoke volumes to his long-time friend and Richard poured him a heavy draught of grog from a stone jar.

"When a woman's involved, there is only one medicine. Distance may help, but nothing beats a goodly portion of drink." He grinned.

"You sound like my lad Trevor." Cameron scowled while Richard shrugged.

"Maybe he's right. Drink up, man! But you know, Cameron, drink will not cure what ails you. Only a decision will do that."

"And what then? To be caught in a trap like my father, realizing his mistake long after it's too late to amend it? No thank you." Cameron drank down the fiery liquid, banging the table with his tankard for emphasis as he spoke. "My father went through hell with that woman. Deborah Brent was the perfect match for him, everyone agreed. She was known in all the right social circles, had all the right connections . . . her family had the King's ear, it was rumored. But she was like a glass diamond, pretty on the surface, but cold and false beneath." Cameron's voice betrayed the pain he felt, and Richard quietly refilled his cup.

"Now they've sent you Caroline," he remarked.

Cameron shrugged. "It has been long assumed we'd marry, but I never gave it much thought. Now . . ." Cameron could scarcely admit to himself that until a few months ago, the thought of marrying Caroline had not troubled him unduly. 'Twas true that her face was comely enough, her blond hair quite pleasant to look upon, and she had the manners and deportment of a lady. But was it because of his acquaintance with the Irish lass that he now saw her movements as studied and unnatural, her glances as warm as thin ice and her voice too brittle to provide him with comfort? He found himself comparing Caroline's voice with Kerry's warm Irish lilt, and he winced. Between his recent conclusions about Caroline and Charles's pointed jabs, he could scarcely wait for this torture to be ended. Even her perfume annoyed him—roses. The smothering scent of wilting summer flowers filled the foyer until George understandably leaned out the door for a breath. But Philadelphia was occupied, and it was not safe for Caroline there. She was counting on him. With a heavy sigh, Cameron drank down his refilled cup and stood up, a bit unsteadily.

"Well, my mind is made up. I shall set sail on the *Morning Star* in a few days hence. Will you join me?"

"Need you ask?" Richard grinned, rubbing his hands in

anticipation of the adventure. Together they trod a rather jagged path to Cameron's horse. Caledonia stood completely still as her master climbed awkwardly into the saddle, and when Cameron pulled the reins to both the left and the right, she ignored his tugging and started down the well-trodden path toward home.

Chapter Eleven

The following morning, Kerry was awakened by a voice calling to her out of the darkness. "Are you awake?"

"Who?..." she muttered, sitting groggily up in bed, suddenly grateful for the thickness of the homespun sheet as she saw Cameron's handsome and unsmiling face peering out of the darkness. "What are you doing here?" she asked, then snatched up the sheet indignantly, her awakening consciousness slowly taking in the fact that he was in her room. Suspiciously she eyed him, unaware of the fetching sight she made, her hair tumbling about her shoulders, her creamy breasts pressed into an even more enticing display by her meager attempts at modesty.

"Don't get your temper up." Cameron chuckled. "I knocked first, but there was no answer. When I tried the door, I found that it was open." Without giving her a chance to vent her feelings, he continued quickly. "I want you to accompany me this morning. Richard Westcoat is selling the cargo of a prize, and I plan to look it over. Can you be ready in an hour?"

"Certainly," Kerry responded, rubbing her eyes in sleepy confusion. She glanced at the night-blackened window panes, then turned back to her employer, puzzled. "But why do you want me to go?" Her voice dripped with sweetness.

"Surely your fiancée would be more appropriate company."

"I want you to come," he said abruptly, and as Kerry opened her mouth to object, he sent her a sardonic smile. "If you insist, I shall order you to come. You are my servant, remember?" Kerry's mouth dropped, and Cameron smiled. "I shall wait for you downstairs." With that he turned and walked swiftly away, his bootsteps ringing sharply on the wooden floor.

Damned English! Kerry thought. He seemed to go out of his way to annoy her. She wondered at his motives. Tugging on her best cotton dress, she felt a vague uneasiness over this trip. 'Twas not like Cameron to secure anyone's company for a business dealing. A small hope arose within her, but she quickly squelched it. He belonged to Miss Caroline now, and she would do well to remember it. Her anger rose as she thought of his silence concerning his fiancée. No doubt he had planned to use Kerry as his mistress, while his wife-to-be was cozily ensconced in Philadelphia! The thought sent a flush to her cheeks and she finished dressing quickly.

Her hair hung in wild disarray about her, and thinking unwittingly of Caroline's smooth coiffure, Kerry paused for a moment to brush the sleek mass of it until it gleamed. Then she braided the long strands, allowing a few shining curls to escape and frame her face with artful wisps. Although she was unpracticed in the art of hair dressing or, indeed, in many other womanly accomplishments, the mirror told her that her efforts were most pleasing so she nearly skipped out the door. As she approached the steps, a command caused her to halt, and heaviness weighed her down for it was Caroline's voice she'd heard.

"Maid! You there, maid!"

Reluctantly, Kerry turned back and mounted the additional stairs that led to the next floor. There, in the first doorway, stood Caroline, wrapped in a sumptuous blue velvet dressing gown that cost more than all of Kerry's simple wardrobe put together.

"Fetch me some water for my room and, maid, I'd like a cup of tea before I come down." The Englishwoman's eyes flickered coldly over Kerry's unusual garb, then her golden eyebrows lifted as her gaze traveled to the hallway containing only three doors.

Kerry involuntarily tapped her foot as she tried vainly to protest. "But the master had asked me—"

"Whatever he asked you to do can wait." Caroline's eyes once again traveled back to those doors. Then she stepped out of her room slightly, leaning back against the doorway. "Is your chamber there, in the first hall?" Her voice was even more brittle than it had been the previous night.

"Yes, miss." Flushing a bit at the unspoken accusation, Kerry faced Caroline defiantly, her green eyes a curious mixture of gold and blue fire. "Is there anything else, miss?"

"We'll see." A small, secret smile crept across Caroline's face. It seemed that her cold gaze had remarked upon Kerry's dress and the reason for it, and that her mind had found a sure-fire way to prevent whatever activity Cameron and Kerry had planned. After all, the girl was but a maid. "Let's start with the tea and water for now. And perhaps a bit of freshly baked bread, and some of that strawberry jam. I could smell it as soon as I walked in last night." Slowly, she stepped back inside her room, closing the door with a soft hush as if to assert her superiority.

Kerry's cheeks burned and stinging tears sought to escape from her eyes. She walked slowly downstairs, her chin drooping, wiping her eyes with the cuff of her sleeve. Kerry had no doubt as to Caroline's intent, and she feared the Englishwoman would see her wishes carried out. Yet this woman was a guest in Cameron's house; it was Kerry's duty to see to her needs. Aware that Cameron wouldn't wait too long, she hurried into the kitchen, hoping to complete her chores as quickly as possible, but this hope was soon dashed for Helga was not even about yet and the fire was only a small pile of glowing embers. To start a full fire would take some time, as would boiling water for tea. Dough was rising in a bowl, but it would have to be rolled out, shaped, and baked before fresh bread would be ready. Kerry threw a wooden spoon across the room and stamped her foot at the injustice of it all. Just then the door swung open, and Cameron's quizzical glance followed the spoon, watching it clatter to the floor.

"Miss?" Cameron questioned, amused. His quick glance took in her charming appearance, simply clothed though she was. "Does the thought of going out with me distress you to this degree? I should think you'd appreciate a day off from work." He smiled as she threw him a well-earned glare. "Shall we go? I wish to get an early start."

"I can't." Kerry fought back tears as she tried to keep her feelings to herself. It would not be to her advantage to speak unkindly of Cameron's fiancée, or to imply that the woman's motive in setting her to work was anything but just. Cameron would certainly not appreciate criticism of Caroline and he might even be inclined to blame Kerry for causing trouble. Taking a deep breath as she saw the rather forbidding narrowing of his eyes, she hastened to explain, however.

"Miss Caroline needs water and tea for her room. Cook is not yet up, so I have to start the fire first. I know you are in a hurry, but if you don't mind waiting a wee bit, perhaps I can finish quickly."

Amazement fought with anger in Cameron, and his eyes changed from a sparkling silver to an icy gray. "Wait here a moment," he ordered, his voice tense. He strode quickly to the rear of the house where the chambermaids were quartered, and Kerry could hear him calling. A tall, buxom blonde answered his summons, rubbing her fists against her eyes as she stared sleepily about.

"Miss Caroline is awake and needing someone to tend her this morning. Tell her that I assigned you to her today, and she and I shall discuss future arrangements tonight, when I return." Dismissing the startled girl with an abrupt sweep of his hand, Cameron returned to the kitchen and, with a gentle shove, guided Kerry outside.

"Master Cameron, are you sure?" she asked as he rushed her toward the carriage. "I don't mind, really."

"I do," he replied firmly, holding open the door. "Nobody runs my house for me. 'Tis a fact that Miss Caroline has apparently forgotten, but I will take care of that when I return." He seemed to be talking to himself more than Kerry, for when he finally looked up, his anger was gone and a brief smile flashed across his face. "Would you like to get in, or do you need help?"

"Where's George?" Kerry asked suspiciously, seeing the empty seat and Cameron shrugged.

"I thought it a bit early to rouse George, so I will drive. Have no fears, miss. I've done it before."

"'Twas not that." Kerry grinned, pointing to the seat on top. "'Tis just that I am used to riding up there with George, and not inside. Would you mind?"

Cameron shrugged, then gestured to her dress and hair. "I would be delighted," he ventured. "But what about your dress? Your hair? Most ladies are reluctant to be exposed to the dust and sands of the road."

"My hair is braided and will scarcely come loose, and I have a shawl that can cover the dress," Kerry reminded him. "Besides, I am not a lady, but a mere servant, remember?" Her chiding tone caused Cameron to give her a thoughtful glance, and he came around to her side of the carriage.

"Whatever you wish." With a courtly manner, he took her small white hand in his large brown one, helping her up to the driver's seat with the care due a great lady. For the first time in her life, Kerry understood the desire women had to be courted by such a man. Even thinking of it was thrilling. He settled himself beside her, carefully arranged the shawl over her dress, then smiled down at her, the newborn sunlight playing over his handsome features, and Kerry experienced a rapid beating of her heart. She turned away, afraid that the expressiveness of her face would betray her. "Shall we?" he asked, and at her brief nod, he slapped the reins, sending the horses in a spirited canter down the sandy lane.

Riding atop the carriage was decidedly advantageous. The day was sun drenched and warm, and on the horizon was a promise of greater heat to come. Cameron pointed out items of interest as they traveled, from a newly erected paper mill to the notorious Bodine's. The latter looked innocent and sleepy this morning, its gray shutters closed like eyelids. Few horses were tethered outside and Kerry could only surmise that Jack had departed, along with the local workers who could scarce afford to play after George's winnings at cards. She giggled at that thought, then glanced about with awakening interest as they crosed the plank bridge that spanned the amber-colored Mullica.

"Down there are the Forks." Cameron pointed in the direction of the river, to a place where the Mullica sported several wheat-colored islands of cattails and reeds. At this point the river twisted and turned like a huge, copper-hued snake, its waters gleaming in the sunlight.

"Sand bars," Cameron said in reply to her questioning gaze. "'Tis easy enough to traverse them if one knows the way. But if one does not . . ." He let the rest of the sentence go unspoken, and Kerry could easily see that many an unwary ship had run aground on one of these obstacles.

"Do many ships have cause to come this way?" She could see little reason why they should, but the sandy beaches were filled with tracks and the area itself had a well-traveled air.

"They do now. This waterway has become important since the war. You've probably noticed the many crossroads about?" At her nod, he continued. "Wagons loaded with supplies for the armies travel across the land, while ships come up the river here." It was on the tip of Kerry's tongue to ask where the ships came from, but something in Cameron's manner told her the question would not be welcome so she kept it to herself.

Rounding a bend, they came swiftly upon a clearing in the pines and cedars, and a tavern and a small store came into view. Behind these buildings was bustling activity that seemed inappropriate to this rustic setting, but from the steady jostling of the crowds Kerry could only surmise it was a common occurrence.

Seamen from the sloops and schooners anchored near the shore carried burdensome barrels of rum and sugar, sacks of coffee, boxes of tea, and barrels of molasses, all the while shouting and laughing heartily among themselves. Kerry could guess that the rum was being freely sampled, for the sailors seemed in unusually high spirits despite their heavy loads. Sides of beef and pork, salted hams, and bundles of cloths in every color were paraded before her eyes—a dazzling array of sapphire blue, red, gold, and green—while other foodstuffs and linens, rare luxuries in the colonies, were arranged and displayed. There was a carnival atmosphere about, and Kerry could barely hear Cameron's offer to help her down, the sailors were so boisterous.

She suddenly spied Richard Westcoat near the shore, shouting orders to the men and directing the mayhem. He held a small slab of wood upon which was tacked a parchment. He checked off items on this, and made notes, occasionally stopping an overzealous sailor while appraising the boxes of goods. He quickly spied Cameron and Kerry, and with a hearty swing of his arm, he waved them over.

"Cameron, old chap. 'Tis a fine haul so far. We have every reason to be pleased." He indicated the parchment, which Cameron looked over in a careful manner, asking a pertinent question or two concerning some of the figures. Ever quick, Richard noted that Cameron casually placed a hand on Kerry's shoulder, while holding the parchment with the other. Smothering a smile, he favored Kerry with an appreciative gaze, surveying her garb.

"You are a lovely sight this morning, Miss Kerry," he said sincerely, for indeed the soft green color of her cotton gown caused her eyes to sparkle and emphasized the startling clarity of her skin. The crewmen from aboard the ships were also enjoying the sight of her, their long time at sea lending considerable enthusiasm to their whistles and cheers. Cameron returned the parchment to Richard, then directed a silent frozen stare to the seamen. One by one their voices quieted, until one salt was heard to mumble under his breath, "That rogue ain't a bit of fun, he ain't." The others were inclined to agree, but with Cameron's gaze upon them, they did not voice their sentiments, saving them for the tavern later.

"Thank you, sir," Kerry turned to Richard, smiling brightly. "'Tis kind of you to say so, especially after the sands sought to do their worst."

"If this is your worst, I'd be enchanted to see your best," Richard continued, playing the English swain to the hilt while Cameron cleared his throat.

"Richard," he said somberly, "your tongue betrays the looseness of your mind. There are several figures here you should double-check." He gestured to the parchment, his eyes twinkling despite his stern demeanor. "See to them instead of the ladies for once." Cameron's voice was light, but his words contained a message that Richard could not overlook and the Englishman's brow wrinkled.

"Would that such a day will never come," he replied in much the same vein, bowing politely before Kerry but not before she saw the amusement dancing in his eyes. Not wishing to arouse Cameron's wrath unduly, he took himself off, returning to the shore and shouting to the struggling seamen.

"I've never seen so much stuff!" Kerry said in wonder as the area continued to fill up. Sailors and ships' officers stood proudly near the tavern, expounding on the guns and the swivels of their ships, while interested businessmen discussed terms. A uniformed captain strode toward Cameron, his bearded, sunburnt face attesting to his time at sea, and Cameron warmly shook his hand.

"Kerry, this is Captain Marriner. Quite a local hero in these parts." Kerry clasped a coarse hand and smiled up into a weathered face.

"Hardly that, Cameron," he said with a twinkle in his eyes. "Just doing my job."

"He set out with only nine men and a whaleboat, just a short time ago," Cameron said to Kerry, "and with those limited resources, he managed to recapture the American ship, the *Black Snake,* and at the same time he took the British *Morning Star.*" Kerry stared at the captain, amazed by this feat. Marriner smiled, then modestly changed the subject, speaking to Cameron of ships and of the troubles of privateers.

While he talked, Kerry's eyes drifted freely, coming to rest at last on the men straggling from a longboat. Besides the gleeful crewmen, she now saw at least a half-dozen pale men who were tethered together, their feet in chains and their hands in ropes. Their tattered naval uniforms were barely recognizable, but Kerry knew these men were English. Some bore signs of the lash, and a guttural German accent came from one man, a Hessian, one of the German soldiers spoken of with such hatred by the colonists. Cameron saw where her attention was fixed, and he broke off his talk with the sea captain, leading her away while the men disembarked from the ships.

"Come. I have something I wish to show you." Taking her down to the shore, he walked along the white sand beach, past the sloops and captured vessels, to a small cove nearly hidden from view. Without pause, he stepped through some brush and onto a small dock at which a glistening schooner was moored.

Care had been taken with this ship, Kerry noticed. The decks were clean, the sails neatly folded, the ropes coiled and in place. A white stripe ran up the side of the vessel, and from the dock Kerry could see the name, *Morning Star*. To her amazement, a cabin boy climbed out, and she saw that it was Trevor!

"What in the world? . . ." She turned toward Cameron, who nodded in return.

"'Tis a grand thing, isn't it?" Trevor announced proudly, as if he himself owned the ship. "Come aboard, miss. I'll show you around mesel'." He first gave a questioning glance to Cameron, who reluctantly nodded before a seaman's question took his attention away from them.

"A fine piece of workmanship, it is. And the master keeps it in the best shape." He gestured to the spotless decks, the polished floors. "Here are the cabins. Those below are for the crew, while this one here is for the captain." Trevor opened a door to display a warm and spacious cabin containing a desk, a stove, a washstand, a chair, and a bunk. It was to the bunk that Kerry's eyes were drawn, and she unwittingly thought of the times she and Cameron had shared a bed together. A heated flush spread through her cheeks at the thought, and she moved quickly away from the bunk.

"Kerry? Where are you?" Her musings were shattered as Cameron strode into the passageway behind them, casting a suspicious glance at Trevor. "What are you doing here, in the cabins?" he asked, his eyes never leaving the Irish lad's face.

"I was just showing her around, sir." Trevor's voice was properly deferential, but his eyes told a story of their own. "After all, you gave me permission." He kept his sparkling glance on the deck while innocently scuffling his feet. "'Twas by your leave, sir."

"Aye. And speaking of leave, you have my permission to take yours. I'll speak with you later." With a grin, Trevor complied, softly closing the door behind him.

"Master Cameron?" Kerry asked, her voice formal, for she

was suddenly aware that they were completely alone in the tiny cabin. She hated herself for the breathless excitement she felt in his presence, but forced her voice to remain cool. "Is there something you wish?"

Cameron felt annoyance rise in him at her tone. She spoke to him as if, indeed, she was nothing more than a mere serving girl. She stood near the round window, artlessly unaware of the sunlight dancing through her hair. His eyes roamed the fullness of her bosom as it rose and fell, the simplicity of her gown only drawing attention to her form. He noted the puritanical braids she wore and experienced a fierce desire to undo them, to run his fingers through her hair and spread it about her in a swirling cape. The warm sweet scent of her, no perfume but the scent of woman, filled his mind, and he wanted to tear her coarse cotton dress from her body, to make love to her wildly and possessively. Furious with himself and with her for arousing him, he walked to the door and braced his hand on the frame, his eyes like cold steel as they caressed her.

"Yes, I wish your presence," Cameron finally answered, his voice cold. "Is that too much to ask from my humble servant? Or are you in a hurry to see Richard again?" His anger at himself goaded him, but Kerry's face flew up at his accusation and her eyes locked with his.

"Richard?" She laughed incredulously. "You accuse me of . . . of all the nerve! Now that you have your affianced so comfortably ensconced at Brentwood, you think to accuse me of your crimes? Ha!" Well fired with anger, Kerry ignored the hardening silver of his eyes, the twitch of his jaw that betrayed his darkening rage.

"What crime is that, miss?" Cameron questioned coolly. "I don't recall treating you badly. I did not accost you the way that taproom hooligan did. In fact, you responded quite willingly to my caresses! What was I to think?"

"Why you lowdown English . . ." Beside herself with rage, Kerry reached for a brass spittoon that graced a nearby table. Without thinking, she hurled it toward his head, glad to see him duck and brace an arm across his face as the thing clanged against the door, then rolled across the wooden floor in an awkward path. Cameron crossed the floor in two long strides, his hand catching hers to prevent her from seeking further weapons. Rebelliously, she twisted and turned, ignoring the pain in her wrists as she fought him, wanting to get away. He was far too close, the masculine, clean scent of him filling her mind, the hardness of his body caressing hers as he changed his tactic and pulled her into his arms.

"No!" Kerry fought more frantically now, guessing his intent, but her actions served only to arouse him more. She felt him, hard and hot against her soft thighs, little guessing the effort he was making to control his baser desires. But she was too soft, too warm and too close.... Groaning, Cameron kissed her, his mouth finding hers as his arm tightened about her waist. Kerry tried to pull free, but his tongue broke through her moist, parted lips, raping her mouth and demanding a response.

Fighting the passion his tongue was igniting in her, Kerry pressed her hands against his chest, pushing and struggling, but his body was virile and iron hard. A craving seeped into her anguished mind, and somehow her arms lifted and placed themselves about his neck, drawing him closer. Some other woman seemed to take control of her, some wild and wanton creature. She felt his desire harden even more, and an ache began between her thighs. His hand moved, slowly, tantalizingly, down around her hips, then up to capture the fullness of a breast. Kerry's body weakened under his assault. She felt his impatient tug at her braids, then her shining mass of hair tumbled down and his fingers slid through it in a languid caress.

"Kerry, oh God, Kerry." In a voice she could scarcely recognize as his, Cameron uttered her name, and Kerry shivered as his fingers found the buttons of her dress and undid them one by one. Helplessly she let him slide the dress from her shoulders, aware that someone could walk in but too lost to blind desire to care. His lips traveled from her mouth to her throat, then nuzzled an earlobe as he gathered her warm body against his own. His mouth lowered suddenly and he was kissing her breasts, his tongue and teeth teasing the nipples into hard, taut peaks.

As desire flooded through her Kerry began to struggle anew, but his arms imprisoned hers, holding them firmly to her sides as he knelt before her. His lips traced tantalizing patterns over her young body, arousing her, burning the flesh they touched, then returning to her breasts. Though she pleaded with him to stop, his tongue flicked lazily over one round breast, then the other until her nipples ached and she was no longer struggling, no longer even protesting, but was surrendering to the heated flush that spread through her like wildfire.

With a strange urgency, Cameron doffed his own clothes, then returned to her, his hard and muscular body promising ecstasy but teasingly withholding it. He lowered her to the bunk, then stroked the silken skin between her thighs, driving her wild, making her writhe against him and beg for release. She heard his light chuckle and finally he touched her where she wanted him the most, bringing her wave after wave of fulfillment. She cried out incoherently.

Before she could return to earth he was inside her, driving into her easily for she was still moist from the pleasure he'd lavished on her. Their bodies merged, Kerry's rising against him and demanding the fullness of his manhood. He drove even deeper into her, his hands caressing her feverishly, her own digging into the hardened muscles of his back. They were oblivious to all but the heated desire that drove them. Their bodies acknowledged what their minds could not, a passion they could not deny. Cameron cried out hoarsely, and he felt Kerry shudder beneath him. He had again taken her to fulfillment. Slowly, their breathing became more regular as they drifted back from the whirling madness of lovemaking to reality.

Kerry's eyes opened and a harsh dawning came to her. In spite of her convictions, of the brave words she'd thrown at him, she had fallen into his bed after little more seduction than a kiss. Shame and embarrassment crept over her, engulfing her in despair. It was a game he played, torturing her in this manner when another awaited him at home. And what would come of it all? Eventually, he would marry Caroline, who would no doubt toss Kerry out of the house. Where would the former mistress of the ironmaster be then?

Tears crept down her face in spite of her determination not to cry, and Cameron stared down at her, amazed. "Kerry, for God's sake, what's the matter?" His hand traced the path of one small tear, but she quickly pulled away from him, not trusting his compassion or the warmth reflected in his eyes. Snatching up her dress, she pulled it over her head and, feeling less vulnerable, faced him.

"Nothing's the matter," she replied evenly, but her words were choked. "I think we'd best be going, before nightfall is upon us."

"Kerry." Cameron spoke commandingly as he rose and grasped his clothes. "Come here."

"Nay!" Kerry backed away, her own sense of shame and horror growing. "I will not! You stay away from me."

"Fickle wench." Cameron shook his his head, obviously displeased. "One minute you're soft and warm and giving . . . the next you act as if something vile has been done to you."

"You have your precious fiancée to return to!" Kerry reminded him. "So that gives you no rights to me! Heaven help me for bedding down with you like some dockside trollop!" Seeing his anger rise, she quickly opened the door. "We have to leave."

Cameron slammed it shut, so hard it reverberated. "Miss, we shall have this out."

"Oh, shall we?" Kerry whirled toward him, mortification feeding her rage. "You see fit to take me to your bed whenever the whim hits you, yet you said nothing to me of your fiancée? Why? And why this now?" She pointed to the bed. "What manner of man are you, Master Cameron, that would have his wife-to-be and mistress in the same house?"

"Kerry." His voice held a warning tone, but Kerry ignored it.

"And when you marry? What then? Toss me and your bastard children out into the cold, so you can comfortably wed your true bride?" Kerry choked, and Cameron took a step toward her.

"Is that what you think of me? That I would do such a thing?"

"I've seen little to convince me otherwise!" Tears flooded her cheeks, and bringing her fist to her mouth, Kerry turned away. The rising knot in her stomach grew, overwhelming her; then she felt Cameron's hard, muscled arms come around her, his hands caressing her, comforting her.

"Kerry. You don't understand . . . about Caroline, that is."

"Aye, you're right." She faced him, her eyes brimming with tears, and Cameron found himself speechless. How could he explain to her, when he had no grasp of his feelings himself? Until a few months ago, he'd had few qualms about marrying Caroline. Logically, he could still specify no objection. Yet he had only to be within a few paces of this Irish lass and his resolve vanished, leaving him more confused than ever.

Unable to find the words to comfort her, Cameron opened the door, then gestured to it. "We should go. It's getting late." He reached for her arm, but Kerry pulled away, retaining this small ounce of pride.

"I can make it on me own, Tory. I need no help from you."

Deciding that now was not the time to take issue with her, Cameron allowed the remark to pass but it angered him.

What was the matter with him? Why did he want to kiss this girl, and at the same time throttle her? Why did she continually affect him so? He knew he lost control in her presence and he did not like the feeling. Nonetheless he returned to her again and again, seeking out the same exquisite torture.

A pub loomed in the distance and Cameron tugged at her sleeve to indicate that she should follow him inside. Scowling and walking carefully behind him like any good servant, Kerry entered the place, which was filled with sailors and seamen.

As Cameron placed his order, Kerry glanced up in surprise, for he'd bid the boy to bring Kerry tea and himself a double whiskey. He was not normally wont to indulge in hard liquor, but his moodiness had returned. He stared off into the distance, not inviting a query. When the order did not arrive within a few moments, he got to his feet, grumbling, and went in search of the lad. Soon after he'd left, the seaman sitting next to Kerry swiveled about in his chair, facing her with a friendly grin.

"Now, miss. I'll be thinkin' you could settle a bet for us. This lug 'ere, he claims that Blackbeard's treasure is buried right 'ere, in Burlington. And I say—"

"It don't matter what you say." His companion leered. "You wouldn't know Blackbeard's treasure from Batsto's iron."

"Is that right?" The barrel-chested seaman stood up, rubbing his grizzled beard in glee. Kerry saw all the makings of a good fight here, but Cameron was approaching and she well knew that would not be to his liking. With a sigh, she got to her feet and stood between the would-be brawlers.

"Sit yourselves down!" she commanded, her eyes glinting with the colors of the sea. Indeed, she was magnificent in her outrage, feigned though it was. Her cheeks were flushed and her breasts rose and fell with each breath.

"That's better," she declared as they reluctantly complied.

"You ask me a simple question, and the next thing I know, I'm in the middle of a brawl. Have you been so long at sea you don't know how to handle a lady?" She raised her finely arched eyebrows to accentuate this implied insult, and the men stumbled over their tongues to reassure her that such was far from their minds.

"No, miss. We're sorry, miss. Truly." Shamefaced sailors hung their heads while Kerry took her seat.

"Good. See that it doesn't happen again."

Cameron, who'd been watching this display from a few feet away, now joined her and he could not disguise the admiration glinting in his silvery gaze.

"It appears you are talented in more ways than one," he remarked, handing her the hot tea while flashing a rare smile.

"I just broke up a fight. What of it?" she replied pertly while Cameron filled her cup.

"Many a meeker lass would not have spoken up, and such a brawl would have caused considerable damage. You have much courage, Kerry O'Toole. It even rivals your beauty."

Kerry felt her cheeks grow warm, but she did not entirely trust his statement . . . or him. Was he trying to make amends for taking her in the boat cabin when he had sworn not to? Unwilling to give him the benefit of the doubt, she sipped hurriedly from her cup, burning her tongue in the process. "Dammit!" she said, and was delighted to see him scowl. She found that much easier to deal with than his appreciation.

He shook his head in mute exasperation. "Finish up there," he commanded and Kerry complied, not wishing to push him too far. For some reason, he seemed to be holding his temper in check, but his dark moodiness returned. His elegant face was so brooding it caused the seamen to mutter into their ale.

When they left, Cameron headed directly for the unpacked cargo. He stopped beside a pile of merchandise stacked haphazardly beside the tavern. A work-weary seaman who was lounging in the shade nearby came over to him then. Kerry paid little attention to the proceedings as Cameron ordered tools for his ship, barrels of flour, sugar, and rum for the mansion. He told the sailor to put aside several flasks of brandy for Charles, along with some tobacco for himself. Then he looked over the display of arms, some fitted for ships. An assortment of rifles and muskets were dutifully examined, and to Kerry's surprise, he ordered the seamen to set these aside with the rest of the goods. Then he held up a thin lace kerchief for her to see.

"Do you think Helga would like a few of these?" he asked and Kerry nodded.

"She will that. And mayhap some of the spices as well." Her quick eye had caught the tins of nutmeg and cinnamon and other spices.

"Excellent idea." He nodded, procuring the tins. As he stacked those with the rest, the seaman lifted a tiny decorated flask, and grinned.

"Perfume for a liedy at 'ome?" He shook the bottle enticingly.

Kerry wasn't sure, but she thought Cameron sighed reluctantly. "Do you have attar of roses?" His grimace was real, however, and Kerry knew that whatever Cameron thought of his fiancée, he didn't like her perfume.

"Aye, that we do." The sailor tossed a flagon of the heady stuff to Cameron, and without testing its scent, he tossed the bottle on top of the pile as if it was of little concern. Then he gestured to the sailor.

"Seaman, bring me that."

Kerry watched bemusedly as the seaman obligingly retrieved a jewel case from among the crates, and set it atop a box for Cameron's perusal. Her eyes grew wider by the moment as pearls, lustrous and gleaming, were withdrawn, then bracelets of gold and silver, and necklaces encrusted with rubies. Her heart sank as she thought of the delight

Cameron's fiancée would exhibit upon receiving this gift. She turned away as Cameron made his selection, unable to bear the thought.

Several moments later, when Cameron had completed his transactions, she followed him to the carriage. The seamen carried his purchases to the coach. Then Cameron turned to her with a questioning glance. "Do you not wish to see your present?" he asked softly, and Kerry gazed up at him, confusion wrinkling her brow.

"What present?" She pulled her shawl more closely around her in the evening chill, and Cameron smiled, his hand dipping into a pocket. He withdrew it and his fist opened to display a gold chain. "'Tis yours," he stated, then pressed it into her hand.

Astonished, Kerry stared at the piece of jewelry which twinkled in the dim light. In a moment, her eyes met his, and a spark of anger flamed within her. She tossed her head back, pressing the chain back into his hand.

"You have much to learn about me, Master Cameron, if you think I can ever be bought, no matter how pretty the price!" Defiantly she faced him, ignoring the trembling that began within her at his angry scowl.

"I had no such intention in mind when I purchased the piece," he declared coldly. "Kerry, I realize that a large part of what . . . happened between us was my fault. I simply want you to have the necklace."

"I won't!" Kerry's eyes blazed green fire and her foot tapped out her anger. "I am not a besom, Master Cameron, no matter what you think of me! Give your trinkets to some willing lass, or to your fiancée. I have no right to such."

"Kerry, don't push me!" Cameron threatened, and his tone made Kerry back down a bit. He eyed her boldly, then a strange smile came to his lips.

"You are my servant, is that not correct?"

Kerry sensed his game, but a denial would have led her further into trouble. She nodded.

"I didn't hear you." Cameron continued hatefully.

"I said yes!" Kerry shouted back, drawing the amused attention of the seamen nearby.

"Then I order you to wear it." He drew nearer. "I want to see it on you at all times! And if you do not comply, you will answer to me. Is that clear?"

"You can't—"

"I asked if that was clear?"

"Yes!" Kerry snapped, enraged that he had so cleverly outmaneuvered her.

Smiling in satisfaction, Cameron undid the clasp on the necklace.

"Turn around."

"But—"

"Miss, are you testing me already?"

His voice was as calm as the moments that precede a storm, and Kerry thought it wise to obey him. She whirled about, stamping her foot in rage while Cameron chuckled coolly behind her. The necklace dangled, cold and hard against her throat, making her feel that she had been branded by him in some way.

"Turn around," he commanded, and forcing back a retort, Kerry obeyed, hating the self-satisfied grin he wore.

"If you think to appease your conscience with your gold, then you are much mistaken!" she said coldly, but Cameron appeared not to hear her.

"It looks beautiful, as do you. Now you are truly my slave—I have you in chains. Come, slave." He gestured to the carriage, and Kerry, little appreciating his humor, jumped inside with the packages, preferring the cramped comfort to sitting on top and seeing his grin.

Chapter Twelve

The following morning Cameron had gone. Kerry heard of his departure not from him, but from Helga. "Never a stranger thing," she told Kerry, punctuating her words with a ladle. "Taking off like that on some ship, right in the middle of a var. Master Brent's taken leave of his senses, he has."

"What was that, Helga?" Charles shuffled into the kitchen, still in his dressing gown and yawning painfully.

"Oh, nothing, sir. Just remarking on Master Cameron's sea trip. It is an odd time for him to be taking off like that. It is not like him."

"No, it isn't," Charles said gleefully.

If he felt any remorse over Cameron's departure, it was not evident. He went into the dining room, and indulged in a huge breakfast.

His hunger was somewhat sated when Caroline glided into the room, and he soon found reason to hide himself behind a newspaper. Caroline had been living at Brentwood for only a short time, but she had made herself felt. Always polite and mannerly, she nevertheless had no compassion for anyone she did not consider her equal. The servants suffered under her imperious orders, as did the village workers when they had to perform certain tasks.

The storekeeper grumbled later that day when he saw her approaching, and he felt the sharp bite of her tongue when he explained that satin thread and other luxuries were not readily available during the war.

"You simply must make more of an effort," she scolded, her glance as warming as the January sky. "I am certain Cameron will hear of this." Giving Kerry a decidedly glacial glance, she lifted her yellow brocade skirt and sauntered from the store to the mansion on the hill. Through the store window, Kerry watched her go, muttering a curse under her breath.

"That miss ain't right, she ain't," Jeremy Cramer remarked, as he counted out the tins of coffee and the bags of sugar Helga had ordered. "When she marries Mr. Brent, there'll be hell to pay."

"I can't understand what he sees in her," his wife remarked, coming from a rear storage room and polishing a pewter cup. "She's beautiful, to be sure. But that's like reading a book because it has a pleasing cover. It may look attractive, but it is the heart which provides sustenance?" Her husband agreed.

"Maybe it's because she's a society girl," Kerry said. It was true that many of the local workers had been in awe of the woman, but that awe had vanished when they'd been subjected to her tyranny. "Other men have married for such."

"Aye. And Cameron Brent . . . he's a puzzler. We've seen him out riding that horse late at night. You know"—he leaned forward with the air of one about to impart vital information, and Kerry grinned—"they say he knows more about the Devil than he lets on. I'd wager that he consorts with such, out in a moonlit clearing late at night."

"Jeremy!" His apple-cheeked wife slapped him amiably on his broad shoulders. "'Tis not kind to believe such nonsense."

"Aye," Jeremy agreed. "But you have to admit, he's got

that look about him. He's a man I'd not like to cross."

"Well, I don't believe that either," Kerry replied, gathering up the goods Helga had ordered. "Now if you have all the entries for the workers' goods"—she indicated her ledgers—"I'll be on my way. With Master Cameron gone, Cook needs all the help she can get to keep up with Miss Caroline." With a fond goodbye, Kerry made her way up the hilly lawn to the mansion.

Sure enough, Helga and the chambermaids were struggling to maintain their own schedules while completing the additional work Caroline had imposed on them. With the summer months drawing to a close, Helga was busy putting up fruits, drying herbs, clearing the cellar, and preparing for winter. A mountain of laundry was piled high on a chair while several flatirons were being heated on a Franklin stove.

"I'll take the ironing," Kerry volunteered, and Helga nodded approvingly.

"*Ja*, that's good. The maids can help me vith this stuff. She has us all running all day, she has. That woman has too much energy!" Kerry laughed at Helga's disapproving grimace, then she proceeded to sort the laundry.

The day was warm, and the kitchen was stifling due to the additional heat from the irons and the stove. Sweat dripped down Kerry's face and arms, and it trickled between her breasts. Her dress clung to her tenaciously, and her legs and arms ached from standing and from working with one iron after another—as soon as one cooled, she placed it back on the stove and retrieved a hot one. Her irritability mounted when she realized that almost all of the items she was ironing were Caroline's.

"How many handkerchiefs can one body have?" Kerry asked in amazement, as she folded the eleventh and placed it beside a pile of ironed clothing. Helga snorted a German response that Kerry suspected was not fit for genteel ears, and Kerry wiped the sweat from her brow. Finally she was finished. She felt dizzy and she wanted to go to her room for a cool sponge bath. But as she was approaching the stairs, she ran right into Caroline.

"Maid, come here immediately."

Kerry was about to protest, but she saw the icy glimmer in Caroline's eyes and thought it best to comply. The woman disliked her because she had seen Cameron all but embracing her in the hallway. Now Caroline led Kerry up the stairs to her room, where she gestured toward the floor with a soft white hand.

"Do you see that?"

Kerry glanced at the floor, puzzled. She knew the chambermaid had just cleaned it the previous day for she had heard the girl grumbling about how picky Caroline was. The floorboards were sparkling, and a soft sheen of beeswax still gleamed from their freshly scrubbed boards.

"Is it not a mess?" she asked Kerry, her clear eyes seething.

Kerry looked again, then said simply, "It looks clean to me." She was about to be on her way when Caroline stopped her, pointing again to the floor.

"That is simply because you are not genteel. To a maid, I suppose it is clean. I would like this floor clean before I retire." Without another word, she swept down the stairs and into the kitchen to remonstrate further.

Kerry's shoulders slumped and her body groaned. With a whispered curse, she walked back downstairs to the pantry to secure a bucket and a scrub brush. She did not answer Helga's questioning look. She was afraid if she gave vent to her anger she would be unable to stop herself. Hauling the cleaning implements behind her, she went up the stairs and into Caroline's room.

Sometime later, Kerry stood in the hall, surveying the fruits of her labors. The room was now immaculate; not one speck of dust was apparent anywhere. Knowing Caroline's disposition, Kerry had made certain that the English lady would have no reason to complain, and indeed, when

Caroline arrived a moment later, she seemed almost disappointed as she inspected the floor by running a long white finger over its smooth surface. When her finger came up spotless, she stared thoughtfully at the braided rugs rolled up in the corner.

"I daresay, it would not be too good to replace those rugs in that condition." She smiled, showing large, catlike teeth, while Kerry glanced up in disbelief.

"What?"

"Those rugs." Caroline gestured to them with a flick of her wrist. "I don't want those placed on the clean floor without being beaten."

"But that was just done. . . ."

"I'm afraid I require them to be done again." Caroline sighed as if truly sorry while Kerry fumed.

"Pardon me, Miss Caroline. But I am very tired. Could we not leave the rugs until the morning and I will take care of them first thing? It's dark outside and with the rugs rolled up, they will not soil the floor." Kerry tried to use reason, but Caroline's golden head turned back and forth.

"No, that simply won't do. I'm afraid I shall have to demand that the rugs be done tonight." Taking a seat on the far side of the room, Caroline lit a candle and bent over her needlework. Yet Kerry saw her smile as one by one she carried the rugs from the room and carried them down the stairs. Helga had reason to look askance this time, for into the night the Irish lass took the carpets, to hang them with only the aid of an oil lamp, and if she beat them unmercifully, the cook really couldn't blame her.

The *Morning Star* sailed down the Mullica, a bright speck on the tea-colored waters. On the main deck, Cameron stood beside Richard Westcoat, a spyglass held to his eye.

"Anything?" Richard asked, and Cameron replied in the negative.

"No, just that bit of white sail we identified as a Continental schooner." Replacing the glass, he strode across the deck, breathing deeply of the pine-scented air. Of all the places he'd ever been, Cameron decided this was the most beautiful. Red cedars and spicy pines rushed up to greet the shores, while mysterious coves and dark hanging cypress lent an air of secrecy to these waters. Now that he was gone from the mansion, Cameron's mind was at ease, no haunting presences demanded things he was not willing to give. Yet he also was forced to admit a longing, a peculiar absence in his life. He had grown used to a spritely presence, a face full of laughter. Like nutmeg in rum, Kerry added a spice to his existence. He sighed, freeing his mind and allowing himself to think of the lass. He pictured her transfixed by the beauty of the scene before him now, her eyes sparkling with excitement and delight. Everything was like that to her, new and to be reveled in. He felt burdens lifted from him just from being around the lass, as if through her eyes he could see the world anew.

"Nonsense!" he said aloud.

Richard turned away from the seacoast and looked at his friend.

"You said something?"

"No," Cameron replied. She has inserted herself into my mind! he thought, annoyed. Yet try as he might to eschew Kerry her image returned, bubbling up from the river—two sparkling green eyes, and seaweed waving in the ripples like black silk hair blowing in the breeze.

"Schooner! Redcoat at nine o'clock!" a seaman's excited voice rang out, interrupting Cameron's train of thought. Snatching up the glass, he peered toward the bay. A schooner greeted his eyes, English to be sure, and loaded to the nines. Shouting out commands, Cameron positioned himself behind a swivel gun, and prepared to take the ship.

* * *

It seemed to Kerry that she had scarcely fallen asleep when morning broke and Caroline's arrogant voice penetrated her dreams. Heaving herself out of bed, she glanced outside at the gray sky, reminding herself that at least one good thing would occur today—Cook had promised that Cameron would return. That thought eased her mind a bit for he seemed to be the only one who could control the cold blond woman.

Kerry sat up in bed and then frowned as she felt the gold necklace drop down between her breasts, its links leaving a trail on her skin. Once again she wondered about Cameron's motive in presenting the gift to her. "'Tis likely he thinks to foist me off with trinkets now, with his beloved awaiting him," Kerry through shrewishly, and her fingers tangled in the chain. She intended to yank the thing from her neck, but suddenly she stopped and let the chain fall back into its former resting place. What if she was with child? It was a possibility. Although she had escaped unscathed in the past, there was no assurance that her luck would continue. The necklace would bring a good price in any tinker's shop. She might need that money in the future.

With that thought Kerry rose, washing and dressing quickly, the cold metal feel of the necklace continually reminding her of its presence. She quit the room, not wanting to dwell on her plight, but she stopped in her tracks when she spied Caroline's face at the stairwell above her, her complexion pale and sallow at this early morning hour.

"Maid! Maid!" She called, and although Kerry tried to pretend she didn't hear her, Caroline was persistent. "Leave off the furnace duty today. I have much I want done in this house and I will need the additional help."

Kerry stared up at her in disbelief, knotting her hair behind her as she asked, "What could you wish to have done today?" From the maids' reports, Kerry was sure everything within the somber mansion had been cleaned within an inch of its life.

"I'm redoing some of the rooms," Caroline said with a haughty air. "I've brought some draperies with me from Philadelphia, and some of my other articles arrived by coach yesterday. I wish to brighten up this place for Cameron." As she claimed her right to the man with that possessive sentence, Kerry's eyes widened with disbelief.

"You mean you wish to change his house around? Don't you think you should wait and ask his permission when he returns?" As the words slipped out of Kerry's astonished mouth, Caroline gave her a hateful glance.

"How dare you speak to me like that? You forget yourself, girl! I am to be mistress of this manor and you are a servant. Where do you get the right to question any of my doings?"

Her shrill voice rang through the open staircase, waking a disgruntled Charles who strode sleepily from his room. "What goes on, old girl?" he asked Kerry, yawning while tugging at the belt of his blue satin dressing gown. "Can't a body get some sleep? Oh, hello, Caroline."

"Good morning, Charles." Disapproval rang out in her voice as she glanced meaningfully toward the rising sun. "I was merely correcting this maid and I do not require your assistance. She seems to feel that I have no right to redecorate this house. She should be lashed for her impertinence." Clear blue-gray eyes glared through gold lashes while Kerry bit back a reply.

"Well, I surely don't care if you redo this whole mausoleum." Charles sniffed. "But the maid does have a point. Cameron is liable to feel quite differently. He has memories he likes to preserve."

"Memories better forgotten," Caroline said decisively. Her anger no longer seemed aimed at Kerry, but at Charles's amiable expression.

"Touché, my dear," Charles replied, sweeping low in a bow. "Now I hope you don't mind if I borrow your servant for a while. I am simply no good in the morning without my tea." Before Caroline could object, Charles led Kerry down the stairs and away from her ranting voice.

"Thank you," Kerry said gratefully, and Charles flashed her a benign smile.

"Certainly. There's a good girl. When is my dear brother returning, anyway?" Charles glanced about the hall, as if suddenly aware of Cameron's absence.

"Today, I think," Kerry replied.

"Well, that will be advantageous for you." At her puzzled frown, he continued. "Caroline tends to get out of hand without Cameron's presence. My brother seems to intimidate her, an awesome task, you must admit." He seated himself at the dining-room table, then expanded on his remarks. "But I'm afraid it is not advantageous to me."

"Why is that?" Kerry asked.

"Because I was indeed looking forward to having you all to myself," he said smoothly. Kerry glanced up, startled, then smiled as he did also.

"Sir, I must grant that you are an outrageous flirt." She grinned while Charles chuckled.

"Outrageous," he agreed, but he was no longer smiling, and a touch of sincerity lingered in his suave glance.

Charles's intervention did help somewhat, but Kerry could not hide from Caroline long. The Englishwoman caught up with her as soon as she had finished clearing away Charles's breakfast plates.

"There you are. I have the other maids assembled in the library. I plan to give instruction only once so hurry in there." Helga and Kerry exchanged a fearful glance while Kerry hastened to obey.

The rest of the day was spent in time-consuming and tiring chores: switching carpets, changing draperies, and rearranging furniture. Caroline thought nothing of demanding that Kerry move the same piece of furniture three or four times before she decided she liked it best where it originally stood. Pictures and clocks were moved, vases and ornaments exchanged, until Caroline was satisfied with the changed appearance of the house. Although her taste was excellent, Kerry could not ignore her feeling of foreboding. Cameron was most particular about his possessions and he resented tampering.

The sun, slowly sinking, was sending feeble orange streamers through the windows when Kerry finally finished her chores. She'd only rested for a few minutes when Jane Clark had stopped by for tea and had invited the entire household to a husking bee the following evening. Caroline had been most impatient at this slight interruption, and she'd hurried the poor woman to such a degree that Kerry could only wonder if indigestion had been the result of Jane's visit.

Kerry glanced about the newly decorated library. White satin draperies hung at the windows, blue and white oriental rugs graced the floor, oil lamps were placed strategically about the room. It wasn't badly rearranged, but the warm familiarity, the masculine feel of Cameron's darker colors and braided rugs, was missing. She no longer felt welcome in this room and tired as she was, she started for the stairs, her legs climbing the oaken steps slowly.

"Just a minute, maid."

Kerry glanced back and sighed as Caroline rushed up, her arms aflutter. "I want everything perfect when Cameron returns. Do follow me to the parlor. There is a bit of dusting to be done, and then I want tea prepared."

Kerry knew better than to argue. Expecting no sympathy, she followed the demanding woman obediently, hoping only that the work would be finished quickly.

"Start with the lamps; then do those tables." Kerry obeyed, hiding a yawn as she raised a weary hand to the lamp. When she did so, her neckline gaped slightly, and the golden chain dangled in the lamplight. Within an instant, Caroline was at her side, snatching at the necklace.

"Where did you get this?"

Kerry's face went pale as Caroline fingered the gold chain, her crystal-like eyes wide and blazing. "Tell me. I demand it. Wherever did you get this trinket?"

Kerry was nobody's fool. She knew instinctively that it would be disastrous to tell Caroline the truth, so she shrugged, acting as if the matter were of little importance. When she took refuge in silence, Caroline yanked at her arm in an unladylike manner.

"You stole it, you slut! I know your type! I knew it the first time I laid eyes on you! You have every man you see lusting after you, but that's not enough. You even had to take the room right next to Cameron's so you could play your nasty little games with him. Well, I'll see to it that your indenture papers are sold off and that you are soon gone!" With a sharp crack Caroline's white hand met Kerry's face, and the Irish lass stepped back in surprise.

Having suppressed her own anger far too long, Kerry was now wrathful. Her fist delivered a neat cut to Caroline's chin. The English girl fell to the floor between two of her neatly arranged tables, and tears of anger came to her eyes.

"What in the devil's going on here?"

The deep voice broke through Caroline's harsh breathing, but Kerry stood with her arms folded, stubbornly refusing to answer Cameron.

"That—that little ruffian! She attacked me!" Tears poured freely down Caroline's smooth white cheeks as she rose from the floor and threw herself into Cameron's arms. Her sobbing was the only sound in the room for an inordinately long time, and when Cameron spoke, his voice grated, flintlike, and Kerry winced.

"Is that true, Kerry?"

"Yes," she answered defiantly. Cameron set Caroline aside, and strode across the room to face the recalcitrant Irish lass. He stopped midway, however, and his eyes fell upon the tinkling glass lamps, then the curtains, the rugs, and the furniture. He whirled about in disbelief, but everywhere his gaze fell there was evidence of Caroline's work.

"What have you done to my house?" he demanded.

"Why, I merely brightened things up a bit. Really, Cameron, the furniture and rugs were as old as the house. I simply couldn't—"

"Silence!" he shouted, his jaw tight with rage. His eyes locked with Caroline's and under that frightful glare even she looked away. "What right, Caroline, had you to tamper with my belongings? Did I give you permission to do so?"

"No," Caroline said meekly. "I was just trying to please you."

"Well, you can please me by returning the house to its former state. And in the future, I would appreciate it if you discussed with me any change you wish to make—before making it. Now, will you leave?"

Caroline assumed an injured air, then swished haughtily out of the parlor and up the stairs. Seizing this opportunity to escape, Kerry sidled toward the door.

"Stay where you are."

Kerry froze, her hand on the doorjamb, so close was she to her goal. She drew it back just as Cameron slammed the aperture closed. He then stood glaring at her.

"Sit!"

Kerry reluctantly took a seat, her courage quickly flagging as he came to stand before her. He seemed towering in his rage, his cloak thrown over one shoulder, his hand locked over the silver horse's head tapping his cane. Kerry stared at that hand, at his whitening knuckles, and she jumped when he spoke again.

"After everything I've told you, everything I've tried to show you, you still react in such a manner that you strike another woman? Why, Kerry? What would make you do such a thing?"

"Did I ever ask you for anything? Did I?" Kerry leaped to her feet, in her anger forgetting her fear. She looked like an ancient sorceress, her black, silken hair falling about her shoulders and her sea-green eyes blazing. Without a thought of the consequences, she faced her employer. "You take me for some common tavern wench, then because you feel guilty about it you try to foist off your hoity-toity manners on me! Well, I'll not be needing them, thank you very much! I can manage just fine, all on me own!"

"You can?" His teeth were clenched, so angry was he, and as Kerry tried to pass him, Cameron grabbed her shoulders, turning her toward him. "You can manage by yourself? And what if I hadn't purchased your indenture? Do you think Mr. Jacobs would have let you remain innocent for long. Hardly. He declared as much a few minutes after I'd met you. And what of that night at Bodine's? I'm sure Jack had more in mind than a midnight conversation. You were locked in his room, and he was tearing the clothes off your back. You run off half-cocked to save Trevor, but you still won't trust me! You won't even tell me what happened here tonight, though I know damned well something did! But by God you're going to!"

"Let go of me!" Kerry yelled, pulling away.

He was shaking her in his rage, and he then clutched her wrists, drawing her toward him until she stumbled forward. The contact caught them both unaware. Wide-eyed, her red mouth open and gasping, she glanced up and saw the metal coldness of his rage melt from his eyes. Something different burned there now, something she could feel down the whole length of his body. His right hand dropped from her wrist and slid down her arm to her waist, pulling her even closer. His muscular thighs pressed most intimately against her. His chest, clothed in ruffled linen, rubbed against her breasts. His face, handsome and forbidding, was only inches away. The effect was devastating, like one long caress. Kerry's pulse raced, and a throbbing need for him overcame her.

"Kerry." Her very name was a caress. His dark head lowered. She was sure he was going to kiss her and that thought was wildly exciting. But just before his mouth made contact, he suddenly let go of her and, with an oath, strode across the room to stand alone before the fire.

Kerry's lower lip dropped, and she placed a hand on the wall to steady her shaking nerves. Stunned by the way her rage had been transformed into passion, she felt that her world had gone mad. None of this made sense! None of it! She had missed him while he was gone, but she refused to admit it. Now, with him here, she was forced to face reality. To a proud Irish lass, that thought was unwelcome, and she strove for composure.

"Sir?" she asked shakily. "May I leave now?"

The look upon his face was her answer, and she scuttled quickly out of the room before he could change his mind. Kerry O'Toole had courage, but she was not a fool.

The following day, Charles was not in evidence, due to Cameron's return, and Caroline was unusually subdued, which made the maids gleeful. Even Helga was in a better frame of mind, and she grinned as she served up the midday meal.

Because Kerry resided at the house, she took all of her meals there while the more important furnace workers, Bill Seldon included, also had their meals there. Due to her dislike for the man, Kerry was wont to take her meals with the cook, avoiding his leers and threatening glances. "Ya, that man eats like a pig!" Helga declared, setting a full plate of chicken pie aside for him. "He'll finish dat up and vant more. That is certain!"

"Is the family eating now?" Kerry was just as eager to avoid Caroline, especially after the scene last night, but

Helga shook her white-capped head.

"Not yet. Cameron—he's out of course. Charles is abed. I think he returned last night with some French bordello girl. I heard Cameron shouting about it this morning."

Kerry smiled at this last, and sipped her cup of hot coffee. A moment of relative peace passed before she heard Cameron shouting angrily outside. She glanced out the open window to see her employer charging up the lawn, his manner foretelling some disaster, and when he entered the dining hall, his booming voice echoed through the house.

"Where's Trevor? That damned fool Irish lout! Trevor!"

At the sound of Trevor's name, Kerry dropped her coffee cup with a clatter and raced to the doorway. Cameron glanced up and, with an icy stare, noted her presence and the probable reason for it. Trevor stood on the other side of the table behind the smirking Seldon, clutching his tricorn and glancing fearfully about.

"What is it, sir?" he said.

"Did you leave the stable door open! Answer me, did you?"

"No!" Trevor replied, startled. "I distinctly recall that the door was closed, sir."

Cameron's granite features softened a bit, and he searched the Irish lad's face for a lie. Finding no indication of one, he swore under his breath and slammed his cane to the floor.

"Sir? What's happened?" Kerry ventured, while the workmen kept their gazes fixed on their plates. For a moment, Cameron said nothing and it appeared he wouldn't answer.

"Caledonia. He's gone," he then declared rather reluctantly.

"Caledonia!" Kerry said wonderingly, and Trevor gave a low whistle.

"D'ya know how much that horse was worth?" Trevor sighed, then quickly cut off his careless words when Cameron gave him a dark glance.

"But how?" Kerry asked.

Cameron shook his head. "I have no idea. I just went to take him out for a ride, and the horse is gone." Thoughtfully, he glanced back to Trevor. "Did you see him this morning?"

"I really didn't look, sir. I usually tend to the horses later, after ye return," Trevor anxiously assured him, not wishing to take the blame.

"Did you hear anything during the night?" Cameron persisted, but Trevor shook his head.

"Not a thing, sir. But I sleep like a baby, I do."

"Aye. A-squalling and a-kicking all night," Bill Seldon muttered, and the furnace men responded with muffled laughter.

"What is all the disturbance? A body can hardly sleep around here." Charles sauntered into the dining room, casting a dubious glance at Bill who was eagerly slopping up his food.

"Caledonia is missing," Cameron said.

Charles's smile vanished. "You don't say. Caledonia! Why that Scottish steed is worth . . . more than I can easily count and that's a great deal. Who is in charge of the stables?"

"No one, but Trevor sleeps there."

Charles favored Trevor with a distinctly suspicious glance. "Is that so? Well, my lad, I daresay a few extra quid wouldn't do you any harm would it?" He gazed at the dark Irish lad with an accusing air, and Trevor glared back at him.

"I'll not be called a horse thief by you or anyone else. Either take me to the magistrate and prove it, or say nothing at all!" Trevor was shouting now, and recalling Trevor's last encounter with Charles Cameron interrupted him. The Irish lad's face had healed, but obviously his memory still pained him.

"No one is accusing you of anything. Are you, Charles?"

Charles's blond eyebrows lifted. Then, with an air of extreme boredom, he passed Trevor and the others to pour a cup of coffee. Stirring it complacently, he said, "You'll not be guilty of anything until it's proven." A few of the workmen gave Charles surly looks, but the Englishman ignored these underlings, took his coffee, and departed.

"Would you like me to take the mare and search the grounds?" Kerry said, knowing how much the horse meant to Cameron and hoping to ease the blow. "Mayhap he's still wandering about."

Cameron's gaze fell on her for a moment; then his face darkened ominously. "No. The roads are not safe, and I'll be damned if I'll be looking about for you when some highwayman abducts you, though you need no such help. Good day." With that he strode out of the room and slammed the door.

Kerry blushed hotly. It seemed all eyes were on her, and stinging tears threatened.

"Come on." Trevor took her arm and led her to the door. "And what are you all looking at?" he yelled.

One by one, the workmen looked away and began to eat.

Once she was outside, Kerry's tears fell freely. Not just from today, but from weeks past. The days with Caroline, her unnerving experience with Cameron—all had been pent up and were now released. Trevor held her comfortably, patting her arm and saying, "There there. It does a soul good ta cry."

"That man!" Kerry shook her fist at an imaginary opponent. "He has no call to say those things. I don't understand him, I don't! He reminds me of the metals the smithy forges: one minute as hot as red iron, the next, plunged into water and just as chill." Roughly Kerry brushed away the tears tumbling down her face, as if angry at their very existence.

"Let's walk down by the lake," Trevor suggested, and together they ambled down the sandy path, the sun gleaming hot and white upon it. When they reached the sparkling sapphire pool, Kerry splashed her face with the water, then wiped it dry with her apron. Trevor picked up a stone and tossed it. The pebble skimmed the surface until it fell with a plunk into the dark blue depths. "Do you feel better?" he asked, and when she nodded, he spoke slowly.

"I've not known Master Cameron long, but a wee bit longer than you have, and I've seen a change come over the man, since the day he brought you back from the city. In some ways he's calmer, more open with the workmen and more concerned about their needs. I know you have something ta do with that, but it's as if he sees us in a different light now. And Miss Caroline . . . well, she's been coming up every summer for years now, but I've never seen Cameron raise an eyebrow when we talk to her—or try not to. Yet he gives me a murderous stare, ya know, like he's jealous or somewhat whenever I say anything to you, let alone touch you."

Kerry was listening thoughtfully, so Trevor shrugged, then continued.

"It may mean nothing, but then again, it may mean everything. I do think the man cares for you more than he's willing ta admit to anyone, even himself."

"That's nonsense!" Kerry shouted. "He's betrothed to Caroline. She has money, sophistication, style—everything a man like the master would want."

When Trevor laughed, Kerry tapped her right foot agitatedly. "What's so funny?"

"Have you taken a look in the mirror lately?" Pointing to the lake, he drew her over to it, then gestured down to the water. Green eyes stared up from a frame of black lashes, and they were complemented by a perfect nose and an inviting mouth. Black tendrils fell in charming wisps about her face, accentuating her startlingly white skin as black velvet sets off pearls. "And you don't think Master Cameron would want that? He would be mad if he didn't." Trevor snorted, then eyed her appraisingly. "Maybe if you acted like a girl for once, he wouldn't have such trouble remembering you are one."

"And what's that supposed ta mean?" Kerry snapped, aiming a well-balanced kick at Trevor's shins. The Irish lad laughed, then removed himself from this deadly threat. Crossing his arms, he spoke in a lecturing tone.

"Like that. And ya know, Miss Caroline always dresses to the hilt. It wouldn't hurt your cause none if you wore something other than that damned work dress—and if you fixed your hair." He gestured to Kerry's black mane which was pulled carelessly into a knot.

Kerry's hand wandered self-consciously to the knot. She recognized the grim truth in what Trevor said. Most men treated her as a lad or as a favorite sister, despite her beauty. Even Cameron only recognized her femininity when he was forced to, like that night in the tavern and even last night when she'd practically fallen into his arms. Kerry blushed violently, and noting Trevor's knowing smirk, she got to her feet, refusing his offer of help.

"I'll need no more advice from you, ya pest. Let's return ta work before I inform them of yer lounging."

"Yes, miss." Trevor replied, but there was laughter in his voice and it lingered in Kerry's mind.

Chapter Thirteen

Kerry returned to the house at the twilight hour, and she was amazed to find the place aflutter. "The Bee!" Helga called, pausing from her stirring of a flour-filled pan. "Ve're all going tonight! To the corn-husking bee at the Clark's. You do recall?"

"Yes." Kerry smiled. A night out would be sorely appreciated after the past few days, and her smile curved more at the prospect. Then Caroline's demanding voice echoed through the kitchen and a chambermaid rushed in, fetching a kettle of water.

"She wants another bath! D'ya believe it? She ain't moved from the house all the damned day and she wants another bath!"

"I'll take it," Kerry volunteered. "I'm going up anyway." The chambermaid gave her a grateful glance, and Kerry hoisted the kettle herself up the flights of steps.

"Just pour it in the tub," Caroline ordered, then turned about when she saw Kerry framed in her dressing-table mirror. "Oh, it's you."

"Yes, miss," Kerry responded. She filled the tub as quickly as she could, eager to get out of this room which chilled her to the bone. Ice blue draperies and a white quilt graced the bed, and Kerry knew instinctively who had selected these

215

colors. On the bed Caroline's dress for the bee was laid out. It was a velvet, of a soft mauve color, the same shade the sky turns after the sun has set. Kerry stared longingly at the dress. The color would not look good on Caroline, her blond looks only paled under such shades, but it would be very becoming to Kerry. Caroline saw her glance and lifted the sleeve of the dress, displaying the workmanship.

"It is lovely, isn't it? I'm sure Cameron will enjoy seeing it on me tonight. But then, he always appreciates my gowns." Her eyes flickered and Kerry bit back a reply, nodded, and then rushed out of the ice chamber.

"I'm sure Cameron will love this dress," Kerry mimicked, now safe in her own room, and with an oath, she tossed a boot across the floor. Snatching off her own gown, she washed her skin vigorously in the cool water on the washstand, allowing that refreshment to ease her anger at Caroline. When she took out another cotton work dress, the other gowns Cameron bought her—the ones she stubbornly refused to wear—glimmered inside the drawer and she was again reminded of Trevor's words. "Aye, as if it would make any difference," she said aloud, but she opened the drawer and pulled out a frock.

The burgundy one. It was simple enough for this affair, yet much richer than the cotton gowns she wore everyday. She was about to toss it back, her pride screaming, but she could not forget what Trevor had told her and she reluctantly withdrew the gown and pulled it on. The dress felt strange: she had to lace it down the back instead of buttoning it, and the material was soft to her skin. When she finally had it done up and had shaken out the skirts, Kerry glanced absently into the mirror. Then her eyes widened in disbelief.

Instead of a maid, a woman of beauty returned her stare. The burgundy gown set off her white skin, her dark hair, and her eyes, making them mesmerizing. The neck was low, lower than Kerry would normally have dared wear, and it pressed her snowy bosom upward. In spite of the good cut of the dress, the remarkable workmanship, it was the lass herself who was the gem, the gown merely emphasizing her charms. Taking up her comb, Kerry removed the restraining knot from her hair and worked with the tresses, trying to arrange them in the stylish sweeps she remembered from Philadelphia, but without much success for she was unable to secure her wanton mane. "Dammit!" she spat out, and a slight giggle sounded from the hall.

"Something the matter, miss? Gor, looky at you!" The chambermaid whom Kerry had helped earlier stepped into the room, her eyes wide and admiring. "You're a right beauty, you are."

"Do you really think so?" Kerry asked, excitement in her voice. The maid nodded quickly, then came to stand beside the dark Irish girl and gaze into the mirror.

"Aye, you are that. Let me help you with your hair, miss. After all, you helped me today and if we're quick about it, no one will be the wiser."

With a nod, Kerry agreed. She took a seat near the mirror, placing the candle to the maid's advantage. The chambermaid, who had considerable experience in the art of dressing hair, now plied her talents with unusual zeal. It was not often she had such a pretty lass to work upon, and one with such a pleasant disposition, never. Sweeping the hair into a becoming style, she allowed several tendrils to accent Kerry's face and to fall down her neck, thereby giving a seductively innocent appearance to this young lass. "What d'ya think, miss?"

Kerry gazed into the mirror, open-mouthed at the results. She'd never realized the difference a hair style and the right clothes could make. "It's wonderful. Thank you." She bestowed a kiss on the chambermaid who smiled with pride at her creation.

"You'll be the loveliest lass there. Oh, she's callin' again. I have to go." Bidding Kerry goodbye, the maid rushed out of the room.

Kerry finished her dressing, and then started to go below. She hesitated at the door, however, and rushed back to lift the mattress of the bed. Underneath, the gold chain shone like a crescent moon. Quickly Kerry placed it around her neck. Her toilet complete now, she hastened out the door to the carriage—after taking the servants to the bee, George would return for the Brents—and inside the coach, she fought hard to quell her excitement.

Jane Clark was at the door to greet her guests, smiling and extending a fond hand to the serving girls and maids. "Kerry my dear! Don't you look lovely. I'm so glad you came." She ushered them inside and through the house, directing them to the path to the barn.

"Do you need help with anything? Can I carry some of those for you?" Kerry pointed to a pile of pies, their scents unbearably delicious in the close kitchen. Apple, mince, and pumpkin were all neatly lined up against the wall on a wooden bench, like soldiers in a drill.

"Why, yes." Jane smiled gratefully. "I've had so much to get ready."

Kerry took three of the pies, one in each hand and one on her arms, not daring to carry more, and she hastened across the lawn to the brightly lit barn.

Music poured out over the dried grass, and beneath each window was a puddle of light. Candles, lanterns, and torches had all been pressed into service. When Kerry entered, the noise was already deafening, so she placed the pies out of the way and gazed about. Girls of all ages were there, dressed in their best frocks: bright blue chintzes, calicoes, a few muslins, yellow or green, and many homespuns, brown or beige. The maids were already dancing, making a game of leaping over the bundles of unhusked corn that covered the floor of the barn. With a roar of laughter, some of the men in the loft dumped additional bushels of the Indian corn down onto the floor, prompting the maids to squeal and run for safety. One table was lined with food, including many pies, cakes, and tarts for there'd been an abundance of fruit that year, while another table was lined with ciders, hard and sweet. Apple whiskey, known locally as lightning, was already being sampled, and the furnace workers, as well as the local farmers and gentlemen, discussed the quality of the liquor while they sedulously quaffed it. The Clarks had bound boys as well as indentured servants, and they were also present, singing and joining in the fun.

After looking about, Kerry returned to the house and fetched more pies, then she helped Jane bring out the other refreshments.

Little by little more guests were arriving. With the war and the harvest to be got in, there were few social activities at this time of year so everyone looked forward to this event. In this crowd, Kerry made her way around a table, and ran right into Trevor. The Irish lad gazed up at her in astonishment.

"Look at you, miss. Why I almost didn't know ye."

Kerry winced and waited for a teasing remark or an "I told you so," but Trevor supplied neither. Instead, the lad seemed bemused by the lovely woman before him and he gallantly took her hand, leading her past the admiring lumber workers who were wont to block her way.

"Ya have ta promise me a dance, miss. I will not let you go until you do."

"Trevor!" Kerry snatched back her hand, and then, recalling his previous words as to her manners, she continued in a more genteel way. "There's Maggie Cramer, Trevor, and she's looking this way. Isn't she your lass?"

Trevor's face reddened, and he waved rather awkwardly to the young girl who was, indeed, watching his every movement. As he departed, however, he whispered over Kerry's shoulder. "I still want that dance." Then he went to explain things to his lady.

Kerry couldn't suppress a grin, and she hoped Maggie wouldn't give Trevor too much of an ear burning.

The crowd roared and clapped as Eliah Clark entered the barn, and the white-haired old gentleman nodded appreciatively, smoothing the front of his good suit in the face of this applause.

"Kind people," he began, and the room quieted respectfully. "I do indeed thank you for your presence tonight. Now the moon is almost in position and we are ready to begin. Take your places everyone. Lads on this side, girls on that."

While he spoke, Kerry glanced about, seeing a few familiar faces. Richard Westcoat was present, as was John Cox, and she recognized a few townsmen. They had been standing in small groups and talking, but now everyone began to take the floor, men going to the far side of the room. Not knowing the dances, Kerry sat on a bench beside a housemaid of the Clarks.

"Is there no other place for me but here with the maids?"

When the sharp voice rang Kerry froze, recognizing the familiar, frost-bitten tones. She could well imagine Jane's discomfort as that good woman replied in the negative, but she restrained her tongue and gave Caroline a polite smile.

"Hello, Miss Caroline. I thought I heard your voice," Kerry said sweetly, although she'd have loved to crack her one right on that uplifted nose. Lord, this manners stuff carries a stiff price, Kerry thought resentfully, her eyes sparkling with wrath. Trevor sat nearby while Maggie was a few seats down, a fact that consoled the lass somewhat. The Irish lad, who was always ready with a joke, provided a buffer from Caroline, and since Maggie was close by, the girl could not accuse Kerry of any wrongdoing.

"All right now. Listen close," Eliah called out happily, while the lads shouted joyful jests. "We will pick the captains. Nominations, please."

"Westcoat. Clark. Cox," the men shouted.

After much haggling, it was decided that Richard Westcoat would captain the men's team while John Cox's wife would lead the women. "Ready . . . set . . . go!" Eliah

Clark shouted, and at his command, men and women dived into the corn, husking it with a vengeance. Laughter and much gaiety followed, and jugs of cider and cakes were pased. Gossip was freely exchanged, and the women whispered gleefully about the town scandal.

"Aye, the widow Murphy is pregnant all right. She went right up to the furnace, demanding to see Mick and claiming it was his."

"The nerve of her!" A young girl laughed. "All the same she was in a hard way. Without a husband, her monies were cut off and she hadn't much of a choice." The women concurred with this, tossing empty corn husks into the barrels beside them as they talked.

"And did you hear of the death of Enid Leeds? Sad that," the maid beside Kerry put in, and John Cox's wife nodded.

"It was sad. Imagine, being subjected to all that talk about the demon, then being forced to live out there alone in the woods, finally to die in such a mysterious manner."

"What does she mean, about the demon?" Kerry asked, and the maid shrugged.

"You've heard of the legend?" she asked. At Kerry's nod she handed her an ear of corn, then continued. "Well, Enid was supposed to be the mother of that Devil."

"No!" Kerry said, startled. "Enid was the Mother Leeds of the legend? Are you sure?"

"As sure as can be. Anyway, from the way the townspeople treated her, it was not hard to believe."

Enid, Kerry thought sadly. I hope you are at peace now.

A joyful shout broke into her thoughts, and Kerry glanced up to see a growing pile of corn husks beside Trevor. "We're gaining," the Irish lad shouted, while the maids laughed and doused him with a bundle of empty green husks. The barn, though crowded, was still filling slowly, the newcomers diving into the work with much merriment. It was pleasant here, amid the noise and laughter, and Kerry's eyes slowly swept across the room. Caroline was at the far end of the barn, separate from the group and pressing her pale fingers to her forehead as if it ached. She was obviously bored, and she glanced repeatedly outside to the moon, as if judging the time by its brightness.

Nearby stood the minister and Eliah Clark, both gentlemen egging the crowd on, alternately cheering each team and inspiring high toasts at each cheer. Each toast grew more joyful and the hands became a little freer with the cider, sloshing the amber liquid into pewter mugs then sipping cautiously from the top. Richard Westcoat, being captain of his team, was knee deep in corn, shouting orders in a jesting manner and tossing a handful of ears to any lad who seemed to be lacking. She saw Trevor husking for all his worth, his whispered comments causing many a maid to blush and drop her corn, which seemed to be his purpose.

Charles stood alone, sipping his drink, his cold blue eyes touching everyone. When his gaze met Kerry's, she gave him a quick smile, then her own gaze wandered only to be caught as if spellbound. Cameron Brent stood a few feet from his brother, beside John Cox who seemed to be discussing some matter of urgency with him. But Cameron Brent heard him not; his eyes were fastened on Kerry with a mesmerizing stare, the heat burning from behind his cool facade visible only in those eyes! They swept across her with fiery warmth. Like sipping wine, it was heady, intoxicating. It whetted the palate and left it hungering for more.

"Lord!" Kerry thought, turning away. "He seems inside my very soul!" Yet even as her eyes fixed upon the corn she was being torn into pieces, she could feel him watching her, his gaze penetrating into the very heart of her.

"Yer supposed to husk the corn, not rip it apart!" Trevor teased, but Kerry hardly heard him. So shaken was she by the effects of that silvery gaze, the corn actually slipped from her hands while across the room the lads shouted with glee.

"A red ear! He's found a red ear!"

Kerry's conscious mind registered the fact that some lad

would leave happy tonight, for the discovery of a red ear meant he could kiss the lass of his choice. These cheers were soon joined by others and when Kerry glanced up, she saw more than one lad was displaying his prize.

When the last of the ears were collected and the baskets were being tallied, Trevor was already jubilantly dancing upon the bench.

"We've won! I just know it," a maid shouted, but Trevor was not daunted.

And sure enough, when the count had been done, the male team had three more baskets than the women. "Cheers!" the men shouted, hoisting Richard Westcoat upon their shoulders, while that fine Englishman tossed his mug into the air, catching it with a rare show of bravado. "Hurrah!" the winning team shouted, stamping their feet while the maids giggled, cheering. Then Richard toasted the ladies, their beauty and their sportsmanship.

"Music!" a workman shouted. "Bring on the whiskey!"

"Not yet," Eliah declared, stepping into the crowd with the minister, their steps markedly jagged. "Before the dance, we have . . ." His voice drained off as the minister whispered something into his ear. "I know that," he replied impatiently, while the workers roared with approval. It was not often they had the chance to see their employer benefit from the beloved Jersey lightning and the experience was most rewarding. "We want to award a prize first. To the worker with the most corn." Eliah held up a jug of the best, and the lads waxed gleeful, rubbing their hands in anticipation of the lethal brew.

"Trevor Shanahan!" Eliah shouted and the lads guffawed, then shoved Trevor forward with envious words. The Irish lad was indeed pleased with this gift, hoisting it high for all to see before pulling out the cork with his teeth.

"Drink, drink, drink, drink . . ." the crowd shouted, stamping their feet while the fiddlers strummed along. Trevor obligingly lifted the jug and gulped the fiery liquid down for several minutes before pulling it away and wiping his mouth amid cheers. The workmen followed his lead, challenging each other's capacity until the wagers grew high indeed.

At a signal from Eliah, the fiddlers began a reel and the floor, once covered with unhusked corn, was now filled with swirling skirts and tipsy men. Kerry was pulled onto it by Trevor's overly zealous hand, and she glanced at Maggie for approval, which the lass smilingly gave. The dances were slightly different from the jigs Kerry knew, but the reel was fun, breathless and dizzying. The furnace workers sent her many appreciative glances, though some were astonished that the young slip of a girl they'd taken for granted had been transformed into this wanton beauty.

"Ah, yer a delight to me very heart," Trevor slurred as Kerry swung neatly around him, dancing with a quick agility. "Yer the light of me life. A more winsome lass I ne'er laid eyes on."

Trevor looked handsome himself tonight, his stubborn dark hair dampened and combed back, his white teeth ever showing in a sparkling grin. But that grin was a little too wide, and his dark eyes were a bit too warm. Kerry's own smile deepened.

"And I'd say you laid yer eyes on too much lightning," she said teasingly. "But I thank you for the compliment."

"You do me no justice!" Trevor cried as if cut to the quick. "Drunk or sober, these lips cannot lie! These eyes are ne'er deceived." As a slow waltz began, Trevor seized the opportunity and swept Kerry into his arms, dancing smartly past Charles who was approaching with purposeful intent. The blond Englishman appeared puzzled for a moment, then shrugged and turned to walk off the floor. As he was leaving, Caroline appeared, tapping her satin-slippered foot in a pointed motion. Ever the gentleman, Charles took her hand and joined in the waltz, but his expression was none too happy.

"Serves him right," Trevor remarked as Kerry glanced up. "Let 'im have the ice queen for a spell."

"Trevor!" Kerry exclaimed, but the Irish lad merely laughed and swept her gaily across the floor. He adeptly dodged all other appropriate suitors and would-be partners, claiming her for himself until a rather stern voice cut through his lilt and a bronzed hand fell upon his shirt.

"Excuse me, Trevor. Miss O'Toole, are your dances taken for the night?"

At the slight shake of her head, Cameron smiled. "I see. Then do me a service, Trevor. Miss Maggie Cramer is in need of a partner. I'd say she's been somewhat neglected tonight."

"Certainly sir." Trevor grinned, and with a courtly bow he took himself off, smirking as if he had planned this whole thing himself.

"Irish dolt," Cameron murmured, a smile still playing around his lips. "Dancing and drinking are his main accomplishments."

"That's what we Irish are best at," Kerry replied spritely. Glancing down at the Irish lass he held in his arms, Cameron could not suppress a grin. Her eyes sparkled, mirth dancing in them, and he was reminded of the elves and fairies he'd heard so much about. Her lashes were so thick and black they seemed a fringe, while her cheeks, flushed and laughing from exertion, bloomed like a wild red rose. Her lips were parted to reveal even white teeth, and her softly curving smile titillated his imagination. Holding her was a pleasurable torture, for his hand rested on a waist that was impossibly small yet curvaceous, while her dress revealed a snowy, full bosom. His height gave him the advantage of viewing this treasure, but the thought that Trevor, or any other man, had the same right annoyed him.

To Kerry, dancing with Cameron was a dreamlike experience. His garb was striking, but not overly elegant, and the dark colors flattered him, accentuating his classic features, the decisive chin, and the smooth brow. He danced surprisingly well, stepping lightly and easily around the other men whose whiskey-inspired steps led them in many directions.

"You can dance," Kerry said, a note of surprise creeping into her voice.

"We English are good at some things." He smiled and Kerry blushed, then looked quickly away. His gaze was too knowing, too confusing for her present state of mind. His hand was now smoothing the back of her dress, his fingers evoking a warming tingle. This whole experience was new to Kerry, dancing under the moonlight with an elegant handsome man whose touch quickened her blood. It was thrilling. She was, therefore, quite sorry when the music ended and the crowd clapped for more.

The next dance was a jig, and Trevor staggered up, still afoot somehow. "Ah, you'll not be wantin' to try this one, sir. I'll take her off yer hands."

Cameron held Kerry's small hand in a tight grip. "I'll manage," he stated evenly.

"An Englishman doing an Irish jig?" Trevor said, incredulity playing over his face.

Cameron did, indeed, manage, quite well in fact. Kerry laughed outright as he kept up with the intricate steps, dancing with an abandon that put Trevor's drunken maneuvers to shame. "Ah, the English." Trevor sighed. "First ya take our land, then our dances. What next?"

"Your women," Charles declared bluntly, taking Kerry from under Cameron's nose with a deftness due to long practice. "Miss, I've been waiting for you all night."

Cameron started to follow them, but a hand tugged on his dark waistcoat. "Cam dear, have you forgotten me tonight?" He turned to see Caroline's piercing stare, the glitter of her diamond earbobs. Reluctantly he offered his arm, but his eyes never left the Irish lass enfolded in his brother's arms.

"Damn him!" Cameron muttered.

"Did you say something?" Caroline asked.

Cameron shook his head violently. "No."

Kerry was having troubles of her own, for due to the influence of cider, Charles's reserve was gone. His hands sought contact with her curves, and his eyes devoured the breasts that seemed about to burst forth from her dress. "Come outside with me," he whispered, placing a drunken kiss upon her neck. "Let me hold you, touch you."

"Master Charles! Are you mad?"

"Mad, crazy, insane for you, my dear! Surely you must have known that. All these weeks I've been wanting you. I only took that French girl because she looked a bit like you, but she was not you, Kerry. I must have you." His hands crept slowly upward while Kerry fought to keep them down.

"Charles." She scolded him politely, but he appeared not to listen. She caught one of his hands and held it firmly to her waist, but the other was other was already dipping inside her dress, caressing her sweet young flesh. "Charles!" Kerry snatched up the offending hand and held it firmly at her side, her eyes snapping with outrage, all pretense of gentility gone.

"If you don't keep yer hands to yerself, I'll knock you right where you sit."

Charles glanced up, his boyishly handsome face showing his surprise before he broke into laughter. "A lass with spirit! I like that. Now really, Kerry. You must allow me. I simply cannot bear—"

"Charles." Cameron's voice rang out sharply, and Charles sighed, still claiming her hand but turning aside to greet his angry brother. "I think the lady made her wishes clear, but if she needs any help in doing so, I will be most grateful to assist her."

The two brothers stared at each other with frightening intensity. Slowly, Charles smiled, then laughed. "Cameron, you always could ruin a party. Good evening, lass. I pay fair tribute to your beauty and offer you my condolences for such company." Bowing deeply, Charles departed, his laughter still ringing behind him.

"The red corn! The red corn!" A mule driver shouted and Eliah Clark nodded and stepped up to the platform that housed the fiddlers. "Now then, ladies and gents. This is the time when anyone lucky enough to receive a red ear gets to kiss the partner of his choice. Are ye ready?"

"Aye, aye!" Came the shouts, and the villagers approached the platform to get a better view. "Now the winners are . . . Mickey Cross, Maggie Cramer, Eliah Clark, and Cameron Brent."

Kerry gazed about at the mention of Cameron's name. She had not noticed that he had husked an ear of red corn. Caroline sent her a knowing smile; then the blonde Englishwoman took a dainty step between two coal workers and stood beside Cameron, publicly claiming him as her own. Kerry's eyes closed and she wished to be a million miles away so she didn't have to stand there and watch Cameron kiss Caroline.

The fiddlers played a low tune as the lights were dimmed, and a maid squealed as Mickey Cross claimed her. Then, when the lamplight was no more, Kerry heard Trevor's laugh. Maggie had found him. Catching up her dress, Kerry rushed outside, unable to bear the thought of Cameron and his fiancée kissing.

After a moment, the lights flashed back on, and there was much good-natured banter. Kerry walked slowly to the carriage, but it was vacant, George being inside somewhere with the others. Leaning against the wheel, she stood, waiting for this night to end.

"Would you like a ride home?" A voice broke the stillness and the mare whinnied. Then Cameron approached, gesturing to the coach with his hand. "I'd not disturb George, but I will take you myself."

"I'd like that," Kerry said softly. "Are you sure?"

"Yes." He smiled. "Charles has taken Caroline. She preferred the other coach, the one lined in leather," he explained as Kerry glanced up, confused. "If you're ready?"

Not willing to soil her dress, Kerry rode inside, alone. She was only too glad when they rolled into the driveway and she could see her room from the window. She sorely needed that refuge. As she stepped gracefully from the carriage, Cameron proffered a hand.

"One moment," he said quietly, after she'd descended. He had not yet released her hand. "You know that I won a red corn?"

Kerry nodded and he smiled strangely, an odd light coming into his eyes.

"Well, I never did get my reward."

With that he swept her into his arms, his lips claiming hers in a fierce, possessive manner. His restrained passion was now unbridled, his mouth insistent and so full of a hunger it left Kerry breathless. Her world swam giddily as his arms tightened about her and his lips tasted the sweetness he'd been denied too long. Then her own arms crept up to caress the back of his neck, the powerful muscles that rippled through his fine garb. Their kiss was more intoxicating than any potion, and once tasted, it begged to be sampled further.

"No!" Kerry tried frantically to resist the spell of the moment, yet her own passion lurked within her like a starved demon, urging her on. "Unhand me, sir. You are promised to another!" She struggled against his well-muscled chest, but as before, physical resistance proved useless. She knew he, too, was thinking of that day aboard ship, and she no longer seemed able to control what was happening.

"Kerry..." Cameron's lips traveled down her neck, his hands loosening her silken tresses meanwhile and letting them cascade down her back. His fingers slid into the black shining mass of hair. Then his lips claimed hers once more.

"Cameron!" The brittle voice shattered their moment of passion, and Kerry broke away. There, on the lawn, stood Caroline, and beside her the grinning Charles!

"My dear Cameron," Charles said smoothly, a trace of

reproval in his voice, "you had only to say you wanted the wench for yourself and I would never have interfered. Really, Cam, you have no cause to berate me for bringing home one wench, when you have two waiting you here."

"Charles, shut up." Cameron's tone was murderous, and even Caroline turned upon the smirking Englishman a not-too-kind glance.

Kerry blushed hotly and, without saying a word, sped quickly across the lawn.

"Kerry!" Cameron called, but Caroline stepped forward to lay a restraining hand upon his arm.

"Let her go," she said coldly, her eyes as narrow as crescents. "I demand an explanation. I am entitled to that."

"You shall have it." Cameron glared at the arrogant woman, then strode briskly toward the house with his fiancée at his heels.

Kerry had rushed into the kitchen, had poured out some water, and had splashed it on her face. Its coolness helped, and she decided to go to her room. Voices suddenly rent the silence, and upon recognizing Caroline's, Kerry froze on the stairs.

"How could you dally outside with that slut, when all night long you acted as if I wasn't even present!"

"Don't call her that!" Cameron's harsh words were clearly audible, as was Caroline's rejoinder.

"And why not? If the shoe fits! I know what's happening. I've been expecting it! You want that girl because of Peggy! Your blood—it's tainted from that maid, that Irish girl your father took! And now his son is following in his footsteps!"

"I am not like my father!" Cameron's voice boomed out, and the sound of breaking glass sickened Kerry. "I feel nothing for the girl! How could I? She is but a servant!"

A harsh silence followed and then Caroline's voice came, hesitant and halting. "Cameron, I didn't mean . . . you won't, I mean—"

"Don't worry. I will not send you away and throw you to the wolves. Marriage with me is what you want and that you shall have. Now leave me. Leave, I say!"

Caroline rushed out of the room, up the stairs and past Kerry. In her haste she never even saw the Irish lass, and she slammed her door shut immediately. Kerry walked slowly up to her room, her feet leaden. Her weary glance fell on the dress she wore, the first nice thing she had ever owned. With an oath, she tore the wretched thing from her body and flung it far across the room, free of its hateful reminders.

Chapter Fourteen

In the wee morning hours, a young girl, garbed in a ragged blue calico dress stained with spatters of blue ink, carefully made her way across a lawn sparkling with early autumn frost. Her cloak was as old as the dress. Only her boots bore signs of a recent purchase, their shiny new leather contrasting curiously with the rest of her ragged garments. She paused only once, to stand in the midst of the great lawn and glance up at the three-windowed room where the master of the house slept. All was silent, and in the gray dawn, the square-paned windows were dark, ghostlike, and eerie. With an abrupt motion she turned her back on those windows and headed for the stables.

A horse whinnied fretfully as the young woman intruded on its sleepy domain, but placing a tattered black bag near the loft, she hiked up her skirts and climbed the ladder to the top. There lay a dirty Irish lad, snoring. His rumpled suit of clothes reeked of whiskey. Straw was imbedded in his dark hair, but the lad cared naught for that. He sighed in his sleep, and gathered a bundle of hay in his embrace, a wistful smile upon his lips.

"Trevor!"

As Kerry's voice penetrated his blissful state, the Irish lad slowly opened one reddened eye and then the other. He groaned as he recognized his tormentor, and he immediately sought to bury himself once more in the pain-free state of slumber.

"Trevor!" Her voice was insistent.

Wincing, the lad sat up. "Not so loud, for the love of Pat! Ya sound like a thousand trumpets!" Grimacing, he yawned and rubbed hay-covered hands over his face.

"Serves ya right." Kerry O'Toole settled down in a heap beside him, sniffing the odorous air indignantly. "The joys of the evening—"

"I know! Are well bought with the pain of the morn. I come from the same place as you." His eyes gradually clearing, Trevor glanced outside and became aware of the newness of the hour. The gray fogs of dawn still drifted amid the bogs. "What are you doing up and about at this hour? Is something amiss at the house?" A worried frown replaced his agonized exprsesion, and Kerry bit her lip, shaking her head. "Then what's wrong? What are you doing here, dressed like that? With yer hair stuffed up inside that cap I can't tell if yer a lad or a lass. For that matter, you could pass for a weary vagabond."

"Yer of the same mind then as Jack," Kerry said caustically while Trevor sent her a confused glance.

"Beggin' yer pardon, miss?"

"Never ya mind. I've come to say goodbye."

"Yer not leaving, miss?" Trevor's mouth gaped, and he clambered to his feet like an encumbered billy goat, nearly toppling over in the process. "But why?"

"I think it best." Kerry turned quickly away, but not before the Irish lad saw the glimmer of tears in her huge, green eyes. Sitting erect and fearless on the bed of straw she seemed an ancient Druid heroine, a Joan of Arc prepared to meet whatever should come her way.

Trevor cleared his throat several times, then finally decided on an approach. "Master Cameron will not like it," he said quickly and was rewarded with an angry glare.

"I will not cheat him, if that's what you mean!" Crooking her thumb toward the road, Kerry spoke in a calmer voice, gathering her courage as well as her resolve. "I plan to return to Philadelphia. Now that the war has turned southward, I should be able to find employment. When someone buys my indenture paper, I shall arrange to have the money sent to him to repay him for his expense."

Trevor found it hard to find a flaw in her plan but he did try.

"Who will protect you? There are dangers about, highwaymen and ruffians. Tory spies and worse. How will you travel?"

"With this." Glancing about, she displayed the gold necklace Cameron had given her. "I plan to sell it. It should more than pay my passage by coach, and when I can afford to, I will repay Master Cameron for it also."

Staring at the shimmering gold chain that shone in the dusky light, Trevor shook his head, then tried to ignore its pounding. "But why? You still haven't told me why?"

"I have to go." Kerry stood up in the straw but Trevor caught her arm. "You have to promise not to tell them where I'm going," Kerry commanded, directly returning Trevor's troubled gaze. "Promise."

"Not until you tell me why," Trevor insisted.

Kerry hesitated for a moment, then reluctantly nodded.

"I just think it would be easier for all. Caroline will make my life intolerable here, and Master Cameron feels obligated to me because of a misunderstanding we had some months ago. I doubt he'd sell my papers so it would be best if I left." Tucking the cap determinedly behind her ears, Kerry lifted her chin while Trevor crossed his arms in disagreement.

"Why don't you ask the master himself? He's a big boy. I think he can take care of himself."

"Aye. And he's also a gentleman. I think my leaving will be the best thing that's ever happened to him." Kerry recalled Cameron's words of the night before, the surety of his declaration to Caroline, and she winced once more. She had decided to go for another reason, one she dared not mention to Trevor, for she could scarcely admit it to herself: she had no desire to remain at Brentwood and watch Cameron marry this pale blond Englishwoman. Yes, for her own peace of mind, it was best to go.

"Goodbye then, Trevor." Bravely, Kerry smiled, softly curving her mouth, but her red lips trembled and Trevor fought for his own composure.

"I'll never see you again, miss. I know it. Is there no way I can change yer mind?" He followed her over to the ladder and watched her shimmy down. Dropping the last few feet to the floor, Kerry glanced up, shaking the straw from her cloak.

"No. Will ya wish me luck?"

Nodding toward her, Trevor saw the young lass smile and blow a quick kiss. Then she slipped quietly out into the gray fog. Trevor scrambled through the hay to the one window at the top of the stable, and he waited until the tip of her black cap disappeared over the hillside.

"I did promise, did I not?" With a wee smile, Trevor uncrossed the fingers of his left hand, which was hidden in his trousers pocket, before scurrying quickly down the ladder to run for the house.

"She what!" Perched on the edge of his bed, Cameron pulled on his boots, while Trevor edged toward the door.

"Aye, sir. Less than a half-hour ago. She made me promise not ta tell ya, but I am fearing for her. Ya know, these are bad times—Indians, wild animals, British soldiers, though not in that order ta be sure." Trevor's smirk disappeared at Cameron's glare, and he sought comparative safety outside the door.

Cameron struggled into his trousers and, with an oath, snatched up his coat. "Get the horses ready. Dammit! I wish

Caledonia hadn't been stolen. Get moving, lad!"

Trevor hastened to obey, a smile curving his lips. He'd been observing Cameron Brent for some time now, and he had some suspicions regarding the man's concern for the pretty Irish lass. They seemed justified now, as Cameron hastened him out of the house like a man possessed, ignoring Caroline's pertinent inquiry from the window of her room.

"Damned fool Irish lass. This is just like her. Hurry back with the saddle." Cameron chafed at the wait, striding to and fro in the stable and tapping his riding crop against his boot.

"I'm hurrying. Me fingers can fly only so fast, sir," Trevor protested, all the while fastening the strips of leather around the mare. "But why, sir, are you in such a rush? The lass is a bit of a pest, is she not? I'm sure you needn't concern yersel'. I would be happy to look for her."

"I have no doubt of that," Cameron replied dryly. "Saddle the roan for yourself and you may accompany me, although what good that will do only time will tell."

"Surely, sir." Trevor grinned, and quickly readied the smaller roan, leaping onto it with dispatch for Cameron was already galloping out of the yard.

Together they took to the main road, racing past the furnaces and the forge towns, the taverns and the salt works, then following the stage coach route to the Forks where Samuel Marryote ran the line to Long-a-Coming, Haddonfield, and Cooper's ferry in Camden. From Camden, it was only a ferry ride to the city of Philadelphia, and Cameron well knew that should his quarry reach the city it would be unlikely that he would ever find her. Amid the inhabitants of that great port, a mere serving girl would hardly be noticed. She could hide for years, if not forever.

"Hurry it up, man! We may yet catch the coach!" Cameron called, and Trevor waved to indicate he'd heard. Galloping into the yard of the Tavern at the Forks, Cameron swung down from his horse while the confused mare still tore up chunks of earth, trying to please her perplexing rider.

Trevor scarcely had time to stop before Cameron was already banging at the tavern door to rouse Richard Westcoat. That noble Englishman appeared immediately, sliding open and window and leaning out upon seeing the man below.

"The coach!" Cameron shouted. "Has it come?"

"Aye!" Westcoat yelled back. "Only a few moments ago. Wait there!" He closed the window, and soon appeared in person below, puffing from lack of breath as he raced out the door. "The coach departed just before you arrived," he repeated breathlessly, while Cameron shook the poor man in frustration.

"Did you see a small lass enter the coach? The one who came with me the day of the sale?"

"The pretty one? I cannot be sure." Richard broke from Cameron's frenzied grasp, then spoke more clearly. "A small servant did take the coach, but from a distance I could not swear it was she."

"She was wearing a cap and a cloak. Black," Trevor added helpfully, but Richard shook his head.

"Let's check with the tavern keeper. She was about early this morn. If the lass awaited the coach inside with the others, she would have seen her. Abigail!"

Richard cupped his hands as they entered the tavern, shouting the name in the echoing stillness. At once a small round woman appeared, polishing a glass on a small cloth and holding it up to the light.

"Aye, gov'ner. You called?"

"Yes. Abigail, did you see a small Irish lass take the morning stagecoach?"

"That I did. If you're meaning the one who sold me the necklace. Pretty young thing she was."

"Necklace?" Cameron asked, pushing Richard aside to question the old woman. "May I see it?"

"Oh, it's you, Mr. Brent. You gave me a start, ya did, shoving aside poor old Richard like a sack of potatoes. Sure,

I'll show it to you." Scuffling off to a worn wooden counter, Abigail dipped behind the concealing wood and retrieved a shimmering gold piece.

"That's it!" Trevor yelled as the golden chain sent oval lights dancing around the room.

Cameron examined the necklace, recognizing it at once as the one he'd given to Kerry.

"Damn it to hell!" he muttered, digging into his pocket for the appropriate coin. "I'd like it back." But before he could toss Richard the coins, Westcoat declined.

"Keep it, Cameron. 'Tis not fitting that you should pay for it twice. When you get the lass back, see that she keeps it. Otherwise we may all wind up in the poorhouse."

Trevor sauntered forward, not one to long endure these Englishmen bragging. "And how do you know she'll be back?" he demanded, provoking an enraged glare from Cameron.

Placing a hand on his friend's shoulder, Westcoat gave the Irish lad a knowing look.

"I've never known Cameron to fail once he sets his sights on something, be it a ship or a lass. And I'm not about to worry now." Smiling confidently, Richard nodded to Trevor who nonetheless faced Cameron defiantly.

"Well, I don't think she will come of her own accord, so what will you do now?"

"If I travel alone I may outdistance the coach and arrive at Long-a-Coming before it does," Cameron said thoughtfully but Richard interrupted, taking Cameron aside.

"Aye, but Cameron we have trouble of our own. You see—"

"It will have to wait," Cameron declared. He started outside, but Richard followed determinedly, grasping his arm and forcing him to listen.

"You don't understand. I just got word this morning from General Benedict Arnold in Philadelphia that the British have set sail from New York and are heading for the Jerseys."

"What?" Cameron halted abruptly and turned to face his friend. Disbelief played over his dark features and his gray gaze was slatelike, his jaw tight. "When? And how many ships sail?"

"Twenty. They departed last night. Washington has sent troops to protect Elizabethtown, but we've got to get the ships out. Chestnut Neck is virtually unprotected. And should they get so far up the Mullica—"

"They could reach the iron works and destroy the village." Cameron finished the sentence, then swore in mute frustration. "All right, Trevor," he called to the waiting lad. "I'm sending you to catch the coach. Should you reach the lass in Long-a-Coming, bring her straight home. I trust you can see to that much, after you let her walk off this morning." Cameron cocked a dark eyebrow at the squirming lad who protested in vain.

"What was I to do? She told me—"

"And I'm telling you to bring her back. I've business to tend to, but I will join you at home as soon as I can."

Cameron's brow was knitted in anxiety; his usual complacency was gone. "Sir, is something wrong?" Trevor asked, worried by his employer's look, and Cameron nodded.

"The worst has come. I have no time to explain. Be off! And don't return without her."

As Trevor scurried off and jumped onto the horse, Cameron stood with Richard and watched him ride away, hearing the heavy clomp of hooves in the peaceful morning quiet.

"Maybe they don't intend to come here," Richard said optimistically but Cameron shook his head grimly.

"No. Since the *Gazette* published reports of the capture of the *Rising Sun*, the *Governor Henry*, and the *William* and the *Nancy*, the British have been enraged. Up until now we've tried to keep our privateering operations quiet and the British have considered us an annoyance, much like a Jersey mosquito. But publicly advertising the capture of some of their prized vessels and the sale of their cargoes, that was a bit much for our loyal cousins to take. They will come here, and we can only hope they will not venture upstream to the furnace."

"I'm afraid you're right." Unable to escape Cameron's logic, Richard followed him back to the wharf, there to plan the defense.

Kerry O'Toole leaned back on the uncushioned seat of the stagecoach, bracing her feet against the scuffed wooden floor. When the coach hit a rut in the dirt road, she lurched against the rotund merchant beside her. That man's snores continued uninterrupted, however, and as Kerry pulled herself upright she was grateful for his girth. She noted that straining silver buttons attempted to hold the two sides of his waistcoat together. Then, placing her bag at her feet, she sighed, drawing her slender form into the far corner of the coach, but sleep eluded her.

I've escaped! she thought, but no elation followed. The same sense of duty that had driven her to leave the verdant island she missed terribly, but never so much as this moment, haunted her. Ghosts of the past mingled with those of the present and the thoughts they precipitated were too much for Kerry to bear.

"And where might you be going, lass?" A voice from across the coach interrupted her private perusals, and Kerry glanced up, grateful for the intrusion. A silver-spectacled man peered out of the darkest corner of the coach, his gnarled hands resting on black homespun trousers as he leaned forward. He had glistening white hair, a sanguine smile, and twinkling blue eyes. A worn book was clutched between his fingers and hooked between that and his thumb, Kerry could see a thinly concealed clay pipe.

"Philadelphia," Kerry answered. The man was surveying her as intensely as she perused him. Kerry smiled, feeling suddenly awkward.

"Philadelphia?" He nodded, drawing closer as the merchant snuffled in his sleep. "And why would a lass like yourself be traveling to that great city?" A kindly light shone in his round sparkling eyes, like the flicker of a candle, and Kerry responded with the same warmth.

"To find work," she said candidly. "I need to find employment." Self-consciously, she drew the ragged black cloak about her shoulders as the man's eyes flickered over her poor garb.

"A lass like yourself must have many talents. I suppose you cook and sew?" At Kerry's puzzled nod, the man smiled and tamped a curiously spicy mixture down into his clay pipe. "Have you ever tended a bar?" he asked, puffing on the pipe while wiping the tobacco residue on his sleeve.

"No." Kerry said hesitantly. "But I'm sure I can learn whatever skills I'd be needing."

"Good." The man smiled as if something was settled in his mind, and he leaned back, still surveying the lass with that odd smile while puffing contentedly. "I come from a place called Haddonfield. Have you ever heard tell of it?"

"Haddonfield," Kerry repeated thoughtfully, then a bit of conversation drifted back to her and she recalled Trevor's mention of a tavern in such a place. "Yes, I have. It is a stop along the coach route, is it not?"

"Yes. A small town, but a very nice one if I might say so. There is a tavern on the main highway called the Indian King. Only it is not called the Indian King now—it is called Creighton House. Do you think you might like to work there?"

Kerry glanced at the worn clothing the man wore, at his work-hardened hands, his callused boots. A vague suspicion crept into her mind, and indignation arose in her for she felt this man was mocking her. "And who are you to be offering me a job there?" Kerry snapped, her eyes wide with suspicion. "You may find my circumstances amusing, but I can do without the like of your jokes!" Her color high and her teeth clenched, she was amazed to see the man melt into laughter. He chuckled deep within his belly while the young girl stared.

"Begging your pardon, miss." He wiped away a tear while his midriff still shook. "It has been so long since a lass accused me of being anything but honorable that I could not help myself. I am Hugh Creighton, owner and proprietor of Creighton House."

He extended a coarse hand to Kerry while confusion, and although embarrassment played across the young lass's face, she shook it wholeheartedly.

"I apologize, sir. But I have learned to be careful and not take anyone at his word. These are not the best of times." Her cheeks still flushed and her hair tucked under her cap, she resembled a poor urchin, but the elderly man found himself smiling at her.

"Aye, you said a mouthful there. But I am sincere about the work. I cannot promise employment far past spring, for I have a man enlisted in the Continental service and I've promised him his job when he returns. Until then, though, the position would be yours."

"As a serving wench?" Kerry said distrustfully and the man chuckled once more.

"I do keep a tavern. But it is also an inn, with a dining room, a ballroom, and several guest rooms upstairs. I have a few servants, but many of them fled when the British occupied Philadelphia and I have need of a girl." The man held the pipe between his teeth as he spoke, and Kerry watched in fascination for that object did not interfere with his speech in the slightest.

"I don't know," she mused. "You see, I had a different plan. I was looking for something more permanent."

"Well then." He leaned forward a bit, bracing his hands on his wide legs as he spoke. "Why not work for me throughout the winter? The air is chill outside today and it will grow colder still. You can weather out the winter months and journey to Philadelphia when it is warmer." Seeing indecision in those large green eyes, Creighton pressed his point. "A street corner in Philadelphia can be mighty frosty when the northern winds blow."

As if to reaffirm his statement, the wind whistled up from the bogs, penetrating every crack in the stagecoach.

"Think on the offer, my friend." Hugh smiled. "We have some traveling time before we arrive."

Kerry nodded, grateful that he did not insist on a quick answer. Drawing the cloak more closely about her, she curled up in the corner and fell asleep, but silver-colored eyes troubled her rest.

"Long-a-Coming!" a voice shouted, and Kerry came awake, sleepily surveying the town. A log chapel and a tavern stood near the road, the latter attracting the travelers who leaped off the top of the coach to quench their thirst. Hugh Creighton joined them with much enthusiasm, as did the other passengers of the coach. Even the slumbering merchant roused himself enough to stumble out, but Kerry disembarked last, pausing to count out the remains of her coins.

Tossing the bag over her shoulder, she started for the tavern in a stooping position, struggling to keep the cloak closed against the wind and her bag in place. The thunder of hooves stopped her, and with her back to the frightful breeze, she cupped her hand over her eyes to observe a familiar-looking roan charge into the tavern yard at full gallop.

"Trevor!" The word burst from her lips as the Irish lad swung down from the horse. He ran to greet her, somewhat breathless.

"Kerry! Am I glad I found you! I mean . . ." He huffed, struggling for air while Kerry's foot tapped angrily upon the cold dirt ground. "I mean . . . he found out! He sent me, Kerry! What was I to do?"

"And you naturally told him just where I was going." Her words struck Trevor like flint on slate and the poor lad, confused, wiped away at his sweat-streaked face.

"Ah, Kerry lass! 'Twas no great feat for him ta see himself! There is but one coach and one place where you would be safe! Please return now before it's too late!" Trevor smiled ingratiatingly, but Kerry remained unaffected.

"Not on yer life, Trevor Shanahan! To think you betrayed me! You, of all people! Well, I'll be taking no memories of friends I thought were mine!" Kerry started indignantly for the tavern and Trevor ran behind her, his voice harsh in the cold air.

"Kerry lass, don't be saying such things. You know I'm yer friend. If I was not, why would I come? Say you'll come back."

Beside the tavern door, she faced him squarely, her shoulders erect, even under the weight of the bag. "That I won't do and you well know why."

Stepping inside the tavern, she ignored Trevor's protests and ordered hot coffee, sipping from the steaming mug while he made a last-ditch effort to change her mind.

"Kerry, he wants you back! He flew into a frenzy when he found out you'd gone." Wisely, Trevor kept the information on how Cameron had found out to himself. "Why he was all set to come after you himself."

Tossing her head, Kerry asked pertinently, "Then why didn't he?"

"Well, ya see . . . some emergency came up at the Neck and he had to tend to his ships—"

"Tend to his ships! Why that English . . ." Kerry choked on her righteous rage. "He ran after you fast enough! Tend to his ships . . . why I'm sure he's glad to be rid of me! No, Trevor! Nothing you can say now will change me mind! Let him tend to his old ships." With a huff, she shoved aside the bench just as the Irish lad was taking a sip of his frothy beer, making him spill half of it. Stamping to the coach, Kerry stepped quickly inside, Trevor following her, mug in hand.

"But, Kerry me darlin'."

"Coach leaves!" the driver called, and with a lurch, the carriage started down the lonely dirt trail. Kerry peered out of the window to see Trevor waving his ale behind her.

"Damn it!" she thought, and huddled back into her seat. She was certain now that Trevor had told Cameron, and that her former employer knew of her destination. And he has connections in Philadelphia, she thought, recalling the solicitor he'd stopped to see. It would be a simple matter for him to trace me. Her gaze then fell on Hugh Creighton, whose bespectacled eyes were fixed on his book. Haddonfield, Kerry thought, and an amusing light danced in her eyes. He would never think to look there! That prospect was most pleasing. She laid a hand on Hugh's leg, startling him so he nearly dropped his book.

"Sir? About the position we discussed . . . I would be most happy to accept."

"Wonderful." Hugh smiled, placing his rough hand above her small one. "Haddonfield is a more lovely place than any . . . well, than any I've ever seen. And I have a niece close in age to you. You will like her, I know." With a pleased grin, Hugh shook her hand to seal their arrangement.

Chapter Fifteen

As the carriage rolled into town, Kerry peered out the coach window, pleasantly surprised by the scene that greeted her. Narrow cobbled streets were flanked by tall, three-story brick buildings, their shutters open to welcome the meager evening light. Basketlike buckets of iron hung from tall posts, filled with coals that burned with a warm orange glow in the darkening fall night. The stagecoach pulled up adjacent to the tavern which was to become Kerry's new home. This one was larger than Bodine's and far more stately. It had a whitewashed brick front and bold red shutters, and a sign—Creighton House—swung lazily in the cool night air, creaking as it did so.

"It's not much, miss," Hugh Creighton said in an attempt at modesty but pride was in his voice. "Just a tavern."

"And a right fine one it is, from the look of it," Kerry responded, and Hugh's face glowed with pleasure as he leaped out of the coach, followed by the lass.

"The taproom is to the left, the dining room to the right." Kerry stepped up a single polished white step and entered the tavern, as filled with awe as she'd been when she'd entered Brentwood. The comparison entered her mind but she quickly discarded it. Brentwood was of the past now, and best not thought of.

"Is this the kitchen?" Kerry entered a cheery room that boasted a huge fireplace, a cold stone floor, and an assortment of kettles. A serving wench scuttled in and placed a dirty dish on a long table.

"Aye." Hugh frowned as the lass departed with much speed. "And upstairs are the bedrooms and the ballroom." A cook, easily as large as a comfortable armchair sauntered out to the kitchen and surveyed Kerry suspiciously before turning away to stir the contents of a pot. "They're arriving, suh" was her only remark. And she did not raise her eyes but continued stirring, her white cap staring at Kerry in place of a face.

"Of course." Hugh did not seem to take exception to the woman's manner, but he turned to Kerry.

"The tavern closes from four until supper. It is beginning to fill now. Will you be able to begin tonight or are you too tired from the ride?"

His voice told Kerry that answering in the negative would be a mistake so although her bones ached from the jostling she'd received on the journey, she forced herself to smile and nod pleasantly.

"I can begin at once, sir. There is no need to wait."

"Very well." Hugh smiled expectantly. "If you put your things upstairs, I will instruct you as to your duties. The girl will show you where."

The serving girl had reappeared, and upon hearing this news she rolled her eyes. Grabbing Kerry's elbow and giving it a decided pinch, she shoved her toward the stairs.

"Up ya go. Come on then. We ain't got all day!" Her rude push almost sent Kerry to her knees. Turning about angrily, Kerry met her companion's astonished face, and she pointed at the wench's long nose.

"You listen ta me. If ya want ta keep that hand, ya'll keep it ta yersel'!"

The serving wench, once she'd gotten over her initial shock, paused to take a second look at this brazen Irish girl.

New servants were usually docile and easy to manage, but this lass brooked no abuse. She was small of stature, but this Irish girl meant what she said. If any doubt of that remained in the serving girl's mind, the sight of the Irish lass's fist tightening meaningfully around the handle of her bag did much to alleviate them.

"Oh well, miss, I'm sorry then. I did not think you the stuffy kind." She cackled when the fire dimmed a bit in Kerry's eyes and the Irish girl smiled.

"No matter. I just don't like ta be shoved. Now if you'll show me the room we can both get ta work."

The serving wench nodded. She appeared in no hurry now that Hugh Creighton was no longer about, and took her time in climbing the stairs. Stopping before a door, she fitted a key to the lock and turned the knob.

"The servant's rooms." She smirked and made a mock curtsey that Kerry politely ignored. Stepping inside, Kerry tried hard not to show her dismay. The room was so cold a mantle of frost made the windows sparkle. An involuntary shiver shook Kerry as she set her bag at the foot of a narrow bed, one of three sandwiched together.

"Cold, ain't it?" The wench smiled. Kerry saw two missing teeth. "'Tain't all that bad now. But wait until winter, when them winds blow."

"You mean we cannot have a fire?" Kerry asked, incredulous, and the wench shook her head.

"At night we're permitted. But firewood is scarce and costly since the war, and Mr. Creighton says we must conserve. *We* must, if ya get my meaning!" Shaking a pitcher, then turning it upside down to display the block of ice inside, she shrugged. "But ya get enough ta eat and we only work fifteen hours. That ain't so bad. Nancy's me name, girl. What's yours?"

"Kerry. Kerry O'Toole." Kerry's gaze danced briefly around the room once more before returning to the serving girl. Her own shabby clothes seemed quite good by comparison for the lass's dress was badly worn and a tear under one arm was visible as the girl stretched out a roughened hand to clasp Kerry's.

"Glad ta meet ya, miss. Since we'll be bunkin' together, it's best we get along. I've got ta get downstairs now. Mr. Creighton, he's a good man, but he keeps 'is eye on the clock." With a wink, Nancy sidled out the door, but she still watched as the Irish lass packed away her few belongings.

It's a good thing I sold that necklace, Kerry thought, for it was not until she sent Nancy a questioning look that the wench gave her a birdlike nod and disappeared. "For something tells me 'twould be gone by morn," she said softly.

By morn. And what would that hold here? All of a sudden, Kerry began to doubt her rash impulse to leave Brentwood. But there was no turning back now, and being an O'Toole, she had only one alternative. She would have to make the best of it.

"All right lass. Get them drinks out," the bartender growled. He was an amiable enough man, but he saved his friendliness for the paying customers, wasting none of it on the girls who raced about serving drinks. Still, working in the tavern was far better than being assigned to the dining room. "You don't get all the food ta cart," Nancy had said in the hall.

Unbearably delicious odors came from the dining area, but the servants could not eat until after the diners left. Then the taproom girls and the dining-room girls grabbed a quick meal.

"It's best to wait until they are well in their cups. Then they don't realize so soon that you're gone." Eileen, a buxom blonde, gave Kerry this advice as she passed her with a tray of foaming ale.

"Over here with that tray, lass," a booming voice shouted, and Kerry glanced over to see a drunken man shouting at the blonde.

"See what I mean?" Eileen smiled, then pushed past grasping hands to place the tray on the table.

Kerry found that she had much to learn about being a barmaid, for she'd been working only a few minutes when a shopkeeper from the town, known for his generosity with his coin and his prowess with women, leaned over and pinched her soundly on her round bottom.

"Aye, me pretty lass. You must be new. I don't recall—" His next words were drowned in a cascade of ale, and the man seated with him stared, horrified, at Kerry.

"Did you see that! The bitch nearly drowned me! Well, I'll see to you, miss!" He clambered to his feet, golden droplets trickling from his lacy jabot, his silk waistcoat, and his brocade trousers.

"Is there a problem here?" Hugh Creighton appeared out of nowhere, and Kerry breathed a sigh of relief as the shopkeeper turned his reddened glare to him.

"Yes, indeed! This lass poured a pitcher of beer all over me!" The merchant huffed indignantly while Hugh turned his blue gaze on Kerry. His eyes were not so friendly now, but when Kerry opened her mouth to protest and tell her side of the story, he sent her a warning glance then smiled benevolently on his customer.

"Rest assured that it won't happen again, sir. Your drinks tonight are on the house and the price of them will come out of the lass's wages. Will that satisfy you, Mr. Ferguson?"

The Scotchman, mollified by this offer, nodded and returned to his table with a satisfied air.

"I trust this will not happen again?" Hugh Creighton asked and Kerry stammered her reply.

"No, but . . ."

"Good." Considering the matter done, Hugh returned to his duties and left Kerry staring wonderingly after him.

"My drinks, wench! Bring up the drinks!" a burly man shouted, and Kerry scuttled back to the bar to retrieve the tray. More wary now, she stayed well out of the reach of the patrons, ignoring their comments on her beauty or their questions as to the cost of a night with her. A tall, dark man of about twenty-five years drank more freely than his companions and from his guttural speech, Kerry guessed him to be one of the Hessians who'd fled the British army to join with the Continentals. Such men abounded here. They spoke in hushed tones of Washington and the war, few of them optimistic, and they drowned their fears in liberal quantities of cider, rum, and ale, staring gloomily into their tankards as the evening lengthened.

"Cheer up lads!" Eileen smiled as she swept by, balancing a tray on her arms as one of the men tried to pull her into his embrace. "None of that if you be wanting yer drink!" She laughed, and the men gazed at her appreciatively as she stooped to place the tray.

"Get yerself some food real quick. I think I can hold them off a bit."

Kerry did as she was told, racing back to the kitchen to procure a few cold scones, a chunk of cold beef covered with congealing gravy, and a slice of cheese.

"Wot's that you got, miss?" the cook asked without turning her head. "Meat's for the diners. It ain't for the likes of you."

Defiantly, Kerry plopped another piece into her mouth while the cook bellowed. "Get out of 'ere missy before I takes a strap to you mesel'! The master will hear of this, he will."

Placing a scone in her pocket, Kerry darted back to the taproom where Eileen, six tankards clutched in her two hands, smiled gratefully.

"Here, give me three." Kerry relieved the comely blonde of the tankards and placed them on the table. The Hessian muttered something unintelligible to his companions; then, as Kerry tried to leave, he swept her into his lap, his hands traveling boldly over the neckline of her faded blue dress.

"Get off me!" she shouted, and the other men roared as if

this was a fine joke, slapping their legs with glee. She struggled to rise, but the German's arms were like a steel vise gripping her about the waist.

"I like you, Liebchen." The Hessian grinned, white teeth shining in his swarthy face. "You come vith me tonight."

"I will not!" Kerry yelled, but the huge man merely laughed and slid a hand up her skirt, refusing to be daunted. Kerry grabbed at the hand, but now the other was opening the front of her dress, fondling one round bosom while the enraged lass gasped.

"You come vith me, *Liebchen*. I vill make it verth your trouble—" The Hessian howled with pain and quickly got to his feet, dropping the lass to the floor in order to hold a throbbing foot. "Vat do you think you are doing!" His face was a mask of rage mingled with pain. His black eyes blazed with anger.

"I'm so sorry." Kerry smiled, got up, and curtseyed politely. "'Twould seem me balance is not so good when I'm pulled about by a jackass. Indeed the same fate befell me donkey when he tried such."

The men guffawed, while the Hessian turned a confused glance on his equally swarthy companion.

"Vat does she say?" he asked quizzically, scratching his dark head. It was a moment before the laughter stopped and the man alongside him could speak.

"She says you're the most handsome man she's ever laid eyes on, but she's taken for the night." His companion laughed. Kerry smiled, and the Hessian turned an ear-to-ear grin on the lass, patting his firm belly and nodding appreciatively.

"Goot lass. Know a goot one vhen I see one." He was chuckling in his ale as Kerry left the table, the others raising a glass to her in a mock cheer.

The night dragged on in much the same manner, and by the time Eileen told Kerry she could retire to her room, the young girl ached right down to her bones. Climbing the stairs was agonizing, and she fell into the icy bed, the coarse blanket providing little protection from the cold. Her exhaustion was such that she fell immediately asleep, however, not realizing until morning that her drawer had been rifled and the last of her coins taken.

Daybreak, October 6, 1778

Cameron Brent stood at the prow of his ship, a spyglass fastened to his eye. At his elbow was Richard Westcoat and on shore, in the surrounding red cedars and dried summer ferns, a company of about one thousand men were secreted. Scattered from the village of Chestnut Neck to the fort between the Little Egg Harbor River and Nacote Creek, this company was made up of tired recruits under Pulaski, raw militiamen—those very same drunken lads that Kerry had seen "practicing" at Bodine's, a handful of men from Philadelphia, and troops under Colonel Furman. Supplemented by iron workers, this ragged defense was all Chestnut Neck had to oppose the mighty British Navy as its ships glided into view.

"How many?" Richard whispered and Cameron frowned.

"Two, three, five sloops. Smaller craft and flags." Cameron's voice dropped as he pronounced this vision and the men reacted as if doom were upon them.

"Five sloops! Holy Mother of God! Five! Did you hear that!" they muttered and then became silent once more.

"Dammit! If only I could have gotten a cannon!" Richard opined, while Cameron shrugged impatiently.

"If they believe we have one, perhaps they'll retreat."

"What are the chances of that?" Richard asked hopefully, and Cameron snorted.

"Next to none. Wait...." Adjusting the spyglass, Cameron gazed at the scene before his eyes, and a small smile crept across his face, enlarging as what he saw became a certainty.

"What is it, Cam?" Richard asked, his excitement barely suppressed.

"They . . . they've grounded! The *Granby* and the *Greenwich* have grounded!"

A small cheer arose from the men, growing stronger as they rushed to the river. The two huge sloops, armed and weighty, were soundly entrenched on the thick sand bar separating the Mullica from the bay, as motionless as sticks submerged in mud.

The Continentals clasped hands and danced with glee along the shoreline. Richard and Cameron were less enthusiastic, however, and with the glass positioned firmly on the channel, Cameron saw the flagship, *Zebra,* break through the bar.

"They're coming!" he shouted to the men while Richard charged down from the ship, heading for the village to warn the others. A grim quiet replaced the merriment of a moment ago, and the men dove beneath the brush, tension gripping their very bones. Those who had not faced the Redcoats feared the unknown, while those who had met them felt a much greater fear, that of a relentless enemy.

"Vigilant! The flatboats, tenders, and other craft are through! Now the *Nautilus!"* One by one Cameron called out the names as the fearsome ships slid slowly through the narrow and tricky river. Positioning his musket, Cameron took aim at the massive *Zebra.* The vessel moved with agonizing slowness through the swampy waters, but Cameron did not move, keeping his head turned toward the oncoming threat and praying as he had not in years. The *Zebra* slowed as it neared the fort, then waited for the *Nautilus* and the *Vigilant* before turning purposefully and bombarding it. Cameron winced at the gunfire, all of it from the British ships. Any hope of an English retreat died with that gunfire, for now the troops realized that the Continentals had no cannon. They knew they could proceed with ease.

The Redcoats swarmed up the beach, pouring out of the ships in a red tide and swarming over the shores. The Continentals, armed only with muskets against the British bayonets, found themselves retreating while Cameron fired furiously from his ship. "Fire!" Westcoat was yelling, but tired and worn, the troops vanished into the woods, leaving the village virtually unprotected.

Cameron's musket peppered the murky waters with lead, keeping the Redcoats from reaching his ship, but only for a short time. The men on board dove over the side, their splashes punctuating the gunfire as they hastened to escape. "Come man!" a seaman at Cameron's elbow called. But Brent rudely shook him off. He concentrated with all his might on the twenty-foot-square patch of water beneath him, oblivious to all else. In his mind he saw the village aflame, the iron works destroyed, and Kerry . . . Cameron cursed his foolishness. He had refused to admit what he felt about her, and now she was probably back at Brentwood, in danger. Fuming at his belated recognition of the truth and at his inability to help her, he swore if he ever got out of this, things would be different in spite of the Irish lass's stubborn pride. Strangely, his reluctance to wed had disappeared. He smiled grimly as he pictured Kerry's response to his proposal.

Cameron saw the last of the Continentals disappear into the safety of the surrounding woods and the British boarded his ship. Dropping his musket, he waited as the British naval officer, garbed in the hated scarlet took him captive.

"You decided to go down with your ship?" The officer smiled nastily while the men tied Cameron's hands with his own rope. "Well, you will have the pleasure of seeing it burn, along with the rest of this place. Take him to the *Zebra!*" he shouted and the marines rushed to do his bidding, leading Cameron down to the shore. As he stood on the sandy ground, he saw the marines take torches to his ship, their faces gleeful and triumphant.

"There she goes!" A young man shouted as flames slowly licked the sides of the vessel, then crept over the deck and the mast. Instantly the night was illuminated by a flaming tongue of fire that scorched the air like the breath of a fearful dragon. Then all was still, only a charcoal skeleton of a ship remaining. The other vessels met the same fate, all captured English ships that could not be gotten out of the channel in time.

"You see that?" a marine whispered at Cameron's shoulder, provoking a frozen stare from the ironmaster. "That's what comes of your Continentals. You joined the wrong side of the war." The marine laughed while Cameron looked at him, unsmiling.

"The price of freedom was never cheap," Cameron finally replied, and the man's laughter sputtered into angry silence. "And I would gladly pay that price a hundred times."

"You talk big now, lad. But you just might pay with your life. Inside with you now." The marine shoved Cameron toward the *Zebra,* and he stepped up the gangplank of the sloop with the dignity of a lord. The marine muttering behind him, he was ushered down into the hold, then pushed into murky darkness. A door slammed shut and Cameron was alone.

It seemed as if hours had passed but actually it was a short time later when Cameron heard the slamming of a door. From his cramped position on a crate, he could make out men's voices in the passage, and a rat scuffling around in the cargo.

"I think we should go for the ironworks," a cultured voice suggested, but another interrupted vehemently.

"No! I have it from the best authority that the countryside has been notified of our attack. Troops are being sent while we speak, and should we advance farther upriver, we would be trapped between the Mullica and the bay. No, it is better to content ourselves with burning the village. We should not risk all for the works."

The village, Cameron thought. His throat tightened as he thought of his home and of those waiting there. He pressed his ear to the damp wood of the wall and listened carefully.

"Aye, the village of Chestnut Neck. That stands no longer, to be sure! But Brentwood is just upstream..."

"And I say you've gone mad!" The other man responded angrily. "Dammit Colins, my spy was Tory and familiar with the area! He told us right of Osbourne Island, of the sand bar, and of the village! If we pay no heed to his words now, all of this may be for naught!"

After an agonizing minute, the man named Colins agreed. "Yes, you're right. We should turn our attention to the island and to freeing the *Greenwich* and the *Granby*."

"What of the bloke below?" It was a coarser voice. The man Colins, obviously the officer in charge, spoke once more.

"Take him to Ellis. We haven't the time for prisoners, or the accommodations. We will turn him over to the general. He is not camped far from here. He will see to our patriotic hero."

"Brilliant!" The other officer chuckled. "Yes, it would be rich to see him hanged, rebel fool! A lesser fate he does not deserve."

This last sentence brought forth mutual laughter, then the door closed and Cameron was once again alone.

"Bring us another beer, miss."

The familiar words rang out, and Kerry glanced up from the bar, smiling to the patron to indicate she'd heard him. The tavern was full this Saturday night, the third since she'd come to work at Creighton house. Grasping the foaming pewter tankards on one hand, the Irish lass hastened to the table and placed the ale before the ample-bellied merchant.

"Aye, you're a fine little lass. Comely, too." The merchant grinned, his round blue eyes twinkling with a naughty gleam. Kerry's mouth curved politely, but she stayed on the opposite side of the round table, next to the printer who dozed on his folded arms.

"Thank you, sir. Will that be all, sir?" Kerry smiled and the man sighed lustily, sipping the frothing ale for solace. A small tinkling sound drifted in from the street, and pausing at the next table to pick up two empty mugs, she listened to the lilting music.

"A fiddler!" announced the elderly gent near the window. Polishing the steaming glass with his lace sleeve, he pered out, clapping his gloved hands in time with the tune.

"A fiddler!" The cry resounded through the tavern as the sweet wafting music came to the ears of the crowd. Kerry stood near the window, entranced by the sound. If there was anything dearer to the Irish heart than a fiddle she did not know of it. The music reminded her of the pubs back home, and she felt nostalgic.

Obviously the patrons were of the same humor for the fiddler was escorted inside despite his protests, and was given a place of honor near the huge brick fireplace.

"Play us a tune, lad," the men shouted. The fiddler, a tiny elfin-looking man with a twisted nose and a golden smile, acknowledged the crowd with a whimsical nod, then, ever practical, he placed a battered, black felt cap at his feet. Sentiment was one thing, but a good meal and a warm bed cost money. He was not disappointed, however, for the townspeople longed to hear the old tunes and they kept his cup full and the coins falling.

"'Greensleeves'!" In response to the shouted request, the fiddler took up his instrument and sweet, soulful chords wafted through the tavern. There was not a dry eye by the time he was done. The crowd shouted for more.

Kerry saw a wagonman lift a thick finger and she rushed to the bar for his stewed Quaker. "Make me a hot toddy while yer at it," a soldier at his table shouted. Kerry placed the order at the bar, then took the poker and thrust it into the fire, her eyes never leaving the fiddler as he played. When the poker was a bright blood red, she thrust it into the cup, heating the rum until it sizzled and foamed. She took the hot rum to the soldier, the Quaker to his tablemate.

"Ah, a hot drink on a cold night. Nothing like it to warm a man's bones." The soldier sighed and then sipped the hot drink cautiously. The tavern grew warm from the heat of the fire, and the turnspit dog ran futilely after a hanging bone, while the metal wheels clanked in the fireplace, rotating a roast of beef that sizzled and sputtered. The bartender occasionally sliced off several huge slabs of the meat, setting them aside for those who wanted food with their drink. He also siphoned off some for himself in the process, but as the innkeeper never noticed, no one was the wiser.

"I daresay it's been a long time since a fiddler graced our halls," Hugh Creighton's voice boomed out right behind Kerry, and she nearly dropped a tank of ale.

"Sorry, lass. I did not mean to frighten you."

Kerry glanced at the wall, then at the corridor behind her that led to the kitchen. Hugh had not come from the corridor.

"You . . . I know you did not come from the kitchen," she said thoughtfully, "so that leaves but one thing . . ." Kerry suddenly recalled Trevor's bragging about this tavern and about the secret passageway it contained.

Hugh's eyes clouded and he watched the lass closely. "And where do you think I came from? Thin air?" His voice was jovial, but the expression in his eyes was not.

Kerry grinned. "Aye, ya must have come out when I wasna' looking. Scared the life from me, sir," she teased. At the sight of this smiling wench, her sea-colored eyes framed in thick black lashes, Hugh forgot his annoyance and sent her toward the bar.

"See to their wants before they tear down the place. The

fiddler should bring us a good night."

His words were prophetic for the patrons imbibed freely of the ale and rum, scarcely giving the fiddler time to sip from his own cup before they clamored for more tunes. "Meat!" called the elderly gentleman tamping a fat cigar on the table's edge. "Lass, bring me meat!"

Kerry hastened to do his bidding, waiting near the fire while the barkeep sliced the meat. "It's getting a bit cold," he advised her, subtly placing his own lot in his pocket. "Ask for hot gravy in the kitchen."

Nodding, Kerry took the dish and ventured to the kitchen. The cook did not acknowledge her presence or even look up from her stirring, so Kerry got the gravy without interference and then made her way back to the bar. A group of military men lounged in the passageway, and something about them, something different, struck Kerry. Upon closer inspection, she gasped audibly. They were wearing the scarlet uniform of the British regiments!

"Redcoats!" Kerry exclaimed, and the closest young man heard her and glanced up, giving her a penetrating look.

"Something wrong, miss?" he inquired politely. With a firm shake of her head, Kerry rushed past him and handed the gentleman his meat, her hand trembling.

"What's the matter, lass? You look as though you've seen a ghost!" the white-haired man wheezed, laughing at his own joke. But then his eyes followed Kerry's and he saw the reason for her fear. One by one the men in the tavern grew quiet, and finally the fiddler stopped playing and glanced about in obvious confusion until his eyes fell upon the hated scarlet coats.

The soldiers were filing in the front door now, openly claiming the bar as their own and taking over tables and chairs. Kerry's hands gripped a tankard of ale so hard her knuckles were white. She watched this dread intrusion with a sick feeling. Even Eileen, eternally gay and laughing, now looked like a ghost of her former self.

"Sir! May I have the reason for this intrusion?" Hugh Creighton's voice rang out easily in the silence, and the officer in charge stepped forward.

"Prisoner escort. We have orders to quarter the men along the way."

Hugh flushed a brilliant red, his face nearly matching the man's cloth. "In spite of my objections, of course. This happened back in June, and in the spring. . . ." Hugh's voice trailed off, for the officer waved a hand, dismissing this commoner, and stepped up to the bar.

"You will see to my men," he ordered.

The barkeep scowled, but the Redcoats bayonets left him little choice in the matter and he served up the drinks with dispatch, the metal tankards clanking against the wooden bar.

"Play," the officer ordered. Standing before the fire, his face oranged by the flames and his silver buttons gleaming like tiny suns, he appeared satanic, and the fiddler openly quaked. "Play, little man!" he shouted, and with amazing swiftness, the fiddle was crooked in the man's arm and music came forth.

Eileen and Kerry resumed their work, filling the soldiers orders while trying to avoid their advances. Days and weeks on the road had left these men famished for the sight of a woman, and the two wenches working in the tavern would have tempted less brazen lads. Kerry dodged groping hands and used her foot to dissuade many a lad from molesting her.

"That's one mean hellcat," an English voice remarked, and the other men roared. Speaking of her as if she were not present, the Redcoats made a wager as to who would be taking this wench for a roll this very night. Kerry's cheeks burned and it took a massive effort to maintain her silence, but instinct told her they were hoping to goad her into a display of temper.

"Hot wine!" they called with a vengeance, and Kerry heated the poker until it was white hot, boiling the purple liquid into a volcanic noisesome mixture. Satisfied, she innocently placed the cups before the Redcoats, secretly amused as they sputtered. "That wench tore the roof off my mouth!" A young blond cried, while the others guffawed at the lad's lack of prowess with drink.

"If you can't keep up with men don't drink with them." An officer of about thirty-five years solemnly advised. Taking up his own cup, he met a similar fate and fat tears started from his eyes.

"It's fine," he choked out, and the others laughed, then tested their manhood on the boiling liquor. Kerry stood far away from the group during this proceeding, grinning with pleasure, and she was surprised to see the cook standing beside her, a satisfied smile upon her heavy lips.

"Serve them right." She grinned and patted Kerry's back. "Them's what killed me old man, they did. That's why I'm stuck here, cooking for the rich folk. You did good, miss." Then, as if surprised at her own garrulousness, she slipped back to the kitchen leaving an amazed Kerry behind her.

"More ale!" a Redcoat called, and the barkeep waved her over. As she stepped around a group of the soldiers sitting in the hall, Kerry felt a slight tug on her dress. She pulled back, but the hand held persistently onto her gown. Kerry angrily turned to face the man.

"Let go of me dress," she shouted; then her mouth fell open and the blood drained from her face. There, chained and on the floor between the Redcoats, was Cameron Brent!

Chapter Sixteen

Recovering from her initial shock, Kerry blinked to make certain it was really him. But his elegant profile was unmistakable. His chiseled features were calm and emotionless, but he gave her a slight smile.

Holding up the chains for her inspection, he waited until the soldier beside him looked away before remarking, "Good evening, Kerry. I would get up, but I do not think they'd allow it."

Kerry started to reply, but a soldier appeared, holding an empty mug out.

"Do you think we may get some drink tonight?" he asked.

"Surely," Kerry answered, distractedly. "I'll be back," she whispered to Cameron, then took up a pitcher and filled the outthrust mugs.

While Cameron watched her every move, Kerry tried to calm the thudding of her heart. He was here! So many times she'd unconsciously looked for his face and now—she glanced toward the wall—there he was. Chained and a captive, he nevertheless appeared in good health. He might be waiting for tea! Kerry thought. He shows no fear or consternation. He even smiled politely at the jest of a soldier who lit a cigar and placed it in Cameron's chained hand.

Running back and forth between the men and Cameron,

she got his story piece by piece.

"How were you captured?" she whispered while filling the mug of the man beside Cameron.

"On board the *Morning Star*. We tried to get the ships out before they attacked."

"They attacked?" Kerry gasped. The soldier beside Cameron glanced up, but the Irish lass was now filling his mug so he shrugged, then turned back to his companion.

"Chestnut Neck," Cameron whispered. "Not Batsto or Brentwood."

"Thank God." Kerry raced across the room to help a merchant, her mind whirling. Ships, the Neck, that day in port . . . slowly it all began to add up. She was amazed that she'd not fitted the puzzle together before! Of course! The maps and notes in the study, Cameron's secret employment . . . smuggling! This practice was an asset to the Continental Army. Capturing ships off the coast of the Jerseys was slowly crippling the massive Royal Navy, depriving it of much-needed goods and supplies and ships. Yes, it would take men like Cameron and Richard Westcoat to pull off such a scheme, men of daring . . . but now Cameron was a captive of the unforgiving British. Kerry knew what his fate would be: they would hang him, as an example to the others still operating as privateers. She had to get Cameron away from them.

Glancing about the steaming room, Kerry saw the townspeople staring gloomily into their cups. They watched the British intruders with open resentment, but afraid to speak or even move, they clung to their ale as if it were a life support. The Britishers were beginning to look bored now that their initial conquest was over, and Kerry shuddered as roving eyes perused her body as if it were naked. Slowly, carefully, an idea grew in the back of her mind, becoming stronger as she glanced about the room. There was the bar, the hallway where Cameron was chained, and beyond . . . somewhere along the wall . . . was the passage! Kerry cursed herself for not having looked for the secret door before, but at least she had an idea of where to look. What she needed now was a diversion. . . .

Humming prettily to herself, Kerry stepped up to the fiddler, swinging her hips seductively. Whirling about, she was gratified to see the eyes of the men on her. Their collective, penetrating stare made her shiver, but keeping her cause firmly in mind, she placed her hands on her hips and lifted her skirts slightly. As all eyes focused on her exposed ankles, she curtseyed, then smiled at the men before her.

"Methinks you could use a bit of cheer this night," she began, and a flood of applause arose, followed by appreciative whistles. She hummed aloud and the fiddler took up the tune, accompanying her. Starting at the table nearest her, Kerry leaned over until the man's eyes were fastened completely on her round snowy bosom, which was nearly bursting from her dress. Then she sang:

"There was in me town a young maiden we knew—
She'd sing for the men for a drink and then two.
Araisin' her skirts and displayin' her knees,
She'd make the men want her as quick as you please!"

With the expertise described in the song, Kerry lifted her dress and danced about the table while the men cheered and whistled. She took up a British lad's hand, and he flushed a bright red as she continued:

"Singing in the tavern and the streets of the town,
She let down her hair and then let down her gown.
'Whiskey makes 'em frisky and liquor does it quicker
But 'tis rum that makes a boy defy the vicar."

Kerry crooked her index finger meaningfully and the men roared. The young lad sighed as his comrades teased him, but he never took his eyes off the comely Irish wench. Kerry grabbed the tallest and broadest of this group, and taking up his arm, she led him out to the floor. Then she sang the chorus:

> "Singing Falala, falala,
> Ale or some rum.
> Fallala, falala,
> Let's have some fun!
> We'll sing through the night to the drink we adore,
> And when morning comes we'll just drink up some more!"

The British cheered this sentiment enthusiastically, while Kerry dragged more men onto the floor, swaying with them to the music. Eileen joined in enthusiastically, as did the village men who saw a chance to salvage some merriment from the evening. The fiddler warmed to the tune and the music grew louder, and the Irish girl rushed about, pulling everyone in and accepting no excuses. She approached the Redcoats who were holding Cameron, luring them with a flick of her dress and with the lilting promise in her eyes. It was a desperate game she played this night, a game clothed in gaiety.

The British glanced dubiously at their prisoners. But the chained men appeared to be dozing or just watching the dancing, their fetters making it impossible to do otherwise. The Redcoats shared a look of mutual agreement, and as Kerry's skirt lifted higher, they leaped to their feet to join in the merriment. She hid her sigh of relief behind a welcoming grin and joined eagerly with them, taking their hands and leading them deep into the fun.

It was a strange scene at the tavern. The British, enjoying a welcome respite from duty, threw caution to the winds and danced as gaily as their colonial counterparts. Rivers of ale and wine continued to flow, and even Hugh Creighton, forgetting his anger at the soldiers' intrusion, looped arms with a red-jacketed Briton and joined in the fun.

Slipping away unnoticed, Kerry worked her way through the singing men to the hallway where Cameron waited, understanding in his silvery eyes.

"There's a doorway hidden in the wall," Kerry whispered as he struggled to his feet, his movement unnoticed in the clamor. While her small hands felt along the plaster wall, she smiled, and sang choruses of the song being played. Finally, a small section of the wall moved, just a chink, then an inch, and a bit more. When the opening was wide enough to permit a man to pass through it, Kerry dashed back to the floor, to ensure that the revelry was continuing. Sure enough, the men were still dancing, ale was being sloshed about. A young lad, emboldened by drink, tried to take her into his arms, but all he got for his effort was air. The Irish lass had scampered away as quickly as she had come so the lad returned to the less elusive drink. But his eyes flitted about the room, following her movements.

"Come on!" Kerry reached the hallway, and taking Cameron's chained hand, she helped him into the black tunnel. Thankful that his feet were not hobbled, he hurried ahead of her while Kerry worked the panel back into position.

They found themselves in a corridor, narrow and black as moist velvet. Holding Cameron's hand firmly behind her, Kerry felt along the wall, taking only a few steps at a time. A spider raced lightly over her fingers and she fought back a scream.

"Is something the matter?" Cameron whispered, and it took all of Kerry's control to reply in the negative.

"No. Let's keep going. They may discover you're missing at any time." Gradually, the darkness went from inky black to gray, and then a small wedge of light became visible at the end of the passage. Seeing the square outline of a door, Cameron stopped Kerry from rushing ahead.

"It might be best to listen first. We have no idea what lies on the other side of that door."

Crouching motionless near the welcome light, Cameron pressed his ear to the door. The ray breaking through lit up his face, and Kerry saw a satisfied gleam in his eyes.

"What is it?" she asked.

Cameron got to his feet. "The guardhouse . . . of the Continental Army."

A triumphant grin came to Kerry's face and with mock ceremony, she released the latch, pulling the door wide open.

"What in blazes . . ." A very young Continental lieutenant glanced up from his desk, amazed to see a dark-haired lass step through the secret door. Right behind her was an elegant-looking man, his dress and manner bespeaking his wealth, but his hands manacled together.

"Cameron Brent of Brentwood, the iron works." Cameron extended a chained hand and the lieutenant took it, gazing awkwardly at the chains. "We had a bit of a skirmish down at Chestnut Neck and the British saw fit to supply me with these bracelets. Would you be so kind as to remove them?" Cameron's manner was so cordial that the lieutenant glanced at Kerry first, to see if this was some kind of a joke. Noting her earnest expression, he fumbled through some nearby crates and, finding a hammer, commenced to pound awkwardly at the chains that bound Cameron. Fortunately, exposure to salt water had weakened the links and with a few swift raps the chain was broken.

"Ah, that's better," he declared feelingly. Though the iron bracelets remained and a length of chain swung from each of Cameron's wrists, he could now move his arms freely. "If we may borrow a horse, or some means of transportation, we'll be on our way. . ."

"Certainly," the lieutenant mumbled. Impressed by the restraint and urgency in Cameron's manner, he sensed impending danger. "I'll go outside and check right away." The slender blond man started for the door, but before he could reach it the panel flew open and an older, gray-haired man stepped into the room.

"What is going on?..." He stopped short upon spying Cameron, and recognition mingled with understanding in his clear blue eyes.

"Cameron Brent. I should have known."

"Jason Winthrop." Cameron extended a braceleted hand. "I haven't seen you since we captured that freighter last summer."

"Aye, you never could stay out of mischief." Jason's eyes twinkled as he spoke, and he gestured to the cuffs adorning Cameron's wrists. "Another ship?"

"No, Chestnut Neck," Cameron explained. It was Jason's turn to look surprised as Cameron related the previous day's adventure. "They took me prisoner and burned the ships," he concluded. "If it weren't for Miss Kerry here, I'd be a prisoner still. She helped me escape from the tavern."

"Helped you..." Jason turned to Kerry, his gaze measuring her slim frame. "This young girl..." As Kerry flushed under his admiring regard, Jason turned to the lieutenant, his manner businesslike.

"Secure a carriage for Mr. Brent and the young lady. We must get them safely home before the British realize they are gone."

When the lieutenant rushed to obey, Cameron gestured about the empty guardhouse. "Your men?"

"Fighting in Morristown," Jason answered. "It's just the lieutenant and myself here now. But fear not, Cameron. The British know nothing of this passage. You are safe here."

Safe. Kerry didn't feel safe, and she prayed the lieutenant would hurry.

Back at the Tavern, the young Briton rubbed the pipe smoke from his eyes and gazed once again at the wall. The lass had disappeared right into it, seeming to melt into the solid stone barrier! Slowly he got to his feet, then followed in the footsteps of the lovely dark-haired girl.

The lieutenant had not yet returned, and Kerry was pacing restlessly about the room.

"He'll be here soon, lass." Jason tried to comfort her.

"The sooner I see the backs of these Redcoats, the better," Kerry answered. "There's something about being so close to them that gets my Irish up." She ignored the frown Cameron sent her.

Jason chuckled. "I can't say I disagree with you, miss."

The words had scarcely left his mouth when Kerry saw her worst fears materializing. The secret door flew open and a young British officer stepped into the room!

Back at the tavern, Hugh Creighton leaned against the bar, breathing heavily. It had been a long time since he'd kicked up his heels like that. Suddenly his thoughts wandered to the pretty Irish girl who'd started the revelry, and he frowned when he did not see her about. The Redcoats seemed not to notice her absence. Their bellies full of ale and their bodies exhausted from the dancing, they lay about on the table tops . . . except for one. Hugh watched the young Redcoat as he made his way to the hall; then the tavern owner's eyes widened and he nearly choked on his ale when the young man found the catch to the hidden door. Slugging down the last of his ale, Hugh started purposefully after the man. The discovery of a nest of rebels beneath his taproom boded ill for everyone, especially himself.

Kerry had barely recovered from her shock when the Briton strode across the three feet of floor that separated them and laid a hand on Cameron's shoulder.

"You, sir, are under arrest."

"What is the meaning of this?" Jason said quickly, while Kerry's eyes flew to Cameron. "This man is a personal friend of mine, a landowner at Brentwood."

"What!" The Redcoat still clung to Cameron's coat, but some of his certainty seemed to leave him as Jason continued in the same manner.

"That's right. He's been here for the past few days. We have some business to discuss regarding the iron works." Jason gestured to the pile of papers on the desk behind him while Cameron kept his wrists well hidden.

"A carriage is waiting outside. . . ." The lieutenant entered the chamber, his words trailing off as his eyes fell on the red-jacketed Briton. For a moment, time hung suspended like a drop of water waiting to fall. The lieutenant and Jason exchanged glances, trying to decide the fate of this British lad, while the object of their thoughts was beginning to realize the precariousness of his situation. Jason had taken one step toward the lad when a rumbling noise sounded at the door and Hugh Creighton barged in.

"I thought I'd find you here." Hugh fixed a red-eyed stare on the young Briton; then he gestured to Kerry and the colonials. "But I'm telling you, you don't get the wench without paying me first. Mr. Brent and the others paid in advance for her favors. But you, lad"—he turned once again to the young Redcoat—"I haven't had a farthing from you. And your superiors are upstairs, looking about for ye. When I tell them . . ."

Understanding dawned on the Britisher, and as he glanced about the room, the lieutenant's face flushed crimson. Kerry had started to protest Hugh's words, but she had suddenly realized the desperate farce he was playing, hoping to delude this youth. The colonials did not have the means to hold a Redcoat, yet they could not have him spreading an alarm.

The plan worked. The Redcoat bowed out of the room with a broad grin, winking at Kerry who blushed deeply. Cameron and Jason dared not speak until the sound of the

Briton's footfalls echoed overhead; then they burst into laughter.

"You were terrific, Hugh!" Jason slapped the tavern owner's back, while that imaginative man grunted mirthlessly.

"Aye. Well, the last thing I'll be needing is trouble from the likes of them."

"Are you sure he'll say nothing?" Kerry asked fearfully, and it was the lieutenant who answered her.

"Fear not, miss. That lad wouldn't want his superiors to think he was dallying with some tavern wench down here." He grinned.

"Aye," Jason agreed. "There'll be hell to pay tomorrow when they awaken, but they'll be out of here soon enough." He chuckled at the thought.

"Well, lass, are ye ready to get back to work?" Hugh fixed his gaze on Kerry, but Cameron stepped between the girl and the bulky innkeeper.

"She'll be working for you no longer. She's coming back home with me."

"She is not!" At the thought of losing such an attractive wench, Hugh whirled toward Kerry, his fist clenched. "I'll have you arrested! You run out on me and you'll pay! I paid yer wages for the week and"—seeing the expensive cut of Cameron's clothes, Hugh saw a way to regain his losses for the damage upstairs—"me pewter's gone."

"That's a lie!" Kerry shouted, but Hugh continued.

"And since you're an indentured servant, 'tis likely you'll be deported. See what happens when ya run out on me, miss."

"Deported!" Kerry gasped, her eyes like emerald saucers. "You mean send me back—"

"That's it." Hugh nodded, his desire for vengeance increasing as he thought of the mess the Redcoats had made in his taproom. Somehow he had come to blame Kerry for all of it.

"You can't!" For a reason Kerry could not name, the thought of being sent back to Ireland distressed her greatly. She did not stop to examine her feelings, nor would she admit they had anything to do with the handsome ironmaster who was enraged by the tavern owner's threats, but her hands flew to her mouth and she turned to Cameron, hating to plead.

"Master Cameron"—Kerry spoke softly—"can he do that?"

"Yes, I can," Hugh declared.

"Ordinarily," Cameron replied, his sparkling gray gaze meeting Hugh Creighton's amused stare, "he would be right, but I think he will find this case is an exception."

"And how's that?" Hugh asked smugly.

"Because you cannot deport a citizen."

"A citizen! Why this wench, this taproom servant—"

"Is to be my bride."

A thundering silence fell over the room. Four pairs of eyes swung to Cameron but he calmly smiled.

"This must be a joke," Hugh blustered. "That's it, a joke." He slapped his knee and began to laugh, but his laughter died under Cameron's ominous glare.

"Are you mocking my choice of a bride?" Incredulity played over Cameron's stern features.

"Why, no, sir." Hugh backed away a few feet, an unreasoning fear racing through him. "I meant no offense. It's just I thought—"

"Well, it appears you were mistaken," Cameron said coldly while Jason hid a smile.

"Yes, sir. Right, sir." Hugh sidled toward the door, then paused, his hand upon the brass handle. "Sir? There is a matter of money here. The wages for the wench—I mean the liedy. Thirteen bob for the week." Hugh embellished the amount. "And we'll forget the pewter. Consider it a wedding gift."

"Why you . . ." Kerry snapped, but Cameron's look kept

her in check.

"I will send you a note for any amount you deem fair, plus interest. I have been relieved of my coin." The fine coat, the lace shirt, and the good wool of his trousers testified to Cameron's wealth and Hugh nodded, satisfied.

"Thank you, sir. That's good of you. If I can do something for you, sir, you just name it." Hugh beamed. Rubbing his hands together in anticipation of the money he'd receive, he scurried out the door.

"I think you'll get a large bill from him," Jason remarked with a chuckle. "That's the happiest I've seen Hugh in years."

Kerry nodded. "But, sir, you didn't have to go so far as to tell him you'd marry me. You might have made up a more likely tale."

"On the contrary, miss," Cameron replied. "I was merely speaking the truth."

Noting the astonished lass before him, Jason wisely withdrew, taking the puzzled lieutenant with him. As anger began to build in Kerry, she tapped her foot warningly on the floor. Cameron smiled.

"I don't think it a wee bit funny, sir," she snapped, her eyes glistening with anger. "I don't care to be mocked."

"Miss, you wound me to the quick," Cameron declared, and before Kerry could give vent to a host of well-chosen adjectives describing his character, or the lack thereof, he placed a long finger to her lips, silencing her.

"I don't want Hugh or anyone else to have the power to take you away from me. Therefore, I judge it best we wed."

"But you can't marry me!" Pushing his finger aside, she faced him boldly and without fear, determined to see the matter through. "I'm your servant!"

His answer puzzled her. He withdrew a quill and a sheet of parchment from a nearby desk, and brushing aside his chains, he began to write. For a moment, the scratch of the pen on the bumpy paper and the rattle of his chains were the only sounds in the chamber. Finishing at last, he tossed the sheet toward her and Kerry read it.

> "On Kerry O'Toole, in reward for my safe return from the British army, I bestow the sum of five pounds, to be paid in full upon my return to Brentwood."

The document was signed "Cameron Brent."

"That relieves you of your indenture," he stated flatly, gesturing toward the sheet of parchment. "You are now free to wed."

"Why?" Puzzled, Kerry stared into his face. "Why would you, an Englishman, deign to wed me? I am nothing but a serving girl—an Irish one at that."

His brow darkened and his jaw tightened, and he stared down at the lass before him for several moments, his eyes touching her everywhere, branding her as with a scorching flame. Kerry blushed in embarrassment at his thorough perusal, and she wished she wore something more concealing than her serving dress. The front was not fully buttoned due to the heat of the tavern, and the curves of her breasts gleamed in the tallow light. His gaze rested on them before returning to her face.

"I can think of several good reasons," he whispered, a mocking leer on his face, then he laughed at her outraged glare. "Come, miss. We are to be wed and 'tis best to make the most of it. You should be happy. After all, I am to make an honest woman of you."

Glaring her gratitude, Kerry snatched back the hand he'd deftly secured. But her mind considered his words. True, she would be safe, but from what? Ireland seemed a distant memory to her, and her troubled mind refused to explore that further. The debt would be paid. That was a source of untold relief to her. But something else, a warming within her, caused her heart to flutter. It was a hope that together they might find happiness. She buried that thought within her and looked up to find Cameron watching her intently.

"All right," she agreed, a twinkle coming into her eyes. "That is, as long as an Englishman like yourself doesn't mind being married to an Irish rebel?" Her grin deepened and Cameron returned it, warmth sparkling in his own gaze.

"Miss, had we but the time, I'd prove how little I'd mind it." Laughing at her startled glance, he took her hand and led her to the door. "Before I forget, there is something else I owe you." He pressed something into her hand, and Kerry stared in surprise at the gold chain glistening in her palm.

"But how—"

"Never mind," he said sternly. "But if I ever find it out of your grasp again, you will answer to me. Now come, wench. Let's be free of this place."

Cameron and Kerry traveled home in a decrepit black carriage that rattled every inch of the way. But she did not seem to mind. Indeed, she leaned back upon the seat and sleep came to her quickly. It was invaded only by a pair of silvery eyes.

"Kerry." When the tired lass murmured an unrecognizable answer and snuggled deeper into the tattered carriage seat, a pair of strong arms slid under her knees, scooping her up in a warm cradle. Kerry sighed and placed her arms around Cameron as he transported her to the house. Only when her feet slid reluctantly to the floor did she realize what had happened.

"Cameron!" A shrill voice jolted Kerry awake, and she glanced up to see Caroline rushing down the stairs. The blond woman brushed past Kerry as if she weren't there, and she stood before Cameron, her face was flushed, her crystal-like eyes blazing. She clutched her hands together as if to keep from slapping him.

"How could you! You made a mockery of us all! I heard all about it. Cameron, I would have never believed it of you. How could you forget your family, your friends?" Her gaze fell to his manacles and she gasped, her hands flying to her lips in horror.

"Where's George?" He turned to Kerry with a polite smile. "Would you fetch him for me, sweet? I'll need some help with these."

"You!" Caroline's gaze settled on Kerry and her rage soared. Hatred in her eyes, she stepped forward, her fists clenching and unclenching.

"It was you, wasn't it. You put him up to it! Fighting against the English, our people, taking the side of a bunch of dirty, sneaking rebels! I should have known you were involved, you Irish—"

"Caroline," Cameron cut her off decisively. "That's enough. I owe you no explanation, but if it would relieve your mind, Kerry wasn't present at the battle."

"I don't believe it!" Caroline continued, her eyes flickering back to Cameron.

"Believe what you must," he snapped, his patience gone. "But it happens to be the truth. I have not disowned England or the memory of my father, but England does not seem to realize that these colonies are a country within themselves, not simply a place to be bled of its resources. For business reasons as well as matters of principle, there was only one side I could take."

"Fine." Caroline raised her golden head and she spoke coolly and contemptuously. "Then I am breaking our engagement. It is as simple as that. I do not want to be associated with a traitor." She waited to see what effect her words would have upon Cameron, fully expecting him to rush into her arms and beg her forgiveness. She was stunned when he shrugged.

His own words cool, he responded. "If that is what you wish. You are welcome to stay here as before, however. I realize that you have nowhere else to go."

Caroline's mouth dropped open. Then she glanced at Kerry, at the listening servants, at Charles, who was smirking in the hallway, and she lifted her skirts and rushed up the stairs with what dignity she could muster. But once in her room, she stared at the door, her hands twisting like writhing snakes.

"Do not be mistaken, Cameron," she said, and the look in her eyes was not quite sane, "this matter is far from over."

Chapter Seventeen

The excitement in the Brentwood household had reached a feverish pitch when Kerry glanced outside, having heard the crunch of a carriage wheel on the gravel. Jane Clark alighted from a coach, pulling her dark cloak about her in the chill November wind. Yet the breeze from the sea whipped her unmercifully, and it was with considerable haste that she scurried inside, away from the harsh weather.

Her footfalls sounded a moment later outside Kerry's room, just before she knocked lightly and then entered. "Kerry, my dear." She smiled warmly, her wrinkled face smoothing into a warm prettiness. Then her eyes fell to Kerry's dressing robe and to the black hair tumbling about her waist, and she sighed with exasperation.

"You haven't even begun? My, my child! The wedding is in less than two hours. We haven't a moment to delay." Calling a maid, Jane ordered a bath and she requested the assistance of two chambermaids before closing the door again.

"We have plenty of time." Kerry laughed, her bright teeth glistening. "I don't think I've ever spent more than a half-hour getting dressed in me whole life."

"Well today is different, my dear." Jane nodded, took off her cap, and placed it on the bed. "It is your wedding day and we really must begin. No arguments now!" Jane winked reprovingly when she noted the rebellious twinkle coming into Kerry's emerald eyes. "Unless you want Caroline to show you up!"

Jane was forced to chuckle at the disgusted glance Kerry gave her, but the stratagem worked. Off came the black stockings, the boots, and the dressing gown while a buxom chambermaid poured water into a copper tub. "I was hoping she'd want to stay home today, but she insisted on coming. I think she wants to see the ceremony because she still doesn't believe Cameron would want to marry me."

"Well, never mind her," Jane said reassuringly. "Caroline will be returning to Philadelphia as soon as the Continentals win. We shall be rid of her for good." And none too soon, Jane thought, having felt the bite of Caroline's aspish tongue herself. There was something wrong with that woman, something unnatural about her, and Jane couldn't help feeling that the sooner she was gone, the better.

"What's that smell?" Kerry breathed deeply of the scented water, scooping up a handful and letting it trickle through her fingers. The water felt soft and silky, and the fragrance of wildflowers drifted up with the steam.

"Lavender and wildflowers," Jane answered. Kerry glanced up at her questioningly, then slipped into the tub. The warm, hauntingly scented waters enveloped her, and she sighed blissfully. The soap had the same fresh scent, and Kerry luxuriated in it, lathering one shapely leg, then another.

"Scent in the water!" She smiled like a contented kitten. "I never heard of such a thing."

"Well, you may as well get used to it," Jane remarked, laying out Kerry's blue brocade wedding dress, along with a sheer chemise and silk stockings. "Cameron is not a pauper and he can afford such things."

"I wonder if I'll ever get used to it," Kerry said thoughtfully, and a bright chuckle escaped Jane Clark's lips.

"You will be surprised how easily one does get used to

such things." She grinned, her blue eyes twinkling like cornflowers from behind her silver spectacles. "Why I was just as poor as you are when Eliah and I married. We struggled together in the early years, but we are now able to enjoy a few luxuries and I don't think I could get on without them. Hurry with the bath, child. You must get dressed and have your hair done while we have time."

Regretfully, Kerry left the warm embrace of the tub, allowing the chambermaid to dry her. The fire crackled warmly, lending a rosy cast to her scrubbed skin while she tugged on the chemise. "Help her with that," Jane said to the chambermaid, who stood idly by.

"Aw, it's just Kerry," the buxom lass complained. Jane lifted one snowy eyebrow, and the maid shuffled resentfully to Kerry, smoothing down the ivory undergarment. The sheer material seemed a gauzy cloud over the Irish lass's body, parting to show full round breasts that thrust impertinently through the low neckline, clasping an impossibly slender waist, and allowing a glimpse of small white feet. Jane Clark, not being of an envious nature, smiled with maternal fondness at the vision of loveliness before her while Kerry, oblivious of her beauty, tossed her dress about this way and that, trying in vain to find the concealed hooks. The chambermaid stared resentfully at the firm curvaceous form, however, comparing her thrusting breasts and pert bottom with her own rather ponderous parts. Resentful, she stepped a few feet away from Kerry, toward the fire, and whispered to the other attendant, just loud enough to be heard.

"That 'tis the reason the bloody bloke wants her," she hissed, crooking a thumb at Kerry's slender form. "Tis for naught else."

"I beg your pardon maid." Jane began to reprimand the girl, while Kerry's hand froze, the dress clutched between her fingers. "Did I hear you correctly?"

"And what if you did?" the maid retorted saucily, tossing back her blond, strawlike hair. "I'm entitled to me own opinion, I am. Why else would a bloke like Master Brent want with a common lass like 'erself?"

"I suppose you would know all about that," Jane continued, and the wench burst into a grin, displaying uneven teeth. Her companion nudged her warningly, but the maid's obvious jealousy got the better of her.

"I know what a man wants," she declared. "And Master Brent—he ain't no different than most men."

"I see," Jane Clark said thoughtfully. Kerry opened her mouth to retort, but Jane sent her a warning glance and faced the maid directly. "And has Master Brent approached you in such a manner? Or has he proposed to marry you?"

"No." The maid was aware that the conversation was turning against her. "But he might have."

"Yet he didn't." Jane smiled triumphantly. Her hands on her hips, her silvery hair glinting in the firelight, she looked like a disapproving schoolmarm. The young maid squirmed. "Cameron Brent has asked Kerry to marry him and marry him she will this very day. Kerry O' Toole will soon be Kerry Brent, mistress of this manor. I understand that this is quite a change for you all, but I warn you, my dear"—Jane was no longer smiling, and the wench turned a dismal shade of gray—"she is to be treated with the respect due the lady of this house. I will not report your behavior today, but I promise you Cameron Brent will be notified of any further lapse and you will find yourself unemployed."

The girl's eyes widened, and biting her thin lips, she nodded fearfully, her cap bobbing. "Now leave the room," June ordered, pointing imperiously to the door. "I don't want such as you attending Kerry on this day."

The maid raced to the door, only too glad to be free of this interfering woman. As she quit the room Kerry gazed wonderingly at Jane Clark.

"I don't believe it," she murmured. "We used to be friends."

"I'm afraid you will find many of your former friends

envious of your new position," Jane warned, taking up the gown and helping Kerry into it herself. "But do not fret much over that. Those who really care for you will accept your new status and be happy for you. But you, my pet, must show them the way."

"How?" Kerry asked, her nose crinkling as the voluminous skirts fell into place.

"Don't be afraid to ask the servants to do things. That is why they are here. If you think upon the time you spent working in the furnace, you will recall that men are happier when they know their duties and perform them. Do not tempt workers by accepting less than your due."

"I see," Kerry said, grateful for the advice. It was just beginning to dawn on her, what it meant to be married to this man. Her fortitude came to her rescue, and with a confident grin, she faced the mirror to adjust the dress.

For a moment, she was stunned by her reflection. The gown, modeled in the French fashion and sewn by a colonial dressmaker, was a delight of beauty and sophistication. The neckline was a jewel cut, and it displayed the creamy roundness of her bosom. The demure ivory lace trim tempted the eye and exposed more than it concealed. That same lace etched the pleated ivory ruching that rose from the tightly cinched waist to just below her breasts, while cool blue brocade, a slender hoop beneath, fell to the floor. Tiny matching slippers peeked out from beneath the skirt, their silver buckles glinting blue in the firelight. A string of pearls accented her throat, while tiny pearl earrings, reportedly the new rage in Paris, shimmered from her dainty ears. Kerry's huge green eyes, like twin mysterious gems, stared back at her. There was no sign of the ragged serving wench in the glass. This woman was sophisticated, poised, but with the beguiling air of a temptress. Kerry flushed at the exposure of her bosom, the flood of pink color rushing down to the scant neckline.

Kerry whirled about to face Jane Clark, and the older

woman smiled, fully pleased. "Is this all there is?" she asked.

"You'll not need much more on your wedding night," Jane reminded Kerry with a grin. "And, I hope you don't mind, for your wedding gift, I took the liberty of purchasing a few negligees for you. They are in that box on the bed."

"Negli . . . what?" Kerry cocked her head, and Jane laughed warmly, then pushed the lass down into a chair so the other maid could proceed to style her hair in a cascade of satiny black curls, with tiny seed pearls set among them.

"Negligee . . . nightgown." Jane displayed a sheer ivory creation that featured a plunging neckline. Tiny pink ribbons were tied beneath the breasts. "This will make a shy man into a bold one." She grinned, and the maid tittered.

Recalling the times she'd spent with Cameron, Kerry smiled wryly. She had little doubt that Cameron needed any such aids. He had proven his lust. Unwilling to impart this knowledge, however, she smiled her thanks as Jane Clark finished the preparations and made ready to go.

The church, built by Eliah Clark and known as Clark's Little Log Meeting House, was a tiny country affair. Glancing up, Kerry saw the afternoon sunlight playing across the red cedar beams, its tiny prisms dancing between the stern posts. Nervously clutching a bouquet of chrysanthemums and winter ivy, Kerry looked back at the handhewn pews, saw Jane's wrinkled smile, her husband's nod. Behind them sat the workmen, Trevor nudging the lad beside him and waving heartily until Jane, noticing, thrust his hand back down to his side. Across the way sat Charles, his amused grin causing her to smile back, and Caroline was beside him, clothed royally in pink and green, her fur-trimmed cloak tossed casually aside. The blond-haired woman refused to look at Kerry, but fixed her eyes on Cameron.

"You could have stayed home," Charles whispered to her.

"There's no need for you to extend yourself." His voice was polite, but Caroline sensed the laughter in it and she sent him a frozen glance.

"'Tis the least I owe Cameron," she said, her voice tense. "Why should I stay home? It is of little concern to me who he marries. After all, 'twas I that broke our engagement. I do not want him to envision me pining at home for him while he takes his Irish bitch to bed."

Her words crackled with venom and Charles chuckled.

"Careful, my dear, your claws are showing. Oh, I think the service is about to begin."

Kerry saw them whispering, but it mattered little to her. Her gaze went to Cameron, and she was again amazed at how ruggedly handsome he was, at how his elegant stance lent him dignity and poise. Clothed in deep blue, so dark that it bordered on black, he was a magnificent specimen of a man. His face was serious, but his sparkling gray eyes were as clear as the lakes of Ireland. His nose was finely formed, his mouth was firm yet sensuous, and his teeth were even and white. By his very manner, he seemed to control the situation, and if he had any misgivings, he did not display them.

Feeling Kerry's gaze on him, he sent her a glance that warmed her, and the minister, observing that look, hastily opened his prayer book and fumbled for the right page. He was accustomed to wedding the coal and iron workers, but it was a rare day that gentry had need of his services and the thought of a good coin and a hearty meal hastened his words.

Kerry repeated her vows after Cameron, a strange chilling sensation rushing through her as she promised to love and obey him as long as she lived. Glancing at him out of one eye, she felt suddenly shy and uncertain. Despite the fact that she was no longer a virgin, she knew there was much to marriage she had yet to experience, and the odd, tingling sensations that raced through her blood at Cameron's sensual glance aided these feelings. 'Tis but curiosity, she thought, her eyes playing upon the tanned hand that covered hers. Having sampled one dish she couldn't help but suspect there was far more to the feast.

As if reading her mind Cameron turned slowly toward her, his eyes burning like twin lights. Kerry was drawn to them as a moth is to a flame, and she barely heard the minister declare that the groom might kiss the bride. With a torturing slowness, Cameron's lips met with hers, that first touch sending shivers up her spine. He clasped her to him, oblivious of the stares of their guests while his mouth plundered hers, legally tasting her sweetness as Kerry tried to still the pounding of her heart. His kiss was insistent, demanding then teasing as he eased the pressure of his mouth due to sudden awareness of the surroundings. The minister cleared his throat, but glancing at the lovely Irish bride, he could well understand the groom's demonstrativeness.

"Congratulations, son." The minister shook Cameron's hand; then he took Kerry's, warming it between his own, while a smile danced in his eyes. "Congratulations to you, madam. May you be blessed with many children." The minister believed it likely that she would, for the Irish girl possessed strength as well as beauty and, judging by the passionate kiss her new husband had bestowed upon her, he felt sure she would need it.

"Congratulations!" The word rang out as Kerry and Cameron were escorted by the exultant workers to the waiting carriage.

The men from the furnace smiled fondly at Kerry, pleased beyond measure that their new mistress was to be their favored companion. Pointedly ignoring Caroline, they hugged Kerry, and the young lass's cheek was scraped pink by their congratulatory kisses.

"Aye, and a right fine day this is," McIntire proclaimed contentedly, leaping up to assist Kerry into the carriage but her new husband possessively claimed that honor. "Aye, a fine day," the Irishman continued, undaunted. "Never thought I'd live to see such a fair mistress here at Brentwood."

"Yes." Charles's clipped voice rang out as he stepped forward from the circle of furnace men and other well wishers. In fact, there was little need for him to do so, his winter white satin brocade coat made him stand out amidst their black woolen garments. "And the mistress is a serving wench. I daresay there is opportunity in America, wouldn't you agree, mistress?" He spoke the word tauntingly, and Kerry's cheeks burned while her husband's lean jawline tightened threateningly.

"Charles," Cameron's voice was threatening, but Charles merely laughed dryly, doffed his tricorn, and bowed with exaggerated deepness, his nose nearly touching his knee.

"Fare thee well, dear sister," he said. "It will indeed be a treat to have you in the family." At this last, his voice dipped flirtatiously, and he was pleased to see Cameron scowl.

"Aye, like a hen loose with a fox," Cameron replied, and Kerry laughed as she nestled her small hand in his coat. "We'll see you back at the house, Charles. There's no need for you to gape out in the road."

Indeed, Cameron did not exaggerate for all the while Charles was preening, his gaze was fastened on Kerry's winsome form. At Cameron's words the workers guffawed and Charles flushed angrily. Trevor's fist clenched threateningly, but then the Englishman's brow arched and the young lad replaced the errant hand in his pocket.

"Blithering idiot," Cameron remarked, referring to Charles, and Kerry giggled, sounding like a sparkling brook. "Now, Mr. Brent, that is no way to talk about your brother," she admonished teasingly.

Cameron's face relaxed and he allowed his gaze to travel freely over his bride. Her cloak of warm gray wool was open slightly, allowing him a delicious sample of the wench beneath. Soft creamy glimpses of her bosom pressed up from the neckline of the rich brocade, providing a tempting sample of what was concealed from his view. A memory seared him, of a warm and willing wench in his arms, a lass of incomparable beauty and passion writhing in his embrace. He took in her warm and sparkling gaze, her lilting voice, her captivating mouth, so soft and red and kissable. Cameron was amazed that he'd ever entertained the thought of marrying Caroline. This merry Irish lass, this warm and realistic girl was like fire and Caroline was like ice.

"What are you scowling at?" Kerry asked, her brogue rich with the musicality of the Irish. "Are you so soon a disgruntled groom?"

"Hardly that." Cameron found himself smiling. "I am, in fact, an eager one. How long do they plan to keep us at this wretched party?" He thought of the mile-long table of cakes, meats, ale, and wine that Helga had been fussing over all morning and his scowl deepened. "Those damned ironmen will likely prevent the consummation of this marriage until well into the morn."

"Control your lusts." Kerry grinned. "The men have been looking forward to this for the last few weeks. And Helga's been working so hard to have everything nice for us." She giggled at Cameron's pained frown, then snuggled closer to him.

As he gazed down into her laughing green eyes, her dark ebony curls teasing his nose, Cameron became aware of the perfume she wore, the scent he had purchased for her. He'd tested the scent then, little realizing the effect it would have when worn by this lass. Struggling to mainting his control, Cameron looked into her eyes and spoke the truth.

"Kerry"—his voice was hoarse—"it might be better if you removed yourself a bit, that is, unless you'd like to miss the party and retire immediately?" His hopes were dashed by her laugh.

"There is a time for everything," she said pertly, but she wisely withdrew her hand from his pocket and moved a few inches away.

"A philosopher in petticoats," Cameron retorted, his gaze still traveling over her in that ageless manner. But the coach had arrived, and already guests were clamoring at the doors. With obvious regret, Cameron handed Kerry down, then dismounted himself.

"You look beautiful!" Helga exclaimed, greeting Kerry at the door with a kiss. The groom was left to his own resources as she hurried Kerry into the dining room, eager to display her mastery with the cakes. Shrugging helplessly, Kerry allowed herself to be drawn along, but she was honestly impressed with Helga's efforts and expressed her appreciation of the assorted delights Helga had concocted. The coal and iron workers were already sampling them, and Helga snatched away a slice of angel cake just as a coalman was about to demolish it.

"Pigs!" Helga declared, offering Kerry a sample while a cup of wine was thrust into her hand. This wine was new to Kerry. Pale and bubbling, it tickled her nose while she sipped it.

"What is this?" she asked, giggling at the bubbles. Her new husband claimed her arm and firmly withdrew the glass from her hand.

"Champagne," he replied, holding up the glass and critically surveying the swirling liquid. "Don't drink too much of that or you will have a headache tomorrow."

"Aye," Trevor, the expert on liquor, declared. "Devilish stuff, Kerry. I'd stay away from it." But his own glass was full and he drank the bubbly stuff with lusty delight.

The music started and Kerry found herself much in demand as a partner for supposedly it was good luck to dance with a new bride. But lads that were too eager found themselves discouraged by the master of the estate. A young coal worker gulped at the imposing sight of Cameron and he hastened quickly away, leaving the bride and groom together.

"I had scarcely a minute to dance with the lad," Kerry reminded Cameron as he took possession of her, swirling her out onto the floor of the parlor. This room had been cleared for the festivities, and without rugs and furnishings, it was magically transformed into a ballroom.

"For the first time since I've known you I have the right to claim you," Cameron said seriously but his eyes sparkled. "And I find I enjoy asserting that right."

"Beast." Kerry smiled. "You'd deny your workers luck in the coming year?"

"Let them look for shamrocks," he declared, gazing down at the sprite in his arms. She was too damned enticing by far, and he found himself longing for the night. "I have my mind set on more fruitful endeavors."

"And what, master, are they?" Kerry asked, her eyes slanted in a captivating manner.

Glancing about, Cameron saw the minister and his wife dancing beside them, and not wishing to shock the man further, he replied, "'Tis a subject much better demonstrated. I find myself wishing for the demise of this affair so I might explain myself more fully."

"I shall eagerly await that revelation." Kerry grinned, knowing full well of what he spoke. His gaze warmed at her response, and his senses filled with the sweet scent that clung to her, the beauty who'd engaged his mind these many days past. When the musicians began another reel, he reluctantly gave her up to a workman, then stood at the side of the room and drank a solitary cup of champagne.

Cameron needn't have worried for the night had wings, as do most nights of merrymaking and it seemed only a short time later when the village women called for Kerry. As the Irish lass approached them, the housemaids gathered her up and led her upstairs in the customary manner. Cameron watched her departure over his cup, smiling good-naturedly at the lewd jests that the men sent him, the first informality any had dared. But he understood that Kerry's trust of him, her free manner, dispelled many of the workers' trepidations and he was amazed at his luck in choosing such a bride. Charles is right, he told himself. I do have trouble seeing what is obvious to others.

Deposited in Cameron's room, Kerry glanced about at the unfamiliar surroundings. A huge fourposter bed claimed most of the wall, while a few comfortable arm chairs were set before the fire. The mantel was packed with books, as were the shelves opposite the bed, and a single picture graced one wall, a large oil painting of the woman depicted in the miniature Kerry had found in her room. Cameron's mother smiled reassuringly at her, seeming to promise that all would be well.

The maids were busily unhooking her dress, and giggling over what was to come. Their knowledge on the subject amazed Kerry and set her to wondering where these girls had learned so much. But they were now thrusting her arms through the slits of the sheer nightgown, curiously examining the material and snickering at the purposeful arrangement of the ribbons. Growing uncomfortable with their attitudes, Kerry dismissed them and the maids curtseyed out the door. "Here's your wedding gifts," one of them called, pointing to a bundle of letters from well wishers. "In case you get bored." A resounding laugh issued from the other girls, and Kerry heaved a thankful breath when the door closed on the maids.

Alone now, she felt a rising trepidation as the hour of the consummation drew near. She stood near the window, idly fingering the rich fabric of the drapes and keeping her eyes from the massive bed behind her. That day on board his ship was but a distant memory, and this night was somehow different and frightening. She blushed as she recalled her own wantonness and her eager participation in their lovemaking, but tonight . . . tonight she would no longer be simply his lover, but his wife.

And what if he should tire of her? She was from a different social level, a different nationality, a different breed. True, he now seemed to find the differences fascinating, but would he continue to do so in the future, especially when he'd given no indication as to how he felt about her? He had married her to repay her, to make her legal as he put it, but was there more to it?

A warming grew in her breast as she thought of what he'd done at Haddonfield. He had relieved her of the debt. Her fears calmed as she thought of this, and she suddenly knew everything would be all right. A secret smile curved her lips as she thought of the grand figure he'd made at the wedding, his masculine presence overshadowing all else, and then an odd thrill coursed through her veins, an excitement and anticipation that grew with each passing moment. "Ah yes, my lustful Tory." Her smile turned into an impish grin. "I do love you and I think it only a matter of time before you love me." With a delicious giggle, she tossed back the quilts and climbed beneath them, awaiting the arrival of her husband.

"Think she's had enough time?" a coal worker asked, and the men cheered lustily.

"You can always assist her if she needs help," another told Cameron.

"If you'll be needing a hand, mate, I'll be happy to lend both of mine," an iron worker offered, and emboldened by the drink, the men roared, clapping Cameron on the back and wishing him well. Raising the groom above their heads, they carted him ceremoniously up the stairs, thrusting him through the door and into the room where his bride awaited.

Regaining his balance, Cameron glanced around the room, looking for his bride. The bed curtains were drawn and it was to them his gaze wandered as he tugged furtively at his lace jabot. Dipping the wick of a candle into the flickering fire, Cameron placed the chamberstick beside the bed, then brushed aside the diaphanous curtain to greet his bride.

The sight of her near took his breath away. She was reclining on the bed, clad in a sheer garment of ivory batiste that was caught beneath her breasts with a pale blue ribbon. The plunging neckline, trimmed coyly with filmy lace, revealed her ripe breasts, their rounded curves thrusting wantonly against the filmy fabric. One of her legs was crossed over the other and fully exposed, its supple curves tapering with alabaster perfection to a small bare foot.

"Kerry." Cameron's voice caressed the name like a treasured jewel as he drew near his bride, his eyes dark silver with the intensity of his passion. He removed his clothes, the lace shirt and the dark blue trousers, his eyes never leaving the vision before him, and when he approached the bed, Kerry rose to meet him, letting him draw her into his embrace. His fingers caressed the splendor of her black, silken hair which fell in a cascade about her, then he brushed that seductive curtain away and placed teasing kisses upon the nape of her neck and throat. Kerry forgot all her trepidations, all thoughts of English and Irish, master and servant. She reveled in this new relationship of husband and wife.

Lifting her tresses aside, Kerry let his fingers undo the fastenings of her gown, and when the light fabric fell like a cloud to her feet, Cameron buried his face in her shoulder, smelling the fresh, clean scent of her mingled with lavender. When he had been a captive of the British, he had dreamt more than once of Kerry, had smelled and tasted her as if she were with him. Now she was. His arms enfolded her, bringing the softness of her against him as he kissed her. His mouth leisurely possessed hers, his tongue tasting the sweetness of her lips, greedily devouring them until he felt her respond. Then he wanted more.

Cameron buried his hand in her hair, holding her still while his lips moved to her cheek, to trace the delicate outline of her jaw. She shivered with anticipation, her senses spinning, her body trembling, as his mouth moved, hot and moist, down her throat, teasingly, to her shoulders, then to her breasts. Kerry moaned as his lips found a burning pink tip, his tongue flicking mercilessly at the small nipple until it was tight and erect, then he turned to the other, arousing it in the same manner. His hands slipped lower to fondle a bare buttock, then he pressed her closer to him and she was fully aware of his own heated desire. Opening her eyes slightly to peep through a fringe of black lashes, she saw the lustful gleam in his as they caressed her. Consumed by that fiery glance, she lifted her mouth to meet his.

Cameron crushed her to him, eagerly sweeping her into his arms and tumbling with her onto the bed. His mouth seared her, his kiss fierce and impatient, and Kerry's ardor equaled his. Her bosom pressed against the light fur on his chest, the nipples achingly sensitive, and a warm heat arose between her thighs where his leg rested. As his lips eased away from hers, Kerry felt the heat of him against her, and she closed her eyes as his lips traced searing patterns across her breasts and down to the curve of her waist, then lower. Her body quivered as his hands caressed her, branding her with their touch, heating her flesh, and causing her blood to race. The warmth within her became unbearable, waxing ever hotter as he stroked the sensitive flesh of her inner thighs, delighting in the womanly softness that trembled beneath his hand.

Her thighs parted, allowing him access, and she strained against him, longing for release. "Cameron," she whispered, pleading, hearing his light laugh as he moved against her.

"Hush, love. This is our wedding night. We've scarce begun."

"Teach me then," Kerry whispered, seeing the hard shining desire in his eyes flame even hotter as her hands, cool and arousing, tempted him with each touch. "Teach me what pleases a man."

He groaned as her fingers found him, her hands gentle and smooth, softly arousing, stimulating, moving instinctively until his passion raged out of control. With a purposeful motion, he parted her thighs and Kerry knew her waiting was at an end. Her legs moved to accommodate him, and she felt his hardness probing, searching, then plunging deep within her. Kerry gasped, her body arching against him and matching his ardor with her own.

Passion played with pleasure as the consummate fire devoured them, drawing them into a cauldron of rapture. Still Cameron held back, his hands moving to her breasts, the tingling sensations they created almost unbearable as he drove deep within her. He was gentle at first, caring, until the driving need overtook them both and he gave in to his senses, taking her with heated passion. Kerry's fierce responses astounded him. Free with her emotions, she gave herself to him in every way possible, her woman's body drowning in pleasure. At last Cameron could no longer delay his ultimate release, and furious blaze of love consumed them.

Time stood still. Then Kerry heard Cameron's whispered words of love and she smiled. Nestling beneath the heat of his body, she lifted her face to his.

"You are everything a man could want, Kerry Brent. From the first time I laid eyes on you, I knew the delight you would bring, pleasure unmatched. I think it was always my intent to make you my wife, though it took me a while to realize it."

"Only centuries." Kerry laughed softly, her hand tracing the classically formed face that peered into hers. "Not bad for a Tory," she teased.

"Still beset by Englishmen?" He grinned, one eyebrow arching at the question, and Kerry snuggled happily against him.

"More so than ever. But as you once said, I'll survive." Her grin displayed a row of perfect teeth and a mouth far too enticing to go unkissed. Cameron lowered his lips to hers, luxuriating in their languid kiss, and the coals of passion flamed anew.

Chapter Eighteen

The first rosy flood of dawn found Kerry sighing in her sleep as she sought the warmth of the man beside her. Her eyes slowly opened, and aware of a delicious sense of fulfillment, she stretched, catlike, then smiled at the dark head pillowed beside her. One leg lay possessively over hers, its muscular strength comforting.

Seizing the opportunity, Kerry let her gaze fall freely over Cameron's lean frame, a warm blush coming to her cheek as she did so. He was magnificent, like some ancient Saxon god embodied in sinewy dark flesh. The sheets had been kicked away during the night and his chest, lightly furred with dark curling hair lay open to her gaze. His waist was trim, not soft like that of a more leisurely man, and his hips and flanks tapered to vigorous legs. She sighed as she recalled the previous night and the pleasure she'd found in his arms. Realizing where her musings were leading, Kerry slipped her white limbs out from under his leg, and climbed out of bed.

A few remaining coals still burned orange beneath the flaky gray ash so she tossed several logs into the grate, then fanned the sparks to flames. For a moment she stood in the warmth of the fire, her hands extended to its heat. Warmed, she puttered about the room, picking up the hastily discarded clothing that littered the floor.

A pyramid of parchment caught her eye and Kerry

remembered the chambermaid telling her that this was a pile of wedding gifts and letters of congratulations. With a small curving smile, she leafed through the pile, sifting through the letters until a peculiar scrawling hand caught her eye and she withdrew it from the lot. There was something oddly famliar about this note, and turning it over, she saw a Philadelphia postmark. This message was directed to her. Chewing her lip thoughtfully, Kerry dropped into the wing chair near the fire and opened the envelope, facing the fire's light to read.

It was from her father—Kerry had only to read the salutation to determine that—and with shaking fingers, she read on.

"My dearest girl," it said, "this is the first letter I'll be sending to you, Seamus just returning and taking up the care of the house. Your mother passed away, I'm sorry to be telling you. She's been sickly these past few months. I nursed her myself, there being no money for the doctor . . . damn these English!

"When Cathleen lay in her grave, her soul in a better place than I was ever able to give her, I took it upon myself to seek out the landlord, to tell him of the damage he'd done to me and my own. I went to Thornton House, and much to my surprise I learned that man wasn't the true owner of the lands after all! You'll be thinking he was lying to me, I thought as much myself, but he showed me the paper. The lands, it seems, belong to a family named Brent. 'Tis a big lot of them, some in England and even America, Mr. Thornton says. I swore on the grave of your sainted mother that the day I lay a hand on a Brent is a day he will rue. I hold them accountable for your mother's death, that I do.

"Enough. I do not wish to lay any more troubles upon your shoulders, Kerry. I've left Ireland, and come to this America, to seek work and a better lot in life. Seamus is looking after the wee ones. Worry not for me, Kerry my darling. I will survive."

A knot had formed in the pit of Kerry's stomach by the

time she'd read the letter. The Brents. They were the landlords that ruined her father. They had brought about her mother's death and her own indenture! It couldn't be! She reread the letter, hoping in the back of her mind that there was some mistake, but there was not.

Brents! Kerry's face flamed as she thought of all the times she had eagerly lain with him, abandoned in his arms. He must have been secretly laughing at her, knowing how much he had taken from her family, and even herself! Kerry's face grew scarlet at the thought. She had little doubt that he knew, for Cameron was a careful man who went over his accounts and his books. Surely he was aware of his family's holdings in Ireland.

And now I am his wife! Outrage built within her. Could his desire to wed have had something to do with those lands, with pacifying the Irish? Or was it a new excuse to raise rents?

His duplicity irked her, and she trembled with rage as her gaze rested on Cameron's slumbering form. Just last eve she had thought she loved him! Helplessly her head fell back and she laughed at the irony of it all. But it was a laughter without mirth, and the odd sound of it dragged Cameron forth from his rest.

He awoke with the reluctance of a man sated with love and content with the dreams that invaded his sleep. But now his thoughts turned to more earthy matters, and he hungered for the Irish lass before him, her dark hair flowing wonderfully about her shoulders, her eyes sultry and flaming with passion. He turned over to scoop her into his arms and caught only air.

Fully awake now, he sat upright in the bed, glancing about the room. A movement from the chair caused him to smile, and wrapping the sheet deftly about his hips, he strode to her and placed a kiss just above her right breast.

"Good morning, love," he began, then stopped as he saw her face. Her expression was anything but sensuous or loving. The sound that had awakened him suddenly came back to his mind, but before he could think, she dashed out of the seat and pounded him full in the chest.

"What the hell?" He snatched her up in his arms, forestalling her blows while Kerry squirmed and raged in an attempt to get loose. "Kerry, what is the matter?"

"As if you didn't know," she said nastily. She was held against him, her breasts pressing into his chest, her eyes sparkling with wrath. "But since you seem so determined to hear it from me own lips, I'll tell you, Cameron Brent of England. Your family is responsible for me mother's death, me father's poverty, and me own disgrace!"

Her brogue thickened in her anger, and as Cameron stared down at her, still puzzled, she slammed the crumpled and tear-stained letter into his hand. Knowing his quarry well, Cameron refused to release her, but dragged her over to the candle in order to read the scrawled words.

Kerry knew he had finished when the parchment slipped to the floor and she looked up at him, her eyes shimmering with tears.

"You knew all along!" she declared, not wiping away the tears but allowing them to tumble, like clear crystals, down her cheeks. "You knew! Well, I'll be out of here the first thing this morning! I'm leaving, that I am! I will not stay here!" She tugged at the hand that clasped hers, but found it as unyielding as the iron made in the furnace.

"You will not!" Cameron shouted. "You will listen to me."

"I won't!" Struggling in earnest now, she kicked and fought frantically, pulling at his fingers. "I will not stay here. Your family murdered my mother! I will—"

"I forbid it!" Cameron's voice was thunderous, and Kerry glanced up at him in amazement. She found herself being drawn inexorably closer to him until her body was pressed full length against his and her legs were trapped between his own. His bold blade of passion seared through the thin gown she wore and she was suddenly aware of his desire.

"No!" she cried as he clutched her to him, but her struggles only increased his craving for her. Sweat beaded his forehead as he fought to keep himself from carrying her to the bed and making love to her. But reason told him that to give in to his lust or to her determination to leave would result in losing her forever. With a firm shake, he thrust her backward.

"Be still," he warned, and Kerry felt a thrill of fear. Indeed, Cameron's eyes burned with rage, and his jaw was tight. Gone was the composure she knew. A frightening stranger held her. Forcing herself to stand still, Kerry glared up at him.

"That's better." His voice was calmer now, but anger and frustration still glimmered in his eyes.

"That's why you married me, isn't it? You want to further ruin my family. Or was it guilt? Guilt that you took me, ruined the virginity I'd saved for a proper husband. Or perhaps it was guilt for what you'd done to my family! I'll bet you had a good laugh, thinking all the while to protect yourself and to hell with me!"

"Is that what you think?" His hands clamped like vises on her shoulders and Kerry winced with pain. At once his grip eased, but his anger did not.

"Kerry, you will stay with me."

"No!" she declared.

But he continued in that purposeful manner. "Yes, you will. You will stay with me until I get to the bottom of this. I was aware that my family had holdings in Ireland, but I did not know until now that you or your family were involved with them. You may believe me or not, but mark my words well: I will not let you go until I have some answers. And should you fly, I will seek you out and bring you back. Do you understand?" he asked, penetrating her with his smoldering gaze.

"I do not," Kerry shouted, defiance shining in her eyes. "I

will not stay! And there is nothing you can do about it, nothing!"

"Don't be too sure of that, madam," Cameron said gently, his voice trembling with rage. "You *are* my wife, and I can force you to comply."

"You call this a marriage?" Kerry's laugh was short and angry.

"Yes, I do. Legally, religiously, and morally."

"Then you plan to keep me here as your prisoner?" The words left her mouth in a startled gasp for, indeed, he was locking the door.

Tossing the key onto the dresser, he turned to face her. "For the time being," he answered, giving her a leisurely smile. His gaze ran over her in a way that made her shiver. As she stood before the fire, her hair falling to her waist, her eyes blazing, she looked like a beautiful witch, ready to cast a spell. Every inch of her bare flesh was visible through her filmy gown, and Cameron's smile turned wicked. "I think, after last night, that you will not find reason to hate your forced confinement with me."

"Why you . . ." Rage flamed higher in Kerry and she looked about for something to throw at him. To think that he had taken her in his arms, that she had responded freely, only to have him remind her of it after what happened this morning. Her hands fell upon a candlestick, but before she could toss it as his grinning face he was beside her, seizing the weapon and disarming her. His grip on her wrist was like a band of steel, but it gave her no pain as she struggled furiously against him.

"This is the way of the English, is it not?" Kerry chided, furious and frustrated. "Crush those weaker than yourself! If I were a man you wouldn't handle me this way!"

"Madam, if you were a man you wouldn't find yourself in this predicament."

Whap! Without thinking, Kerry swung her free hand and struck him. Then her eyes went wide as she saw him flinch.

As the evidence of her Irish temper, a red welt, appeared on the side of his face, his hand tightened about her wrist and fear replaced anger for she realized the foolishness of her act. She was his wife, completely in his power both legally and morally, and from the hard brittle gleam in his eyes, she knew she had pushed him too far. She trembled as he reached for her, but instead of striking her as she expected, he pulled her against him and his hard, angry kiss left her breathless.

Kerry tried to pull away, but he held her firmly against him, one hand behind her head, the other holding her wrists at her back. He kissed her savagely and thoroughly, his tongue ravaging her mouth, bruising, arousing, demanding —all gentleness gone. Kerry fought him mentally, resisting any response, but she was nearly swooning. She had never been kissed like this before. It was as if Cameron was trying to force feeling from her, to make her admit something physically that she couldn't say out loud.

Suddenly her rage transformed into passion, and without knowing why, Kerry molded her body to his. "Kerry, Kerry . . ." he groaned, and his hand went to the top of her gown, fumbling awkwardly with it. Then, with an unaccustomed impatience, he tore it from her body. The flimsy material gave way easily and he tossed it aside, his hands like burning brands against her bare skin.

He held her close against him, one arm slipping down to catch her beneath the knees so he might lift her and carry her to the bed. Kerry's mouth opened to utter one last protest, but the words went unspoken for his lips covered hers, taking her mouth with an all-consuming kiss. Kerry's head fell back, resting against his arm; then they tumbled onto the bed.

All thought of resistance or of escape left her, but Cameron still held her pinioned beneath him as if not entirely trusting her. His shirt was still on and it trailed across her bare body, teasing her until he tore it free with an impatient tug of his hand. Throwing it across the room, he tossed one leg over hers to keep her captive, then his hands, rough and warm, began their exploration. He kissed her again, and she could still taste the fury that raged inside of him, but she no longer cared. His hands found her breasts, the tiny nipples springing into life as his fingers moved like flaming fire over them. When his mouth replaced his hands, she writhed against him, straining, moaning, her hands reaching up and helplessly pulling him even closer to her. One of his hands traveled over her flat belly, then lower still.

Suddenly, it was between her thighs, stroking the silken flesh there and causing her to tremble with emotion. Instinctively she tried to pull away, embarrassed as the morning sun poured through the window, illuminating the most intimate part of her, but Cameron was having none of that. With a strength that she'd only guessed at, he held her legs apart, wrapping his arms around each knee, and then his mouth found her. There, where his hands had caressed her so deftly only moments before.

Shocked, Kerry struggled again, but his mouth was arousing her and she could only moan, her objections dying as wave after wave of sensation flooded through her. She had no idea that it could be this way, that people did these things, but Cameron was teaching her once again that there was more to love than she'd suspected. She let him have his way, shuddering at the intense passion that surged through her, then trembling at the explosion that ensued. She muffled her cry of pleasure with her hand, his lips replacing it a moment later in a soothing kiss.

"Cameron, why? . . ."

"Just another way of loving you, sweet," he murmured, his thighs lowering between hers, the hard gleam of passion in his clear gray eyes. Her legs twined eagerly about his as he plunged deeply and effortlessly into her, for her pleaasure had prepared her for him. Beneath him, Kerry felt a driving heat pulse through her, a throbbing in her loins, and he took her with lazy slowness, savoring each moment until she thought she would go out of her mind. He smiled as she moved with him, her body encouraging him to give her the release he'd taught her to crave. But stubbornly he resisted, making her crave it even more. He withdrew, then drove into her again, more deeply this time. Almost sobbing beneath him, she let her hands travel across his back, down past his tensing muscles to his thighs, tempting him with cool, arousing caresses until she heard him suck in his breath in what sounded like a groan. She was rewarded with the demise of his tarrying, for the full heat of his passion now flowed forth. Each thrust, forceful and hard, brought her higher and higher until she writhed beneath him in wanton abandonment, and within moments they knew mutual fulfillment. They lay in each other's arms, sated with love, for what seemed like hours before Cameron lifted his head and peered down at Kerry.

"Madam, I think you'll have to work harder at convincing me how much you despise my English name. If you keep going about it in this manner, I'll be hard pressed to take you seriously."

"Are you starting that again?" Kerry smiled when she saw the teasing glint in his eyes, and he shook his head in negation.

"No. I just cannot resist the urge to test you on this. You look so beautiful in the daylight, your hair falling freely about you, and when you cry out my name like some wild thing, I—"

"Cameron." Kerry blushed, unable to bear the way his eyes raked over her, but his fingers touched her chin and raised it up, forcing her to meet his gaze.

"At least there will be no more secrets between us. I mean to straighten out this mess with your father."

He sounded determined, and a hope arose in Kerry. Perhaps they could have a happy married life? Though her doubts and fears returned, she still felt regret when he climbed out of bed and searched about for his clothes.

"Leaving?" She raised herself on one elbow, watching as he dressed, then blushing when his eyes found her and he grinned.

"Don't look away." He laughed. "You have a right to see me as I am."

"How long will you be gone?" Kerry asked, eager to change the subject.

"Just for a short time this morning." Fully clothed, he unlocked the door, then tossed the key to her. "See that you are here when I get back."

He strode out of the room, and Kerry heard a door slam below, then a horse's hooves on the gravel. The sound slowly died, and alone in the unfamiliar masculine room, Kerry pondered her fate and the future of her marriage.

It was well into the noon hour when Cameron returned, and Kerry was seated in the kitchen, partaking of the pork Helga had roasted in a pungent concoction of apples and onions. Hearing Cameron's firm footfalls, she blushed, then whirled about just in time for him to see her daintily licking her fingers. Wiping them on a cloth, she sent him a flustered glance, but preoccupied with his own thoughts, he did not seem interested in correcting her manners.

"Where is Charles?" Cameron asked, glancing about as he spoke. When his gaze settled on her, Kerry shrugged.

"He went out for a walk in the woods. He said he'd return later." An impatient groan issued from Cameron's lips and he tossed his frost-encrusted cloak aside, then stood before the fire, warming his reddened hands. As awareness came to him, he turned to Kerry, his brow raised in disbelief.

"Charles? Out walking in the wood?" Cameron glanced at the steamy window, an additional testament to the chill outside.

"That's what he said." Kerry spoke softly, for she was a bit puzzled. "He claimed he'd be back shortly."

"Very well." His impatience returning, Cameron frowned. "I would like you to start packing," he said. "We are going on a trip."

"A trip!" Forgetting all else, Kerry scampered from her fireside perch and came to stand before him, her green eyes wide and uncomprehending. "Where?"

"Philadelphia," Cameron announced, blowing on his slowly warming fingers. As understanding slowly gleamed in the pert face of his wife, he smiled bleakly. "I told you I plan to get to the bottom of this."

"But a trip, at this time of year! And with the war? Cameron, are you sure it is safe?"

"It most certainly is not." Charles stepped uninvited into the red brick room, tossing aside his tricorn contemptuously. "Cameron, you cannot be serious."

"I most certainly am." Cameron's stance was purposeful. His hands rested on his lean hips, and one leg was braced forward. He looked directly at his brother. "I expect you to maintain the grounds and house for me while I'm gone. Do you think you can manage that without a workers' revolt?" Although he spoke in a jesting manner, the seriousness of Cameron's question was apparent. Charles brushed the matter away with a flick of his white hand as if it concerned him little.

"I cannot believe you plan to take this girl with you on such a trip. Tories range the woods, as you well know, and Hessian soldiers. Why the chill itself is enough to kill you! And have you considered the ice and snow of December? These roads are impassable. The trip is brutal in the summer months, but in winter it is pure folly. Cameron, I do believe you've taken leave of your senses." Charles returned Cameron's stare with a horrified look.

"When I want your advice I'll ask for it," Cameron said smoothly. "I've made many such journeys successfully, as my presence here testifies."

"And you plan to leave me without a carriage? 'Tis bad

enough that the only decent horse we owned was stolen, by those Irish workers, no doubt." He ignored Kerry's bristling glance and continued in the same vein. "What am I supposed to do for transport?"

"Do not concern yourself," Cameron replied testily. "Richard Westcoat has offered me the use of his coach for the trip. You shall not be prevented from gadding about."

"Ah, Westcoat! I should have guessed that he would be involved in this. No doubt he has a carriage laden to the roof with illegal cargo. Yes, a tidy sum can be procured by furnishing the Continentals with arms and munitions." At Cameron's heated glance, Charles turned to face Kerry. She appeared none the worse after her wedding night with his mysterious brother . . . indeed, she possessed a beauty and radiance that captivated him. She was dressed in a burgundy gown with a neckline of gratifying depth, and Charles allowed his gaze to linger on her snowy bosom before reluctantly fastening it upon her face. Her black hair was drawn back with a ribbon, and the color of her dress made the greens and blues of her eyes merge and melt together like waves. Clearing his throat, Charles attempted one last plea.

"If you do not think of yourself, Cameron, think of the lass. She would not long endure such a trip." The prospect of having such a fetching wench under his protection while her hawk-eyed husband was across the river was most pleasing.

"Sorry, Charles," Cameron replied, laying a possessive hand on Kerry's shoulder. "Kerry has already made the trip at a warmer time of year and she should manage quite well. She is made of much sterner stuff than you give her credit for." Amused, Kerry smiled at her husband while she noted the frustrated gleam in Charles's eyes. When his brother opened his mouth to protest further, Cameron shook his head, refusing to hear his objections.

"It is all decided. We shall leave in the morning. Is that enough time for you to make ready, sweet?" One black eyebrow lifted, he gently questioned the girl. Warmed by this endearment, whether or not it was spoken for Charles's benefit, Kerry's red lips curved into a spritely smile.

"Of a certainty," she replied. "I've been a lady for but one day; I am used to much less time for preparation." She spoke truly, and the grateful warmth in her eyes was not missed by Cameron.

"Good. If you find you need anything else, let me know. I can see to a few purchases before we depart, if given the time."

Kerry nodded and then went to make ready for the journey. That he would go to such lengths to investigate her father's troubles confused her and stirred something deep within her. But she would not allow herself to think that their future rested with what they found in Philadelphia.

The gray morning was sharp with winter's chill, and Kerry huddled deep within her cloak, a fur-lined black wool garment that was a present from Cameron. She appreciated its warmth for her expelled breath turned to an icy fog and from the carriage window she saw only slate-colored sky. Shivering, she burrowed deeper into a corner of the coach, nearly jumping out of her seat when the door swung open suddenly.

"Cameron!" she exclaimed, then managed a weak smile. "Are we leaving now?" Her teeth were chattering, and observing her predicament, he gathered up several thick fur pelts and tossed them over her knees.

"Bundle up," he warned, climbing inside. "'Twill be several hours before daybreak." He chuckled at the rueful glance she sent him, then raised his arms. "You could always follow Charles's suggestion and stay behind."

"Not on your life." She smiled sweetly, but the chill returned and she could not speak without a chatter. "I will see this matter through to the end!" Her sea-colored eyes sparkled determinedly and she braced a chapped hand firmly on her knee, much as a man does when he is fully resolved. She was unaware of the charming picture she made, her hair swept up under her fur cap, and only a few strands escaping that restraint and curling softly against her cheek. Her lips were full, and when they curved into a smile as they did now, they seemed to beg for a kiss. She was child and woman combined. With a strained smile of his own, Cameron moved closer to her. "It will be warmer with me beside you," he said seriously, then smiled at her surprised glance. "Or do you so despise the English that you'd prefer the chill?"

"Far be it from me, master, to deprive you of your comfort," Kerry said smugly, as she snuggled against his warm body. She felt secure beside him, especially when his arm slid down to pull her even closer to him. Her warmth increased no small degree, Kerry glanced up, and was amazed to find a pair of intensely gray eyes burning into hers. But when he spoke, his voice was casual, aloof.

"Then that is your main concern, my comfort?" At his penetrating glance Kerry felt her color deepen but she refused to say him yea or nay. "Fie upon thee, madam," he continued, undaunted by her silence. "Methinks you cherish much more than an English bedwarmer."

"I don't have any idea what you mean," Kerry replied loftily, but her breath caught as he claimed her hand, warming it between his own before pressing a kiss to the back of it. The hand at her waist gave her a featherlike caress, and the other rose momentarily to caress the black silk curl that brushed against Kerry's neck, tracing her well-shaped jawline before returning to recapture her hand. Her racing pulse betrayed her as he smiled down into her eyes with a seemingly endless warmth.

"You almost tempt me to prove it." His smile was charming, easy and sensual, and Kerry found herself caught in its spell. But he spoke again, this time with resignation and almost to himself. "But that would be a mistake, wouldn't it, my Irish rose? I would win the battle and lose the war, and such is not my way." He placed her hand upon her lap and withdrew his arm, turning from her to gaze at the landscape he'd seen a thousand times, as if it was suddenly keenly interesting.

Gathering the furs around her once more, Kerry had much to consider. Her hand was trembling so she tucked it inside the woolen cloak, her mind whirling. How could she respond so readily to this man who was responsible for the suffering of her family—an Englishman at that. She would have to find a way to control this weakness.

The woods flashed by, the trees leafless and barren in the wintry morning, their branches outstretched like the mourning arms of the grief stricken. Secret hidden lakes glimmered with the sparkle of ice. They were invisible in the summer months when leaves provided a camouflage. Cold winds sighed through the bogs, occasionally punctuating those muted sounds with ghastly cries. After one such heartrending sound, a sudden shout rent the air and the carriage lurched, bounced across the frozen road, and thudded into a briar-filled bog.

A click drew Kerry's attention and her eyes grew wide as she saw Cameron withdraw a loaded horse pistol from beneath the carriage seat, his face granitelike. "What is it?" she whispered, growing more frightened by the moment when she heard George exchanging heated words outside. Horse's hooves stomped the ground, and before Cameron could reply, the door was wrenched open and a face concealed by a black silk bandana peered inside the carriage!

Highwaymen! Kerry squeezed back into the corner as two shining black eyes glimmered at her over the mask, and with the crook of his pistol, the holdup man gestured for them to come out.

"Leave the lady be, Mulliner." Cameron's voice was cool and determined, and he stepped out of the carriage, not addressing the man who'd peered into it, but the one still astride his horse. That man appeared puzzled. He waved his gun in the air and his light-colored eyes narrowed. Even from inside the coach Kerry could see that he was an extraordinarily handsome man who was wearing an elaborate uniform of undetermined origin. An ornate sword rode at his hip and tucked in his belt was a brace of pistols. "Who is it that speaks my name?" he asked, his clipped tones as brittle as the morn. "Speak man. Who are you?"

"Cameron Brent." Standing before the horseman, his gun concealed within the folds of his cloak, Cameron faced his fellow Englishman, a barely hidden sneer on his lips.

"And how do you know of me?" the highwayman continued.

The briefest of smiles crossed Cameron's face. "I make it my business to know Tory spies, thugs, and cutthroats."

"Careless words." Mulliner sneered. "Take heed, Cameron Brent. For I would as soon kill you as look at you."

"No!" Kerry shouted, jumping out of the coach. She missed Cameron's angry glare but not the highwaymen's sudden interest as their eyes turned to her. Beside her husband in the morning cold, she stood defiantly, the wind lifting her locks and thereby accentuating the beauty of her finely formed face.

"Gor! 'Tis a blooming beauty!" the first man shouted while Mulliner's dark eyebrows perked up with interest.

"She is that," he conceded, his eyes roaming over the all-encompassing cloak, the arresting face. Seeing the glare she directed at his man, he gave vent to laughter and sidled the horse up closer to the girl. "She would bring a good price in the city." He spoke musingly, his eyes like two pieces of chipped ice. "Remove the cloak, lass, that I might better judge your worth."

Kerry's outrage provoked further laughter, but his mirth suddenly died when he found himself staring into the barrel of a well-aimed pistol.

"The woman you speak of happens to be my wife,"

Cameron stated, with his left hand bringing Kerry closer to him. "And should you lay a hand to her I will surely kill you."

Mulliner's gaze flickered from the lass to the gun pointing at him. Then he considered drawing his own pistol. Finally he shrugged. Cameron Brent would waste no bullet on his man; the gun was aimed at him. He desired this lass, not only for the profit he'd make on selling her, but she was not worth his life.

"We shall meet again, Cameron Brent," he declared, his voice full of hate. "I never forget a foe." With a tilt of his head he indicated that his man should remount, and together they backed away from the carriage. At once Cameron lifted Kerry inside, but as he was climbing in himself, a shot rang out and Kerry gasped when Cameron clutched his arm. Jeering laughter followed, then the highwaymen disappeared into a screen of briars.

"Cameron, let me see." Kerry pulled away his cloak, revealing a bloodstained shirt as George's face appeared at the window, worry etched into his features.

"I'm sorry, sir. There was naught I could do. The other had a gun to me head."

"That's all right." Cameron winced, then tore his shirt away from his wound. "Filthy coward, that man," he declared. "Thank God it's but a scratch."

"A scratch!" Kerry exclaimed, for blood gushed forth from his wound. "We should head back immediately."

"No," said Cameron quietly.

"But the wound!"

"There is an excellent medical hospital in Philadelphia. I will receive the best treatment there. You will recall that at home the best we have is a country doctor, and although he is is adequate to treat furnace burns, he does not have the knowledge to treat a gunshot wound."

"But you should rest!" Kerry said fearfully. She had seen many men in Ireland wounded thus, and the result was often the loss of a limb. "It may turn poisonous."

"It is less than a day's journey to the hospital. My arm will fare no worse for one day's travel." In spite of his condition, his tone was decisive and Kerry knew he would not alter his decision. She glanced about the coach for some material to be pressed into service as a bandage, but saw nothing appropriate. Lifting her skirts, she ripped a square from her petticoat, then folded it neatly into a compress. While she was thus occupied, Cameron's gaze, warmly admiring, was fixed on the slender legs now exposed to his gaze.

"Cool your lusts," Kerry said purposefully, but she had to suppress a grin as she placed the bandage against his arm. From his slight grimace, she could imagine his pain, but as the carriage lurched forward, against him, his good arm slipped about her slender waist and prevented her from being thrown about. As her cloak gaped, he had an unhindered view of her bosom which was straining against her dress.

"Dare I hope, madam, that your eagerness for me extends beyond simple caution?" he teased, although the strain of his injury showed in the tight crinkles around his eyes. Pain forced him to ease the pressure of his arm about her waist, and he involuntarily pressed against the blood-soaked bandage she'd supplied.

"Aye, and if you watched your back as closely as you do me, this wound would not be here," she said smartly, but the amount of blood coming through the bandage alarmed her. It would be quite some time before they reached the city, and she knew a man could weaken in just a few hours. She frowned, testing the wound with a finger, and to her dismay, fresh blood dampened the reddened cloth.

I must stop the bleeding, she thought. As she tried to think of a way something nagged at her and suddenly, the woodswoman came to mind. *Sphagnum moss.* Enid had said it cleansed wounds and held water like a sponge. If the moss would hold water, it would hold blood . . . and keep the wound clean.

"Stop!" she called out the window to George, while Cameron grasped her cloak and pulled her back.

"Madam, what are you about?" he demanded, his eyes peering into hers with a silvery stare, but she paid him little heed, speaking instead to the servant who appeared at the window as soon as the horses could be stopped.

"George," Kerry said evenly, "please stop at the swamp."

"The swamp!" Cameron looked askance, but his wife nodded.

"Yes. You see, George, there is a moss that grows there, a moss that will help his wound until we get to the city."

"Dash it all Kerry! We have no time for heathen remedies! Pay her no mind, George, and go on. I'll have no woman clucking over me like a hen with a chick." Cameron nodded his head as if all was decided, but George remained uncertain, his eyes wavering from the lass to her disapproving husband.

"But, George"—Kerry smiled, and her liquid, green eyes gazed down at the coachman—"please . . . it will not take much time, I promise."

"Aye," George declared, shouting to be heard over the protests that shook the small carriage. "It is on the way! And if the lass thinks it will help, I will stop!"

Cameron raged as the servant climbed purposefully atop the coach, ignoring the oaths below. But Kerry was not so fortunate for she was within the carriage and had no choice but to submit to the wrath of her husband.

"Madam, you deliberately defy my wishes. Worse! You force my servant to defy them. I will not tolerate such audacity." He leaned across the coach, his eyes like heated metal, his square jaw tense. One hand clamped to his wound, the other waving at her as if she were an errant child. That gesture got her dander up, and without forethought, she slapped his gesturing hand away and returned his glare.

"You will not tolerate! Upon my word, you treat your

horses better than yourself! You fret for days over Caledonia's departure, yet you'd let your own arm go untreated just to prove a point! You, sir, have called me stubborn," she continued, unable to see his face for he was looking down, staring in amazement at the hand she'd so boldly slapped away, "but I think I have a way to go before I reach your obstinacy!"

She nearly flinched as his eyes blazed upon her, but she forced herself to remain on the edge of her seat and face him. Her bravado slipped badly at his next words, however, and it was all she could do to maintain her determined facade.

"Madam," he choked out, his voice harsh with anger, "you have tested my limits one too many times. You seem to confuse patience with weakness, and it has been in my mind since the day we met that you sorely need a lesson on this point. I can think of no one better than myself to provide that instruction." He raised his hand, intending to give her a fatherly lecture but Kerry mistook his intent.

"You wouldn't dare!" she gasped, and with a frightened squeak, she ducked under his arm. Refusing to relinquish this opportunity for what he deemed a sorely needed lesson, Cameron lunged toward the floor where the lass now crouched. The quickness of that movement was his downfall, however, for the loss of blood took its toll and he lost consciousness, falling from the seat onto a pile of furs.

Kerry rose and took a seat, as wary of the man below as prey is of a hunter. She waited one minute, then two, and when he made no motion, she caressed his forehead for the briefest instant, quickly withdrawing her hand to see if he stirred. He breathed easily and his eyelids flickered, but they did not open so Kerry tucked the remaining furs about him with a sigh.

"'Tis better at any rate," she said thoughtfully. "For he is less likely to injure the arm now and we can safely apply the moss without his protests." As soon as she'd decided this, the carriage door was flung open and George proffered a handful of the much-needed moss.

Kerry smiled appreciatively, then recalling Enid's words, she squeezed the light green foliage with a firm pressure. Water poured forth and when she repeated that procedure she got the same results. George's amazed eyes met hers, but she kept squeezing the moss until little water remained in it. Finally she carefully removed the petticoat square which was now blood red. Packing the moss firmly about the wound, she used the old bandage to keep it in place.

"This should hold." She patted the poultice, then glanced hesitantly at George. "Let us be on our way. If he regains consciousness and we are late arriving in Philadelphia, I shall never hear the end of it."

"Aye, that is certain." George chuckled and then climbed back up to his seat, wrapping his long woolen muffler about him against the cold. As he snapped the reins, he shook his head, privately amused. He'd never met a man or woman who dared overly much with Cameron Brent. Something about the man did not allow for such a possibility. Yet this tiny slip of a lass had defied him openly. He could only chuckle to himself, and think that Cameron had met his match. But in spite of the lass's fire and determination, she had none of the cruelty of Brent's former fiancée, none of her nastiness or her airs, and for that, George was grateful.

Inside the carriage, Kerry repeatedly checked the wound for the slightest sign of blood. Fortunately, the mossy covering was very absorbent and the pressure created by tying a bandage around it had eased the blood flow. Unwilling to leave anything to chance, Kerry tucked the remaining furs neatly about him, pillowing his head and his injured arm, and bracing them against the movements of the carriage. Once, when the horses slipped on a sheet of newly formed ice, the coach was jolted, and Cameron slid across the seat. But Kerry blocked his movement with her own body, cushioning him against any damage. And when the wind blew cold and wild, she wrapped him even more carefully, fighting the chill that seemed wont to creep into her own bones. Cameron shivered, nonetheless, and his face was paling with alarming speed. Kerry prayed silently that he would be all right, but his lips were blue now and he could not control his violent shaking, even in his unconscious state. Instinctively, she removed the covering furs and slipped her body over his, warming him while she pulled the furs back over them. Taking heed not to injure his arm, she let her face rest against his, her breath warming his cheek. She stayed in this position until, hours later, the carriage rolled into Cooper's ferry.

"Cameron?" Realizing that they'd stopped, she quickly set about waking him, and attempted to revive his color with a tap on his cheek. "Cameron, can you hear me?"

Slowly one eyelid flickered open. It shut and then opened once more. At length he gazed wonderingly about, unable to identify this frosty and damp place.

"Is he up? Ah, good evening, sir." A satisfied smile crossed George's face as Cameron's clear gaze met his searching glance. "Now if you'll be putting an arm over mine, like so . . ." With a deft maneuver George hoisted his employer to his feet and onto the awaiting ferry, while Kerry followed. "Just a short ride, sir."

Cameron was in no state to argue so he followed his servant's directions and climbed aboard the ferry, supported by the coachman and his young wife. His eyes seemed to warm him for a moment when they met Kerry's, but the effort of standing at the rail was taking a toll on him. Indeed, the three of them were relieved when they reached the opposite shore of the Delaware, where they rented a brougham that quickly took them to the hospital, an impressive building with many windows and several wings. George summoned a passer-by, and with the combined strength of the two men, got Cameron inside and out of the chill.

Within moments the physician approached them, a small,

rotund man of middle age, with an air of bustling importance. He waved the men away from Cameron, and with the aid of several strange instruments, thumped and examined him until Kerry thought she would shout.

"It's his arm," she said impatiently. The doctor peered up at her through small spectacles and nodded, amazed at this impertinence.

"I am aware of that," he said smugly. "How far did you bring him?"

"From the Forks," Kerry replied, her worried glance on her husband. Yet she heard the doctor's spectacles drop and turned to see him peer at her with squinting amazement.

"The Forks! In this weather! That is impossible." He puffed as he retrieved his glasses to better view the lass before him. "He would be frozen stiff with such a wound! And the blood loss!" At once he was picking at the gunshot wound, peeling the bandage away as if he thought they were playing a practical joke on him. His amazement increased when he removed the petticoat square and found the grasslike material beneath.

"Sphagnum moss, sir," George said, shuffling his feet. He was now not certain they'd done the right thing. The physician continued to gape while George stutered. "You see, sir, the miss, I mean the madam thought it would help . . . and I couldn't see the harm. . ."

"Madam?" The doctor whirled toward Kerry, his eyes as round as his glasses now. "You are responsible for this?"

"Yes," Kerry stammered, growing more worried by the minute. "You see, I—"

"Madam, you may just have saved his life," the doctor said, his amazement complete. "I know what this is. Some of the soldiers we treated after the Chestnut Neck battle had sought to stem the flow of blood from their own wounds. Unable to find any cloth or such, they used this moss, and found that it not only held the blood but cleansed the wound. As it has done here." He demonstrated by washing away the remaining moss. Although the bullet hole still gaped, the flow of blood had stopped and the wound showed no signs of infection. The doctor probed for any remaining metal and Cameron groaned, fully awake now under the painful exploration. But within moments, the physician gave a satisfied sigh and dried his hands on a nearby cloth, his head still shaking to and fro.

"Consider yourself a lucky man," he told Cameron, as he glanced admiringly at the lovely Irish girl. "But for your wife there, you might have had a stump for an arm. As a matter of fact, you might not have lived. You were fortunate indeed in choosing someone so clever for a bride."

Cameron looked at Kerry as if considering his words; then he smiled wanly. Swinging to his feet, he grasped the table for support while the doctor chuckled.

"You must be newly married; you're so eager to return home." He winked broadly as Kerry took Cameron's arm and George hastened to aid his employer. A slight blush came to Kerry's cheeks as Cameron's eyes met hers; then, with a hearty thanks to the doctor, they returned to the rented coach. It was a strange parade they made, the tall stately man supported by the wee girl and the bulky servant, but together they managed to get Cameron into the coach. At once George started for the inn, while Kerry gathered up the furs and saw to her husband's comfort.

"Kerry," Cameron rasped, and the young girl smiled down at him. "The next time I act in such a foolish manner, do me a service."

"Of course. What do you wish me to do?" She nestled against him.

"Remind me of tonight. Just say the words, 'sphagnum moss' and I will desist immediately." With that his head rested against hers and he fell into a healthy sleep while the lass beside him laughed.

Chapter Nineteen

The inn was but a short drive through the cobbled streets of the city, yet every jar and bump set Kerry's nerves on edge. She sought to prevent any discomfort for Cameron, knowing that his recovery depended much upon the next few hours, and with great care, she plied the furs about him to ease the rollicking motion of the carriage. But her task seemed endless for the cobbles tossed the small coach as the sea does a ship. Indeed, it was a relief to her when the horses stopped and George knocked upon the door of the hostelry.

"I'm coming, I'm coming!" a disgruntled voice, heavy with sleep, called from above. Somewhere within the building there was a clatter, followed by a muffled curse as the innkeeper flung open the door.

"And who might you be, awaking me op in the middle of the night?" the voice cried, and Kerry could hear George's stammering reply.

"'Tis Master Brent, sir. We sent word of our arrival. Are we not expected?"

"Ye are not," the innkeeper declared. "I own the place. If ye were ta come, wouldn't I have known about it?" His tone was belligerent, and Kerry could almost see George's red face.

"Is there some mistake?" She opened the carriage door

and stepped gracefully onto the doorstone. Without further ado she swept her hood from her face, allowing her shining black curls to be tousled by the wind as she peered toward the inn.

A peculiar little man, his face so completely swathed in a muffler that only his watery blue eyes were visible, stood before her. He was so like a badger that Kerry was startled, but she kept to her purpose, rubbing her hands as if they pained her.

"There is a mistake, miss," the innkeeper continued, but there was no mistaking the change in him. His tone was respectful as his filmy eyes surveyed this lady of quality. "I was not warned of your coming, but now that you are here, I do think I could find some . . . accamadations." He nodded, clearly pleased at having recalled this last lengthy and sure to be impressive word. Kerry smiled and nodded politely, then turned a most winsome pair of twinkling green eyes up at the man.

"I thank you most kindly, sir," she declared. "But might we get in from the cold? My hands are near frozen."

"Certainly, my dear! Certainly! Where are my manners? Higby, see to the luggage!" With a bustle, the innkeeper ushered Kerry inside while a shivering lad went out into the cold to bring in their baggage.

"Can you help me?" Kerry said to the boy, gesturing toward the coach. "My husband sleeps. Please assist me." At once the innkeeper's eyes clouded, but his demeanor changed again as she helped the lad escort her spouse into the inn. The man did not appear old, but his gait was heavy and the innkeeper, watching from behind the door, thought that such a comely lass should not be burdened with an ailing husband. In fact, she might welcome a bit of stalwart and able company, he decided, and he set out a bottle of sherry, hushing the clink of glass so as not to awaken his ample wife.

"Right here by the fire. Yes, isn't this nice?" The innkeeper directed Kerry and the lad to place Cameron on a long wooden bench. Loss of blood added to his fatigue, and it was with some difficulty that he glanced about, his eyes slowly clearing.

"Let me show you your room, my dear." Deftly securing the sherry, the innkeeper started for the hallway. Kerry glanced uncertainly back at Cameron, but George had now entered and stood by his side. He nodded to Kerry and knowing Cameron was protected, she obediently followed the tavern owner.

"Right here, my dear. Is it not fine?" He had removed his muffler, and his long thin nose quivered with his words, adding to the mole-like appearance. Kerry glanced about her.

The room was plain, and obviously not a good one, but the kind reserved for less fortunate travelers. The small bed sagged sadly in the center, and a threadbare quilt graced the worn mattress. A single, straight-backed wooden chair was the only other furnishing; there was no washstand, not even a pitcher. An old stove occupied one corner, but even the innkeeper's attempts to fan the coals produced little heat. The warm air was drawn off through the many cracks and openings in the walls.

"Is this the only room available? We'll freeze!" Kerry whirled about, surprised to find the innkeeper amazingly close behind her. "I'm sorry, but we need another room."

"Another room!" the innkeeper wheezed, his eyes blinking in pure amazement. "Do you know what I've gone through to get this one? Why I've had a man waiting for this very room, but I planned to disappoint him, just to help you."

Kerry's shrewd nature immediately came to her aid. Recalling Jane Clark's words, she smiled, a pretty curving of her full red lips, and she laid a hand gently on the man's shoulders.

"I'm sure you have and we are grateful for any trouble you've gone to," she said, effectively hiding her soft Irish accent and mimicking Cameron's decisive tones. "But you have seen that my husband is not well. Can you think of any other room that would be more suited to our needs?"

Lost in the brilliance of that smile, the little man stammered and stared.

"Aye, I can. You have moved my very heart, my dear, just with your presence. I have a room down the hall that was let this morn, but the couple have not yet arrived! I think mesel' justified in thinking they will not come at all, don't you now?"

He clucked and rubbed his hands together, well pleased with his generosity. Then he led Kerry down the hallway. At the end of it was a door, and from a massive pocket, the innkeeper fished out a key and wedged it inside.

"Right here, madam. I think you will find this to yer likin'."

Kerry glanced about as soon as the little man lit a lamp. This room was indeed better, comfortable in fact. A large canopied bed stood to the right, heavy with warm quilts, and a washstand was nearby. The huge fireplace yawned across the room, while chairs and carved tables were placed about it. Warm rugs kept the winter chill from one's feet, and the heat from below drifted up through the floorboards, so the temperature of this room was tolerable before the innkeeper fanned the logs into flames.

"This is wonderful." Kerry smiled, surveying the place with delight, but her smile vanished as the innkeeper closed the door behind them, then withdrew the sherry bottle from his coat pocket.

"A small drink, lass," he crooned, holding up the amber-colored bottle to the light. "For yerself and myself." His tiny narrow eyes were open only slightly and Kerry saw a strange glint in their depths.

"I don't think . . ." she began, edging deftly toward the door. But the little man blocked her way with a lightning-quick movement that belied his apparently quiet demeanor.

"No, No!" The innkeeper nodded, his pointed nose

dipping toward the floor. "Such a naughty thing, such a pretty thing!" His clawlike hand fell upon Kerry's arm, and with a shriek, she brushed it away.

"Sir, have you gone mad? Me own master, my husband, is downstairs!" Kerry exclaimed, her eyes wide with disbelief.

"Aye, and ailing he is." 'Twould seem to me that a young lass like yerself would appreciate a full man upon her for once. Now come here, my dear, I mean to have you, I cannot help myself." The clawlike hand reached for Kerry's cloak, and the Irish girl thought she would suffocate.

Suddenly the door was flung open and the little innkeeper stood aghast, his tiny eyes blinking rapidly in astonishment. There, framed in the doorway, was the dark-clothed figure of Cameron Brent, his cloak thrown over one shoulder, his white shirt riddled with blood. To the innkeeper he seemed altogether too fit as he leaned against the doorframe, his arms crossed over his muscular chest. The smile that flitted across his face was not one of amusement, and the flickering shadows cast by the fire deepened the granite outline of his face. He was satanic, diabolical. The innkeeper dropped the sherry bottle to the floor with a crash.

"A . . . Master Brent," the little man sniveled, his fear obvious, "I was just seeing to the lady's comforts. I thought she might like—"

"You thought she might like what?" Cameron said coldly, his eyes transfixing the squirming man like a pin jabbed through a moth. "Well man? Speak!"

"A fire. And perhaps a wee drop." The innkeeper gestured lamely to the bottle, but Cameron's eyes did not waver.

"Get out," he said quietly, but there was a dangerous tightening of his jaw. "Now!"

"Aye, sir." The innkeeper scuttled quickly out the door, but before he was quit of this frightening specter of an outraged husband, he felt a strong hand grasp his collar and his feet suddenly dangled in the air.

"And if you come near my wife again, I shall kill you."

As Cameron's fingers tightened in the little man's collar, he nodded frightfully, his arms flailing helplessly at his sides. Just then a matronly woman waddled out of the hall below, her round face angry and flushed. She resembled a fully stuffed mattress, but when her eyes fell on the quaking form of her husband she was anything but pleased.

"At it agin, are ye! After the young missus, I suppose! Wait 'til I get you below!" Her years of practice evident, she grasped the innkeeper's ear and led him, protesting and explaining, down the hall. "Sorry, gov," she called over her shoulder to Cameron, ignoring the man in her grasp. "It will not 'appen agin. I'll see ta that." Then, with a firm kick, she sent her husband reeling down the stairs, her own ponderous form following him vengefully.

As Cameron closed the door firmly behind him, Kerry gave vent to her pent-up laughter.

"Did you see his face?" she asked, obviously delighted at the little man's comeuppance. "I swear he thinks you the devil incarnate, the way he shook." She gazed up at Cameron and her smile was dazzling.

"Aye, but I think for him the worse is yet to come." Indulging in one of his rare smiles, Cameron lifted a lock of the black hair curling about his young wife's shoulders. His fingers toyed with it idly, but his closeness, the warmth of his presence, and the strange lights in his gray eyes made Kerry feel shaky. He touched her face, brushing away hair from cheeks that bloomed like a wild rose. "'Tis time we get some sleep," he then said abruptly, speaking with a sharpness that left Kerry wondering. "We have much to do on the morrow."

His hand dropped from her face as if scalded, and he stalked away from her, realizing that only now that they were alone was he favoring the injured arm. He sat on the bed, removing his boots while Kerry sought the comfort of the fire. She was well aware of the meager size of the bed, and her concern for Cameron's weakness had vanished with his treatment of the innkeeper. Staring into the flickering blaze, she doffed her cloak and gown, and hurriedly pulled on a nightdress as an oddly strained cough came from the bed behind her. The gown, one of those given her by Jane Clark, was of rose-colored batiste, sheer and filmy, and when Kerry moved before the fire it seemed she was naked, except for the rosy haze floating around her.

Unaware of the effect her state was having upon Cameron, Kerry sat in the chair before the fire, brushing out her hair. This was a task that she'd longed for all day, for on the long cold trip the wind had ravaged and tangled her locks. With industrious application of brush and comb, however, she chided the mass into willful obedience, and the result was a polished black curtain that fell to her waist.

"Kerry."

Her gaze flew to the bed when he spoke. From her position by the fire she could see that Cameron was between the sheets, sitting up, and he was watching her with burning intensity.

"It is not my desire to force you into anything, but there is a limit to my restraint. Unless you have decided to share this night with me, as my wife, I would suggest you finish what you are doing as soon as possible."

Kerry nodded, but a small smile broke out upon her lips, hidden by the turning of her head. She finished her hair quickly, giving it a few last strokes with the brush. Then she busied herself with putting their garments in order. When the reassuring sound of deep even breathing came from the bed, Kerry smiled, knowing herself safe for this night.

Hearing a noise that came from below, she glanced out of the window and saw a lorry ambling slowly up the road, its driver barely nodding as he drove the habitué of some tavern back to his waiting wife. Lights gleamed from the windows of nearby dwellings, the tiny specks comforting reminders of the life surrounding her. Leaning against the window, Kerry wondered if one of those lights was her father's and if he was thinking of her.

* * *

As it happened, Beagan O'Toole was thinking of his daughter, but not in the way she imagined. The once-handsome man with the mane of snowy-white hair now sat red-faced, his paunch distended from too much ale. "Barkeep, another!" he shouted, slamming his fist upon the wood while the good man behind it sought to keep his glass filled. There seemed not enough ale in all the world to numb the soul of Beagan O'Toole, to assuage his ache.

"Aye, and who'd 'a thought I'd come ta this?" He addressed the ale which flowed upward in a comforting stream of golden bubbles. "Me, Beagan O'Toole."

And indeed, Beagan was the picture of a broken man. His back was bent, not from years of hard labor but from dejection, and his head hung over his glass, but he cared naught. He was beyond that now. His cap was askew, his coat shabby and poor. Its patches barely meeting the frayed ends of cloth, it provided little protection against the cold night air.

"The wager! Are ya in, man?" A voice floated softly back to Beagan and through misty eyes he peered up, staring until the barkeep was no longer two apparitions, but one single man.

"Aye. Count me in."

At once the cocks were loosened and set upon each other, and the air was filled with the shouts of wagering men. A flurry of blood and feathers rent the air as a large bandy-legged bird tore at its opponent, which sought to get in a gouge of its own.

"Come on ye bloody beggar." A stout, half-drunken man shouted. "Paid half a sixpence for ye, ya'd better fight!"

"I told ya none could beat old Joe." A wizened patron warned as the white cock slumped to the floor in defeat while the bantam rooster renewed his attack on its glistening plumage. The white feathers were already veined with red. "None can. Ain't seen a bird like him in my many days."

Beagan sipped his ale and watched the barkeep collect his

coin, cursing under his breath. You'd think I'd be used to it by now, he thought, banging for another mug. But I never do get used ta losing. Drinking down his ale, he waited for oblivion, wanting to be taken from this life. "Ah yes, Kerry me darlin'," Beagan thought wistfully, gazing into the ale, "now that ye are settled in that foin house, you won't mind helping out yer poor father." Finishing up the mug, he slowly slid from the barstool, comforted by that last thought.

Kerry awakened abruptly at a slight knock upon the door. Then two mousy chambermaids entered the room. With a clatter, one poured a bucket of steamy water into a copper tub while the other deposited a tray of food beside the bed. Glancing toward her apparently sleeping husband, Kerry put her finger to her lips, then rose from the bed, wrapping herself in a thick robe against the morning chill. The smaller maid shrugged. Her freckled nose resembled a sparrow's egg, and above it, two tiny eyes nestled together in puzzlement. Then her gaze flew to the bed and widened as she beheld Cameron.

Even asleep he was a magnificent specimen of a man, and the young maid could scarcely take her eyes from him as she tossed the logs onto the fire. Her companion seemed equally impressed, and only when Kerry stood pointedly by the tub, gazing into its shallow waters, did she remember her duty and hasten off to return with two more buckets.

"Will there be anything else, mistress?" she asked, her speech directed at Kerry but not her eyes. Her glance wandered so boldly to the bed that Kerry felt her ire rising.

"No, that will be all," she responded, more sharply than she'd intended. Clutching the robe about her, she went to close the door after the two young maids.

"If his master should want anything," the bolder of the two continued, "such as help with his bathing, you can jest call."

"If he'll be needing any help, I'm the one he'll call," Kerry snapped, her patience gone. With a firm shove, she shut the door, her sea-colored eyes sparkling with something other than laughter.

The fire rose slowly in the ample logs, and the chill set Kerry to shivering. Since thick clouds of steam wafted from the copper tub, she doffed the robe and slipped into the warm bath with a sigh.

Instantly the ache in her toes fled, and she sank deeper into the water, her bliss complete. Content, she did not notice a dark form arising behind her, nor did she hear him come to stand before her. Her eyes closed, her senses absorbing the silky caress of the bath, and her foot braced on the far side for balance while the waters teased her chin. Thus, when she raised her eyelids, she gasped in astonishment to see Cameron seated contentedly on the chair directly in front of her. Before she could prevent it, her foot slipped and she disappeared beneath the surface of the water.

"Oh, you!" She emerged, sputtering, while Cameron gave vent to unrestrained laughter, throwing back his dark head as he did so. But he had little reason to laugh a moment later when a handful of water splashed over his face and dripped down over the collar of his royal blue robe.

"You appear to be in need of a wash." Kerry giggled as Cameron glanced at his robe in amazement, seeing the tiny crystal beads that decorated him. Then he arose and strode purposefully toward the tub while Kerry lowered herself into it as far as safety permitted. He stood before her like some dark majestic statue, his features austere. His hands were braced on his hips, and his lightly furred chest was partially revealed by his blue robe. When he lowered a hand to the water, idly dipping his fingers in it, Kerry's gaze flew to his face. In his eyes burned a longing, a passion, that left her breathless, and his voice came in a husky whisper.

"Is that a welcome to join your bath, my rose?" Her pert nose still harbored a droplet of water and her bosom teased him, her breasts bobbing at the surface, their round fullness enticing him then disappearing in the steamy depths of the bath. His fingers slowly traced their outline, leaving Kerry with a craving for more of his touch. She gazed up at him, her pink mouth half-open.

"I didn't mean . . ." She feigned outrage, and he withdrew his hand. But the heated sensation continued so she grasped at the scented soap, lathering her well-shaped leg with fierce determination while he chuckled.

"No? My apologies then. I merely thought—"

"Aye, I know what you thought, to come sneaking up on me when I had me eyes closed!" She glared at Cameron, but still smiling, he returned to his chair and the comfort of his pipe. His quiet observation of her was unnerving yet his eyes never left the comely form that glistened in the fire's light.

"Would you mind looking away?" she finally asked, but his reply was a calm shaking of the head. Before she could give vent to a well-thought-out assortment of oaths, he spoke sincerely. "Kerry, I have honored your tender sensibilities in not pressing you as to your marital commitments before we see this matter through, but I will not be denied all the pleasures of being wed to thee." His eyes caressed her even as he spoke, and she felt a strange trembling in her limbs. The warming within her grew, and try as she might, she could find no words to deny him this request. Indeed, she was more than aware that few husbands would demonstrate the will he possessed. Once again, she wondered at the extent of his patience.

Finishing her ablutions with some haste, she reached for a cloth to stave off his view. Then she draped the linen around her and arose, a satisfied smile on her face, only to discover that her covering allowed him to gaze at her legs. In fact the cloth scarcely allowed her any modesty, for her bosom almost thrust free of its meager confinement, and her rounded buttocks threatened to peek forth as well. Aware of Cameron's appreciative stare, Kerry dashed across the room to snatch up the quilts.

The crackle of the fire mingled with his dry laughter, as she gave him an angry look. But her eyes quickly shifted when she saw him doff his robe and step casually into the tub, unconcerned about his own naked state. When she dared to look at him once more, he was resting peacefully in the bath, his injured arm elevated above the water.

"Your arm? How is it today?" she asked cautiously. In her embarrassment she'd forgotten his wound. He opened one eye and peered at her strangely, an odd smile coming to his face.

"It is fine, and I have you to thank for that." A glimmer of white teeth showed between his red lips as he continued to study her intently. "Is your hatred for the English waning? You have gone to considerable lengths to see me in good repair." His gaze never left her face, as if he was seeking the truth of the matter.

"'Tis the least I could have done," Kerry answered loftily. "I could not let you bleed to death, as was your wont."

"I see," Cameron said, but his smile remained. Nervous under his stare, Kerry flung open her drawer and hastily withdrew a woolen gown of emerald green. Chosen mainly for its warmth, the dress complimented Kerry's slender figure, hugging her tight curves and emphasizing her tiny waist, and its color deepened the mysterious shades of her eyes, making them swirl and melt together into emerald seas. Having dressed, she pinned her hair into a simple upswept coiffure, allowing a few black curls to dance about her face.

When Cameron rose from the tub, his eyes traveled over her in an ageless compliment. "You look lovely," he murmured, coming to stand before her.

Kerry smiled up in gratification while he toyed with one shining curl. "It's the dress." She replied, one hand smoothing its soft wool. Then her gaze met his once again. "You are very generous."

"'Tis not the dress," Cameron scoffed, striding away from

her and donning his own dark trousers and white shirt, "but the lass who wears it." When Kerry opened her mouth to object, he shook his head and buttoned his waistcoat. "Madam, I have seen many other ladies whose beauty is legendary. But none of them could wear that gown with the same ease you do. Now, gather your cloak. We are off to see the solicitor, and you'd best hurry before I change my mind about taking you with me."

Taking him at his word, Kerry quickly donned her fur-trimmed cloak, grateful for that garment the moment she opened the door. A blast of cold air ripped through the hallway, only a small indicator of the cold to come. She shivered, glancing up at Cameron as they stepped outside. The cold of this day bested that of the previous one, and the sky was an icy blue gray.

Gazing upward, Cameron pointed to the clouds.

"It looks like snow. We'd best hurry if we are to complete the business of the day."

George dismounted from his perch on the rented coach, holding open the door and helping Kerry into the carriage. His eyes widened at the sight of her, and a broad grin creased his fleshy face. "You're looking lovely this morning, mistress," he declared, beaming. "You take the chill from me very bones."

"Thank you." Kerry bestowed a brilliant smile upon him, then giggled at Cameron's scowl.

"Might we get on with this journey before the entire street pauses to proclaim your fabled beauty?" he snapped. He then closed the carriage door with a firm slam, giving George cause to shake his head as he drove off.

"It's certainly changed, has it not?" Kerry remarked, peering out of the carriage window to view the scene unfolding before them. The docks were piled high with rubbish, and the streets reeked of rotting garbage and the remnants of chamber pots. Even as Kerry closed her nostrils to this fetid smell, a white-capped woman leaned out of an upstairs window to empty a pot onto the street. Below her, a scavenger paused and, wiping at his sleeve, shook his fist. Many houses were boarded up. Their shuttered windows strangely sightless, they seemed to be guarding secret memories of their former occupants.

"The British," Cameron remarked, pointing to the wretched filth. "Since they've departed, the city's been a shambles. The new governor, Benedict Arnold, has set about cleaning it up, but it will take time to restore the streets to their former state."

"And those houses?" Kerry asked, glancing at another brick-faced building, boarded and desolate. "What of them?"

She gazed sadly at the once-grand dwellings, aware that music and dancing had filled their halls. Although she had no pity for the Tories politics, she couldn't help but feel sympathy for the families forced to flee.

A stray cow banged into the carriage, and George shouted. Then a group of people bounded into the street after the animal, shouting and brandishing canes in an attempt to corner it. But the cow sauntered idly into an alley opposite an inn, whose sign was bravely lettered Pewter Platter Inn. A pewter plate was the only decoration on the sign, but the description was vivid enough. As Kerry watched, the cow's pursuers rushed by the inn, missing the animal and the alley altogether.

The carriage lurched past a coffee house, then rounded a corner and drove by a printer's shop, a silversmith's, a court house, and a tall church. From there on it slowed, fighting its way around coaches and horsemen before coming to a stop alongside a row of imposing brick houses. White marble steps graced these dwellings while new, square-paned lanterns loomed above them. A small brass plate identified the house before them as that of Jacob Northrop, solicitor.

Kerry had no more time for observation as the door was flung open and a pair of helping hands grasped her, swinging her down to the step. She smiled awkwardly at Cameron, suddenly ill at ease and uncertain. This visit seemed of the utmost importance to him, yet she could only wonder at this solicitor and what news he would bear.

A rosy-cheeked maid answered their knock, and at once, she smiled sweetly at Cameron. "Why, it's Mr. Brent! The master said ye'd be calling one of these days, but I must say, sir, it is very good to see you!" The pleasure in her voice could not be disguised, and Kerry sent an inquiring glance to her husband. Cameron shrugged, then handed the eager lass his hat and cane while she escorted them into a fire-lit parlor.

"And you must be his new missus," the maid continued brightly, scarcely allowing Kerry a nod of acknowledgment. "I'm happy to meet you. I'll take you both right in. He's waiting, you know." With a giggle, she swung open double doors and gestured beyond them.

As Kerry entered, she looked about the room and was immediately aware of its richness. Bookshelves lined the walls, filled with leather-bound volumes that were immaculately kept, and a chandelier gleamed from the ceiling, dripping with crystals that radiated light from their many prisms. Chippendale chairs and tables occupied the corners while leather armchairs stretched before the fire.

A gentleman rose from the far side of an imposing mahogany desk, his broad hand extended to Cameron.

"Good to see you, lad. Good to see you."

Kerry's imaginings of an old, white-haired gentleman vanished into thin air when this hale and hearty middle-aged man with bright red hair and curling sideburns stood up. He was not content with shaking Cameron's hand, however, and he soon came around the desk to embrace him.

"Aye, it's good to see you. You really must make more of an attempt to get here! Yes, I know, I know, I have not been down." Jacob chuckled, thrusting Cameron away and peering into his pale face with a fatherly glance. "But it is difficult for me, what with my practice and such. But you!

You look fit as a fiddle!" His eyes finally traveled across the room to where Kerry stood and they widened.

"Why this must be your new bride!" Dashing past Cameron, Jacob came to stand before Kerry, his pea-green eyes staring, unabashed, into her face. "Cameron," he said, and Kerry heard a strange choking noise in his throat, "she's the very image of your mother. If I didn't know better, I'd think this was Peggy, come back from the grave." He managed a weak smile, and his hand softly caressed Kerry's chin, at the place where her bonnet was tied. The young lass smiled softly back at him.

"You mustn't think ill of me, child," he said kindly, tilting his head to one side. "It is just that you gave me such a start."

"Don't apologize," Kerry replied. She took his proffered hand in her own, feeling the warm strength of it. "I am happy to meet you, Mr. Northrop. In spite of the circumstances."

"Ah yes." Undaunted by her statement, Jacob waved them both into chairs. "Sit, sit! We have much to discuss. I hope you have not found the weather too inconvenient?" He opened a drawer of his massive desk. "I daresay we shall see snow this very day. And where are you staying? Not the waterfront, I hope. Yes, a handsome couple you are. What fine children you shall have! I could not have wished better for you, Cameron lad." Beaming, Jacob tossed an assortment of letters and papers onto his desk, along with a pipe and a tin of tobacco.

"The Rams Head Inn," Cameron responded, answering his friend's bewildering assortment of questions with ease. Kerry sensed a fondness in Cameron's voice that was not present when he spoke to his brother and she wondered about his relationship with this man. "Not too bad. Yes, I think snow also. No thanks, I have my own." He withdrew his own pipe and a small tin. "Try this." He smiled as Jacob removed the lid and sniffed the mixture appreciatively. "You'll not find better."

"Ah, procured from his Majesty's ships, no doubt." Jacob

chuckled, digging his pipe into the aromatic mixture, then sighing with contentment. "Just arrived, I suppose? Good. You must dine with us this eve. My Betsy is eager to see you and to make the acquaintance of your missus. As is Fanny." Jacob grinned, showing numerous golden teeth, and he rubbed his hands as if enjoying some secret joke. "And when they do . . . someone so pretty, so kind . . ." His entire face glowed red with the warmth of the fire and with his own pleasure, and Kerry found herself liking him more each minute.

"You had us worried, before," Jacob continued while Cameron smoked, a single eyebrow uplifted. "We always did think it unfair, the way Caroline forced your proposal, yet being a gentleman, you could not refuse." Jacob turned to Kerry, who was listening pointedly now, and he could not mistake the interest she showed. "'Twas true." He smiled, puffing away while he spoke. "She was the betrothed of Charles, but he ran off, dandy that he is, and spent all of his inheritance, so she flung herself on Cameron's mercy. And with Philadelphia occupied and her family gone, what was he to do?"

"Caroline has broken the engagement herself," Cameron put in, stemming the flow of words. "She found that the idea of marriage with me was not at all what she'd anticipated."

"Pity." Jacob smiled again, but then became serious. "You know that the manor house is gone."

"All of it?" Cameron said, aghast. Kerry laid a hand on his arm, shocked by the paleness of his face, but in a moment, his features were composed and he shook his head sadly. "I should have thought as much. So that is why Charles is staying at Brentwood. He always despised the place."

"Aye." Sitting behind the desk with a businesslike air, Jacob rolled his head from one side to the other. "Always did say that boy was indulged too much. Not by your father, mind you! There was a man of good sense if ever I saw one. 'Tis a shame he died when he did, down at Brentwood. Heart attack, so they say. Yet he never had a problem as far as I could tell. Strange business. And with all those rumors afterward, of the demon perpetrating his death..."

"The demon!" Kerry sat upright, her worried glance falling on Cameron. "You didn't tell me that the demon was involved."

"Silly superstition." Cameron got to his feet, pacing with great agitation. "Nothing will ever induce me to believe such a thing!" He spoke with such vehemence that Kerry and Jacob were silent, and there was only the sound of his pacing mingled with the crackling fire. Calming somewhat, Cameron dropped back into his chair, then took a sip of the brandy Jacob deftly placed beside him. "Thank you. I did not mean to go on like that. Now, back to business. Are you sure there is nothing left of Charles's inheritance?" Cameron gazed into his silver cup as he spoke, but from Kerry's seat she could see his hand tremble and she could tell how much the conversation was upsetting him.

"From what I can tell, yes." Jacob sighed. "To think, because you were an illegitimate child, you were left with nothing. You built Brentwood almost single-handedly, and you were your father's favorite. Yet Charles, the dandy, got all, and he's squandered it before his thirtieth birthday." Jacob's mouth curled in disgust.

Kerry was surprised that Jacob spoke so freely of Cameron's illegitimacy. When her gaze turned to her husband, a wry smile curved his mouth and he nodded at her questioning stare.

"My wife was not yet aware of my bastard state," Cameron said drily and Jacob's expression showed his acute embarrassment.

"I beg pardon, Cameron, I had no idea."

"Do not apologize, Jacob. I had every intention of informing her. I simply haven't had the opportunity." He sounded amused, and realizing that topic bothered him little, Kerry ventured a question.

"Does that mean you are not a Brent?" she asked, confused.

"No, unfortunately." Cameron smiled and Kerry flushed. She sat facing him, alert, her hands in her lap.

"My father was indeed Samuel Brent of Philadelphia. He was a self-made man, with everything but social position. He married a woman from a prominent Philadelphia family, Deborah Chadwick. She was of good stock, had the King's ear, and she was well accepted in society. Beyond that she had little to offer," Cameron said musingly, and a slow understanding dawned on Kerry. "She did not want children. She did not desire intimacy with my father. I did not understand that until much later."

"She damn near killed him, that woman," Jacob said emphatically. "I never saw your father so unhappy."

"Well." Cameron looked aside for a moment, then back to Kerry, his smile sad and secretive. "Then a maid came to work for them, an Irish lass named Peggy. She was beautiful, I hear."

"She was that." Jacob conceded, his eyes glowing at the memory of Cameron's mother. "Deborah hated her from the first, that was apparent. And when your father came to care for the lass—"

"She made her life impossible." Cameron sighed heavily. "My father was in a difficult position. He was unable to divorce Deborah, yet he would not see his love abused. And when Peggy became with child, he sent her to a cottage to live. There he met with her, spending the few happy days he was granted."

"Few?" Kerry questioned.

"Aye." Cameron nodded. "She died when I was born. My father took me into his home then, and shortly thereafter, Deborah became pregnant for the first and only time. I think she resented the closeness of my father and myself, and thought to destroy it by having a legitimate child. She was a troubled, unhappy woman. I see that now."

"May her soul rest in peace," Jacob said sadly. "And now Charles has lost everything."

"I shall have to see to him," Cameron said purposefully. At the anger in his voice, Jacob immediately glanced up.

"Throw him out?" he asked hopefully, but his desire to see the dashing Charles fend for himself was destroyed a moment later.

"No. Charles knows nothing of the business world. To do that would be cruel at this point. I will not throw him out, but I will not allow him to live off my holdings, either. I am sure I will be able to find some source of employment for him." But even as he spoke, Kerry's and Jacob's eyes met, betraying the same doubts.

"Now about the letter." Cameron extended the parchment, and the solicitor retrieved a pair of silver spectacles, then scanned the contents. Tucking the missive into his desk, he scribbled a few notes upon his sleeve before peering at Kerry and Cameron.

His amiability was gone. "When did you receive this letter?" he asked.

"Last week," Cameron answered. "It was delivered to my house by coach this very day."

"Well, that's a help." Jacob nodded. "A delay of one week shouldn't put us off the scent too much. From the paper and the description I've received I shouldn't be surprised if I could lay my hand to the man inside of a week."

"Do you really think you can find my father that quickly?" Kerry spoke so eagerly that Jacob flashed her a brief smile.

"Yes, I should think so. In fact, from the way the letter was written, I think your father wants to be found. It sounds as though he is in desperate trouble. Robbins!" Jacob called, and at once a scrawny seaman entered the room, dragging a bag upon his back. His watery eyes peered from Kerry to Cameron, then rested disinterestedly upon the solicitor.

"Aye?" His gait was a shuffling one, and he stood first upon one foot and then another as if both pained him.

Northrop handed him a single piece of paper with a name scribbled upon it.

"Go down to the waterfront, then to Helltown. See what you can discover about this man." With a nod, the bewhiskered man was gone, and Jacob leaned back in his chair, his hands resting on his ample belly.

"He'll find him, no doubt. Most arriving immigrants make their way to the waterfront, then to the taverns along Race Street. That area's known as Helltown. It's a rough crowd there, what with the Three Jolly Irishmen and the other tippling houses, no place for a gentleman to seek information. I got Robbins out of a scrape some years ago, and he has since worked for me. They'll answer him readily enough."

"One other thing." Cameron rose, his hand resting upon Kerry's and his eyes meeting the solicitor's. "I understand my family has holdings in Ireland. Find out what you can about their state and the manner in which they are run. If injustices are being done, remedy the situation."

"Aye, lad." Jacob Northrop got to his feet and walked with them to the door. "And don't forget our dinner engagement tonight." He smiled, obviously delighted by the thought. "We have a fresh-killed goose about; ye would not want to miss that!"

"I should say not." Cameron smiled. "If it is agreeable with you, Kerry?"

"Aye." The Irish lass quickly responded. "After all, I can scarce refuse the man who is to find my father, can I?"

Jacob looked pleased and he vigorously shook the Irish girl's hand. "It is a date then! Tonight!" he declared.

After the pair had returned to the coach, however, Kerry turned for one last look at him, and she found him staring at the carriage, a worried look upon his face.

The rest of the afternoon passed agreeably. Cameron and

Kerry perused the shops, seeking items not to be found at home. For Kerry, the trip was a long-awaited reprieve and she danced merrily through the milliner's and the shoe store, as well as the Race Street dry-goods shops and the silversmith's. The open-air markets were teeming with folk, and as Kerry strolled about, men's eyes followed her and many an introduction was only prevented by the cold glances of the man at her side.

Cameron enjoyed himself immensely. Previously he'd seen making purchases as nothing but a task, but with Kerry present, even the meanest task was enjoyable. Her gaiety was infectious. Cameron even found himself participating in the joyful bidding, and when one trader let a silver perfume flask go for less than half its worth, Cameron found cause to smile.

As they were returning to the inn, they enjoyed the peaceful moments in the carriage, and Kerry gratefully accepted her husband's affection, curling up to him like a contented kitten when his arm came about her shoulders and his fingers lightly touched her face.

"Kerry," he said softly, and she turned her spritely face to him. "About your father. I just want you to be prepared. Things may not turn out as pleasantly as you hope they will."

"What do you mean? Mr. Northrop seemed confident that he could find him," Kerry said, puzzled by his words.

"Aye. But when you find him, you may wish you hadn't."

"And what's that supposed ta mean?" she cried, indignation flashing in her eyes. His words seemed evasive, and she gazed at her husband with a forthright stare.

"Nothing." Cameron sighed, pulling her closer to him once more. "I just want you to be prepared, no matter what."

Chapter Twenty

Back at the inn, Kerry enjoyed the luxury of a nap before dinner, but she was aware that Cameron slept not at all. She could hear the sounds of his footsteps even as she dreamed, pacing back and forth across the floor. She awoke to find twilight darkening the window, and he appeared pensive, his stern face easing only when she climbed sleepily from the bed.

"Cameron, what time is it?" As she gazed toward the window, Kerry started when the clock chimed below. "Six! We've scarce a half-hour to make ready! Why didn't you wake me?" She flew about the room, splashing water on her face and pulling a brush rapidly through her tresses while Cameron watched in fascination.

"I thought a half-hour ample time. You are already dressed." He indicated the rumpled green gown she'd slept in, and Kerry sighed with exasperation.

"Aye, with a million wrinkles!" She unbuttoned the dress and snatched another from her wardrobe. This was a deep wine velvet, with a square neckline that framed her swelling bosom. Cameron's mouth dropped as he stared at the gown's décolletage while Kerry fumbled helplessly with the hooks.

"Would you like some assistance?" he asked hoarsely, coming to stand behind her. Without waiting for an answer, he brushed her hands away, fastening the bewildering hooks himself. He seemed to take an overly long time at this task, and Kerry felt a soft tremor race through her when he paused, letting one hand creep round to her bosom then come to rest on the satiny throat laid bare to his gaze.

"I think we should be going," she said, amazed at the shakiness of her voice. She turned to face him, but realized her error when she gazed into his eyes, burning like twin tapers. His face was close to hers, his mouth only inches away, and her breath came quickly as his hand slid down to touch the soft skin swelling above the wine velvet.

"Yes, we should," Cameron replied slowly, but it was several minutes before he reluctantly released her, leaving her trembling and quaking. Kerry put a cool hand on her brow, terribly aware of the weakness in her knees and of this man before her. What folly was this? A look, a simple touch left her gasping and breathless, yet one week hence they might be enemies. She would have to keep tight rein on herself, at least until they knew the truth. Gathering her cloak about her as if it could protect her, Kerry hastened to the door and on into the carriage, trying to ignore the feel of the strong hands that helped her.

A lamplighter stood beneath a round globe, his ruddy face illuminated by the warm glow he had just created. A long row of these beacons was already gleaming, wreathed in vapor. They reminded Kerry of a multiplicity of moons. A light snow was beginning to fall. It drifted noiselessly down around the carriage, hushing the sounds of the city and burying the less attractive sights beneath its filmy blanket. Kerry sighed at the beauty of the swirling flakes, nestling within her furs and enjoying the closeness of the man beside her.

In the quieter evening streets, they reached the solicitor's home in much less time, and Kerry was amazed when the carriage stopped. A peek out the window assured her that this was Jacob Northrop's dwelling, and soon the man himself was beaming from the door.

"Here ye be. I was worried that the weather might stop ye." He waved an expansive hand at the softly drifting flakes, then directed it to George. "Drive on if you like, man. I'll see these folk home, and if the snow gets too bad they can remain here."

George glanced down at Cameron, and at his master's nod, he drove on. The coachman was not unhappy to do so. He could now stop at a taproom for a warming cup of cider, and then venture home before the storm worsened.

"Come in! Don't stand out in the cold. Kerry, you look lovely." Jacob's greeting was warm, but he stopped talking when Kerry removed her cloak and his eyes fell on her snowy white breasts, which seemed to hold up her gown. "Yes, what a lovely . . . dress." Nervously, Jacob looked toward the frowning Cameron, and he shrugged apologetically.

"Cameron!" Two voices cried out at once, and Kerry turned to see an older woman and a young girl run out of the hallway, their arms extended. The woman was almost the twin of her husband, round and crimson cheeked, but her hair was covered with scented powder. The daughter, Kerry thought the girl about sixteen, was a pretty little thing with bright coppery curls and a round smiling face. She pulled away from Cameron first, then took Kerry's hands and smiled brightly.

"You must be Kerry. Father told us all about you. You're even prettier than he said. And look at your hair! The color of a raven's wing, that's what I say. My name's Fanny. If we wait for himself there to introduce us we'll be waiting forever. She indicated Cameron with a nod of her head, and Kerry hid a smile as Cameron bent a threatening look on the girl.

"Aye, because you'd not let me get a word in edgewise." He took one of his wife's hands from the young girl, who giggled. "Kerry, this is Jacob's wife, Betsy. And I see Fanny has already made your acquaintance." His stern glance renewed Fanny's giggles, and the girl gazed admiringly at Kerry.

"I give you a bit of credit, being married to him. He'd scare the life out of most the girls, he would! That is, the ones that weren't drooling over him!" At this last remark Kerry broke into laughter.

"Now, now, Fanny! What's Mistress Kerry to think, you carrying on like that! Really, she's not all that silly. 'Tis just the excitement of seeing Caméron again." Betsy smiled welcomingly and then led Kerry into the parlor while Jacob talked quietly with Cameron. "I am so glad to meet you! When Jacob told me that Cameron had taken a bride, I was worried. After the life the lad's had, he deserves some happiness. But now that I look at you all my fears are dispelled. Yes, I think the dear boy has good years ahead of him, and I am never wrong!" Betsy winked.

Kerry sensed the warmth and wisdom of this smiling little woman, and her affection for Cameron was obvious. Indeed, she seemed to anticipate his wants though obviously she was still very much in love with her husband for as she talked, her gaze sometimes met his to exchange a fond glance with him. In all, the Northrop home was wonderfully warm and comfortable, not because of its rich furnishings but because of the people inside.

"Come along with me, dear." Betsy drew Kerry aside, telling Fanny to cease plying her with questions concerning Brentwood and the country life. A stone kitchen adjoined the back of the house and it was there Betsy led her. While surveying the work of the maids, she offered Kerry a cup of hot tea, which the young woman eagerly accepted, suddenly realizing that she had not eaten since noon that day.

The smell of roasting goose filled the house with a luscious scent, and from her perch, Kerry saw the maids ready the enormous bird for the table, along with an assortment of relishes and golden breads. The mouthwatering aromas brought Jacob out to the kitchen and he summoned Betsy and Kerry to the dining room.

"Really, dear! I wanted the poor girl to have a chance to rest before the meal!"

Betsy sighed, but her husband remained undaunted, and everyone was soon seated at the dining table. Jacob carved the goose, sniffing appreciatively as he did so. Betsy had seated Kerry directly across from Cameron, Fanny beside her. A prayer began the meal, then the goose and breads were enjoyed by all.

"Don't you think the streets are a mess?" Fanny continued to chatter while she ate. "It was all those British. Lovely parties they gave though. Plays and concerts all spring. Will you be going to the governor's ball Saturday?" she asked.

Kerry glanced questioningly at her husband, but almost imperceptibly Cameron shook his head. "I'm afraid not," Kerry answered, and Fanny looked disappointed.

"But you must! It's the talk of the season. And you being here this very week, if that isn't fate, what is? Father, you can get them tickets, can't you?" She turned a pleading face to her father and Jacob nodded immediately.

"Aye, an easy matter that. Ye are going, lad?" Jacob peered over the huge joint of goose he was about to bite into. "We all are."

"Jacob, you know how I hate—"

Cameron's ample host waved the joint, dismissing his argument.

"Aye, I know. But you're a married man, son! You may not like these affairs, but think of the young lass! She'd be a treat to show off to all those old dowagers, I should say!"

Kerry smiled at the compliment, and even Betsy entered into the argument.

"You must go, Cameron! Kerry will not be in the city that much. When might she have another such opportunity?"

With a sigh, Cameron pushed aside his plate and stared across the table at Kerry. "Madam, do you wish to go?" he asked. Kerry nodded. She did not wish to put him on the spot, but his abrupt question left her little choice. "Then I yield. But, I'm warning you, mistress, these affairs are not at all what you'd anticipate."

"Fiddlesticks!" Fanny interrupted. "They are fun! There is music and dancing, and everyone is gay. Oh, I'm so glad you're going! Himself there, he hardly goes anywhere. Just stays down in that gloomy old mansion in the pines. . ."

"Fanny!" Betsy admonished her daughter, her crimson face flushing a deeper red. "What you must think of us, Kerry?"

"Fear not of that." Kerry smiled. "I come from a large family myself, and it has just occurred to me that Fanny reminds me of my brothers."

At this statement, Betsy's embarrassment subsided, nonetheless she sent another warning glance to her gleeful daughter.

The roast goose was splendid, and Kerry ate as though famished, unaware of the attention she would draw when she reached for a second helping. "Now that's what I like to see." Jacob beamed, obligingly slicing off more meat. "A lass who enjoys her food. Not for me these mincing maids who live on tea and biscuits, forever fainting and claiming they have no appetite."

"Perhaps," Betsy ventured, "you are expecting a wee one?"

Kerry felt her color rise and her eyes flickered to Cameron. He was amused and his gray eyes twinkled. Kerry stammered, "Not yet, I should think."

"Perhap soon," Betsy said, by way of consolation. "A nice child to carry on the name."

Kerry wouldn't let her eyes meet Cameron's for the remainder of the meal, after which they all adjourned to the parlor for coffee and brandy. The gentlemen smoked, after begging the ladies permission, and Fanny sat on the floor before the fire. They all remarked on the grandeur of the meal. With snow falling outside, a fire crackling within, and good company, the time to depart came all too soon.

Snowflakes were still descending and a glisteningly white carpet greeted Kerry when the door was wedged open. There was only one carriage on the street. Its driver had dismounted and was kicking at a frozen wheel while he cursed with all his might. It took the combined efforts of Cameron and Jacob to free the coach, after which the driver bestowed so many thanks upon them that Kerry wondered if his gratitude was enriched by a hidden whiskey flask. She noted that the vehicle started off down the road at a very slow pace for ice and snow still clung tenaciously to its metal-rimmed wheels.

"I'd say that decides that." Jacob motioned them back inside, and kicking the caked snow from his boots, he said, "You must take the sleigh."

"Good, good! Father, since they're going, why don't we all take a ride in the sleigh? I hear bells outside now, I'm sure the neighbors are out for it's a fine night."

Everyone thought this a delightful suggestion. Even Betsy beamed with excitement. "I'll get my cape," she murmured, returning with Kerry's handsome garment and a warm one of her own. As the men set about hitching up the horses, Kerry watched them from the window, occasionally wiping the glass that steamed with the warmth inside.

"Have you ever ridden in a sleigh before?" Jacob bellowed to Kerry when he summoned them. He ventured inside for Fanny and her mother had already tiptoed through the snow to the waiting conveyance.

"No, I can't say I have." Kerry grinned, for she was keen for this new sort of adventure. She watched the other women parade easily through the snow; then her glance fell on her own dainty slippers. They were already dampened and she frowned slightly, trying to envision how to get to the sleigh without damaging them too much.

Cameron observed her plight, and without hesitation, he climbed to the step, swept her into his arms, and carried her across the white expanse to the sleigh.

"Cameron!" she gasped, her blush deepening at Fanny's delighted giggle and Betsy's promptly averted face.

Jacob's booming laughter rang out in the street, and he called, "Aye, an eager lad, that is. 'Tisn't any wonder, with a filly such as that he cannot keep his hands from her."

"Mr. Northrop!" Betsy admonished, while Fanny giggled again.

Although Kerry protested, being cradled in Cameron's arms was not at all unpleasant and she was vaguely sorry when she was seated inside the sleigh. "There was no need for that," she said primly, annoyed by his all-too-knowing smile. "I could have managed."

"And how would you have done that?" Cameron smiled, his gaze staring down into her own green depths. "Hike up your skirts and make a run for it?"

"Mayhap." Kerry smiled too, a bright curving of her red lips, and her eyes were all innocence. "But if I still had me own boots, I'd have no cares."

"Aye, those ragged strips of leather would have provided no protection," Cameron replied, but his remark was less severe than they might have been for he was lost in the sparkling beauty of his wife. "And I must confess I favor this womanly behavior to the pugnacious acts of the lass who disembarked from a ship." His eyes skimmed eagerly over her upswept curls, her cheeks blooming with color.

"Truly, master?" Kerry teased. "And do clothes make such a great difference?"

"Aye. When one's wife never removes them except within the deepest shadows of the room." He grinned.

Kerry's lips parted in a gasp, but the sleigh, which had been inching its way down the narrow street, now found itself on a snow-covered cobbled slope and it glided madly along. Suddenly pulled into Cameron's embrace, Kerry made no objection for without his protection she would have surely been sent sprawling. The cold wind whipped their faces, the bells jingled cheerily, and only when Jacob pulled the reins to the right, directing the horses to an incline, did the sleigh slow its pace.

"Whew! What a ride!" Fanny clapped her hands together while Betsy clung to the side of the sleigh. Although their pace was now considerably slower, Cameron did not remove his arm and Kerry stared wonderingly up at him. After a moment, his eyes met hers and she saw a challenge in them, as if he were daring her to comment. Fanny was watching them closely so Kerry did nothing to forestall his caresses. She had no intention of letting Fanny, or anyone else, suspect they were anything but loving newlyweds. Still it was difficult to maintain control when his hands moved boldly beneath her cloak and his eyes were innocently questioning.

"Are you cold, Kerry?" he asked, and she shook her head, trying to ignore the tingling response of her body to his caresses. She felt great relief when another sleigh appeared and the folk within called to Jacob and his family. Fanny stood up and waved frantically and a faint tinkle of music was audible, becoming louder by the moment.

"Fiddlers!" Fanny called, turning back to inform Kerry and Cameron of this. "It's the Morrises. They have fiddlers with their party and they've invited us to the public house."

The sleighs glided along smoothly, the horses throwing out their feet and champing with this fine play. Their breath was a misty cloud in the falling snow and they arched their necks, stepping in time to the music. The fiddlers now came into view, miraculously balancing their fiddles upon bundled arms while staying upright on their horses, and their wistful tunes wafted through the streets, mingling with the sleigh bells and the shouts of people. The street lights gleamed through the swirling snow, and light-encrusted flakes danced prettily about them. It was a most romantic scene. Kerry's eyes wandered to her husband's broad shoulder, and she thought it would be grand to lay her head upon it and enjoy his warmth. As if reading her mind,

Cameron drew her closer to him, inviting her to do as she wished. No sign of protest came from her. Indeed, a happy smile curved her lips. White snowflakes shone in her black hair, and unwittingly, Cameron's lips touched one. In response, Kerry glanced up at him and then nuzzled her face against his cloak, her hair brushing his jawline and teasing him with its silken caress.

Her affectionate behavior encouraged Cameron greatly and he fought to keep from rubbing his hands together with glee. The softness of her shape filled his thoughts and he recalled how warm and willing she'd been in his arms, returning his passion with an answering one. Now as she gazed up at him, her eyes swirling like liquid turquoises, his control was sorely shaken and the raging in his loins was almost out of control. When Kerry innocently placed her hand on his thigh to brace herself at a turn, she quickly withdrew it in mortification while his own blood surged.

The sleigh finally stopped at the Bull's Head, a tavern in Strawberry Alley. Neighboring sleighs joined them and there was a great rush as acquaintances and friends jostled one another. Kerry was amazed to find that Cameron was almost as well known as Jacob. In fact, most of the people who knew the solicitor appeared to know his young friend as well. Tucking her hands inside her cloak, Kerry smiled and acknowledged the dizzying introductions, but she was relieved when the party finally started into the tavern.

A matronly wench served up cider and rum, looking none too pleased by this rush of customers. Muttering about "these daft folk," she hastily supplied them with warm drinks, easing the thirst these Philadelphians had acquired on their sleigh rides. The greetings grew more jovial with the passing of time and finally each new arrival was hailed unanimously as soon as he set foot in the door. Kerry enjoyed the fun, and she watched the broad-bellied men vie with the young dandies for the taproom girls' attentions, while these experienced lasses merely slapped at their hands and laughed at their praise.

"Aye, and with each pint of ale I look better," a buxom lass shouted as one overanxious lad accosted her. "Pay up and save yer songs for the birds."

The company roared at this fine joke, and the poor lad skulked out of the tavern. The hours sped by, and soon, in spite of Fanny's protests, Jacob advised them it was time to leave. They drove back in the soft quiet of the snow, the sleigh bells dimming in the distance.

Kerry lost the battle to keep her eyes open, and she barely recalled arriving at the Northrops' and going up a flight of twisting steps to a sleeping chamber. Able and warm hands stripped her dampened shoes and stockings from her feet, while her cloak was dropped to the floor. Her dress followed it, then a cool rush of sheets greeted her flesh and she sighed.

Cameron gazed down at her sleeping form, the flame from a single taper illuminating her fine features, her flushed cheeks, and her thick black eyelashes. Her curves, outlined by the quilts, were tempting even as she slept. Cameron groaned, and snatching up his pipe, he quit their bedchamber, retiring downstairs to the safety of the parlor where he could enjoy a smoke. When fatigue finally overtook him, he again climbed the steps and slipped quickly into the narrow bed, falling into an exhausted sleep.

As the first rays of the December sun struck the eyes of the Philadelphia shopkeepers who were opening their shutters, an odd scene transpired in the less commendable part of town. A carriage of a fine make rolled over the packed snow, its wheels emitting a crunching sound. This carriage did not stop at the finer shops, but continued to roll past them, down to the docks where the sailors were beginning to recover from their nightly merrymaking. Occasionally a seaman glanced at this impressive coach before shrugging and continuing on his way.

Before the meanest and roughest public house—the Three Jolly Irishmen—this coach came to a halt. Inside, the weary tavernkeeper was sitting amid the wreckage caused by last night's drunken bouts, a pewter cup of malt liquor before him as a cure for his pounding head. His headache was not helped by the sight of the black-cloaked gentleman who stepped from the carriage. He paused only to glance up at the sign post, ascertaining the name of the inn, then he strode with fierce determination to the door.

"Blimey." The tavernkeeper grimaced, tossing down the liquor with a vengeance. "That's one bloke I'd not like ta cross." He shuddered as the door was flung open and the man approached.

"I'm looking for him." The stranger tossed a slip of parchment at the owner. "I'd like to see this man immediately."

"And who might you be, the law?" the tavern owner growled, sullenly. His swollen eyes had already taken in the fine cut of this man's clothing, the cultured voice, and the rich walking stick now tapping on the floor. He glanced at the slip before him and saw a name inked across it.

"Exactly the opposite." When the stranger spoke, the tavern owner felt a thrill of fear for the man turned a pair of piercing silver eyes on him, eyes that seemed to bore a hole right through his broad belly. "A lawman would give him his just deserts, whilst I intend to reward him. Bring the man here or the law will do it for me."

"No need for that." The tavern owner pushed the paper back across the table. "I can't read."

"Beagan O'Toole," the tall stranger said. His stick no longer tapped the floor and his stare narrowed. "Now."

"Aye, sir. No need ta make a fuss." The tavernkeeper squealed and he ambled out of the taproom to make the laborious climb upstairs. The chambermaid watched him go, her face portraying amazement for she'd never known the man to comply with such a request. Usually he threw the inquirer out, but this man had presence, even she could see that. She sashayed boldly into the room, swaying her hips.

"I say Gov'." She smiled, showing the spaces where teeth had once been. "Can I be gettin' you anything?"

Cameron Brent stared down at her, suddenly realizing that she was speaking to him. His eyes traveled down over her thrusting breasts, her round belly, her soft hips. The girl was not unattractive. Her hair was a mass of soft brown curls, her eyes were a brilliant blue. When she winked at him, gathering her hands about her waist so that her blouse puckered and allowed him full view of whatever lay beneath, her intent was obvious. Yet Cameron had no interest in bedding her. He shook his head, noting the lass's disappointment before her gaze dropped.

Watching her broadly swaying hips as she departed from the room, he shook his head, a wry smile curving his lips. I think the Irish girl has woven a spell around my heart, he thought, laughing to himself. A few months ago this wench would have served well for a night's toss, but even though Cameron's restraint with Kerry tested him sorely, he was not tempted.

"And who is asking about for me?" The thick Irish brogue came from the hall, and was followed by its owner. Cameron stood erect, waiting for the Irishman who strode through the door, his flushed face enraged.

"Ya don't have a thing on me!" the man said.

A round fist appeared beneath Cameron's nose but he merely inspected it for a moment, then pushed it gently aside and smiled. "I am not the law. Do sit down, Beagan O'Toole. We have much to discuss."

"And how'd ya be knowing me name"—the bandy-legged Irishman sprawled into a chair, his naughty blue eyes twinkling with mischief—"when I'm not knowing yours?"

"I'll remedy that immediately. My name is Cameron Brent." He paused for a moment, allowing this to sink in. The Irishman pondered for only a split second, then recognition came to him.

"Brent! Ye be the one—"

"That purchased your daughter's indenture." Cameron finished the sentence for him.

"Well, if that's not a queer bit o' luck!" Beagan smirked, then pulled a much-used flask from his pocket. He offered Cameron a drink, which was declined, then sampled the contents himself. "Ya know, I was just thinkin' of looking up me girl. Then you pop up!" He shook his white-thatched head as if unable to believe the wonder of it all.

"Mr. O'Toole, let me come to the point. I am a busy man and I haven't much time. I understand that you have written Kerry a letter that has greatly disturbed her, a letter claiming that you were mistreated by my uncle in England, Lord Randolf Brent."

"Aye, that I was!" the Irishman swore, his face flushing with rage. "A raising the rents every month, I could scarcely keep food on the table! Me own sweet wife, she died, an ailing she was—"

"Mr. O'Toole." Cameron braced his foot upon a seat and gazing into the Irishman's face with a pair of forthright gray eyes. "I am aware that some of the landlords charge unfair rents, occasionally outrageous ones. But I have inquired into the matter, and I have here some letters from neighboring farmers who also pay rent to my uncle. They claim the rents are fair."

"'Tis a lie!" Beagan boomed, coming to his feet as his chair met the floor with a clatter.

"Furthermore. I have it on the best authority that your debts are not so much from the rents as from gambling and drink. These notes, if you would please look at them, were made out to a barkeep, and these racing tickets—"

"Bah!" Beagan held up his hand, refusing to look. "All forged. You can prove nothing with those." Then his eyes narrowed as fear assaulted him, and he gazed up at Cameron who was looming over him. "You'll not be . . . I mean, you'll not be saying anything to me girl about this, will ya?" His head was cocked beseechingly to one side.

Cameron indicated that he would not. "Now Mr. O'Toole, I am a reasonable man and I'm willing to make some restitution for a possible overpayment of debt. I have here a note for two hundred pounds, as well as an address at which I'd like you to apply for work. It is a shipyard that I own. Show them this letter and you will be given a job and a place to live. Is that acceptable to you?" He gazed down at the amazed little man whose attitude had changed from belligerence to gratitude.

"Aye, sir. It is, I say so. Thank you, sir." His eyes caressed the monetary notes before he pressed them deep within his coat.

"Good. Then I am satisfied that the debt is settled, and you?"

The Irishman nodded eagerly, relief pouring over his ruddy face as he envisioned his creditor's threats abolished.

Cameron took up his stick and cloak, and strode toward the door while the Irishman waxed gleeful. "One other thing," he called back, securing his cloak and tricorn while Beagan glanced up. "Kerry is just fine." With a meaningful stare, Cameron strode out of the tavern and climbed into the coach, glad to be free of this business.

As Beagan watched the fine coach roll off, his hands caressing the pounds in his pocket, a raggedy man arose from the far side of the bar, where he'd been hidden in shadows. He stepped to the middle of the floor, his fingers itching because of the money he'd seen exchanged.

"Beagan O'Toole, is it?" he asked, and the Irishman started up, warily watching this vagabond's approach.

"Aye, and who are you?" Clutching the bottle tightly, Beagan faced the bearded wretch who came toward him with a leering smile and a stumbling gait.

"Ezekiel Jacobs me name, lad. And you and I have much to talk about, for you see, I know that man. I recall the day he bought the lass and if you settle for that mere pittance after what 'is family's done ta yours, you man are a fool."

"What d'ya mean?" Beagan's blue eyes narrowed suspiciously, and with a gleeful cackle, Ezekiel snatched up a chair.

"He's used yer daughter. I seen that the first day he bought her. Aye, he couldn't keep his hands off her even then. There's money here, lad. Make me a cut and I'll show ya how ta get it."

The promise of more riches warmed the heart of Beagan and blinded him to all else. With a greedy smile, he took the seat beside the ragged vagabond and listened to his plan.

Chapter Twenty-One

A door slammed, bringing Kerry awake, and she found herself alone. Gazing out the window, she saw the carriage drive off, then snuggled under the bedcovers, pouting. He's probably found himself a taproom wench, she thought snidely, tucking the covers beneath her chin. She visualized a well-endowed lass baring her breast to Cameron and it bothered her more than she'd anticipated so she fumed silently.

It must be, she reasoned, for in the last few days he has become secretive indeed.

Mysterious persons called for him downstairs, and when she pressed him as to their identity, he merely gave a laconic smile and asked if she minded everyone's business the way she did his. This alone was enough to drive a lass like Kerry mad, but in addition she did not miss the longing glances that ladies, as well as chambermaids, directed his way. She wanted to pinch every one of them.

But he's my husband, she reminded herself. That knowledge was little comfort, however, for she realized that she had not been much of a wife to him these days past. Kerry's eyes grew dreamy and her face flushed as she thought of their wedding night. He had taken her into his strong arms and made love to her until the dawn. He had little time to dally with other wenches then.

"What am I to do?" she said aloud; then she voiced a muffled curse and sprang out of bed. She had no proof of his doings, and if Cameron would not discuss his whereabouts with her, she was powerless to confront him. In anguish, she thought of the ball to be held that night at the City Tavern. All the society belles that would be dripping from his arm. She could see them now, fanning and posturing before him, peering innocently from behind heavy lashes and begging him to walk outside "for some air." With a vengeance, Kerry tossed a feathered pillow at the wardrobe and a cloud of feathers danced around her.

The wardrobe. Her eyes returned to that oaken chest and she smiled coyly. There was but one thing she could do. Tearing apart her assortment of gowns, she sought the one dress that would secure his attention and make sure his eyes did not wander to other women. Her hand caught it and she drew out a gown of azure blue. Although demure in color, the dress was cut shockingly low in front, its cleavage bringing a bright blush to Kerry's cheeks as she held it up to her before the mirror. Yet her purpose was firm and if Cameron Brent sought to ogle other women, he would not find cause to do so tonight.

Free of the disturbing presence of her husband, Kerry had managed to bathe and dress, draping a shawl discreetly about her neckline while arranging her hair. Pushing aside the scented powder and affected ribbons, she pinned her curls high upon her head, allowing their raven mass to fall free behind her ears. Dainty diamond earbobs nestled on the lobes, a present from Cameron, and with each motion of her head these jewels winked like iridescent eyes.

As Cameron strode into the room, Kerry pulled the shawl higher about her neck, wanting the surprise to be sudden. The neckline of the dress was even more daring than she'd imagined. The soft swelling curves of her breasts were revealed to an alarming degree, and it seemed with each breath they would spill forth from the satiny blue fabric. But the dress held, pressing her bosom into an even more enticing fullness.

Cameron appeared, at first, not to notice, for he tossed his cane and tricorn to the bed and then came to stand beside her, a look of concentration on his face, his black eyebrows drawn thoughtfully together.

"Kerry my love," he said, his hand resting on her shoulder.

Kerry wondered wildly if he had guessed her secret, but when his hand met her white skin, he said nothing, just gazed down into the mirror.

"I have some news," he said finally, and Kerry's eyes flew up, meeting with his.

"About my father?" she asked breathlessly, and he nodded, a look akin to pain silvering his eyes. It was gone in a second, however, and a wry smile came to his lips.

"Jacob Northrop located him last night and I spoke with him this very morn." Kerry's eyes grew wide at this statement and she leaped to her feet, excitement causing her every limb to tremble.

"You spoke to him? How is he? Are the others all right? What did he say?" Her words tumbled out like a waterfall and Cameron laughed, holding her shoulders firmly to keep her still.

"One question at a time." He smiled. "He is fine. I have arranged an interview with him on the morrow at the house of Jacob Northrop. We have discussed the matter of rents and we seem to have arrived at an agreement."

"You have?" Kerry was astonished. "But I thought—"

"You shall hear it from his own lips tomorrow." Cameron did not add that Beagan's words would be carefully prepared by Jacob, nor did he say that the man would be instructed to say nothing of his own vices in Kerry's presence. Cameron sensed that the truth would hurt her immensely and so he smiled kindly, drawing her hand into his own.

"He asked many questions about you, Kerry. He seemed very concerned."

"I can't believe it! Me own father, right here, and you spoke to him." She sighed dreamily, then lowered herself to the edge of the bed and hugged her hands about her slender blue-garbed waist. "Now tell me," she chattered, her eyes bright. "How did he look? What has he been doing here? Oh, it seems so long since I've laid eyes on anyone from home!"

"His hair is very white, but his eyes are a brilliant blue and he seems fit. He has found employment in a shipyard and will be working here for some time, although you may not see him much, for he'll be on this side of the river."

"Aye, I know. But just ta know he's here and that he's well!" Kerry laughed gleefully and Cameron reached out to touch a curl that danced enticingly before him.

"I thought I'd tell you. Perhaps you will enjoy the dance more fully with this knowledge."

"Yes." Kerry smiled, her eyes following Cameron as he began to change his own clothes for the night's event. "Cameron." As his eyes met hers, a mistiness came into her own. "Thank you," she said.

"It was my pleasure," he replied as he fastened a bewildering array of buttons with comparative ease. He chose a dark blue coat and trousers, and a sparkling white shirt and a minimum of ruffles. His garb was fine but not ostentatious, and she realized that no one could call Cameron a dandy. He lent a quiet dignity to his clothes, and they in turn enhanced his masculinity. Kerry watched him with interest, knowing too well what drove women to flirt with him. Indeed, she thought, his menacing glances only added to his allure, for they made him seem dangerous and something of a challenge. She was suddenly glad that she'd chosen the dress she was wearing.

"Are you ready?" he asked softly, pausing to press a kiss to her hand. Kerry snatched it away, half-feeling that he was mocking her with that gallant gesture, and then waved it toward the door.

"After you, sir. I think I should see to your back, in case any bleating chambermaids are lurking about." Cameron glanced down at her in puzzlement, but her brilliant smile puzzled him and, with a shake of his head, he proceeded out the door.

The City Tavern was surrounded by carriages and horses, the walkways around it obscured for blocks. Fortunately Cameron had had the foresight to rent a coach, for the night was chill and a long walk along the icy roads would have caused considerable damage to Kerry's apparel. A butler was waiting at the door, and upon being shown the ticket, he led them to the Long Room that was especially reserved for parties.

Soft sweet music emanated from this area, and Kerry caught a glimpse of a woman in a pink satin dress. This lady's hair had been woven into an elaborate coiffure which had been heightened by wool stuffing, and then powdered a snowy white. She gave Kerry a bored glance, then daintily lifted her skirts and rejoined the party.

Kerry's hand tightened in Cameron's and she fought the urge to run. What folly was this, attending a ball that was sure to attract the cream of society, posturing belles and dandies? Previously she had not given this any thought, but now as they stood framed in the doorway she was frightened. For across the smooth wood floor on which a white carpet of sand had been carefully sprinkled, glided a host of satin and silk begowned women and men. Most of them wore powdered wigs and sported twinkling jewels, and the women's daintily slippered feet stepped in time to the music. This dance was one Kerry had never seen. It required the couples to clasp hands and do mincing steps.

The governor, Benedict Arnold, was seated at the far end of the room, his left leg propped up on a silken cushion. At his arm was a lovely young woman who doted upon him, serving him cupfuls of Madeira and assorted delectables from a nearby tray. Many eyes were upon this couple, and whispered remarks were made about this lady and her benefactor.

The large room was elaborately furnished in the latest London décor, and crystal chandeliers dripped from the ceiling, throwing sparkling shadows upon the dancers. It was with some relief that Kerry saw Fanny Northrop approach.

"Kerry! That man will take your coat. Isn't this grand? Come along with me, I'll show you to the people I know. What a lovely dress! Whoever did you go to? Not Madam Mullan, I should think. She never does so well for me." Kerry grinned at the girl's unchecked flow of chatter, allowing Fanny to pull her into the crowd. She glanced helplessly back at Cameron, unable to tell him where they were going for Jacob had engaged him in conversation. He waved distractedly as she departed.

"Now, there is the governor. That girl is Peggy Shippen. Scandalous, isn't it? They say since he's come to the city, she's been his constant companion. Come with me to meet the Frenchmen. They have been asking for you since you came through the door and they are ever so much fun. Not nearly as stuffy as some of the Colonials."

Kerry noticed that Betsy Northrop sent her daughter a disapproving glance when she saw her dragging Kerry to the circle of handsome young men standing near the governor.

"Monsieur de Beaumont, this is Mistress Brent, the lady you asked about." Obviously delighted to be with all these good-looking Frenchmen, Fanny presented Kerry to a dashing youth whose eyes traveled approvingly to her swelling bosom.

"My gratitude, Miss Northrop, for bringing such a flower to my side. You are indeed ravishing, madam. I had not expected to see the beauties of Paris rivaled here in America, but you have put the best of them to shame."

"A fine bit of blarney that is." Kerry wisely stepped back as the overly zealous captain sought to enhance his greeting by kissing her pink cheek. It was not the kiss that concerned her but his eyes, which were returning to her breasts. She spread her fan demurely across them.

At her words the Frenchman appeared surprised for a moment, then a broad smile crossed his fair face.

"*Oui*, a lady fair from the verdant isle. But it is no flattery, I assure you, madam, only the boldest truth. You are beautiful. A fair rose amid thorns. You must promise me a dance. I am besotted."

"Aye, I can see that." Kerry smiled winningly, and she indicated his glass of champagne. "'Tis said that the beauty of a woman grows with the emptying of each cup. If that be true, you must have seen the bottom of many."

At this remark, Fanny stared in horror at Kerry for the French were held in high esteem by the Americans, who admired Lafayette. But the Frenchmen merely glanced at one another, barely suppressed chuckles, and then threw back their heads in gay laughter.

"You are indeed charming, Madam Brent," Monsieur de Beaumont brushed the tears from his eyes and finally ceased laughing. "It is refreshing to find a young lady who is endowed with wit as well as beauty. Too often the ladies of the court speak of nothing beyond the makes of their gowns or hairstyles." The swain grew bolder now and he pressed his lips to the underside of Kerry's wrist. "I grow more enamored of you by the moment. I must know more about you, where you come from. How is it I have never before met a lady as ravishing as yourself?"

"I am glad you find my wife so interesting."

The laconic voice came from behind her, and Kerry whirled about to face Cameron. The Frenchman seemed suddenly far less bold and he dropped the dainty white hand he held as if it were on fire.

"Cameron, this is Monsieur de Beaumont," Kerry said

innocently, gesturing with her now-free hand to the man behind her. "And this is my husband."

"Ah yes. I had gathered as much. It is wonderful to meet you sir and your wife is . . . most charming." The Frenchman smiled and extended his hand which Cameron took after a moment's hesitation.

"I quite agree." Cameron's eyes, like two shining pieces of steel, sliced into the Frenchman.

"Monsieur de Beaumont was asking where I was from, and I was just about to tell him of Brentwood," Kerry explained, her eyes wandering from the white-satined gentleman to her husband. Cameron's dark blue garb was assertive and masculine, and the simplicity of his garments made the laces and satins of the Frenchmen seem foppish. His forcefulness was enhanced when the now-nervous Frenchman set aside his cup of sparkling wine, the trembling of his obvious.

"Brentwood is my home, in the west Jerseys. I own a good deal of property along the river." Cameron's tone was polite but not overly so. Nevertheless, the Frenchman was so relieved to have this less disturbing topic of conversation at hand that he latched onto it eagerly.

"Land along the river? It should prove valuable when the war ends, if carefully tended."

"Yes," Cameron agreed. "I always see to my property, and protect it from others." His words were completely lost upon Kerry, but the Frenchman understood them; and when Cameron led his wife away he turned to his companions, muttering with disgust about American men. "They are not like us at all—selfish clods." But his eyes followed Kerry as her hips swung gently away from him and he quickly took up another cup.

Cameron took Kerry's hand and gallantly led her out to the floor. "But Cameron, I don't know how—"

"You'll see." He smiled confidently. "It is called the minuet. It is quite easy, you will see." Then as they stood amid a roomful of satin-gowned ladies and elegant men, his gaze wandered to her dress. The shock was sudden and unexpected for his eyes seemed to brand her breasts as they explored their snowy cleavage that rose and fell with each breath. A hot excitement shot through her at his reaction, for it seemed that he could pierce the slim square of blue which barely covered the pink peaks of her bosom and that she lay naked to his gaze.

"Do you like the dress?" she asked coyly, as she copied the motions of the woman beside her. At his sharp intake of breath, she glanced up and saw a sorely strained smile upon his lips.

"Were we alone I would prove how much," he responded, his eyes never leaving the delicious treat that tortured him. But his enthusiasm dimmed when he caught the gentleman to his right gazing raptly at those ripe fruits so beautifully displayed. "I suggest you employ better use of the fan," he said through clenched teeth, as yet another man gaped eagerly at her. "It seems you are causing a sensation."

Indeed a ripple went through the crowd as Kerry became noticed. Her black hair shone in the candlelight, a raven mass in the midst of so many snowy heads. The azure hue of her dress caused her eyes to sparkle with many strange lights, and she moved well in the dance, her natural rhythm coming to her aid and lending her grace. She was like a colorful bird surrounded by pigeons, and Colonials as well as Frenchmen inquired about her.

"She must be of the nobility," remarked an official to the governor. Arnold himself had noted this beauty, and he nodded as the man spoke. "Look at that face! The fineness of the line! You never see such among commoners."

"Aye," another man put in. "Her husband is Cameron Brent. Yes, of the Philadelphia Brents. Charles is his brother. A wonder that noble swain hasn't snatched her for himself."

"No doubt he tried," Jacob Northrop said. He was

amused by the reaction of the crowd. "But you remember Cameron! Determination marks the man."

The others nodded sadly, their eyes following the beauty who swirled and capered before them. Their wives and daughters were less kind with their remarks, and many wished this newly arrived creature would take herself back from whence she came.

When the dance ended, Kerry found herself pursued by a multitude of zealous males and Cameron was forced to relinquish his bride for a time at least. He was none too pleased to do so, and he declined to offer for any other lady except Fanny. As he and the young girl waltzed about the floor, his teeth clenched for Kerry's partner, a young Colonial militiaman, had fastened his eyes on her bosom as if by will he could peel the flimsy material that covered her. And Kerry's next partner pleased him even less. The Frenchman had returned to her side and was pressing his suit. Watching him, Cameron's anger grew, and it was not much lightened by Jacob's hearty laughter.

"Cool down, man! She's only dancing with the fellow." The red-haired man jostled Cameron, then pushed a glass of punch into his hand. "I never thought I'd live to see this day," he said.

"What day?" Cameron drank down the punch in one gulp and accepted another without realizing it. This, too, he dispatched in the same manner and Jacob's florid face beamed redder.

"The day Cameron Brent became jealous." At Cameron's startled gaze, Jacob guffawed and slapped his knee. "Don't try to deny it, man! That tiny slip of an Irish lass has gotten to ye, I can see that for meself!"

Snorting at this wisdom, Cameron folded his arms and feigned noninterest, but even Jacob could see that his cool gray eyes did not leave his wife for a moment.

Shortly after, Kerry was glad to hear supper announced. She watched as a long curtain was drawn aside, revealing tables heavily laden with silver dishes and trays containing hot and cold meats, breads, cheeses, game birds, fish, cold oysters, and clams. Cakes and assorted sweets were also evident. The Frenchman had returned to her side, and before she could object, he gathered up her hand and led her toward the sumptuous display of food.

"Madam, you must dine with me. I find your presence as effervescent as champagne, as intriguing as a fine wine. Do not desert me, mistress. I will be devastated." Kerry's eyes urgently searched for Cameron, but a young acquaintance of Caroline's had cornered him and was asking pointed questions concerning her absent friend. Cameron tried to escape for he found the interview irritating, but the woman would not be refused so he was forced to stand and listen to her inane chatter.

Kerry knew none of this. She saw only a regally gowned woman standing entirely too close to Cameron and lending her own exposed bosom to his gaze as she laughed brightly. To her, Cameron seemed to be enjoying the interlude so she bestowed a charming smile upon the eager Frenchman. Jacques de Beaumont wasted no time but laid his hand upon her lace-encrusted sleeve, seeking to caress her arm while his eyes sought out richer game and clung to her pale breasts.

"I am most grateful. Allow me to select for you." He placed the choicer meats upon her plate and then filled a wine cup to the brim. "And now if we may sit—"

"Monsieur de Beaumont." Cameron spoke quietly, but Kerry's eyes flew up, their sea green depths sparkling with surprise. She glanced about for his companion and found the woman nowhere about. She noted that Cameron's features were set in a manner that was far too familiar and that his eyes glittered with wrath. "It seems I ever find you ogling my wife. I suggest you find yourself a dinner partner who is not encumbered with a husband. Unless, of course, you wish to challenge me?"

Jacques' eyes wandered over the well-muscled form of

Cameron Brent. Although a gentleman, Cameron did not waste time posturing in court and his physical superiority was evident. It was also rumored that he was an excellent shot, and the thought of being felled by a bullet decreased Jacques' ardor considerably.

"By no means, monsieur," Jacques answered quickly. "I was merely conversing with your wife. I had no intention—"

"Then take your leave," Cameron said decisively. The Frenchman took this hint and strolled away, leaving Kerry to stare open-mouthed at her husband.

"There was no need for that," she snapped, her eyes flashing green fire. "The man was merely talking to me."

"Really?" One black eyebrow rose, and Cameron stared boldly into her irate gaze. "And of what did he speak? Tell me, I am most interested." At her sputtering answer, Cameron nodded wisely. "I see. Kerry, please don't misunderstand me. I do not blame you. You, my darling innocent, know naught of this world and for that I am glad."

"And what is that supposed to mean?" Kerry was angry now and she tried to prevent herself from flinging the plate into his handsome face. "Are you calling me ignorant?"

"Not at all." Cameron laughed dryly, leading her away from the listening ears at a nearby table. "But you see, Kerry, in France married women regularly take lovers. That man obviously was approaching you with that in mind."

"You mean . . ." Kerry's eyes widened as she thought this over, and her head turned quickly toward the Frenchman. Jacques caught her gaze and sent her a pleading glance that caused her to blush and drop her eyes.

"Yes." Cameron smiled. "Now enjoy your supper and think nothing of it. I think our Frenchman understands now."

Kerry picked at her plate, unable to believe all that was happening around her. The scandalous Peggy Shippen was consorting with the governor while the dandies postured before haughty ladies. She noticed that the woman Cameron had been speaking to was now with the Northrops, and a sudden worry seized her. She turned quickly to look up at Cameron and found him studying her with great interest.

"Do you think, I mean... I did not embarrass you tonight, did I?" The words rushed out as often happens when fears are voiced, but as she watched in anxious confusion, Cameron broke into laughter.

"Madam, you are the belle of the ball. I have heard only admiring remarks, although for me that has been equally disturbing."

Kerry smiled happily, ignoring his last words and sipping the funny, sparkling champagne. The buffet was scarcely ended when the music once more began. This time, Cameron refused the pleas of would-be partners and allowed himself the privilege of dancing with his wife.

"Madam, you are indeed lovely," he said sincerely, and Kerry peeped up at him in surprise. Warmth radiated from his eyes and his glance held her under its spell. The next dance was a waltz and Kerry melted into his arms, swirling around the floor with an uncontrived grace. The music drifted around them, but these two dancers heard it not, for, lost, they stared into each other's eyes. There were only two people in the ballroom, and Cameron bent his dark head, his lips brushing against Kerry's and igniting fires that begged to be answered. She gazed up at him, her eyes like liquid turquoises and Cameron, too, was spellbound. Only when she heard the spontaneous applause did Kerry return to reality, and she realized with a flustered smile that the other dancers had cleared the floor and were now clapping appreciatively.

At that triumphant moment, the door banged open and an Irishman bounded into the room. Audible gasps came from the clustered men and women, for it was obvious even to the most generous eye that the man was a commoner, a laborer perhaps. His garb was tattered and worn, and his eyes swam in pools of red while his face bore the flush of a drinking man. Without hesitation, he rushed up to the lovely young Irish lass in the center of the room, laying a thick hand upon her white shoulder.

"Kerry me darlin' girl. 'Tis a foin time ta see yer old man, that is sure. But I could wait no longer." His blue eyes beamed in delight as he gazed upon the winsome lass before him.

A buzzing arose from the crowd, growing from a slight noise into a clamor. Jacob Northrop appeared about to burst with anger, and Cameron stepped forward to address the man.

A militiaman then pressed through the crowd, seizing the Irishman in a firm grip. "Mr. Brent," he said to Cameron, "would you like this man arrested? I see he is annoying your wife."

"You'll not be arrestin' him!" Kerry shouted, her hands braced upon her hips. "He is my father. You'll be taking him nowhere."

"Master Brent?" the militiaman gently questioned. With a curt shake of his head, Cameron answered in the negative.

The crowd buzzed anew at Kerry's declaration, and the Irish lass retrieved her cloak and then dashed outside, unable to bear the murmuring around her. The tension mounted as Cameron seized O'Toole in a firm manner and escorted him outside, intending to seek out his bride.

He had not far to look. Kerry stood nearby, her cheeks cooling in the frigid winter air. Beagan approached her, a drunken leer on his face, his eyes fighting to see clearly.

"Kerry me dear. I don' mean ta trouble ya lass. I only came to ask for a few shillings fer yer own dear father. Can ya spare a few?" His head lolled and he gazed at the girl, trying to fit the two swimming figures into one.

Kerry stared at the man before her for a long time. The memories of youth fade hard, but her answers stood blatantly before her. Suddenly she knew why Cameron had been so secretive about his meetings with her father, and why

Beagan had gone so heavily into debt. Worse, she also realized that he had caused her mother's death, though the woman had loved this man dearly.

"Well lass?" Beagan cajoled.

"Ya will not get one farthing from me!" Kerry shouted, facing the little white-haired man. "I understand it all now! What with yer drink and the games too, no doubt. Aye, I recall Seamus saying something about yer gambling, but I wouldna' listen, would I? No, I thought the sun rose and set for Beagan O'Toole. And so ya broke me mither's heart, sold yer daughter into slavery, because of yer own vile habits. Ya don't care one whit about me, yet ya come here asking me for money. Well, I'm sorry, Father, I consider me debt well paid and you'll nae get more from me!" She turned from the man and ran down the street while Cameron called after her. Stunned, Beagan stood blinking in the road, unable to believe his ears.

Cameron caught up with her after she'd run a few blocks, for rage had lent wings to her feet. He grasped her squarely, but she fought his grip, her eyes flaming up at him.

"You knew! You knew of this! Why did you not tell me? Now I've been made a fool before your friends." Tears began to fall, but Kerry brushed them away. "Well, I shan't go back! Not ever! You return to yer fancy friends, ta Caroline, and leave me be!" Pride scorched her as she thought of those whispered comments and she fought to break free of this crushing embrace.

"I didn't tell you because I didn't want to see you hurt!" Cameron shouted, calling quickly for a coach. He picked up the fighting and kicking lass, holding her upright while her feet danced in frenzied anger. "Let me go!" she yelled, but his grip only tightened and he shouted to be heard by the driver.

"The Ram's Head Inn."

Without saying another word, Cameron tossed Kerry unceremoniously into the coach while the driver merely shrugged. He'd seen many a strange happening on his job, but this would be one he'd talk about for years.

"I'll run! You canna' make me stay!" Her rage still in full swing, Kerry pummeled Cameron unmercifully, trying to break free. Envisioning her tumbling out into the street, Cameron grabbed her shoulders and pressed her beneath him on the seat. This ploy stifled her movements, and he easily grasped her wrists with one hand, holding them at her side.

"Be still," he warned. Kerry had little choice in the matter, but the expression in his mocking gray eyes carried more weight than his words so she ceased fighting.

"That's better." His eyes still bearing down into hers, he continued more softly. "We shall discuss this in the privacy of our room. Until then, you will not run. You owe me that much."

"Aye." Kerry yielded reluctantly. But she turned her face away, unable to meet his eyes as she thought of the people back at the ball.

Once at the inn, Kerry kept her promise and did not bolt but climbed the stairs to their room. There she faced her husband determinedly, her eyes reflecting the fire of the hearth. Her hair falling freely about her, and she resembled an Irish warrior woman prepared to fight 'til the death. She still bore the wounds of the evening and that pain goaded her to speak.

"I'm never going back there! Not in a thousand years!"

"Nobody said you had to," Cameron was quick to assure her. "You were the one who wanted to go tonight! I couldn't care less if we ever returned."

"Oh? Now you're ashamed to be seen with me, is that it? Because of me father! Well, an O'Toole he is and an O'Toole I am. I will go off and live elsewhere, earn me own keep."

"In what manner?" Cameron asked, his patience now nearly drained. "As a tavern wench?"

"Aye and what of it?" Kerry sneered. "'Tis honest work, among honest people. More honest than yer fancy friends back there. Those English besoms who drool and fawn for yer benefit."

"Madam?" Cameron said incredulously. "You dare to accuse me . . . you, with that fine Frenchman sighing in your ears! 'Tis a good thing I happened upon you when I did, for that noble man could not keep his eyes from feasting on your flesh and he no doubt would have tasted it before evening's end!" The green monster of jealousy had aided and abetted his words, but he gave a self-satisfied smile at seeing her aghast. "I'm sure you would have welcomed his advances," Cameron continued, in the manner of a besotted lover. "Since he is not English, not of the land you hate. You flirted and preened before him. By God, lass, why is it so easy for you to render unto others what you deny me, your husband?"

Kerry stamped her foot in exasperation.

"You . . . simple-minded Englishman! Do you really think? . . ." Kerry flung up her hand and, turning on her heel, stalked toward the door. She had intended to fasten the bolt, but he was before her in a minute, blocking the exit.

"You shall not leave tonight, madam." His arms closed around her, and enraged, Kerry struggled to be free. But his embrace was iron hard and his eyes glowed into hers with burning intensity, sending warmth flooding through her. "You shall not leave ever."

Kerry's head fell backward, and when she started to shout her objections his mouth swooped down upon hers. Rage fired into passion, and without thought, Kerry's arms slipped up around Cameron, her fingers meeting at the nape of his neck. Cameron's kiss was answered with a heat and passion that left him reeling. He no longer tasted anger, but as his tongue plundered the warmth of her mouth he was greeted by a frenzied response that was wildly exciting.

But was this another game or some sort of a test? Cameron eased the pressure of his lips and his fingers found the fasteners of her cape. He would have his answer now and not be left with another night of unanswered hunger and of ravenous lusts.

Kerry stood still as his fingers released her cloak, her own long-starved passion flaming. This was what she wanted: Cameron was her husband, not some imaginary villain. In a blinding flash it all became real to her and the vision of the heinous landlord vanished, leaving in its stead an awareness of the warm and loving man she'd married. She made no objection when her cloak fell in a disgruntled heap to the floor, merely kicking it aside with her small slippered foot. Then she was fired with heat as his eyes swept her everywhere, his fingers softly caressing the soft flesh of her bosom.

"Kerry, I must have you." Cameron spoke reluctantly, as if hesitant to break this spell. "I cannot continue to live with you as your husband, always wanting but never having this sweetness before me. I've hungered for you since the first day we met, and not a day has passed that you were not in my mind. I have a hundred visions of you. I see you as the tattered and defiant lass who greeted me on the wharves and as the beguiling temptress that danced before me this eve. I am bewitched by you and I cannot risk losing you again, for you see, I love you, Kerry. I think I always have."

As her full red lips parted in astonishment, he turned away from her, standing before the fire as if he'd revealed more than he intended. His back was to her when he spoke once more, resignedly.

"Aye, 'tis true. But I know not what to say to you, how to make you see."

In answer, Kerry stepped forward and unfastened her gown. The silky material joined her cloak on the floor, and when Cameron turned, his breath caught at the sight of her. Her white shoulders gleamed, bare except for the slim straps of her shift. The accommodating sheerness of that garment allowed him a vision of her breasts, which pressed through the filmy batiste, their thinly veiled pink peaks begging to be caressed. Her waist curved inward in a lissome line, and the curves of her well-shaped legs enticed him. "Well, English," —Kerry smiled teasingly, her eyes sparkling with a thousand gold lights—"I think you just did."

Cameron's mind whirled as she placed her arms about his neck, then pressed her curves against him with a torturing slowness. Cameron's lips joined the soft beckoning ones before him, finding them warm and willing, returning his passion. Slipping off his encumbering clothing, Cameron returned to her, his lips meeting hers once more. Kerry's small tongue teased his, and his hands slipped back and fumbled with the ribbons of her shift. Suddenly, his English reserve departed, and with hungry impatience, he rent the flimsy material in two, brushing away the clinging cotton so that it fell to the floor. Now she stood naked before him. She moaned softly as his lips brushed her breasts, teasing the tiny nipples until they sprang into prominence beneath his searing tongue. His arm slipped around her then, and he tumbled them onto the bed, cool sheets meeting the flaming surface of her satiny skin. The flickering orange light of the fire painted their bodies, and Kerry's hands eagerly rose to caress that hard-muscled body kneeling above her. Hoarsely he muttered encouragement while his own hands grew bold, stroking her soft, quivering belly then the silken softness of her inner thighs. Her world dissolved in a frenzy of desire as his lips followed in their path, making her forget all else except assuagement. When her hands guided him between her legs, the raging ache in Cameron found appeasement in her soft woman's body.

The fire crackled, but the incandescent fervor of the entwined couple put it to shame. Cameron moved with torturous slowness, savoring each motion while his lips and hands caressed every inch of her burning skin. Each new thrust brought Kerry to a higher level of passion and she wondered wildly if she could bear it. Then, like the gathering of thousands of white-hot stars, their fires of desire burned brightest. Kerry cried out as Cameron buried his face in her hair, and slowly the stars changed to golden cinders that drifted back to the earth and left them panting in the warm aftermath of their bliss.

When a fire-burned log snapped in two and fell into the flames with a hiss, Kerry's eyes slowly opened and she watched the dancing shadows against the ceiling. She was wrapped in Cameron's arms and a languid smile curved her lips. Her green eyes were smoky and serene, and her fingers caressed the dark hair that curled about the nape of his neck. Cameron arose, stuffing one pillow under his arm while he returned her smile.

"About tonight—" Kerry started, but Cameron placed a finger to her lips, refusing to hear her apology.

"I understand completely." He smiled, a dusky flash of white teeth in the firelight. "More so than you think. I was oft subjected to the ridicule of that society in my youth and I well know the pain it can cause. It is for that reason that I seldom attend these functions, while Charles seems to thrive on them."

"You?" Kerry peered into his gray gaze and found it serious. "But why?"

"Remember, my sweet, that I am what society considers a bastard. For that reason I was not accepted. Now that I have money, they tolerate me, but I find their presence tedious and boring. Jacob and his family were kind to me in my youth and I never forgot them. They are the only people in this place I consider friends." His fingers softly caressed the fine line of her profile, smoothing out her frown.

"And of my father?"

Cameron kissed her hand, warming it between his own.

"I met with him just yesterday. When I understood his . . . circumstance, I worked out an agreement that seemed to satisfy him. I gave him a sum of money and offered him a position at one of my shipyards in the city. He seemed content enough then. I don't know what happened to change his mind and make him seek you out."

"You gave him money! Why, Cameron?" Kerry abruptly sat up in the bed, heedless of the sheet that fell away from her. Her hair tumbled softly about her breasts, very black against the white linen and Cameron found his concentration tested as she continued to protest. "You could see that he was the cause of the trouble! He broke my mother's heart and her body, and you gave him money and a job? Why?"

"He's your father." Cameron shrugged. "And although I have inquired into the rents and found them to be fair, there is always a chance for error. I wanted to be sure he was adequately compensated. After all"—he grinned roguishly—"he did produce you and for that I am forever grateful."

Kerry was not as forgiving, but as Cameron's kiss extended from her hand to trace her arm and then find her lips, she forgot all about Beagan O'Toole and was drawn into the passionate fire that flamed once more.

Chapter Twenty-Two

The morning sun had scarcely climbed above the frozen branches of the trees when Kerry was rudely awakened from sleep, the warm quilts snatched completely off her bare form. "What dya' think yer doing!" She shivered, clutching her arms fruitlessly about her goosepimpled flesh, while her fully dressed husband smiled from the far end of the bed. He held the covers in one hand like a cape and he bowed mockingly, addressing her in a formal fashion.

"Make haste, my dear. We have an appointment this day and we must see it through."

"An appointment?" She gathered the pillows to her round breasts, the nipples tight against the chill. Cameron's eyes gazed appreciatively at this sight, for while the pillows provided a small degree of warmth, they pressed her bosom upward to an even more enticing fullness, the pink crests teasing him from this partially obstructed view.

"Yes," Cameron answered with difficulty. "We are to meet with your father this day and then we will prepare to return home. I think it best to do so before another winter storm approaches."

"I'm not meeting with him!" Kerry's eyes snapped green fire and she rose to kneel on the bed to face Cameron. Still clutching the pillow, she made a charming picture as her lissome curves peeked forth from this barricade, promising to reveal more. "I've had all I want of him! I am not talking with him any more, not listening to—" But her speech was cut off for the pillow had been slowly extracted from her grasp and she found herself naked and vulnerable both to the cold and to his gaze. He smiled wickedly, then held out a gown of deep burgundy and advanced determinedly toward the bed.

"I have not yet discovered if dressing you is quite as enjoyable as undressing you, but I am willing to find out."

With a gasp, Kerry snatched the gown from his hands, then bounced from the bed to retrieve her shift. Pulling the undergarment over her head, she hastily donned the gown while he chuckled merrily. "You have an odd sense of humor," she remarked, facing him now that she was clothed and not so vulnerable.

"Odd? Not in the least." His hands captured her slender waist and pulled her close. Looking up into his face, Kerry wondered at his intent, but he smiled, then turned her around to fasten her gown. It felt right to be in his arms, to feel his hands performing this small task for her, and she shivered as he placed a small kiss on her bare throat.

"I still don't want to go." She declared as he tossed her a cloak.

"'Tis best to leave no loose ends," Cameron replied firmly. "You don't wish to see him now, but in a few weeks when your anger has cooled, you will wonder what became of him. At least this way you will know that you made the effort."

Kerry stared up at him, stunned by his wisdom. Although her fiery nature rebelled, she complied, following him out the door and into the carriage.

The Northrops' maid led Kerry and Cameron right into the study, having been informed of their arrival. Kerry allowed herself a sideways glance at her husband, and she wondered if there was no end to his self-confidence. But she scarcely had time to dwell on the matter, for the study door swung open and Jacob bellowed a greeting. Her eyes fell not on him, however, but on the meek figure sitting before him. At the exuberant sound of Jacob's voice, Beagan placed his hands over his ears, a sweat breaking out on his flushed forehead.

"Mr. and Mrs. Brent! I am so happy that you've come." Jacob extended his hand while Kerry glared at her obviously pained father.

"The noise!" Beagan pleaded and Jacob apologized.

"Cameron, you can sit here," he added, "and Kerry, the seat near your father's for you." Kerry threw a disdainful glance at the comfortable chair he indicated, but when Cameron sent her a meaningful stare she relented and took it, reserving her sneers for the man that deserved them.

"Now, before we begin, Beagan has something he wants to say," Jacob announced quickly, giving the floor to the Irishman. At once Beagan stood up, and sweeping his cap from his white curls, he turned a reddened face to Kerry.

"I fear I owe ye an apology," he began, shuffling his feet in embarrassment. "'Twas true that many of the trials were of me own making. And when yer mither died, saint that she was . . . well, the guilt was too much for me ta bear. I set out for here, thinking that since ye were settled in with this foin lad ye'd be helpin' me out. That's when this gent found me and gave me some monies and an offer. I thought then that the debt was settled, but another lad told me I was a fool fer taking so little when I'd lost so much."

As Kerry's mouth opened to protest, Beagan wisely rushed on with his tale.

"I woulda paid him no need, but I got ta thinkin'. And with the whiskey pourin' free and him tellin' me where ya'd be, well it seemed I saw yer own mither right before me, atelling me ta go. But today I see that I've done ya wrong and I will try ta make it up ta ya. If ya could just see it in yer heart ta forgive me." As his naughty blue eyes widened like cornflowers, it was on the tip of Kerry's tongue to deny him, but a pointed cough from Cameron reminded her of his words.

"If you really mean that and you want to make it up to me, then take that job and stay out of trouble. Only then will I accept your apology and try to forget the rest." Kerry sent Cameron a meaningful glance and her husband smiled, secretly pleased by her words.

"Aye, aye. That I'll do. That is, if the laddie will still hae me?" The old man's pleading eyes now went to Cameron, who nodded, a sternness playing about his lips.

"Yes, the job is still yours. But I warn you, the manager at the yard is a wise man and he will keep an eye on you. Do your job well and there is money to be made there, however," Cameron declared, and Beagan smiled, his gratitude apparent.

"Thank you sir! 'Twas the lucky day when me daughter met with you! You're right kind for an Englishman." Beagan beamed as if he'd bestowed the most wonderful of compliments, and cap in hand, he scuttled out the door while everyone was still feeling magnanimous. As Jacob watched him go, a chuckle shook his broad frame.

"A reformed man if I ever saw one. I will keep an eye on him, lass, and send you a note from time to time. But you have little to worry about. I know your docksman, Cameron, and that hearty soul can wring work out of anyone. You're not leaving already, lad?"

As Cameron drew Kerry's cloak about her, he nodded.

"Yes. We've a long trip ahead and I'm eager to be home. I'm half afraid that Charles may have made a shambles of the place in my absence." Cameron spoke jokingly but Kerry saw real concern in his eyes.

Jacob nodded, clapping his hand to Cameron's broad shoulders. "Then don't let it be so long before you return. Now that you have a bride I trust you'll be returning more frequently?" Jacob asked hopefully, and Kerry smiled to reassure him.

"I'll see to it." She grinned and the red-haired man responded with a smile.

"Oh, I almost forgot. This came for you, Cameron. I found it in with my own letters this morn."

With a frown, Cameron accepted the parchment, breaking the letter open in his haste to be off. A square slip fluttered to the floor and Kerry retrieved it. She gasped as she brought the slip to eye level, for the wording was clear. Lettered boldly in black ink, the message was curt:

Do not return.

"Cameron, do you see that?" Kerry thrust the slip at her husband, but there was little need to do so for he had already seen it. He frowned and, perplexed, turned the note over in his hand, but there was little to be learned from it. The sheet was blank but for those frightening words, and even the envelope provided no clue as to the sender. Silently, Cameron handed the letter to his host and Jacob's mouth dropped.

"Who would do such a thing?" he asked, his eyes wide. Cameron shrugged.

"I haven't the slightest idea. We've had other puzzling disturbances at home, but nothing as direct as this. Do you know how this letter was delivered?"

"No, but I can find out." Jacob rang and the maid promptly appeared.

"Yes, sir?" she said, her gaze wandering from Cameron to her master.

"Do you have any idea who delivered this note? I found it with the correspondence on my desk." When he showed the bewildered lass the letter, she shook her head.

"Why no, sir. But let me think. A small lad come to see you this morn. I let him into the parlor for just a moment and by the time I went to call you he had gone. I thought nothing of it at the time, but perhaps he had an opportunity to slip the letter onto your desk." At her employer's grim expression, the little lass grew pale. "I hope I have not done wrong, sir?" She sounded so worried that Jacob was quick to reassure her.

"No. You could not have foreseen this. Thank you." As the girl disappeared through the parlor door, Jacob turned an apologetic eye on Cameron.

"I am sorry. That lad could be any one of a hundred urchins in the street. Our chances of finding him are slight. But if you wish to try..."

"No, no. We must head back. 'Tis likely that the lad does not know his benefactor at any rate, for a man who seeks to hide his identity would not reveal it to a small, loose-tongued boy. I think it best we return home and find out why someone wishes to prevent our reappearance." He smiled confidently at Kerry, but she could see the concern in his gaze and she wondered what awaited them at Brentwood.

"Godspeed," Jacob called as they climbed into the coach. With a flap of the reins George headed them for the Delaware, where they boarded a ferry and left the city behind.

Night had fallen when they reached Brentwood, but Kerry knew they had arrived before she shook the sleep from her eyes. The aromatic smell of pine mixed with cedar, the soft gentle lapping of the Mullica River, and the clang of the furnace, all gave the place away. She lay nestled in Cameron's arms, warm and secure, and as he lifted her from the coach, she slipped her arms about his neck, pondering the many advantages of marriage. His iron-hard arms carried her as if she were thistledown, through the door and up the darkened staircase, to the comfort of a downy bed. Sleep greeted her there, and she welcomed it for she was at home.

In the morning Cameron was gone so Kerry slipped quickly out of bed to stand before the fire and thaw the icy chill from her bones. A discreet rap sounded at the door.

"Come on in, but have yer coat on," Kerry called, tossing a few twigs upon the meager fire. She had lifted her nightgown and was standing with her backside bared to the newborn flames, but when Helga entered, she promptly dropped the gown, facing the woman with a glad cry.

"Helga!" The cook embraced her joyfully. She smelled good, like flour and tea and baking bread, and Kerry laughed when Helga, realizing this display was unseemly, backed away to stand more formally by the door.

"Ja, it is me! I could not vait to see you, I hope you don't mind." She eyed her charge critically for signs of wear so Kerry spun about in a waltzlike step, allowing her a full view. "Tell me"—Helga spoke sternly but her blue eyes were shining, "you are happy, *ja?"*

"I am happy, *ja!"* Kerry laughed again, and her dreamy expression changing her green eyes to a swirling turquoise blue. "Oh Helga, if only you could have been there! Philadelphia is a grand place. And everything is settled with me father, and Cameron is wonderful."

"Vonderful." Helga's eyes rolled and she folded her hands over her full bosom, an unavoidable smile sparkling on her face. "Then it verked out for the best, you do love him?" She cocked her head sideways and watched her young mistress as a sparrow watches its young.

"Oh yes," Kerry replied. "I think I always did. I was just worried about him."

"You were vorried about him?" Helga nodded as if this made no sense at all, but she thought it best to let that go. "Then tell me vhat you did and vhere you went. I have a minute before Miss Caroline demands her breakfast."

"I'll do you one better. Wait until I wash and dress and I'll meet you downstairs in the kitchen. I'll tell you about it while you work. By the way, did you see Cameron this morn?"

"Ja. He vent out vith the dawn, as alvays. To the furnace

no doubt. Hoodlums! Dey nearly wreck the place in his absence. 'Tis goot that you are back." After fondly patting Kerry's shoulder, Helga stepped smartly down the stairs, and Kerry rushed to get dressed.

Less than ten minutes later Kerry's brisk step was heard in the hall, for when the room temperature dipped below forty, one was inclined to hasten one's toilet. Her emerald green skirts swirled about her as she started down the stairs, and she'd taken the time to weave a matching ribbon through her jet black hair. She made a charming picture, her profile pert and sunny, her nature the same. But one person did not think so, and before Kerry had reached the third step, her voice rang out sharply.

"Ah, I see you have returned. Has Cameron come to his senses yet and thrown you over?" Kerry froze, then glanced back to see Caroline posed in her doorway. Without a rich gown and smartly coiffed hair, Caroline appeared quite plain and the ugly smile on her lips did not make her less so. Her face seemed pale and sallow, her hair tousled and ragged, but her eyes were exactly as Kerry remembered them, clear and as warming as crystal. "If he has, I'm sure you can still find a job, though not here."

"That will not be necessary." Kerry's hand tightened on the banister and she felt her knuckles harden against the wood. She forced herself to smile, but a glimmer of pity for Caroline caused her to answer less harshly than the woman deserved. "I am thinking that you are worried about Cameron, but he is happy, I assure you."

"You assure me? I have known the man for most of my life. I think I can best judge his happiness—or lack of it." She grinned, catlike, showing teeth that glowed wetly. "And how did you find Philadelphia? I'm sure Cameron had better taste than to present you anywhere, you a common servant, so I daresay your visit must have been boring."

"I don't think I'd call the Northrops boring," Kerry said

politely. "But the governor's ball was. Cameron thought so too. Seeing as you know him so well, I needn't tell you that. Will you be coming down to breakfast now? I'm going to see Helga and I'll tell her if you are." Kerry kept a tight rein on her emotions, but Caroline's face whitened perceptibly and for a moment Kerry thought the woman would strike her.

"I'll be down when I'm ready," she hissed, and as Kerry turned away, she heard a final warning. "He will grow tired of you, you common slut! And when he does, I'll be waiting."

Kerry's head flew up. She was ready to respond angrily, but she saw only the sweep of an ice-blue gown as Caroline disappeared into her room and slammed the door. Still the woman had planted a gnawing doubt in her mind, and though she tried to shake off the feeling, the morning was not as bright as it had been a moment ago.

Helga's work was considerably lightened by Kerry's lively chatter, and the small dark Irish lass was dusted with flour for she'd aided Helga with the bread making. The two women now sat beside the fire, sipping tea and enjoying the fruits of their labor. Helga grinned when Kerry spoke of the Northrops, laughed when she heard of Beagan's apology. But the cook grew concerned when Kerry told her of the highwaymen and of Cameron's injury. Her worriment faded, however, as Kerry assured her that the wound had healed completely, leaving only a pink scar.

"*Ja*, and that you would know, being a newlywed." Helga smiled knowingly and Kerry felt herself turn red, that last blissful night in Philadelphia on her mind. "'Tis good," Helga said. "Ve will have children in this house! There are many rooms upstairs. *Ja,* a third ving. It has room for a nursery and sunny vindows. It will be, how you say, grand?"

Kerry laughed, then turned her attention to the fresh bread and jam with enthusiasm. Her teacup had been emptied and her chunk of bread enjoyed, Kerry finally stood up and gazed out the window. "I guess I'd better go down and see what's keeping Cameron," she said. The remark had scarcely left her lips when a maid handed her her cloak. Donning the garment, Kerry slipped reluctantly from the warmth of the kitchen and headed out into the relentless morning chill.

The snows of Philadelphia had reached the pines, but here it was a different snow. Windswept fields and deep sparkling drifts met her gaze. In the morning sun their brilliance was nearly blinding. Shading her eyes, Kerry followed the footprints in the fresh fall and found herself heading for the furnace, as she'd suspected. But before she reached that solemn pyramid, she heard angry voices by the pond. Indecision stopped her, but curiosity won out. Altering her path, Kerry made for the frozen pool of water.

She hadn't come within ten feet of it, yet the voices were clear and easily distinguished.

"I don't care what you have to say! I cannot afford a charity case on my hands! Now if you can show me one good reason as to why you should be exempt from doing your share of labor, I will be most happy to listen!"

There was no mistaking that voice. The clear, precise tones belonged to Cameron. Yet the next voice startled her for the anger in it was naked, and she found herself an eavesdropper on a family quarrel.

"I am no laborer! How dare you imply such! But I might have expected as much from you. You are bred of the laboring class. Do not include me in your menial plans, however. I do not intend to soil my hands."

"Charles"—Cameron's voice was strained—"I have tried to be patient. I ask no more of you than I am willing to do, yet you squandered your inheritance, you lost the family estate. I leave you in charge for a mere week, and when I return, the place is a shambles, the workers are ready to quit, the team drivers are drunk. What the hell did you do in my absence?"

"'Tis not my fault that your workers are so spoiled by your management that they are lazy and disobedient. You would not give me permission to use my fists on them and this is the result." Charles sneered.

Kerry could bear to hear no more. Faced with the choice of sneaking away or letting her presence be known, she chose the latter and risked Cameron's anger by walking into the grove. Charles sensed her presence immediately and his eyes roamed over her, a hungry look in their pale blue depths. But Cameron's gaze narrowed and he went to stand beside her, his cane tapping angrily against his boot.

"Madam, what are you doing? The air is freezing." His eyes flickered back to the place where she'd stood and Kerry could read his thoughts.

"I came to look for you. I did not mean to overhear. At any rate, I thought it best to step forward." She raised her eyes and faced Cameron squarely, her honesty written in her stance, and his annoyance faded.

"Well, since you heard you may as well know the end of it. Charles, I will give you until the end of the month to reach a decision. Either you decide to work for me, here at Brentwood or at the shipyard if you find my presence unbearable, or you take your leave. I will not allow you to remain here unless you take your share of the burden. Do I make myself clear?" Cameron stated this plainly, without insult, but apparently Charles did not see things his way. Drawing himself up to his full six feet, the pale, blond Englishman smiled coldly at his brother. His eyes flickered to Kerry, and with a nod, he took himself off, striding to the house without another word.

Kerry watched his departure, then turned to her husband. "Cameron, are you sure this is the best way? He seems very upset."

"There is no other way, I am certain." He sighed. "I am convinced that it is best for Charles to realize this immediately. It is not as though I can't afford to keep him on, but there is no reason to do that. He is a grown man, and it is time he made his own life." The tension eased from Cameron's face and he smiled down into her darkly fringed blue-green eyes.

"Come, mistress. Since you insist upon running out in the snow, we may as well complete the trip. There is a pest of an Irish lad asking about you at the furnace, as are a host of eager workmen. If I plan to get anything accomplished today, your presence may be necessary."

With a smile, Kerry took the hand he proffered and walked down the path to the furnace. They had scarcely stepped inside when a thunderous applause broke out. Blushing, Kerry glanced awkwardly about and saw Trevor standing in the center of a group of workmen.

"Glad ta have ya home, mistress." The insouciant lad grinned and strode forward, taking Kerry's hand. Then without warning, he twisted her hand about his waist and kissed Kerry, longer and more fully than his age or his meager height seemed to warrant. An abrupt clearing of Cameron's throat cooled his ardor, however, and Kerry stepped back, laughing in astonishment.

"'Tis a good thing we were only gone a week." Cameron scowled, and his hand rested possessively on Kerry's cloaked shoulder. "I should hate to see his reaction if it had been longer." He sent the Irish lad a warning glance that Trevor dutifully ignored, and the other men chuckled.

"Aye, good ta see you, mistress." The others gathered about, to greet her and to clasp her hand. Kerry smiled and nodded at each friendly face, asking about a wife or a child and hearing the most delightful stories in return. Finally when time sprouted wings she grinned and gestured to the office.

"I'll find out tomorrow what you've been doing this past week," she said teasingly. "And it had best be a good report."

"Oh, it will!" They laughed, then their merriment grew silent as a shuffling noise came from the far end of the furnace. Bill Seldon ambled slowly toward the crowd, his yellowed eyes leering, his tone mocking.

"We ain't getting paid to chitchat," he snarled, and one by one the men fell off, returning to their work. Kerry's hand tightened involuntarily on Cameron's as the man looked up, surveying the couple with displeasure.

"So yer back." He wiped his grizzled mouth on the back of his sleeve and waved a thick hand to the men. "Yer brother's been causing a right bit o' trouble down here. I told him I hate the Brents—all of them."

"Mr. Seldon, your feelings are well known to me. But as long as they do not affect your work, I see no reason to discuss them."

"Aye, that's fine, sir. But you can tell your brother ta stop sneakin' down 'ere at night. I seen him coming and going, and I won't be liable for what the laggard does."

"Charles? Coming down at night?" Kerry could see that the words took Cameron by surprise and he stared thoughtfully at the hostile man beside him. "For what reason?"

"And 'ow would I know that?" Bill scowled. "Seems ta me you should know what yer own kin are doing." He ambled to the furnace fire, grumbling aloud as he departed.

Kerry and Cameron started back for the house. Their greetings having disrupted the work they decided there was little for the diarist or the master to attend to that day. Cameron was clearly puzzled by Bill's words, and Kerry interrupted his thoughts with an idea of her own.

"He was probably trying to catch Trevor or Bill at something. You know how Charles is."

Cameron glanced down into her winsome face and nodded. "Yes, you are probably right. I just find it difficult to picture Charles going to all that trouble."

"Unless he stopped there when returning home from his nightly prowls."

"Aye, I forgot about that. You are right, Kerry. One should not judge too quickly."

Yet Cameron still seemed disturbed and he excused himself a while later, to disappear into his study.

Chapter Twenty-three

The ravages of winter soon melted into spring and snow drops appeared, their sparkling white flowers and green leaves a refreshing sight. The air was filled with the cries of migrating birds returning to their summer homes and the skies had assumed a golden hue, losing the icy grayness that marked them in winter.

The furnace was back in full production now, for the ice on the rivers and ponds had melted, enabling the men to dig for ore and to have running water. The villagers came out of hibernation to cultivate their gardens and plant early seeds. The woods were filled with the calls of workmen, the plodding of the teams, the clang of the forge. Winter was an ugly dream, now departed.

Yet the beauty of the land had competition, for the mistress of the manor was flourishing under the warm and loving care of her husband. She was seen often and everywhere like a spring butterfly, in the furnace keeping the books, in the village helping the wives and children of workers, or in the great house itself. And when she saddled her horse, a replacement for Caledonia with the same Scottish blood and that wonderful red-hued color, the men paused at their work, to better view the vision before them. On horseback, wild and free as this new country, her black hair blowing and the wind making color bloom on her cheeks, she seemed the very embodiment of Brentwood. The previous solemnity of the house had vanished, and a warm cheerfulness had replaced it. Indeed, she was the lady for Brentwood.

Cameron knew that. Watching his wife had become his favorite pastime, and he was now more relaxed, more open with the men. Kerry had a way of making everything new and exciting, such as the day she'd decided the weather was too fine to eat inside and she'd had Helga spread cloths upon the ground for a picnic. The men had devoured the huge meal with great enthusiasm and the occasion had turned into a holiday, with all participating except Caroline. She'd watched from the window, a twitch of the lace curtain the only sign of her presence, and Kerry had wondered about the woman lurking above.

"I think she's touched," Trevor declared solemnly, swirling his finger about his head. "Ya never see her about much, and when ya do, she acts like a loon. Crazy as a henhouse, I tell ya."

"You should know," Cameron replied dryly and the workmen guffawed. Their laughter slowly died when Trevor turned to Cameron, a question in his voice.

"'Tis a shame Master Charles decided to leave us. Back to Philadelphia, is he?"

Kerry glanced up at Cameron, concerned about his reaction. But he simply shrugged, took a drink of cool spring ale, and then replied.

"Perhaps it's for the best. Charles was not an ironmaster at heart. Maybe now he'll find his calling." Cameron's words sounded doubtful, even to himself, and Kerry placed her small hand in his.

"You did all you could." She smiled reassuringly at him.

From his position Cameron had an advantageous view of his wife. She wore a soft muslin dress, of a cream color with sprigs of lavender flowers abounding on it. The neckline was a jewel cut, which afforded a grand view of her swelling bosom. Seeing where his eyes wandered, Kerry pressed a hand to his ear.

"You, sir, are a rogue. Are you never sated?" She gave him an enchanting smile, one that teased and promised him all, and it was a full minute before Cameron could answer.

"Not when it comes to you. And if you keep looking at me like that, I will be forced to drag you off so we can have some privacy."

"So roars the lion," she retorted. Her black curls danced in shimmering waves about her face and Cameron's hand rose to caress them. He was just beginning to realize what it meant to be married to this woman, and his blood warmed more than a bit.

A horseman galloped up the path, all heads craning to view this new arrival, and cheers and shouts rang out as Richard Westcoat dismounted, doffing his tricorn at the sight of Kerry. He tossed the hat to Cameron, then laughed at the sight of the spread.

"Is this a private party or can anyone join?" he asked, then without waiting for an answer, he took the seat beside Kerry and smiled brilliantly. "Madam, how are you this day? I swear you blind the very sun with your beauty."

Cameron scowled and tossed the hat to Trevor, who shrugged and threw it on the ground. "First that Irish lad, next my own English brother, and then a Frenchman in Philadelphia. Now you. Is the wench not safe from anyone?" Cameron protested good-naturedly, and Richard grinned.

"Not when she looks like that. You, sir, are going to have your hands full fighting off suitors. I daresay you will rue the day you married this lass," Richard teased. Kerry gasped, and Cameron paused wickedly for a moment, as if considering these words, then he nodded.

"I suppose a less winsome lass would prove less tiring. But I, for one, prefer livelier game." Cameron grinned and Kerry threw him an admonishing look, whereupon Richard threw back his head and laughed, delighted at this wisdom. When he could speak, he addressed Cameron in a more serious tone.

"I did not come by just to enjoy your food, though I will do that. There has been a problem at the shipyard. I think you should know about it."

"What is it? Inspections?" Cameron questioned.

"No. Robbery."

"Robbery?" Cameron's eyes narrowed. "Are you sure?"

"Aye. And a queer lot of things stolen. Some wire. And some of our finest Madeira. I can't make head or tail of it." Richard was truly perplexed and he shook his head as he spoke.

"Anyone seen?" Cameron asked, and Richard's hand absently caressed his own chin as if deep in thought.

"No. But you know where the shoreline extends near the warehouse, the new one we constructed since Chestnut Neck?" Cameron nodded and Richard continued in the same troubled tone. "Well, I saw a footmark."

"A seaman's?"

"No," Richard replied. "It was a boot print, made by a gentleman's boot."

Several of the workmen turned interested eyes on Cameron, their gazes falling idly to the expensive, square cut of his boot. Impervious to their glances, Cameron continued to question Richard.

"Have you called the sheriff?"

"No. I thought I'd speak with you first."

"Well," Cameron said thoughtfully while the workers nudged each other, "it might be best to handle this ourselves. Let me know if anything further develops."

"Right." Richard sounded doubtful, but Cameron was already drawing Kerry up from the ground and ending the conversation.

* * *

After the evening meal Richard departed so the newlyweds sought the privacy of Cameron's chamber quite early. The window was ajar, and the fresh spring breeze carried the sweet scents of lilacs, fruit blossoms, and lily of the valley into the room. It had rained the day before, so a light mist surrounded the moon.

Kerry stood before the lace-curtained window, admiring the view. At this time of night the furnace seemed peaceful enough. Though she knew it still roared deep inside, the bustle of workmen and team drivers had ceased, and only a faint orange glow revealed that its activity was not altogether stilled.

Cameron came up behind her, his hand sliding sensuously over her shoulder. Kerry tingled where he touched her and she gently nuzzled his neck, drawing his other hand about her waist. His lips brushed her hair, stirring from it the sweet fragrance of the pines.

"Ah, wench. The very sight of you stirs my blood. It will be doubly difficult working with you down at the furnace now for I'll be counting the hours until night when you can be mine." Kerry's head tilted upward and Cameron kissed her lips lightly. "You nearly drove me to distraction before, but now! If I can concentrate on my work, 'twill be a miracle."

"Really, master?" Kerry teased. "I had no idea." She drew in a quick breath as her dress slipped to the floor, the swish of loose material the only sound in the room. Dressed only in her light shift, she was as alluring as if she were naked. The filmy fabric clung to her well rounded figure, which had become slightly fuller in the past few days, yet her waistline was narrow. Kerry shivered as Cameron's lips lowered to the front of her shift and his hands lifted those ripe fruits free.

"Cameron, I . . ." Just as Kerry spoke, a low moan arose from somewhere deep within the bogs. It built to a rising crescendo, then ended in a harrowing howl. Kerry turned quickly in Cameron's arms, terrified.

"The demon!" she whispered.

Cameron, too, had paused to listen and he seemed distracted by the cry, visibly shaken. "It is one thing to laugh about that in Philadelphia," he said slowly, "but another to stand here in the Pines and feel it thrill your bones."

He had scarcely finished this statement when the cry arose again, louder this time. Kerry shivered and pressed closer to him, her thinly veiled breasts rubbing his chest. "I am frightened," she murmured.

A firm resolve built in Cameron's mind as he gazed down at her, his mouth set and his gray eyes sparkling with wrath. "No one—no thing—will make me leave my home," he vowed. He clenched his fist and raised it to the window, shaking it at the hideous sound. "Leave, you Devil!" he shouted, and Kerry trembled as the wind caught the sound and brought it nearer, until it seemed to be wrapped around them.

"Cameron! Cameron, kiss me!" Kerry begged, her flesh rising as the strange cries rent the night. Her mouth was open and fearful, and Cameron accommodated her, his lips swooping down and crushing hers. Soon his kiss trailed lower, and his tongue flicked a tiny nipple into tightness. She heard a soft moan of pleasure that she distantly recognized as her own. Meanwhile, his hands caressed her satiny skin, brushing the shift downward to join the dress.

The demon howled outside but Kerry heard it not, for Cameron's hands were moving slowly and deliberately down to her curved waist, across her flat belly, and then farther still. Kerry gasped and bit her trembling lips as his hands caressed her inner thighs, then explored the womanly softness that awaited him. He laughed softly as she writhed against him, and slipping an arm under her legs, he carried her to bed. Tossing aside his own clothes, he joined her, but when she pleaded for him to take her, his mind seemed of a different bent. He stroked and explored her body with maddening leisureliness while she twisted and turned beneath his branding touch, her emotions spiraling out of control.

With an instinct born of passion she reached for him, her hand closing over him and applying a few deft caresses of her own. She felt rather than heard his groan and finding her silken legs parted welcomingly beneath him, he took her fiercely, with a passion that left them both gasping. Mindless except for the urgency of her need, Kerry arched against him, her body tasting freely of the pleasure his hard-muscled body delivered. Together they gave vent to their feverish desire, and achieved the ecstasy lovers know.

When Kerry slowly drifted back to reality, she heard something strange. It took her a minute to realize what had distracted her, then it suddenly came to her that all was silent. Cameron, too, had noticed the change. He was halfway up, his hands still caressing the warm flushed skin of her face and breasts.

"It is still," Kerry breathed gratefully, and Cameron smiled, his eyes gleaming with the silver of the moon.

"Aye. It seems we have discovered a cure for this problem that plagues us."

"And what is that?" Kerry asked, her blue-green eyes round with innocence.

"Why, we simply have to make love each time it disturbs us. The poor beast can't take it."

Kerry laughed softly as she gazed up into the warmth of his eyes. "Cameron, what do you think it is? Are you really in some danger, as the villagers say?"

"I don't know." He picked up her small white hand and kissed each finger lightly. "But whatever it is, this demon will learn that I am not easily subdued. I am not an old woman living alone like Enid. And I am not my father who had a heart condition. I am prepared to face whatever this world deals me, natural or supernatural." He smiled, his tongue tracing fiery patterns along her wrist and arm, but Kerry was still worried.

"Cameron, be careful," she pleaded, raising his head. "I want to have you with me for a long time, especially since it took so long for us to be together."

"Have no fear, madam," Cameron whispered. "I have no intention of leaving you. Now come, wench. No more talk of devils or demons. My mind is set on more earthly matters." He lowered his mouth to hers, and once more the coals of passion were ignited.

The following day a light spring rain drizzled down, coating everything with its silken mist. The new mistress of Brentwood spent the day indoors, after seeing to the furnace and adjusting the books. She had carried those books into the parlor now, intending to sum up the month's entries and make a complete listing of all the coal, ore, and wood used. Then she must record the feed allotments for the horses and mules.

Brushing aside a stray lock of hair, Kerry tore her burning eyes away from her work and gazed about the room. From her seat, she could see the hallway and the coat of arms immediately caught her attention. The horse's head seemed to stare right back at her and she shivered, thinking of the previous night.

Hogwash, she told herself. Must have been the wind. But her Irish intuition told her differently, and she had the uneasy sense that all was not well.

She returned to scratching figures into the books, and continued with this until she was finally interrupted by the clatter of a tray. Glancing up, she found Helga glaring at her with disapproval, and she braced herself for the lecture to come.

"Vat are you doing, vith all those books and no food! You shouldn't bother vith that now! You are lady of this house.'"

"Helga, I am the only one that keeps them right. They

were a shambles when we came back from Philadelphia. And I really don't mind doing something useful." Taking up one of the sandwiches, Kerry gave the frowning woman a pert grin. "Would you rather I was like herself upstairs, never moving from me bed." She winked.

"None of that, mistress. You couldn't sit still if you tried. Now finish that up and get dressed. Or have you forgotten that the Clarks are coming for the evening meal?" Helga cocked her head reprovingly and Kerry's hand flew to her mouth.

"Oh, that's right. I did forget! And I haven't a thing ready, I've been too busy down at the furnace." She dropped her sandwich and started up, but Helga laid a hand on her arm.

"Ya, I know. I took care of that. You vill find your dress laid out on the bed and a bath made ready. Now finish that up so you vill not be starving by the time they come and gobble up everything in sight!"

Kerry smiled her thanks and relaxed, finishing the tea and sandwiches in peace. When the last crumbs had been eaten, Helga smiled with approval, then Kerry dashed upstairs to bathe and dress.

As Helga had promised, the scented bath was ready, and Kerry lounged in the warm water, purring like a satisfied kitten. A flagon of French perfume lay next to her towel, and she lifted the glass stopper, testing the bewitchingly sweet scent. Smiling to herself, she placed a droplet behind each ear and between her breasts. She recalled the day Cameron had reluctantly purchased rose perfume for Caroline. But this scent suited his taste, and once again he'd proved that he settled only for the best.

Picking up the brush, Kerry stood before the mirror and applied it to her hair until her black locks gleamed like satin. Then she donned a shift and put on her dress. It was a warm rose gown that dipped between her breasts, and it featured a cinched waist ruched with pink silk. Tiny rosebuds were gathered here in its folds and her dainty rose slippers matched them. Kerry glanced into the mirror, and satisfied that the color enhanced the natural warmth of her own flesh, her eyes sparkled in the candlelight.

As she stepped down the stairs, Kerry heard the idle chatter of their guests, but when she entered the parlor, all eyes turned her way and a complimentary silence fell. It was broken by Cameron. He strode toward her, and capturing her small hand in his, he led her to the Clarks.

"We've saved the best for last," he said gallantly. "I'd almost despaired of your arrival, but it was worth the wait."

"It was indeed, mistress," Eliah Clark declared while Jane smiled approvingly.

"You look lovely, child. I daresay lovelier than any rose."

Blushing her thanks, Kerry passed the tray set with glasses of wine that Helga had discreetly deposited nearby, letting Cameron handle the task of filling them. Kerry and Jane talked softly about their household problems, while Cameron and Eliah spoke of their plans for the future.

"I hope one day to have several mills here," Cameron said, standing beside the window and gesturing to the wide expanse of pinelands. "I think a paper mill will do quite well. And perhaps a glass factory."

"Glass?" Eliah nodded. "That's an excellent idea. You certainly have the sand for it here, and the water power."

When Helga announced dinner, Cameron escorted Kerry to the dining room while Eliah performed that same service for his wife. The food was good and the talk flowed freely, everyone relaxed by the spring weather and the enjoyable meal. Cameron was just calling for more wine when the most dreaded cry of all was heard from the furnace.

"Fire!"

The cry intensifed and there was a flurry of activity. Cameron and Eliah leaped out of their seats and raced down to the furnace while Kerry and Jane followed.

"Buckets! They will need something for the water!" Jane shouted to Kerry and the Irish lass lifted her dainty skirts and rushed into the barn where Trevor kept the extra pans and pails. Kerry took up two and Jane did the same. Pausing only to fill them at the river, she and Kerry formed a makeshift assembly line that passed the filled buckets to the men working inside as empty ones were handed out. It seemed that hours passed this way and Kerry felt her skirts becoming wet with water, dirt and sweat, but she cared little.

The blaze was mostly concentrated on the bellows' house roof where a red tongue of flame now appeared, licking ever upward over the rafters. With a worried glance, Kerry saw that the barn was altogether too close. With its stalls filled with hay and straw, it could become an inferno. Thinking fast, she called to Trevor and the black-faced Irish lad rushed up, his hands and clothes stinking of smoke.

"Let's douse the roof of the barn," Kerry called, pointing to it. "In case it spreads. The horses—"

"Don't worry, mistress. I'll see to it." Trevor ran around the side of the building and fetched a ladder. Climbing to the uppermost rung, he poured the buckets of Mullica river water they handed up to him over the shingled barn roof, not stopping for a breath until every square inch of it glistened with moisture. Sliding down, he hastened into the barn to find Kerry already tugging on the reins of the mare, but the animal refused to move.

"Come on, ya old bitch!" Trevor yelled, but the horse stared determinedly at him, her ears laid back and her teeth bared.

"It's because of the fire," a familiar masterful voice called out, and Kerry breathed a sigh of relief as Cameron strode into the stable. "It frightens them and they refuse to move." Doffing his white linen shirt, Cameron wrapped the cloth about the mare's eyes, speaking softly to her all the while. The mare calmed instantly under his touch, and naked except for his trousers and boots, Cameron calmly led her outside, past the fire-ravaged furnace and to the house. He tied her to the hitching post, removing his shirt and repeating the process until all the horses were safe.

"We got it under!" the little Irishman called Mick shouted from the rooftop and the workers clapped, relief evident in their blackened faces, fatigue in the droop of their arms. They collapsed by the ore stream, some splashing water over their scorched legs and arms while others seemed too tired to move.

Kerry sought out Cameron and sat beside him on the water-soaked ground. Her hair was askew, her face was smudged, and she little resembled the serene woman who'd greeted her guests just a few hours ago.

"How bad is it?" she asked, and Cameron responded slowly, each word dragged from him.

"Very bad. The roof and rafters appear to be destroyed, and the pacers and all of the top of the gear are injured. At least the bellows were saved, with a great deal of difficulty." He smiled wanly, then nodded to his men. "We should be back in business by late tomorrow, and I have you all to thank for that."

The workers acknowledged his gratitude, then slumped once more to the earth. Eliah joined them there.

"I am puzzled as to how the fire started." The elderly gentleman gestured to the rooftop with his hand. "It seems to have begun on top, but that is not common."

"Aye, and we all know how it started." Mick sat up and, looking important, leaned forward. "'Tis the Devil, breathing his fiery breath upon us."

"Fiddlesticks!" Jane Clark declared, her hands perched on her hips. "There is always danger of fire in the furnace. Don't go believing those tales."

"'Tis no tale," Mick said defensively. "Happened the same as before, when the old man died. The demon is heard at night and he strikes the next day, always a fire. Cursed of the brown waters." Mick crossed himself religiously and Kerry's gaze met Cameron's. She tried to smile, but couldn't manage more than a parting of her soft mouth. Cameron snorted in anger.

"And why did the demon decide to strike now? He's been relatively quiet for the last few months," Cameron said derisively.

Charles Magee answered for him. "'Twas because you were gone, I'm sorry ta say, Mr. Brent. But 'tis said that it is the Brents he's after."

"Jane is right," Eliah chimed in. "We want to hear no more of this nonsense. It puts us on the same level as savages, believing in all this superstition. Now I don't want to hear another word." He directed a silencing glance at an oreman about to impart his knowledge of the Devil, then held up his hand. "Not another word."

Together the Brents and the Clarks walked up the white sand path to the house, and Cameron apologized as to the ending of their meal.

"No apology necessary." Eliah smiled, and Jane nodded in agreement. "What are neighbors for?" As he spoke his eyes were drawn to a slight movement upstairs, the dropping into place of a curtain. "Who is up there?" he asked, squinting as the twilight painted the windows gold.

"Must be Caroline," Cameron remarked. "Her window is on the third floor."

"Strange the fire didn't rouse her," Jane said, her distaste clear.

The window above stayed shut, and the curtain was now closed to the eyes below.

The next few days passed uneventfully. The workers were beginning to recover from their experience with the fire, and business was almost back to normal. Several of the team drivers volunteered to help fix the bellows' roof, and Cameron gratefully accepted, eager to see the building restored once more.

By the week's end, the furnace was fully operational, and new shingles, made of white cedar, gleamed with a rich luster from the roof. To celebrate, Cameron called for a holiday and he arranged a fox hunt to allow the work-weary men a bit of sport. This proposal was met with rousing cheers, and the men made many wagers on the next day's events.

Chapter Twenty-four

As the morning of the big day dawned, eager villagers sounded horns beneath the window. Yawning wearily, Kerry saw with some distaste that her husband, already dressed, was sitting by that window in his hunting garb. His rugged outfit did not detract from his elegance in the slightest. Instead, the sporting clothes lent him a debonair quality that she found most appealing.

"Are you awake yet, sweet?" Cameron's voice was teasing, and Kerry reluctantly parted with the quilts. "I daresay they will be up for us any minute. You should make haste."

When his eyes wandered boldly over her slender form, Kerry felt a mischievous desire to heighten his qualms. "And what of it?" she stretched contentedly. "I don't know what all the excitement is about anyway. Damned English sport. Chasing after some poor little fox!" She hid her smile, but Cameron was on to her game.

"Oh, then you do not wish to go?" he asked blandly. "'Tis a shame, for I had Trevor saddle the new mare for you. But since you despise English activities—"

"I wouldn't miss it on yer life!" Kerry bounced out of the bed. "And don't you be giving my horse to anyone else." She wrapped a sheet around her as his gaze settled on the soft jiggling of her bosom, then lifted an admonishing finger toward him, recognizing the fire in his eyes. "None of that, sir." She giggled as he quit his seat and advanced on her. "The men will be up."

"Yes." Cameron smiled, and his hand reached out to caress the silky flesh that curved above the sheet. Kerry lifted two warmly glowing eyes to him, and her own passion flamed when Cameron kissed the side of her breast. "You'd best get dressed, Kerry," he declared. "Otherwise we might not appear at all." He tore himself reluctantly away from her side and returned to the safety of his chair. Yet his eyes continued to probe the sheet as if by some magic he could cause its disappearance.

Left to the problems of her toilet, Kerry cast her eye over one cool dress, then another. While all were lovely and delicately made, few could withstand any strenuous exercise. As she held out a peach, flowered muslin, a thought dawned on her and she whirled to face Cameron.

"I'm not riding sidesaddle," she stated flatly.

"Oh?"

"That's right. I hate that thing." Her lower lip thrust out in a pretty pout as Cameron objected.

"You are not riding astride in a dress," he said firmly. "I have enough trouble keeping all physically able bucks away from you, without you riding among them with that dress flapping up in front." He held up his hand to forestall the heated retort on the tip of her tongue. "No arguments, madam. I am firm on this point."

"Oh!" Kerry fumed, kicking the bed as her temper flared. Then, muttering a curse, she grasped her throbbing toe while Cameron chuckled.

"I'm glad you think it's so funny." She hissed. "'Tis not you who are forced ta sit cramped upon a horse like some idiot, instead of riding it properly." She did an excellent imitation of an idiot and Cameron's laughter deepened.

"Look in the top drawer of your dresser," he said when he could speak, waving an arm at the Chippendale. "Where you keep those filmy chemises."

Puzzled and curious, Kerry's hand dipped inside, and there she found a strange garment. It was a skirt, made of strong cotton dark brown in color, but instead of flowing free like most others, it was split and sewn up the middle. It was like a combination of pants and a dress, and accompanying it was a jacket and a blouse of ruffled white lace.

"A riding outfit." Cameron grinned in response to her bewildered expression. "I hear it's all the rage in London."

Kerry wasted no more time gazing at the unusual garb, but proceeded to put it on, the skirt first. After fastening the blouse, she raced over to the mirror to view this odd outfit.

Cameron was strangely silent as she did up the buttons on the blouse, for even the severe cut of the shirt could not hide the thrust of her bosom or the tiny curve of her waist. The skirt, though most accommodating, revealed her rounded bottom in a way that the voluminous dresses did not. "What do you think?" she asked eagerly, swirling about to face him directly.

"I heartily approve," he answered, a warm smile playing about his lips.

"Maybe all women should ride the way I do," Kerry quipped when Cameron joined her at the door.

"Aye, but not all could wear that outfit the way you do. Come wench, let's be off." Holding the door for her, Cameron got a rather enticing view as she stepped before him, and his eyes caressed the gentle swing of her hips as she descended the steps.

Below, the house was a-bustle in preparation for the hunt. Helga rushed about the kitchen, preparing a feast and wielding a large wooden spoon to the backs of the overly eager oremen. "Vait outside. You'll not be swilling da food before it's even cooked!" Rolling her eyes at Kerry, she escorted a workman outside by the seat of his pants and Kerry giggled in delight.

Cameron ventured out to see to their mounts, and Kerry helped the cook set out the tempting array of refreshments. Both women were surprised when the door opened and Caroline walked into the room, an annoyed expression in her pale blue eyes.

"Is the hunt on yet? What is the delay?"

Caroline's eyes ran derisively over Kerry, pointedly marking her hunting garb and then returning to rest more favorably on her own dress. Garbed in ice blue satin, complete with gloves and matching silk stockings, she appeared beautiful and aloof.

"Are you joining us?" Kerry asked in amazement, for indeed this was the first sign of sociability that Caroline had shown in quite some time.

"I never miss a hunt," Caroline replied loftily. She patted her well-coiffed blond head, smoothing her curls into a sleek mass. "But of course you wouldn't know that, being so new to Brentwood." Her tone implied that Kerry was only a barely tolerated guest, but saying no more, she stepped out to the dining room to await her morning tea.

Kerry glared at the closed door, then stuck out her small tongue. Helga laughed, but she hastened to prepare the tea before Caroline complained.

The men outside were creating enough of a racket to send any poor fox scurrying to his den, and the small white and tan dogs barked and howled with excitement. Amid the shouts and cheers of workmen, Kerry joined the gathering. The dogs raced around her feet and nipped playfully at the horses that were champing impatiently and tossing their heads on this fine spring day, sensing the play about to come. In the midst of the roans and chestnuts, Kerry's Scottish mare stood apart, the sheen of her coat like carefully brushed velvet in the sunlight.

"I did her up for ye mesel'," Trevor declared proudly, appearing at Kerry's arm as if by magic. "She looks grand, doesn't she now?"

"Aye, she does that," the mistress of Brentwood agreed. Then she searched out Cameron and found him with some workmen who were passing a bottle about. Kerry was about to join him, but seeing the men's obvious interest in the local applejack, she declined, not wishing to spoil their fun. Instead she stood beside the mare, checking the saddle and straps, and talking softly to calm the animal.

Someone gave a signal, and the men fortunate enough to ride hastened to their horses, while the others stood amidst the dogs.

"Are you ready?"

Kerry smiled at Cameron. "Aye." Many helping hands suddenly volunteered to assist her into the saddle, but Cameron's gaze declared that he alone had the honor. As she settled into the saddle, Kerry giggled merrily for Richard Westcoat was sending her a lascivious glance, his eyes falling approvingly over the snug riding habit she wore.

"Richard," Cameron said dryly, and his friend turned to face him. "Your horse." He gestured to the roving steed who, sensing his master's attention was elsewhere, was wandering freely about and nudging the other horses out of place. Red-faced, Westcoat shrugged apologetically while the workmen guffawed, but his eyes returned to the black-haired Irish lass laughing beside him.

"Isn't anyone going to help me mount?" a shrill voice asked. No one had noticed Caroline's presence. The workmen seemed awed by her blue satins and laces, but not a hand reached out to help her until Cameron reluctantly swung down from his horse and lent her assistance. It seemed to Kerry that her hand lingered overlong on Cameron's shoulder as he lifted her onto the small roan, but as soon as she was safely settled in the sidesaddle, Cameron returned to his own mount without glancing back.

Caroline sat erect and proper in her sidesaddle, her skirts draped demurely over her thin legs and ankles. Her pale eyes flickered to the grand horse Kerry rode, but she remained silent and led her horse away from the others for the call.

The hunting horns sounded and the dogs were set free. Baying and howling, they cavorted through the dew-wet grass, down around the lakeside, and were gone.

The horses charged after them, breaking into spirited gallops. At the baying of the dogs, Kerry felt a thrill race through her and her legs gripped the sides of the mare expertly. Allowing the wind to break over her head, she gave the mare full rein, and together they swept over the glistening white sand, flashing by the sapphire blue blur of a lake. Pines and cedars were one dense wall of green, lining the path as the horse galloped eagerly toward the enticing howls. A log suddenly appeared, blocking the path, but the Scottish mare gathered up her legs and cleared the object while Kerry patted her neck and shouted encouragement.

A red flash ahead identified the fox. The frightened animal was racing frantically through the rushes, pursued by the yowling hounds. The dogs ran confusedly around a hollow tree, then started off again, their noses to the ground and whining all the while.

Kerry reined up her horse, recalling something she had seen in Ireland. The fox had deliberately laid a false trail for the hounds, then it had dashed through the opposite end of a hollow tree, disappearing before the dogs realized the trick. With a determined grin, she parted from the pack and slipped down a side trail that led around to the other side of the lake.

No one had noticed her departure, it seemed, for Kerry heard no following hoofbeats. As she galloped freely down a path wreathed with briars and overhanging trees, a small bird darted across in front of her and a squirrel chittered nearby but all else was silent. The path ended in a cool glade, and here Kerry slipped off her horse, her hand still clinging to the reins as she stepped into the center of the clearing.

Here was cool early grass dotted with small spring flowers, purple violets, and white-flowered strawberry plants. A few leafy oaks stood amid the scrub pines, making this an enviable grove for shade. A slight rustle came from the left, and Kerry smiled when a fox scampered through the brush. It paused to give her a quizzical look.

"Fear not," she told the sly little red creature. "I'll not tell a word."

The fox stared one more second, then disappeared under a budding blueberry bush. Kerry walked through the grass, allowing her horse time to cool after her exhilarating run, and she drank in the beauty of the day, the sweet and spicy scent of the pines. She turned slowly toward the path, then froze. A man was watching her, astride a horse!

"Spoiling an English folly?" a familiar voice drawled, and as the horse stepped nearer, Kerry emitted a sigh of releif, then placed her hand to her thundering heart.

"Good Lord Cameron, announce your presence. You'd like to take a year off my life!" she said, but she smiled as he swung down from his mount and came to stand beside her, the Scottish mare nuzzling his jet black steed. Taking both sets of reins in his hand, Cameron tied the horses to a stripling pine, then came back to stand before her.

"I'm sorry I startled you," he apologized. "Did you follow the fox or did he follow you?"

"Oh, I followed him," she assured Cameron. "It seems that foxes are better at getting away from the English than mesel'." Her eyes sparkled with mischief, and Cameron pulled her into his arms, staring into that beloved visage.

"Any regrets, love?" he asked, and she shook her head, turning her face up to his. Her lips were parted, red and moist, and he needed no further invitation to sample them. It was a teasing kiss, light at first, but then a mutual surge of passion overtook them both and Kerry pulled his head closer, locking her fingers in the dark hair that curled about his neck. Cameron's hands slid beneath her riding jacket, tightening about her waist until she was pressed full against him, her rounded form writhing so intimately that all thoughts of the hunt left his mind.

When a small fleecy cloud drifted over the sun and the glade darkened ominously, Cameron eased his lips from Kerry's. He cast his eyes toward the sky and then frowned.

"What is it?" Kerry asked. Her fingers still locked about his neck, she stood on tiptoe.

"That cloud. It could be rain. This time of year it blows up suddenly from the sea." He reluctantly released her from his embrace, and Kerry wrapped her jacket more securely about her slim figure. Without the sun, the glade seemed overly cool for spring and she shivered involuntarily.

"We'd best return," Cameron stated, not too pleased at the thought. But when he retrieved the horses and helped Kerry to mount, his eyes fell to her blouse. Without the aid of a chemise, her full bosom pressed against the clinging shirt, leaving no detail to his imagination. "Kerry," Cameron said hoarsely, and she glanced up at him in wonder. He pointed to her shirt. "Methinks you should return for a cloak. With the chill, that blouse provides no protection." He smiled when she grasped his meaning and pulled the jacket more closely about her, but this only aggravated the situation, pressing the fullness of her breasts into an even more enticing display. Cameron groaned and fastened the buttons with his fingers, while Kerry's cheeks flushed pink.

"Now before I take you down from that horse and into my arms, see to the cloak. I don't want anyone else tempted the way I am. I wish to kill nothing more than a fox this day."

"Yes, sir," Kerry retorted.

Then Cameron led her horse to the path and, with a fond pat, sent it on its way. Kerry waved back to him before she reined to the right and headed toward the manor house.

The yard was lonely and deserted when she arrived, for the servants, having been included in the day's activities, were down at the gristmill to cheer the victors and console the losers. Dismounting, Kerry could hear their bawdy songs drifting over the pines and she grinned as he tied her mount at the hitching post closest to the door.

Inside, the house was deathly silent. Kerry felt a chill for never before had it been so still. Without Cameron's reassuring voice, Helga's scolding, the chambermaids' chatter, the place seemed ghostlike and she hurried up the steps to retrieve the garment she sought.

Her cloak in hand, Kerry softly closed the door to the master bedroom, hushing every sound she might make in the silent hall. She was about to head down the stairs, when something caught her eye, something not quite right. Glancing down the hallway, her gaze flickered over the three doors. Cameron's, then the one she used to occupy—now empty—and lastly, Charles's old room. It was this door that drew her attention, for instead of being completely closed as it usually was, it was slightly ajar.

Indecision wracked Kerry as she stared at the partially open door. She knew she should head on down the stairs and out to join the others, but a thrill of fear shot through her. That more than anything decided her, and she started for the door.

'Tis ridiculous to be frightened of an open door, she thought wryly. It's all that talk about demons and devils. I'll be afraid of me own shadow next.

She placed her hand on the brass knob, pushing the door open a few inches at a time. When nothing happened, she breathed deeply and then stepped inside.

The room was exactly as it had been the few times she'd been sent to clean it, for Charles was as neat as his brother. The bed, while not as large as the one in the master bedroom, was nevertheless comfortable and was covered with a handstitched quilt. Tables and chairs stood in their rightful places and an unopened book rested on the mantel. A picture lay there too, face-down, and Kerry picked it up, a wrinkled frown coming to her face as she recognized the portrait. It was the one she'd discovered when she'd first come to live at Brentwood, the miniature of Cameron's mother.

Must have been the maid, Kerry thought, replacing the framed picture. Seeing nothing else out of the ordinary, she was about to step out of the room when the sun burst from behind the clouds and shone into the room. There, beside the bed, she saw the cold glint of metal.

Curious, Kerry strode over and picked up the strange object. It was like nothing she had ever seen before. Made of iron, the piece seemed to be a cast of some sort, and it had holes for nails in the bottom. Turning it over in her hand, Kerry saw that the underside had two vertical protrusions, they reminded her of something. . . .

Edging closer to the bed, she pressed the object into the quilt and gasped. There on its fluffy surface was a cloven hoof, exactly like the one beside Enid's dead body!

"Curiosity killed the cat."

Kerry's blood ran cold as she recognized the clipped tones, the precise English. Whirling about, she faced the grinning visage of Cameron's brother. Charles firmly closed the door behind him. "And it just may have cost you your life."

"You!" Kerry choked out when she could speak. "You are supposed to be in Philadelphia!"

"Quite." Charles continued to smile pleasantly, as he strode across the room and then halted beside her. "But I decided to come back and claim what is mine."

"This?" Kerry asked, displaying the cast. Charles's face darkened and he grabbed up the piece, his other hand closing firmly on Kerry's wrist.

"Yes, this." He smiled and his blue gaze was not so amiable. "If I had not forgotten this damned thing, I wouldn't have had to return to the house."

"Then it was you!" Kerry felt her blood run cold as she thought of Enid. "You killed Enid and left these . . . marks beside her!"

"You are very perceptive, my dear," Charles said quietly. "Indeed, that was one of the things that attracted me to you. Pity." His eyes ran slowly over Kerry's riding habit, lingering at the open jacket.

"But why?" Kerry continued, hoping to keep him talking while she found a way out of the room. Her eyes flickered briefly to the door, but Charles noticed and tightened his grip on her wrist until she cried out.

"Do not think of escape, Kerry," he said menacingly, and his eyes bore into hers. "As to Enid, well, she discovered my plans and threatened to tell Cameron. I had to kill her." He shrugged as if he'd spoken of killing a fly. "But you my dear will serve a double purpose. I cannot allow you to escape."

"Cameron will come for me," Kerry promised as Charles pulled a leather riding whip from under his cloak and tied it around her wrists. As he pushed her toward the stairs, draping her cloak about her shoulders, she again said, "He will come."

"Mistress, I am counting on that." Charles leered.

Frightened even more by his words, Kerry was beginning to have a dim idea of what Charles had planned and she stumbled as he forced her down the stairs. The door was at the bottom of the stairwell, but as if reading her mind Charles leaned forward, and his arm coming pressing against her throat, he whispered in her ear.

"Do not be so foolish as to utter a sound. I have a pistol beneath my cloak, and if you so much as breathe loudly, that breath will be your last."

Nodding to show him she'd heard, Kerry heard his satisfied chuckle. Then he thrust her out the door.

A team horse was waiting nearby and Charles was about to lead her to it when he spied the new Scottish mare that was Kerry's mount. "How very accommodating." He grinned and pushed her toward the waiting mount. "Get on."

Kerry glanced quickly around, estimating the distance to the grist mill. It was worth a try for she doubted that Charles would want to fire the gun so close to the house. With a sudden movement she broke free, but Charles's hand shot out, and he then flung her up onto the horse himself.

"Try that again, my spirited beauty, and you shall ride

face-down," he drawled as he swung gracefully into the saddle behind her. He kicked the mare's flank and the horse jumped, then raced off down past the gate.

"Help!" Kerry called out, but the wind snatched away her cries and the workmen at the mill still bawled out their songs. Charles laughed softly as Kerry struggled to stay upright in the saddle.

"Yell all you want to out here," Charles said nastily. "There is no one to hear your cries." As she slid about in the saddle, he wrapped one arm about her waist to keep her still; then his hand slowly crept up the front of her blouse. Now that they were free of Brentwood, he slowed his pace, his hands fondling her freely.

"Take your hands off me!" she shrieked, as Charles found the buttons to her shirt and deftly undid them. Laughing at her outrage, he cupped one round breast, his cold hand roughly caressing it. Kerry struggle and fought, mindless of the danger of falling as his hands wandered intimately over her. "Cameron will kill you!"

"Cameron!" Charles snorted. "What right has Cameron to anything? He's a bastard born and bred. He calls himself master of that house and of Brentwood, but what right has he to any of that?" He gripped Kerry tighter about the waist, and as his anger grew, he urged the mare to an even faster pace. "He has no right to anything, least of all to you, and he will discover that soon."

Anger and amazement crossed Kerry's face, and as she glanced over her shoulder, she saw the silvered wig of the man behind her, the rich clothes, the hatred in his eyes. She could not keep a sneer from her voice as she spoke.

"Cameron built Brentwood into what it is today. What have you done but squander your inheritance?" Kerry shrank back fearfully as Charles's eyes blazed and he raised his whip. For a moment she thought he would strike her, but his hand fell to his side and his crystal blue gaze sliced through hers.

"Careful, my pet. I do not wish to hurt you. I should not like to mar that lovely face before I take you. I shall have you, Kerry my dear. I have never been denied a wench before, and I have hungered for you for far too many months." He smiled as Kerry's mouth dropped and then he nodded pleasantly.

"Are you mad?" Kerry asked. "Do you think I will ever give myself to you? Not in a hundred years."

Charles's arm tightened about her until she could hardly draw breath.

"You will have little say in the matter, my dear. Since you so enjoy the caresses of that bastard, you will undoubtedly enjoy a more experienced lover, a gentleman."

"Gentleman!" Kerry laughed. "You dare to call yourself—"

"Enough!" Charles shouted. "I grow tired of your sneers, milady." He used the title sarcastically. "But I promise you this, I know how to treat a woman and you soon will be begging me to take you."

Kerry opened her mouth to object, but she found a lace-scented handkerchief thrust between her lips. Bound and now gagged, she could do little except grasp the horse with her kneees to keep from falling.

Cameron was at the gristmill, waiting for his wife. He glanced at the house once or twice, and when he saw that her horse was gone, he expected her to ride up at any moment. But as time passed he became concerned and called to Trevor.

The Irish lad reluctantly left his companions and the cider. "Aye, sir?"

"Have you seen Kerry? She went up to the house a while ago to fetch her cloak and I haven't laid eyes on her since."

"No, sir," Trevor replied. "I'll take me a run up and look, if ya wish." At Cameron's nod he sped off, while the master of

Brentwood waited at the window. Outside, the weather was more threatening, and his brow furrowed. He saw Trevor heading back down the hill, shaking his head, and he immediately rushed out of the mill, past the curious men and to his own mount. Richard Westcoat followed at his heels, stopping Cameron as he reached for the reins.

"Cameron, what is it?"

"Kerry. She's wandered off and with the rain approaching—"

Richard needed to be told no more. He swung up on his own mount and started for the gate.

A young serving girl rushed out, waving her arms, and Cameron reined up. "Sir, are you looking for the mistress?" she called, cupping her hands to her mouth. At Cameron's abrupt nod, she continued. "I saw her leave on horseback, with a man behind her. I was upstairs in the attic and I couldn't see too good, but he looked like a gentleman. And I think she was forced."

"Forced?" Cameron shouted, and the maid nodded, her head bobbing furiously.

"Aye. She broke away and this man . . . he snatched her back up. Please bring her back Master Brent. They were headed toward the swamp. The mistress . . . she was right kind to me." The young girl hung her head as she spoke and Cameron broke the silence.

"Fear not. And you, miss, have earned the price of your indenture this day." With that he kicked his steed and galloped off, Richard right behind him.

The two horses thundered down the road, past soft spring fields waving with green to where the road darkened and Penn Swamp began.

"Do you know what you're doing?" Richard called, and Cameron slowed his mount, drawing his horse aside so he could respond.

"She said a gentleman," he shouted. "Who would fit that description?"

"Charles?" When Cameron nodded, Richard stared, perplexed. "But I thought—"

"So did I. But I got a letter this morn from Northrop. Charles never arrived in Philadelphia." Cameron pointed to the bogs ahead. "Where else could Charles have been all this time and not have been seen?"

Richard glanced toward the eerie swamp that was creeping up on both sides of the road. "Let's go," he said.

Kerry was seated in a chair in Enid's hut, her hands secured behind her and her feet tied as well. She gazed about the room, seeing that it had changed. The little jars were smashed, the animals were gone. Even the plants had died, as if they'd sensed the evil in Charles Brent.

When the gag was torn from her mouth, Kerry moistened her dry lips with her tongue. She glanced up as Charles thrust a cup of wine at her, while he slowly sipped of his own.

"Drink," he commanded. When Kerry refused to even look at him, he thrust the cup to her lips, pouring the liquid over her until she choked and was forced to swallow some. The wine was a fine Madeira.

"You . . . robbed Cameron's ships," she declared.

Charles nodded. "Yes. They will all be mine soon anyway." His eyes glistened at that thought, and sated with wine, he glanced warmly toward her. Kerry sought frantically to keep his mind on other matters.

"But how?" she asked innocently. "You will be arrested and jailed; then you won't have Brentwood."

"There you are wrong." Charles preened, unable to resist bragging. "You see, I have my share of the Brent intellect, although I chose to apply it in different ways. What happens will never be traced to me." His smile was a satisfied one. He refilled his cup, then held it toward Kerry as if in a mocking toast. "To you, my pretty . . . and very soon."

"But they will find you," Kerry continued whereupon

Charles sneered.

"Did they when Enid died?" He cocked his head as Kerry stared at him. Then he placed his cup aside and started toward her. "Now we have plenty of time before Sir Cameron comes charging to the rescue and, incidentally, his death." Pushing aside her cloak, Charles saw the red splash upon her blouse where the wine had spilled. The nipple was clearly outlined in the liquid and his tongue traced that outline. "It never pays to waste good wine," he murmured.

Kerry gasped and writhed in the chair, but he seemed to enjoy her struggles. Finally, he untied her feet and pulled her up from the chair, letting her cloak fall to the floor.

"It is time, my dear," he declared, "for the Master of Brentwood to receive his due."

The door to the tiny hut was flung open, and Kerry's head flew to it. She was amazed to see Caroline. The blond Englishwoman looked anything but pleased to see Kerry enfolded in Charles's embrace, and she flung out her hand, pushing her back against the wall. "What are you about now, you slut?" Her eyes flew to the wine stain on the white blouse and her teeth clenched with rage.

"You trollop! You're not content to have one man lusting after your skirts, you want every man you see!"

"Do ya think I'd want him?" Kerry asked, her eyes wide and incredulous. "He forced himself on me!"

"Liar!" Caroline grated out, then she slapped Kerry across the face, her stinging blow leaving a bright red mark. "I know what you are. Yes, you and your husband will not see tomorrow, and for that I am glad."

Reeling from pain, Kerry nonetheless understood what Caroline had said and she turned back to face her. "You! After all Cameron's done for you!"

"Did you think I would ever forgive him for choosing you over me?" Caroline's eyes gleamed like cracked glass and she seemed far from insane. "Me. A lady! Yet he chose a common slut! And all the time he thought I was madly in

423

love with him. I just wanted his money, and now I shall have it anyway." She smiled at Kerry's surprised face, then sneered. "And you were all so quick to believe that I was lovesick, pining because he'd rejected me. I did that to stay on at Brentwood, knowing that Cameron would pity my circumstance." She laughed with delight at the thought and Kerry's eyes narrowed with rage.

"You—"

"They're coming," Charles said excitedly, and Kerry smiled, hope springing within her breast. "Do not look so happy," he added, "for he's come to die." With that Charles went out the door, to prepare some horrible fate for his brother.

As the time drifted slowly by, Kerry's hands worked furtively at the knot holding her wrists behind her back. The tight leather slipped and strained, but gradually she felt the first part of the knot loosen and she continued her efforts. Caroline glanced up once, but seeing only Kerry's glare, she strode across the room, shoving her down into the chair.

"Be still, besom!" she shouted. She then produced a slim blade, and broke into an ugly smile. "Your time will come soon enough!"

Determined not to react, Kerry stared at the blade and wondered where Cameron was.

A flash of lightning rent the blackness of the swamp, and Cameron cursed the chilling drops of rain pelting him, the wind howling through the twisting trees.

"Where is this hut?" Richard shouted, but his voice was nearly drowned out by a deafening clap of thunder.

"Just ahead," Cameron yelled. Another flash of lightning split the black sky and thunder boomed again, following upon the heels of the jagged bolt. As darkness descended around them, the trees swayed in the gale, the smaller pines bending toward the dark swamp waters, and rain fell in fierce torrents.

"Take heed!" Cameron called, barely able to see his companion through the slashing deluge. "One step in the wrong direction—"

A clap of thunder drowned out Cameron's words; then the swamp was day-bright as lightning flashed. It was then Cameron saw the horror on Richard's face as he gaped at the bog. Following his gaze, the skies illuminated by an electrical charge, Cameron felt his blood run cold as a monstrous creature burst from the trees. An apocalyptic sight left Richard swearing and Cameron speechless. A horse was galloping toward them, but not any horse mortal eyes had seen before. This animal had wings, and its hideous white eyes rolled in their sockets. The creature's teeth were bared, but Cameron stared helplessly as this horror raced toward him.

"My God, it's real!" Richard hissed as the horse charged closer. A few feet and it would be upon them ... Quickly Cameron sought to rein in his horse, but the poor animal champed and snorted, frightened by the creature thing ahead. Glancing quickly about, Cameron saw that Richard's horse was behaving the same way. The swamp surrounded them and one step in the wrong direction meant instant death.

Suddenly, a roar of thunder shook the earth and a bright flash of lightning cracked the sky. The macabre horse reared up on its hind legs, and with a terrible cry, threw back its head. Its front hooves tore at the air and its rider screamed, then plunged from the back of the winged creature, tumbling beneath its crushing feet and into the murky waters below. There was a scream, then silence.

The storm, having spent its fury, was slackening to a steady rainfall. "Did you see it?" Richard breathed, his face pale and frightened. Cameron did not anser, but he shakily dismounted and walked slowly toward the creature standing calmly in the falling rain. As Cameron approached the animal, it raised a white muzzle to him so he called, "Caledonia!" The horse responded with a gentle neigh, and Cameron laid his hand on the rain-drenched shoulder of the stallion. Even in the pelting rain he could see that the animal's bones were sticking out.

Richard gave a low whistle as he approached.

"He looks half-starved."

"He is," Cameron answered. He slipped a hand under the weighty wing and revealed the thick wire that held the apparatus together. "Here is what happened to our canvas," he said.

"Charles?" Richard asked, and Cameron nodded.

"I always knew he hated me, but I never dreamed to this degree. Only a clever mind could have devised this. Charles evidently thought I'd believe the legend and plunge to my death, but it seems he met his." Staring into the surrounding waters, Cameron saw only the clumps of light green sphagnum moss, and pattering rain drops landed where his brother had fallen. Even now the mosses were filling the vacant spot, obliterating the grave of Charles Brent. "Let's go find Kerry," he said.

It was suddenly so silent that Kerry glanced up at Caroline who was listening intently. When no sounds ensued, she turned slowly to Kerry, withdrawing the knife from her gown. "Something's gone wrong," she whispered, and her voice was deadly. "But at least I shall have my vengeance." Hatred glistening in her cold eyes, she started for Kerry.

"That's what you think!" Kerry shouted, struggling with the leather that bound her wrists. The knot was almost loose. . . . With a jerk, Kerry pulled her hands free and sprung up to pounce upon her attacker.

Her sudden movement took Caroline by surprise and as she fell to the dirt floor, Kerry grabbed for her right wrist, hoping to make her drop the knife. She threw her entire weight against the struggling Caroline, and the blade dropped, falling beneath one of Enid's shelves. Caroline attempted to retrieve it, but Kerry rolled on top of her. Immediately, Caroline's hands closed around Kerry's throat. Forced to change her tactics, she was trying to strangle Kerry to death. Kerry choked as Caroline squeezed her windpipe, but her hand struck the leg of the chair she'd been sitting in and, with a gargantuan effort, she dragged it toward her, then smashed it across Caroline's head. The blonde's hold weakened and Kerry slipped free. She slid a hand under the shelf and retrieved the knife, but as her hand closed upon the weapon she heard a scuffling behind her. Glancing up, she saw Caroline escape through the door. Exhausted she lay back on the floor.

Only a few moments passed before Cameron rushed into the hut and took his wife into his arms.

"Thank God you're all right. He didn't hurt you, did he?"

Kerry quickly shook her head. "No, I'm fine. But Caroline . . . she was with him . . . she ran out of here a moment ago. What happened to Charles?"

"He fell into the swamp," Cameron said after a moment. "He had taken Caledonia and disguised him as the Devil. He hoped to frighten me into falling into the bog. But Caledonia reared and he fell to his own death."

"Oh, no," Kerry whispered, burying her face in Cameron's shirt. "I'm so sorry."

Cameron stroked her bright head, his touch reassuring.

They heard a strange scuffling outside and then the door flew open, framing Trevor and a few of the furnace workmen.

"Trevor!" Kerry exclaimed; then her mouth dropped as Bill Seldon walked into the room.

"Are you all right, miss?" Bill asked while Trevor embraced her eagerly.

"Aye," Kerry answered. "It was Charles and Caroline. Charles fell into the bog, but Caroline ran out of here a few moments ago. She might be wandering out there still."

"We'll search for her now, before she's lost to the waters," Seldon said, and he ushered the men back into the curtain of rain. Pausing at the door, he gave her a crooked smile. "Glad ta have you back, miss," he declared, and then he was gone, taking a bewildered Richard with him.

"Well how about that?" Kerry asked as Cameron took her into his embrace.

"He's not nearly as glad as I am," Cameron said sincerely. "Come, love. Let's return home before this hut is rained out." Indeed, as he spoke brown water was washing over the rush floor so, together, they slipped out into the night and returned to the ill-omened mansion.

Epilogue

The rain continued well into the next day, making the search for Caroline doubly difficult, but as evening drew near, a frantic banging at the door sent George scurrying to answer it. Dripping furnacemen stomped into the hallway.

"'Tis Miss Caroline," Mick told them, and Trevor's wet head nodding in affirmation. "We've found her."

"Found her?" Cameron nearly shouted, but Mick hurriedly clarified his statement.

"Dead, sir. We've found her body. It was in the swamp, she had just started to sink into it when we caught her body and dragged it out. I would have brought her in, sir, but from the water and the time that's passed, it didn't seem fit."

At a choking sound from Kerry, the furnaceman paused and Cameron nodded.

"I see. Tend to her as best you can, and I'll arrange a proper burial. 'Tis the least I can do. And Charles?" Cameron seemed almost afraid to ask, and it was Trevor who answered him.

"I'm afraid that he's gone, sir. The swamp has claimed him. We couldn't find even his boot."

A weighty silence followed his words, and then John Cox spoke. "It seems that Charles has met the fate of the others who roamed the swamp." He turned to Cameron and Kerry, clicked his heels in military fashion, and then followed Cameron into the parlor, where the Clarks and Richard Westcoat waited. When he was seated, he took a sip of brandy, and turning to Cameron, he said, "Now I would like to know what happened."

"I've had suspicions about my brother for a long time," Cameron explained, placing an arm comfortingly about Kerry. "You see, I was well aware of his character, although I did not realize that his hatred was so fanatical. Charles was always spoiled, for he was the only legitimate child my parents had. As a result, he could not stand frustration of any sort. I learned in Philadelphia that he had squandered his fortune. He, therefore, had a motive for causing my death. He hoped to inherit Brentwood. I am not sure what he intended for my wife, for he wanted her as well. Yet he had to realize she would not keep silent about his deed. I hate to think of what he'd planned."

The room grew still as Cameron continued his narrative. "When we returned from the city, I was informed by Mr. Seldon that Charles was entering from the furnace at night, for reasons unknown to anyone. He was apparently making these iron casts—Kerry found one in his room—and attaching them to the hooves of the horse so the animal would leave the cloven hoofprints described in the legend of the devil."

"Remarkable," John Cox said, shaking his head.

"Yes," Cameron agreed. "Charles never wanted for brains. 'Tis a shame he used his wits for such a purpose. Where was I? Oh yes, the casts." He took a sip of his brandy, then continued.

"I was also aware that someone was riding about at night, helping to feed the villagers' belief in the legend. So I took it upon myself to venture out, and though I never managed to catch Charles, I knew he was the only other member of the household who rode about at night. His barroom trysts could not easily be verified, and he did camouflage his nights as the horseman by paying visits to taverns.

"Scoundrel." Eliah Clark muttered, and his wife glanced sympathetically at Cameron.

"Finally, when I asked him to leave, I forced Charles's hand. He pretended to comply with my wishes, but he never went to Philadelphia. And when Richard reported a robbery at our shipyards, a robbery of some odd items, including a quantity of good wine, my suspicions increased, particularly since the only print found at the scene was made by a gentleman's boot. Yesterday, when my wife failed to return from the house when she was fetching a cloak, my fears were confirmed. I had suspected that Charles intended to use her as a lure, and when the upstairs maid told me a gentleman had forced her onto a horse, I was pretty sure I was correct. Recalling Enid's death, when the maid pointed toward the path to the swamp, I thought the woodswoman's hut might be where he'd taken her. We followed, Richard and I, but Charles had a surprise waiting for us."

"You've never seen anything like it," Richard interjected. "I've had my share of frights—been to war, fought pirates, the British. But I will still see that horse in my dreams, charging out of the black bogs while lightning flashed and thunder rolled around it, its huge wings flapping in the wind." He paused for a moment, and Jane Clark shuddered. "It was horrible, just horrible."

"I'm almost sorry you came with me," Cameron said to his friend. "I suspected something of the sort, but nothing could have prepared us for that apparition. The lightning caused the horse to rear."

"Aye, and it was a good thing," Kerry put in. "Had anything happened to you, I don't know what I would have done."

"Well, we're safe now, darling." Cameron's gaze met Kerry's, and they exchanged a private glance while John Cox coughed and shuffled his feet, paying close attention to his brandy. One by one the visitors took the hint and went to the door, and when Cameron glanced up, he was surprised to find them gathered there.

"You're going?" he asked, and Jane Clark led the laughter.

"Yes, my dear lad. There is time for visiting later." She smiled and departed with her husband. John stepped back as Richard took his leave.

"I will file the forms with the sheriff," he said. "But I don't think there will be any further inquiry. Caroline's death is proven, and in the next few days, Charles will most likely be deemed deceased." He put a hand on Cameron's arm and he smiled, his military carriage easing for the moment.

"I am glad you are all right, son. The Pine Barrens need men like you. One thing that still concerns me, however."

"What's that?" Cameron asked.

"You've explained everything except that cry. I've heard it, so have the other villagers. It's been heard as far away as Haddonfield, and the creature, the Jersey Devil, has been sighted in many places. All of that could not have been Charles's work." John Cox's brow furrowed.

"No," Cameron agreed, equally perplexed. "Charles always returned by the next day."

"Yes. Well, I suppose some things will always be a mystery here in the Pines. I think it's meant to be that way." He smiled at Kerry, his hand taking hers. "May God bless you and your children. I feel it in my bones that you will both find much happiness here." Then, as if ashamed he had said so much, he donned his tricorn and walked out into the rain.

"You know what?" Kerry asked, and Cameron smiled down at her. "I believe your friend is right," she said.

But peace had come to Brentwood.